MAGIC UNDER THE MISTLETOE

By Lucy Coleman

The French Adventure
Snowflakes over Holly Cove
Summer on the Italian Lakes
Magic under the Mistletoe

MAGIC UNDER THE MISTLETOE

Lucy Coleman

HEAD
of ZEUS

First published in the United Kingdom in 2019 by Aria,
an imprint of Head of Zeus Ltd

A CIP catalogue record for this book is available from the British Library.

ISBN (E): 9781788541572

Aria
c/o Head of Zeus
First Floor East
5–8 Hardwick Street
London EC1R 4RG

WWW.ARIAFICTION.COM

To Clive, Claire, Ellie and Anna-Sophia for a wonderful day spent at Porthkerry – the perfect setting for this story. Love you guys. xx

I

Come Fly with Me

The channel piping Christmas music through my earphones might be all singalong, jingle bells and goodwill, but I'm trying very hard to contain myself. If I let rip it won't be to spread any seasonal joy. And as I'm in a plane flying at 38,000 feet over the Indian Ocean, it's no place for a meltdown.

As I switch screens on the laptop a message box pops up bearing that dreaded little flag.

> I'm having second thoughts about the opening shot. I think, on balance, I prefer the one you originally selected. Although, I recall seeing a side-angle shot before I turned to face the camera which might look more natural. Can we discuss please?

The mere thought of Solar Powered Solutions' CEO, Mr Cary Anderson, reclining in comfort a mere thirty feet away while he sips his cocktail, isn't doing my blood pressure any good. It's the twenty-third of December and we're flying back to the UK from Sydney. The answer is, *no*, we can't discuss this until the Christmas holidays are over, unless he invites me up to first class.

Sitting in a row of four seats in economy class, with a boisterous toddler to the left of me, is a challenge. His father has the aisle seat the other side of him, but the child is out of his own seat more often than he's in it. Add into the mix a woman to my right, sorting out an oversized bag and it's little short of hell when you are trying to type.

It's unbelievable that Cary is continuing to harass me with messages as if we're still at work. The list of changes he'd like made to the rough edit of the promotional video my company, Dynamic Videography, has been making for Solar Powered Solutions is beyond unreasonable.

What is really incensing me about all this is that if we hadn't over-run on the filming schedule then I'd already be at home relaxing. I had been due to fly back a little over a week ago with my cameraman, and long-time friend, Jeff Martin.

But I reckoned without the interference of a CEO who didn't just deviate from the previously agreed storyboard and script for the shoot but kept insisting I re-write bits of it. And now, when we've finally finished filming, he's still not letting up.

Cary isn't the only workaholic around here, but even I acknowledge that you can't work at full throttle twenty-four-seven. I get the impression that Christmas isn't a big deal for him. However, most of us have family obligations to meet which aren't always easy and I was hoping to unwind a little on the flight home.

Hasn't it occurred to him that after a stressful few weeks at his beck and call, I might actually want to sit back, relax and switch off? If only to get a break from him and his constant demands.

There's another reason my nerves are on edge at the moment, though. Jeff decided – rather wisely as it turns out – not to fly back with me to the UK, but to stay in Australia for the Christmas holidays. Self-professed, long-term bachelor Jeff is going to be experiencing an Aussie Christmas with a rather attractive woman named Tania. She was working on one of the exhibition stands next to where we were filming.

That is good news in a way because it's been a while since anyone caught his eye. Sadly, his little romantic interludes never last very long. Mainly because he's not a wine 'em and dine 'em sort of guy who is prepared to make an effort. Tagging along for a beer at the local and then on to a football match isn't every woman's idea of the perfect date. Even though I've set him up on more than a dozen dates with friends over the years, I've accepted he was a lost cause. So this was a complete surprise, to say the least. He's due back on the second of January and I hope he comes home prepared to tackle Cary's growing list of edits at full throttle.

A message alert signals yet another communication from Cary.

I now have updated information with regard to some of the energy comparison figures you are using. Full spec uploaded to Google Docs for action.

I stifle a groan. Being under contract to him doesn't make me his slave.

Taking a deep breath, I try not to take this personally. I've witnessed up close how tirelessly Cary works; the man is like a well-oiled machine. I get the impression he would never ask anyone to do something he wouldn't consider doing himself because basically he seems fair, but his work ethic is a tad intimidating. He never stops, and – I'm loath to admit – his focus is admirable, if relentless.

Success comes at a cost and I know that myself. But he is a total control freak and I imagine that the employees who report directly to him have proven themselves time and time again. Understanding the way he likes to work and getting onboard with that is probably the only way to survive. I wonder what his marketing director thought when Cary insisted on starring in, and overseeing, the filming of the video himself. This is clearly his sole focus at the moment, so I guess a lot is riding on it.

There you go – figuring out his excuse for acting like a total pain in the ass helps, doesn't it? I ask myself. Ding. Another message alert flashes up.

When Jeff zoomed in on the conference banner did you realise the sign for the public toilets off to the left-hand side is on the screen for a couple of seconds? I'm sure there must be the same shot taken from another angle. Can you sort it, please?

Aarrgghh! Is he going to spend the entire flight lying back and replaying the footage over and over again?

I jumped at the offer to fly to Sydney to make what has turned out to be more of a documentary than a promotional video. It was a first for us and Jeff was raring to go. But the reality is that I've probably underpriced the job, given the amount of time we've been away. Cary has acknowledged the parameters of the project have grown, but whether he'll like the increased bill at the end of it, who knows?

My back is really aching and I squirm around in my seat as much as I dare, given the constant jostling either side of me. To my left the increasingly hassled father has hauled his unruly, screeching child onto his lap. Now I'm having to dodge sharp elbows and kicking feet. To my right, the woman who has taken command of the armrest is spilling out over her seat, as are the items she's sorting from her enormous carry-on.

Snapping my laptop shut, I lean forward to stow it in the seat pocket in front of me for safety. Why me? I ask myself. I don't do kids; I simply don't have the patience, or that well of maternal instinct most other women I know seem to have.

Without warning, a flying fist sends my head rocking. The struggling dad next to me hastily bundles the little nightmare across the aisle and into the lap of his equally stressed wife. He turns to me, looking distinctly hot, bothered and embarrassed.

'I'm so sorry about that. Hayden is a little overtired; you know what kids are like at this time of the year. There isn't much room in these seats, is there?'

I nod briefly to acknowledge his apology but the excuse is a lame one. There are lots of children of varying ages on this flight and I don't see any other passengers being used as a punch bag.

'No, there isn't. Maybe he'll fall asleep soon,' I reply, a hint of optimism in my voice.

The guy looks me firmly in the eye, shaking his head. 'I doubt it,' he admits, sucking in a deep breath. 'I fear it's going to be a long flight.'

He says the words out of the side of his mouth as if he doesn't want his wife to overhear him, which she can't. Hayden is now refusing to be restrained and complaining loudly.

'Darling, I think Hayden needs to run off a little steam.' She turns to her husband with a desperate look on her face and I instantly find myself feeling sorry for them both.

The poor guy doesn't have much choice. Rather reluctantly, he stands to begin grappling with the boy as his wife tries to hand him over. It's the turn of the elderly gentleman sitting next to the desperate mum to dodge elbows and kicking feet now.

'Is there a problem?'

Cary suddenly appears in the aisle to the right of me and I spin my head in his direction. As I do so, I notice that I'm not the only female in close proximity whose eyes have alighted upon him. In fact, the air hostess standing patiently to his right could easily pass by but she's lingering, hoping to be of some help. It's hard to suppress a hint of the intense irritability I'm feeling. If he was her boss, it would soon wipe that fawning smile off her face.

'No, why?' I ask, trying to remain cool and ignore the kerfuffle going on in the aisle to my left. However, when I turn back around I see the screaming Hayden being forcefully carried, with great difficulty, and deposited on the floor. He rebels by refusing to stand and disappears out of view. All that is visible now are his flailing arms and legs. Heads are turning in his direction.

I watch in total disbelief, as the wife begins to accuse her husband of mishandling the situation. Not wishing to add to the poor guy's embarrassment, I turn back around and try to divert Cary's gaze. I should imagine it's bad enough coping with a child throwing a tantrum in such a confined space, without being pulled into an argument over it. That's family life for you, but people don't always realise what they are getting themselves into.

'Everything's fine. Just a tired little boy and two stressed parents,' I inform Cary.

We're talking over the head of the woman sitting to my right and I give her a little sardonic smile of apology.

'You didn't respond to my last three messages. I'm checking you received them.' Cary's tone is clipped.

Is he joking? He can see the situation I'm in.

I nod, unable to answer him for fear that the sarcastic retort in my head will find its way to my lips. Time to remind myself he is a client and maybe I'm not doing a very good job of managing his expectations. Well, reining in his unreasonable demands, to be precise. Like assuming that I'm sitting here ready and waiting to act upon every command he issues.

The woman alongside me glares up at Cary disapprovingly and his frown instantly dissolves.

'Is there anything I can do?' he asks, in a more civilised tone.

Guilt is a wonderful thing.

Considering I've spent the last three-and-a-half weeks working twelve-hour days alongside this man, this is probably only the second time he's said something that makes him sound like a normal human being.

The first occasion was during a brief encounter we had, early one morning. We both happened to be doing an early morning run around the perimeter of the hotel grounds. Ironically, in opposite directions, which says a lot.

Seeing him coming towards me I had absolutely no intention at all of stopping, but as he slowed he yanked out his Rovking earbuds. Inwardly I'd groaned.

'I didn't know you were a runner,' he'd said as he drew alongside, running on the spot. Which set me on edge. Who does that? Rather annoyingly, he hadn't even sounded the teensiest bit out of breath, although his skin had been glistening with sweat. I'd consoled myself by assuming he was on his first lap, whereas I was on my fifth and only pleasantly glowing. Or so I thought at the time, but sweating isn't really glamorous under any condition, is it?

'It's the best time of the day,' I'd admitted, not really knowing what else to say.

I remember wishing he hadn't stopped, just waved and continued on by. I had tried, with limited success, to avoid making eye contact. Instead I'd found myself glancing over those solid, tanned arms of his. Muscles that showed he was as committed to the gym as he was to his work. When I'd looked up at him again his smile had been warm. Engaging, even. And I clearly remember seeing his eyes flickering over me. Was it appreciation I'd seen reflected back at me as I'd quickly looked away?

'It seems that's something else we have in common,' he'd mused. 'Aside from being workaholics and perfectionists.'

With that, he'd given me a rather amused smile, popped his earbuds back in and off he ran. But when we caught up again just over an hour later it had been business as usual – and by then he was frowning again.

A sudden jolt as we hit an air pocket sees Cary grabbing the side of the seat alongside him as he stares at me, awaiting my answer.

'I'm fine, thank you.' My tone infers that I'm not fine at all, but what can I say with everyone around me listening in on our conversation.

Cary frowns. 'Can I at least get you a drink, or a snack?'

Now his conscience is bothering him but not enough to offer to exchange seats.

I declined an alcoholic drink when the cabin crew were doing the rounds but after only two hours of little Hayden's antics I'm in dire need of something fortifying. And I rather like the thought of Cary having to put himself out for me, for a change.

'Yes, please. A gin and tonic would go down *really* well.'

He takes a moment to study my face before returning a polite smile. And then I realise this is the first time he's really noticed me. I mean *me* as a person, rather than a contractor hired to make a promotional video.

'G and T it is, then,' he throws back at me nonchalantly.

Out of the corner of my eye I notice that a little smile is creeping over the face of the woman sitting next to me.

'Your boss?' she leans in to ask as he walks away.

Well, I suppose he is while I'm under contract.

'Yes, unfortunately.'

'Commiserations,' she offers, diving back into that bag which seems to contain a weird assortment of items.

Cary heads off down the aisle, and with two empty seats next to me for the first time since boarding I feel that I finally have room to stretch and breathe. I can still hear Hayden screaming somewhere in the background. But as I look over to smile at the elderly gentleman sitting across the aisle on my far left, I draw in a long, slow breath. It feels good.

'Kids, eh?' The man nods, raising his eyebrows before focusing once more on the book in front of him. The one Hayden was repeatedly trying to kick out of his hands a few minutes ago.

It isn't long before the mother returns, anxiously searching through her bag and retrieving a packet of wet wipes.

'I'm so sorry about the disruption,' she apologises, looking first at the elderly gentleman sitting next to her and then across the aisle at me.

He gives a nod and a little smile.

'It's difficult when they're so young,' I offer, hoping to make her feel a tad less awkward. 'Would you like to swap places with me? It might allow you to make your little boy more comfortable, so he can get some sleep.'

I can see she's delighted but instinctively her head turns towards the rear of the plane where the noise level is elevating by the second.

'Look, I'll move your things over here. You get back to your husband to help out.'

'Thank you so much. We've been dreading the flight as Hayden is going through the terrible twos. Before we were parents we laughed whenever we heard that phrase but now—'

'Just go. I'll sort everything.'

As we're going to be in the air another twelve painfully long hours, now is the time to at least try to come up with a workable solution. Otherwise none of us are going to get any rest at all. I drag my hand luggage from under the seat and grab a few things I stuffed into the seat pocket in front of me.

Squeezing sideways along the row to the aisle on the other side, I see that the elderly gentleman has now put down his book. He's already gathering together a collection of toys to place them on the seat together with the lady's bag.

'That's really kind of you. I'll just carry these things across and then I'll settle myself in.'

When I return, I figure that at least sitting here I'm not dodging anything and I will be able to make a list of Cary's latest revisions. I'm concerned we're trying to pack in too much footage at his insistence. If we don't get the pace of the video spot on, it will diminish the overall message. He should stand back now and let me finish the job in the right way.

Catching a sudden movement out of the side of my eye, I glance across to see Cary doing an about-turn in the far aisle. I can't help suppressing a little grin at the thought of him waiting on me. Moments later he appears carrying a small tray that is almost brimming over.

'The supplies have arrived,' he declares with an engaging smile. 'Wise move,' he adds, lowering his voice to a whisper.

'It looks like you ransacked the drinks trolley,' I exclaim but I'm happy enough to take command of three single bottles of gin and three small cans of tonic.

'I played the pity card and told her you were nursing bruises. When I explained where exactly you were sitting her face visibly sagged.' Cary raises his eyebrows mockingly and I begin laughing. I didn't realise he had a sense of humour.

'Actually, I asked if there was any chance you could be moved to give the family a little more space. Unfortunately, the plane is full, but she was very apologetic and kept loading up the tray. I also have these.' He pulls a selection of snacks from his pocket. 'Crisps, mini chocolate chip cookies and Godiva chocolates. Help yourself.'

I hold up my hand and he deposits enough packets to make them spill over into my lap. Then he offers the contents of the tray to the nice gentleman sitting next to me, who declines with an amused smile on his face and indicates towards the still untouched drink in front of him.

Cary gives him an acknowledging nod and gazes down at me.

'I'll see you later, then.' With that, he turns on his heels and hurries off. As I glance behind me I can see why – the family are heading back in this direction. Well, they're trying their best to steer Hayden forward but it's slow progress.

Surveying the stash on the tray in front of me, it seems Cary can be very persuasive, rather than dictatorial, when he wants to be. But then, grabbing a few freebies is one thing – upgrading me to first class is another, and it's clear that hasn't even crossed his mind.

Cary and I haven't seen eye to eye on a few things during filming, but I was butting heads with him for a reason. Namely, I care because I'm a perfectionist too and I do know what I'm doing. He might think he knows best, but he could at least extend me the courtesy of listening to my advice before he steamrolls through the decision-making process.

Quite frankly, at times I've found him overbearing and intensely annoying. I can now add totally self-absorbed to the description.

'I should imagine that will hit the spot.'

I turn to look at my new companion.

'Absolutely! I'm Leesa, by the way, Leesa Oliver.' I offer an outstretched hand and we shake.

'George Richardson. Lovely to meet you, Leesa. And that was very kind of you to accommodate that young family. Takes me back a bit but I can't remember my boys, or the grandkids comes to that, being quite so… energetic.'

I can't contain a chuckle and I lean in, keeping my voice low. 'Self-preservation, actually. That little guy certainly packs a punch!'

It's George's turn to laugh. 'Are you heading home for Christmas?' he enquires.

'Yes. I've been working in Sydney for the past few weeks and we over-ran the schedule. Otherwise I'd already be back home listening to Christmas oldies on MTV, I suspect.'

'Ah! No avoiding them, I'm afraid. I've been on a whistle-stop tour to catch up with two of my three grandsons and their families. Might be my last trip to Australia, as I find the jetlag a bit much these days,' he admits.

'Get them to come to you in future,' I reply with a smile.

'Now there's a thought. But I'm not sure I could cope if they all arrived at once. So what line of work are you in, Leesa?'

'My company makes promotional videos.'

George's eyes light up. 'You're not in the market for any help, are you? Grandson number two, who lives in the UK, is having a career crisis. In his spare time he posts a lot of videos on YouTube – mainly featuring his other hobby: buildings that could be restored but have been abandoned. I had no idea people found that interesting, but they do and he attracts a phenomenal number of views.

'He works in finance and I think it's a waste because basically he's a creative person. I keep telling him that while he's still single, now is the time to try something different. He's passionate about the videos he films and it gives him a real buzz. A little hands-on work experience would be invaluable to him at this stage.'

George's face is animated as he talks about his grandson with great fondness.

'I'm all for encouraging people to follow their dreams and sometimes you just have to go for it, or you'll never know where it might have led,' I say. 'I'll give you my card and if he does decide to make the break, send me an email. I can't promise I'll be in a position to take on some additional help, but I can always ask around.

'I know a lot of people in the business. Some are office-based but there are a growing number of businesses like mine who employ contractors to work from home. It keeps the overheads low and there's little point in having an office, as most of the work requires us to travel around the UK when we aren't in front of the PC.'

'That's very kind. It's a tough industry to break into, that's for sure. How did you start off?'

'My ultimate dream was originally to become a screenwriter and producer but even starting at the bottom the job opportunities were thin on the ground. After university I began making edgy, low-budget music videos for YouTube. They were supposed to launch some previously unheard-of bands and would, in the process, kickstart my business. Well, that was the idea until reality set in and I grew tired of living like a perpetual student. There isn't a lot of money at the lower end of the market.

'I was lucky in that a friend of my father's mentioned he was looking to hire a company to do a short promotional video to upload to his website. I managed to persuade him to let me have a go and that's how it all began. My first photoshoot featured the latest in bathroom and kitchen designs. After that, a lot of my work came from word of mouth recommendations. Your grandson sounds like he's made a really good start, though, and realises it's all about hard work and commitment to build a reputation.'

'I've always told him straight, if you want something, you have to be prepared to work for it. The trouble is—' he looks at me and smiles '—I retired three years ago after more than forty years in the printing business. I sat around twiddling my thumbs for a couple of days and decided I'd had enough already. I guess one's work ethic isn't something that can be switched off just like that. I run a proof-checking service these days. Guess he takes after his granddad when it comes to motivation.'

I raise a toast to his grandson and we clink plastic cups. As I take that first, wonderful sip I realise Hayden has stopped moaning and, finally, peace reigns.

We will be arriving in Qatar airport at eleven-thirty this evening, which is three hours ahead of UK time. But our body clocks will still be on Sydney time, which is eight hours ahead of Qatar time.

'I hope they have more gin,' I half-whisper to my companion who raises his eyes to the heavens.

Fortified by a nice little buzz as the alcohol begins to kick in, I can at least settle myself down now and my body can finally relax. I glance across at Hayden. Well, this experience has confirmed that having kids isn't something that's right for me. But I think I had already sussed that one out.

2

It's Going to be a Long Night

After another brief chat with George, I dig out my business card and we do an exchange. His bears the company name Proof Positive. Then it's time to assemble my thoughts and get to work. George's nose is in his book again and I leisurely glance through my hastily scribbled notes. I see that the first half of the page is covered with stray lines where my arm kept shooting across at an angle from a shove or a kick. Oh well, at least now I can write without threat of stabbing the pen into my own leg.

As the hours pass my eyes grow weary so I pack my notebook away and nestle back into my seat.

Unable to sleep, my thoughts wander. Cary Anderson is a very attractive man, I will freely admit that. Annoyingly, he has an inherently broody yet enigmatic appeal that, to me, is dashed the moment he begins speaking. It's the tone he uses that comes across as arrogant and demanding.

With his short, curly brown hair and hazel eyes with a hint of green to them, he turns heads. He doesn't tower over me at around five-foot-ten, some four inches taller than I am, but he carries himself with a sense of purpose. It makes him stand out in a crowd.

Or maybe it's his passion for his work that gives him that air of absolute confidence; even though he's probably only in his mid-thirties and young for a CEO. He doesn't suffer fools gladly. Or people who won't step up when it matters, and he is demanding, I can vouch for that fact. The other side to that, though, is that he makes things happen and expects those around him to do the same.

When his assistant at SPS – Solar Powered Solutions – initially made contact to arrange a meeting at their London office, the first thing I did was to look the company up online. They are one of the UK's leading manufacturers of solar panels and remotely controlled wireless thermostatic controls. The SPS website was impressive and their mission statement grabbed my attention: *profit from securing a cleaner future, today.*

They have re-designed the whole heat exchange and absorption cooling system to reduce costs and improve efficiency. Apparently, it's a game-changer as the installation consumes significantly less energy than anything else currently available. The resultant power savings mean that even a modest-sized home could expect a very good return, over and above the amount saved on their domestic usage, from day one. As with other systems currently on the market their combined installation can be controlled from a phone, iPad or PC. But they are offering a real option aimed at the mass market – the average man in the street who can now benefit significantly in the same way that the bigger users have in the past.

I will admit I was impressed and that was before I had the benefit of the many presentations Cary made at the Sydney Self-Build Exhibition.

He's passionate about the need to reduce greenhouse gases and the damage it does to the planet, which is very commendable. If only he would climb down out of that tower of his occasionally, it would be easier to warm to him as a person. But maybe that's the whole point. Keeping everyone at arms' length is a clever way of remaining firmly in control and getting your own way.

I will be honest and admit I'm not looking forward to the eight-hour stopover at Doha Airport in Qatar. Cary and I will just be hanging around at the airport while we wait for the connection. That means making general conversation and, from what I've seen so far, that's not something Cary's inclined to do.

I find myself shaking my head at the thought.

Settling back against the curve of the seat I feel too tired to sleep. That wired feeling gives everything an edge and it's hard to shut down. I figure that closing my eyes might help and while resting isn't sleeping, it's better than nothing.

Half an hour later and there's still no change. My eyes flick open when the seat begins to wobble and I stare at George, who is shaking. With laughter, thankfully. One look at the screen in the back of the seat in front of him tells me why and I start laughing, too. A grumpy-looking, furry, lime green character with attitude is doing some very mean things.

He slips out one of his earpieces.

'It started a few minutes ago. *The Grinch*. He's out to steal Christmas.' He leans in to whisper. 'Benedict Cumberbatch is the voice and they cast that very well. He's certainly making me laugh. You should watch it. Beats tossing and turning in your seat and I'm sure he won't really steal Christmas.' He winks at me.

I put my earphones back in and George assists me in getting set up. It isn't long before we are both stifling our laughs, as the majority of the people around us are snoozing.

I give him a thumbs-up, and settle back to watch the onscreen antics. George is right, Benedict Cumberbatch is so the right voice for *The Grinch*. Yo! Ho! Ho! Let the festive fun begin.

I learnt a few new things during the flight. Firstly, that a child awakes with renewed energy after only a couple of hours sleep. When I say energy, I mean Hayden turned his attention to climbing up the back of the seat in front of him. He almost succeeded in launching himself over the top at one point. But there was one more surprise to come and that was Cary stepping in when both of Hayden's parents were reaching desperation point. We still had well over an hour to go before landing and they were seriously flagging.

To my surprise Cary's head suddenly appeared around the galley curtain, one row in front. He was talking to a flight attendant and pointing in the direction of Hayden. The boy was jumping up and down in his seat as if it was a trampoline. She pushed back the curtain, giving Cary a very generous, full-lipped smile as she did so. Yes, lady, you can smile but you wouldn't if you had to work with him. Looks can be deceiving.

As I surreptitiously watched him out of the corner of my eye, Cary seemed to be vandalising one of the inflight magazines. He was tearing out page after page. I noticed that Hayden was watching him, too. The little boy clambered over his dad's lap for the umpteenth time, eliciting some loud groans – the guy must be black and blue with bruises. But the little lad wandered up to stand in front of Cary, who simply smiled down at him and said 'Hi, little fella.' Cary waved at Hayden's father, who gave him a thumbs-up. Then he continued what he was doing.

It turned out he was making paper planes and when he launched the first one Hayden's face lit up. As little legs scampered away to retrieve it, Cary continued making them until he had half a dozen on the tray next to him. Every time Hayden brought one back, Cary launched another with amazing precision. I almost laughed out loud as it was very reminiscent of a dog with a ball, but it worked.

One of the flight attendants was so impressed that he joined in to encourage the toddler and rewarded him with an apple. Hayden glowed under their approval and his mood lifted. Cary played with him for about twenty minutes, moving on to entertain him by juggling paper scrunched up into balls this time. I mean that man can really juggle!

Much to Cary's mortification, when Hayden's mum finally went to reclaim her son after the seatbelt sign was switched on, she gave Cary a hug. He turned to ruffle the boy's hair and high-fived him before heading back to his seat.

As I prepared for an anticipated bumpy descent, I found myself wondering if Cary was married and whether he had young children of his own. I certainly wouldn't have had a clue about how to keep a tantrum-inclined toddler occupied.

After I catch up with Cary on landing, we follow the snake of weary travellers through the terminal. 'That was some juggling show earlier on,' I muse.

He smiles and shrugs his shoulders.

'Hayden is a bright little boy. Full of energy and too young to understand being cooped-up on a plane for all those hours. It's about defusing situations and distracting them, at that age.' He sounds like he's quoting from a textbook on children's behavioural management. Is everything in life that simple, to him – find the key to staying in control?

However, I am amazed by his response and sense of acceptance, as if Hayden's behaviour was to be expected.

'I guess, with a lot of ex-pat families heading home for the holidays, there were a number of youngsters on the plane. Yes, there was a bit of crying and scrambling around admittedly, but he was the only really disruptive one. That can't be normal, can it?'

Cary's face lights up with a quirky smile.

'Clearly, you haven't been around many young children. Even the angelic ones have their moments, believe me.'

'Well, no, you're right there, I haven't. Children aren't really my thing,' I add, drolly.

Cary looks amused. 'It's a pity it's such a long wait until we board our connection to Cardiff, but my PA has booked us into the Oryx Lounge. I'm hungry, how about you?'

A sigh of relief escapes my lips at the news as Cary indicates to a sign advertising the lounge. Hopefully, the facilities will help to make our wait a little more bearable, at the very least. I follow as he tucks in behind a steady stream of people all heading in the same direction.

'I feel rather grimy. I'd like to freshen up before I eat,' I admit.

'No problem. The showers here are great. Endless hot water and immaculately clean.'

There speaks a seasoned traveller who understands what really matters after a lengthy flight, in the early hours of a new day. As we approach the entrance to the lounge it's exactly what I would expect from this sleek and modern airport. Flanked by two very tall ceramic pots on plinths and with a sign you can easily spot at a distance, it certainly looks promising.

We follow the queue of people inside and wait our turn to check in. Then Cary and I head off in the direction of the showers. Agreeing to meet back in the lounge area, which is almost full already, it's pretty optimistic to assume we will be able to find a couple of unoccupied seats. We might have to sit separately, which would be a relief in one respect. At least it will mean not having to make polite conversation.

Standing beneath the steady stream of hot water without the overhead shower wetting my hair isn't easy but it's so refreshing. By the time I've dried, changed my underwear and donned the crease-resistant, long-sleeved top rolled up in my hand luggage, I at least have a bit of my sparkle back. A quick brush of my hair, a squirt of deodorant and then perfume, and I'm done.

Making my way back into the open area of the lounge and scanning around the sea of occupied seats, I look for

Cary. His head appears above the crowded masses as he stands to wave at me and I head in his direction. He, too, is looking a little more refreshed, I notice as I sink down very gratefully into the squishy leather seat next to him.

'I was hoping to grab four seats so we could put our feet up and lay out as some have already done but it's just too busy at the moment. If you want, I'll stay here with the bags and you go and have a look at the buffet. Water and soft drinks are off to the side in the fridge. Coffee is at the far end, over there. It's all a bit calorie-laden but it will keep us going until we board.'

Sauntering off, I resist the temptation to turn around to see if Cary is watching me as I walk away. His brisk business manner and hmm… how can I describe it? That almost uptight, driven vibe I'd come to expect from him is diminishing by the second. I don't recognise the much more relaxed and normal human being he's turning into. Even his tone of voice is beginning to lose that slightly caustic, haughty edge.

The buffet is immaculately presented but it is all rather stodgy food. There are little cakes and pastries, sandwiches and wraps, with a few bowls of different types of salad. But there is also a platter of dates, which I love. The coffee machine is the push button sort, but the cups are on the small side and it seems to only dispense what looks like a double espresso or a smaller Americano.

Looking around as I walk back to Cary, I see predominantly Westerners surrounding us. There are several men dressed in thawbs, the long white shirt over loose pants. I can't see any women in the traditional long, black abayas at all. Most travellers are flying out to the UK or European destinations, no doubt eagerly heading home for Christmas.

As I sit down to savour the dark, pleasingly bitter coffee, Cary heads off in the direction of the buffet area. When he returns he's bearing a plate piled high with food.

'I know I've passed over the healthy stuff, but I need carbs,' he comments as he settles down next to me.

I watch as he stuffs a whole mini croissant into his mouth in one and I guess a look of surprise flickers over my face.

'Sorry. I really am starving,' he admits.

I nibble on a vegetable wrap rather daintily as he watches me.

'You're obviously a lot more relaxed now the exhibition is over,' I say as soon as my mouth is empty.

'Am I?' He seems surprised by my remark. 'Look, I'm sorry if I've seemed a bit… uptight but it's been the year from hell. I guess I didn't realise just how wound-up I've been and I'm sorry if you've felt the effects of that. It wasn't my intention, I can assure you, and I value your opinion and your professionalism.' The look he gives me is genuine. For some stupid reason it makes my stomach flutter. An apology and a genuine look of remorse – I'm overcome.

In an attempt to move on rather quickly, I say the first innocuous thing that comes into my head.

'What are your plans for Christmas?'

He frowns. 'Taking part in the obligatory family festivities. And you?'

I nod. 'I wish I could say I was looking forward to a wonderfully relaxing break, but I'd be lying.'

He shoots me an apprehensive look. Eek! I didn't mean to be quite so blunt, or to sound so depressingly negative, even though that's the truth.

I'm dreading Christmas and once I'm on the plane my fate is sealed. But I've surprised myself, as I don't usually let down my guard like that with a stranger. And especially not someone who is a client. It's the tiredness taking over and for a moment I forgot who I was with.

'Would you like to talk about it?' Cary has demolished everything on his plate in record time and he looks at me in earnest. What is he? A professional counsellor all of a sudden? Now I have to explain away my momentary lapse. A lapse inspired by the way Cary's eyes connected with mine for a second. The sincerity reflected in his words made me regret having been so harsh in judging him.

'Umm, that sort of tripped off the tongue. I'm not usually a person who sounds off easily but there's something about Christmas, isn't there? I guess it can bring out the best and the worst in families.'

He glances at me, his eyes sparkling with the merest hint of amusement at my sidestepping response. Suddenly seeing him in a different light, am I finally glimpsing the man beneath the armour?

'Amen to that. Coming from a dysfunctional family myself, I quite understand.'

I can't hide my surprise as our eyes meet once more. I find myself, unwittingly, growing a little hot and bothered by his attention.

'Oh, I'm not being unduly critical, or unfair here,' he clarifies. 'I'm just as much to blame. It's simply a statement that happens to be true.'

Sensing a little discomfort coming from my direction he settles himself back into his seat, extending his legs out in front of him. 'Guess we'd better try to get a little sleep, then,' he remarks, thankfully drawing the conversation to a close.

3

Cold Comfort

'Ladies and gentlemen, this is Captain Wilson speaking. I have a further update on the adverse weather conditions currently being experienced on the western side of the UK.

'The snowstorm continues, but I'm informed by Cardiff flight control that they are managing to keep the runways clear at this time. We are approximately an hour away. Forecasts indicate that the storm is worsening and it's very likely we will experience some turbulence ahead. Please buckle up and make sure all hand luggage is stowed safely in the overhead lockers. Thank you for your cooperation and let's get you all home safely for Christmas.'

There's a steely determination in his voice. Please God let it be safe to land when we do get there. Inwardly I groan. That damned Cary Anderson has a lot to answer for; it's his fault for delaying my departure. I could have avoided what is now threatening to become a potentially nightmarish situation.

'Not the best news, is it?' the elderly lady sitting next to me declares. But I notice she doesn't seem overly concerned about the problems we're facing. 'I hate flying anyway and for me this storm is my absolute worst nightmare come true, I'm afraid. Even if we don't end up having to divert, if they can't keep the roads clear, onward travel will be impossible. Adding to all of that it's a Sunday and the day before Christmas Eve.'

Why would Cary choose to cut it this fine? Unless he, too, isn't relishing the thought of the Christmas break. Perhaps he was secretly hoping the plane would be diverted, delaying his return.

'The timing of this storm couldn't have been more unfortunate. It's going to be chaos with so many people affected. We're all in the same boat, though, so there's no point in stressing, I suppose. I guess the main concern is a safe landing at this point,' the woman admits. 'Don't worry, try to relax because I'm sure it will all be fine.' A brave smile accompanies her words.

If that's supposed to calm me down, it isn't working and my heart thuds loudly in my chest.

A huge shudder ricocheting through the body of the plane has me grasping both armrests in alarm, dispersing all other thoughts.

'It's only an air pocket. Nothing to worry about,' my companion informs me with the calm voice of a frequent flyer.

'Thank you and sorry to be such a wimp but my stomach is in knots.' My knuckles are now white, as the bouncing continues. The rising fear level has my heart racing inside my chest. Then the cockpit intercom kicks into life.

'This is Captain Wilson speaking, again. We'll shortly be climbing to get above the current turbulence we're encountering. We will continue at that altitude until the final descent, once we have been cleared for approach and landing. Conditions are worsening as expected and road conditions around the airport are not good, I'm afraid. No further updates will be issued at this point, but I can confirm that it's looking good for arrival at our scheduled time.'

Looking good? We're flying in blizzard conditions by the sound of it and they're about to close the airport. In my book that isn't reassuring. My breathing is out of control and a feeling of lightheadedness comes over me.

'This really is nothing out of the ordinary given the weather conditions and if he didn't think it was safe the pilot wouldn't even attempt to land. So, sit back, take a few deep breaths and try not to fret, my dear.'

Fret? I know she means well but I'm on the verge of having a full-on panic attack. The last place I want to be is inside a huge chunk of metal with snow no doubt pitching on the wings and obscuring the pilot's view as we land. Okay, so maybe they don't even need to see where they're going because it's all done electronically, but it's still deeply concerning.

Sucking in a huge breath, out of the corner of my left eye I see that her hand is tentatively hovering over mine. I'm gripping the arm rest between us for dear life. I stay rigid, focusing on my breathing and she withdraws it after a couple of moments. I know I must look like a total idiot, but a quick glance around reveals more than a few anxious looks. I close my eyes and start counting backwards from one hundred. Why, I don't know exactly, but it helps. A little.

The joy of having my feet planted firmly on solid ground is so great I could weep. After surviving the bumpiest landing I could ever imagine, any other worries and concerns simply fade away. However, it's pandemonium inside the airport terminal as the roads have all ground to a halt. People are clamouring around customer service desks trying to arrange overnight accommodation.

'What are you going to do?' Cary asks and I glare at him.

'There's little point in joining one of these ever-growing queues. I need to sit down while I think; that was harrowing to say the least and my legs are still shaky.'

He shrugs, as if this is nothing at all to do with him and wheels his luggage over to a quiet corner. I follow on behind, feeling exhausted and almost too tired to care.

Even though my nerves are now much calmer, my head is in a spin. Suddenly, I spot a man wearing a supervisor's badge walking past and I jump up out of my seat to hurry over to him.

'I'm really sorry to waylay you but it's the first time I've flown into Cardiff International airport. I had a hire car booked to take me to Caerphilly. Is there any movement at all on the roads at the moment?'

He shakes his head. 'Nothing except for the gritter lorries and they can't keep up. You'd best prepare to settle down for the night, I'm afraid. All of the local hotels are already fully booked and struggling, anyway, as the staff can't get in. Even those with rooms they've previously booked will probably end up having to sleep here overnight. There are abandoned cars everywhere and it's a fair trek on foot to the closest hotel, for those brave enough to venture out. There's a lot more snow to come I'm afraid, and the advice is to stay off the roads.'

Walking back to Cary, I can see by his face he overheard every word and he's not happy. I collapse down onto the seat next to him, tiredness washing over me in waves.

'Where were you hoping to stay tonight?' I ask, out of interest.

It wasn't a trick question but it's thrown him. He pauses for a moment as if considering his response.

'About a mile away; my grandmother's house.' He runs a hand over his chin, his mind elsewhere. His phone buzzes and he focuses on the screen.

Even a mile is hard-going on foot, I reflect, if there's nothing on the roads because of the amount of snow on the ground. And dragging a suitcase wouldn't even be an option. We all know the UK grinds to an eerie halt if we get more than an inch of that dratted white stuff and the man said there's more to come.

'I'm thinking that the floor is going to be a better option than this plastic seat. It wouldn't be quite so bad if it was padded.' I cast my eye over the weary throng of people, many now sitting huddled next to their luggage as the queues aren't moving. They seem unwilling to accept the inevitable but it's only a matter of time. Those with children are already using whatever they can from their suitcases to snuggle them up.

Cary looks up, giving me an uncomfortable glance. 'I'm getting a lift back.'

'Really, in this? I thought the roads were virtually impassable.'

He breathes out rather sharply, then heaves a sigh. 'Look, this isn't ideal for reasons I don't really want to go into, but I can't let you sleep on the floor. You'd better come with me and we'll sort something out.'

Why is he talking to me like I'm some sort of encumbrance that has been forced upon him?

'I'll be fine here, I can assure you.'

He stands, slipping the phone into his pocket.

'Leesa, I'm too tired to debate this, just grab your things and follow me.'

I don't know whether it's shock, the effects of jetlag, or having reached the point of not caring less what happens next, that makes me give in.

'Okay. But I have a phone call I need to make first.'

He at least has the decency to move away a few feet while he waits – rather impatiently, I might add, and looking more than a little put out.

The background noise is at least beginning to subside as people realise there's no point in getting angry. I look around thinking that this is all so unexpected. I don't even know how to react as I wait for my ex-mother-in-law to pick up.

'Gwen, it's Leesa.'

'Hi darling. I've been worrying about you and watching the clock. I checked online and was relieved to see the plane had landed safely. The snow won't delay you, will it?' The hopeful note in her voice makes my heart plummet.

'Yes, it will, I'm afraid. I'm sorry you've waited up for nothing. The roads around the airport are closed, apparently, and there's a lot more snow to come in the next few hours. I hope to get out at some point tomorrow as I'm sure the snow ploughs will clear the main roads and then the gritters will be out in force.'

'Oh dear, what a disaster! You are safe for tonight, though, aren't you?'

'Yes, I'm safe. No need to worry. I'm been offered a bed for the night and I'll get over to you tomorrow as soon as the roads are open again. This is a major airport so I'm sure they will work quickly. How are you doing?'

There's a telling pause. 'Oh, you know. Up and down. Nothing feels quite right at the moment and I wish you were here.'

Guilt kicks me in the gut, reminding me this is an emotional time of the year for so many different reasons. I can almost feel her anxiety and fear that I won't make it. There are things we need to talk through but… well, I can't dwell on that now.

'I'll see you tomorrow and don't worry. I will get to you as soon as I can, I promise.'

I don't even wait for Gwen's response before I end the call and walk over to Cary, who is now easing on his thick jacket. I slip a jumper over my head, then undo my suitcase and pull out a slightly rumpled padded coat.

'I nearly didn't pack this as it takes up such a lot of room but it's very lightweight and now I'm glad I did. I was expecting to come home to minus temperatures, but I really wasn't expecting snow.'

'Me neither,' Cary agrees, 'but we'll need to cover up as best we can as our lift is an open-topped, rough-terrain vehicle. It's one of the few forms of transport safe enough to venture out in during a snowstorm.'

He pulls a beanie hat from his pocket and with the other hand grabs the handle of his suitcase.

'Right, let's head in the direction of the exit.'

It isn't easy navigating our way through the mass of stranded travellers and luggage trolleys. As we approach the exit, even in the darkness we can see the snow is falling fast and the flakes are large. It's a sight to behold but rather intimidating.

The strong wind is sculpting huge white mounds that are so powdery they change shape quickly. After only a couple of minutes the outline of the front of a vehicle suddenly appears out of the darkness and it looks suspiciously like an old army jeep. Considering the Arctic conditions, it's approaching quite fast and I wonder how safe it can be as it looks rather basic.

'Okay, let's do this.' Cary heads out through the door and I follow as best I can. Being buffeted by the wind is no joke and it's a struggle to move forward. With each step I'm falling further behind and the eerie silence when the wind isn't gusting is unsettling.

A sudden change in the direction of the icy blast takes my breath away for a moment. I'm being pounded full-on and the intensity of the Arctic chill leaves me gasping. The jeep is only a couple of feet away now and a guy approaches; well wrapped up and wearing a ski mask and goggles, so not an inch of skin is showing.

He holds up a gloved hand in acknowledgement and immediately takes my case from me with a nod and heads off to stow it in the rear of the open vehicle. Cary deposits his case next to mine and then takes my arm to help me climb into the back seat. He leans in to fasten my belt, double-checking it before giving me a thumbs-up. There's little point in trying to talk as the wind would disperse our words as soon as we tried to speak.

Worryingly, the snowflakes are getting bigger by the second. Drawing the hood around my head tighter with both hands, I keep blinking away what now feels like icy missiles being fired directly into my face.

Our driver turns the vehicle around and we head away from the terminal. All we can see is a few feet of the white landscape ahead of us, against the curtain of night. Visibility is deteriorating quickly and it's just us, a lone vehicle on a deserted road – the boundaries of which can't even be seen, so we follow the quickly fading tracks in the snow to lead us out of the airport.

I half-turn to take a quick glimpse behind me; already the airport terminal is just a massive blur; mere pinpricks of light shining out into the hazy darkness. There is nothing at all in the sky other than the battering snow as it falls relentlessly. It will be hours before anyone is going anywhere. It feels like the heavy, dark-grey sky above is going to engulf us and my heart begins to race as the chill takes a hold.

I'm not feeling at ease anyway, what with being whisked off to Cary Anderson's family home. I hardly know the man and he's already made it abundantly clear he's not happy about it. But I fleetingly wonder how many people will end up sleeping on the floor at the airport tonight. I'm beginning to realise how lucky I am, even if I would have preferred the anonymity of a room at one of the hotel chains in the area.

It's a bumpy ride and at one point we slow while the shovel-like apparatus on the front of the vehicle is lowered to clear a section of the road. The drift is way above the bonnet of the open vehicle. We smash into it and the wind quickly sends a spray of powdery snow swirling in all directions. I've heard of the term *whiteout* but never in my wildest dreams thought I'd ever experience one here, in the UK. It's even more daunting with the pervading darkness all around us. It seems to accentuate every little sound, as if we're travelling in a tank and not a vehicle stripped down to the minimum. But those chunky tyres are doing their job and the grip, for the most part, is reassuringly firm.

With the obstacle removed we continue, albeit at a slower pace now, along what looks like a main road to the rear of the airport. We travel along parallel to the link perimeter fencing, beyond which is a large snow-covered bank extending up and obscuring any view of the airport itself. To our left I can only make out the odd swathe of skeletal winter trees. They are interspersed with evergreens that are now weighed down by their heavy white coats.

Beyond that the landscape falls away slightly, disappearing into the darkness as if it's been swallowed up. Abandoned cars litter what I assume is a grass verge at the side of the road. They stick out at differing angles like some weird parking configuration. After being unable to gain any traction on the slippery surface they only came to a halt when something solid prevented them from sliding any further. Often, that was another car and in one case, a wall.

We pass the outline of a very grand house with a collection of stone buildings nestling behind an impressive gateway. Travelling onwards, the jeep takes a left turn into a single-track country lane. After a few hundred yards of ploughing through crisp, virgin snow I spot where we're heading. My jaw would have dropped if I wasn't already cradling my entire face. It's a constant battle to avoid the sting of icy white missiles coming at me from every angle. This isn't a house, it's a huge Victorian country manor.

The vehicle pulls to a halt and Cary literally heaves me out and bundles me under an open, extended porch. It's flanked by two enormous stone lions that now look more like polar bears. Small, red Christmas lights, like glowing berries, hang from the canopy turning this little haven into a colourful grotto. He lowers his collar, glancing at me in earnest.

'Are you okay? I'll get the bags.'

It's actually a relief to hear his voice and my shoulders sag a little, grateful to have made it here in one piece. At the same time the large door behind me is flung open.

Suddenly I'm hurried inside by a gentleman who looks most concerned as he escorts me over the doorstep.

Seconds later Cary, me, our very competent driver, and a pile of damp luggage are all creating a puddle on a very old and beautifully tiled floor. A woman steps forward to greet us. Her smile is warm and her demeanour one of graceful elegance. Long, silver-grey hair is coiled up into a perfect French twist and her face is beaming, clearly delighted by Cary's arrival. Behind her the man who helped me inside is standing attentively awaiting her command. I'm rather surprised, as I thought butlers were a thing of the past.

I glance upwards to see that above our heads isn't just the customary token piece of mistletoe – oh no! It's a massive orb, no doubt lifted by a cherry picker from the top of a very stout tree. It's suspended some forty-plus feet in the air. As my eyes continue to take in the surroundings, I note the grand sweep of the staircase and the wide, galleried landing.

Above that is a beautifully detailed ceiling with ornate plaster coving. I've stepped into the film set of a Christmas film and they are about to begin shooting.

'Cary, my darling boy; it's so good to have you home. And welcome, my dear, I had no idea… but I simply love surprises and this one was well worth the wait!' Her eyes dart between both Cary and myself and before he can introduce me properly she begins talking again. 'You must both be exhausted. Nicholas, can you kindly grab their coats and take them to dry off? Robert, I insist you stay for a drink, you extremely brave man,' she continues, turning to face our driver as he pulls off his woolen ski mask. 'Thank you so much for saving the day and rescuing Cary and his young lady.'

4

The Introduction

His young lady? I don't know whose head jerks back the furthest – mine or Cary's. He casts me a warning glance, but does that mean I should jump in and correct her or not? To be honest, I don't care. She can call me anything she wants as long as there's a spare bed upstairs.

The house is warm enough that my hands and face begin to sting as the heat starts to permeate into my freezing flesh. A pair of soft hazel-green eyes flicker over me and I feel a little embarrassed under her scrutiny.

'Ah, you're half-frozen, my dear. Welcome, I'm Cary's grandmother. We have a roaring fire. Let's get you warmed up.'

She is very charming and reminds me of someone, or maybe a composite someone. You know that cosy, motherly individual who is always putting her guests first and making sure they have everything they need. In fact, she looks vaguely familiar. Maybe she has a doppelgänger, as they say, and it's someone I've seen on TV, or in a magazine.

As I turn, there's an enormous Christmas tree that is probably twenty feet high standing proudly on display, dripping with a collection of silver and white baubles. It's a work of art and I can't take my eyes off it. Topped with a glinting silver star, it couldn't be more perfect. This really is like something out of a film. Lavish, romantic, country-style Christmas decorations, tastefully arranged. The sort of thing you only usually glimpse in expensive magazines while you're waiting to see the dentist.

Walking through the immense hallway we follow her through an oversized, oak door into a spacious room with very tall, and deep, box sash windows denoting the proportions of the room. It looks like the wooden shutters are original and have been painstakingly returned to their former glory. I think this is what would be referred to as a drawing room. Our hostess hurries us across to a large log-burning stove surrounded by an oversized, Victorian feature fireplace with inset ceramic tiles. Delicate lilies adorn the tiles which are in pristine condition.

A realistic, although it's not fresh, garland graces the mantelpiece. In the centre is a large vase full of burgundy-red roses, with sprigs of blue spruce sending out a gloriously festive smell. As my eyes travel around the room it's obvious that this country house has been lovingly restored and money was no object at all.

Before his grandmother turns around to face us, I look at Cary and shrug my shoulders to indicate it's about time he said something. He frowns and I wonder why he feels this is a real dilemma. Cary clears his throat, nervously.

'Grandma, this is… um… Leesa Oliver, the owner of Dynamic Videography. We've been working together out in Australia.' Cary emphasises the last sentence. It draws a halt to my casual gaze around the room and I turn to offer my hand.

'How lovely to meet you, Leesa. I'm Cressida. What a terrible experience for you both, tonight. You were in safe hands with Robert, though.'

Cressida's handshake is surprisingly firm and as we exchange eye contact there's a genuinely warm smile reflected in those hazel eyes of hers. They are so like her grandson's it's easy to spot the family resemblance between them.

'And this gallant man who came to our rescue is Robert Jones, my grandmother's neighbour,' Cary jumps in and I can't help wondering why her initial reaction was to assume I was *Cary's young lady*. If he was seeing someone surely his grandmother would be aware of that fact?

Actually, Cary does look rather nervous and flustered, which is unthinkable and so out of character. I'm beginning to find this rather funny seeing him floundering and clearly worrying about what she's going to say next. Is that a little mean of me, or is this karmic payback time? No, that's unfair. The man has been stressed and this is in such sharp contrast to the last couple of weeks.

Glancing at Robert, I can see that he's much older than I assumed him to be. Probably around Cressida's age, which I would put at seventy-something. It might even be closer to eighty. The old army jeep struck me as being a bit of a... boy's toy, I suppose, because you don't often see them around. But it most certainly has its practical side and maybe you need something like that when you live in such a rural area. A handy acquisition for a gentleman farmer.

From the little I've seen of the area there don't appear to be many properties in this location. I should imagine that not only are they expensive properties to buy, but they also come with acres of land.

I extend a hand towards him and offer a sincere and very grateful smile.

'Thank you so much, Robert. That was some journey and not for the faint-hearted.'

He tips his head back and laughs, a hint of embarrassment flashing over his face. 'A bit of snow is nothing. It's just the fools who insist on having a go at driving when they are in the wrong type of vehicle, who cause the problems. They aren't suitably equipped for the conditions, which makes them a danger to other people. You only have to look at the number of abandoned cars along the main road. Each one was a potential accident in the making.'

As I take a step back, Cary moves in to grasp Robert's hand and give it a firm shake. But I am a little surprised that it all looks rather perfunctory.

'Good to have you back, Cary,' Robert adds before pulling away. His tone might be matter-of-fact, but his smile can't hide how pleased he is to see him. Cary seems oblivious, almost dismissive as he turns away.

'Don't I get a hug?' Cressida moves forward, and Cary immediately throws his arms out towards her with genuine enthusiasm.

'You see what I have to put up with, Leesa? But then, I expect he is much more thoughtful when he's in your company. I haven't seen my grandson for what, four months? And then I have to ask for a hug. He's just like his grandfather!'

'Yes, but Grandma—'

She almost knocks the breath out of him as she launches herself into his arms.

Cary glances at me over his grandma's shoulder with a grimace on his face. Clearly, he's very fond of her, so it must be the reference to his grandfather that has annoyed him. Suddenly I feel distinctly uncomfortable being thrust upon his family like this with hardly any notice. Cressida doesn't seem to have grasped the fact that I'm not Cary's girlfriend and we know nothing about each other beyond our working arrangement. And that hasn't been smooth running.

Fortunately for me, Robert asks when the family are arriving and Cressida is distracted. Cary looks a little relieved.

'Laurence and Sally arrive with their brood tomorrow lunchtime. It's going to be bedlam as usual. It will be so nice for them to meet Leesa for the first time. I knew this was going to be a special Christmas but I didn't quite appreciate *how* special.'

Cary opens his mouth to speak at the exact same time as I'm just about to jump in to correct her. A split-second of hesitation and it's too late.

'Remind me of their ages,' Robert asks. 'It doesn't seem that long since Jackson arrived and here he is, one of three.'

Cressida's eyes gleam. 'Well, he's eight now. Daisy has just turned six and little Chloe is a very determined little three-year-old. She still doesn't sleep through the night, though, and poor Sally doesn't get much help from Laurence. Both of my grandsons work way too hard and are obsessed with their careers to an unhealthy extent. One of them is too busy to even think about settling down, or so I thought.' There's a wicked gleam in her eye.

She casts an amused look in Cary's direction and I steal a quick glance to check out his reaction. He looks exasperated and mightily embarrassed. While now is the moment to come clean, it is rather fun watching him squirm and I'm rather enjoying this.

'Grandma, I lead a busy life at the moment, what can I say?

'Life is all about balance, my dear boy. You can't continue to put work ahead of your relationships; don't you agree Leesa?'

I swallow hard as all eyes are suddenly trained on me. Why I'm letting myself get pulled into this, I have absolutely no idea. I should clear up the misunderstanding now but as soon as her eyes alight on mine, I'm sunk. She's just so *lovely* and besides, it's not my job to point out she's made a mistake. That's down to Cary.

'Um… well, yes, I suppose so but it's seldom that simple, is it? I mean fate comes into play, too, and sometimes it's a bit of an uphill battle. But when things do fall into place I suppose that you have to grab…' I'm wittering on and decide it's best to simply shut up.

Cressida claps her hands to her mouth. 'At last, someone under my roof who understands what I'm talking about.'

I was merely trying to point out that things can't be forced and unwittingly Cressida now thinks I agree with her. It's easy to see that this larger-than-life character has a big heart, so how can anyone possibly take offence when she means well?

I can see that both Robert and Cary are wearing polite yet distinctly forgiving smiles, so maybe this is their normal banter. I make a concerted effort to appear relaxed, so Cary thinks all of this is going over my head as it's none of my business. My growing concern is that I don't want to unwittingly say the wrong thing when a question is levelled directly at me.

Cressida is a woman driven by her love for the people she cares about and, coupled with that formidable energy she exudes, it's an overpowering combination. It's easy to see where Cary gets at least some of his traits from.

'We've been travelling for hours, Grandma, and I think we both simply want to drop into bed.'

The moment Cary stops speaking he looks horrified, instantly realising he didn't quite phrase that correctly.

'Fortunately, the blue room is made up if you'd like to take that one?' Cressida offers and Cary's jaw drops a little. Now she thinks we're sleeping together. I might be mistaken, but is that a flash of embarrassment he's trying to fend off?

'There… there's no need, Grandma. I'll use my old room and perhaps Leesa would be comfortable in the second guest room.' His face is set into a deep frown that isn't very flattering but thank goodness he put her right on that one.

'Well, that's a pity, but it's up to you. In my opinion it has the best view of the garden.'

Cressida gives him a truly wicked smile and Cary looks appalled, then flustered. I have to stop myself from laughing out loud.

Robert jumps in to fill the uneasy silence.

'Right, I'd better get off. The men are due in shortly. We're going to plough the lane and then hook up the gritter. Hopefully, that will mean everyone will be able to get out in the morning. I doubt your company will be too impressed if they have to walk down from the top road with their cases. And the milk tanker will need to get through, so the quicker I make a start, the better.'

Cressida leans in to place her hand on Robert's arm.

'Thank you for thinking of us all, Robert. We're so lucky to have you around to get things sorted. I bet a lot of small communities are cut off right now. The children will love the snow, of course, but this fall was a lot heavier than I think any of us could have anticipated.'

She pulls back, and he gives her a friendly nod. As their eyes meet, I can see there's a real connection between them. Suddenly Cressida turns her head in my direction and catches me watching them.

'Right, it's very late and everyone is tired,' she declares. 'I'll show Leesa to her room so she can get some sleep now she's warmed up a little. Cary, can you ask Nicholas to bring up Leesa's luggage, please?'

A look of relief flashes over his face and he nods, as Cressida takes my arm, walking me off in the direction of the hallway.

Once we are out of earshot she leans into me, speaking in a conspiratorial tone.

'It's so good to have another woman around, Leesa. And aside from a week at Easter and two at Christmas, I only get a rare visit from Cary these days. But it's all work and no play, from what I can see. It's not that I want my grandson to be constantly running back home to me, but that I'm the only person to remind him life is much shorter than we think. It makes me happy to think he's been having some fun while he's been away.'

Fun? It was a lot of things, but fun isn't one of the words I'd use to describe the experience.

'Just between us, my big fear is that he feels he can put his personal life on hold as if it's something he will be able to pick back up when he's good and ready. What you said was classic, simply classic and it wouldn't have gone over his head. Of course, he no longer listens to what I have to say, but that doesn't matter now. This is all so exciting!'

I immediately go into panic mode as my foggy brain decides how to answer that.

'We've just been together in Australia filming the promotional video. It's no big deal, really.' Well, that is the honest truth.

'I understand and this is a bit like being thrown in at the deep end. Anyway, you know by now that he's married to his work and we need to change that. And I'm sure we will.'

Her response is distinctly worrying and her eyes are firmly fixed on my face as if she's expecting me to confirm that. I try to remain impassive and ignore the reference to 'we'. But I'm feeling so drained that none of this is making sense any more.

Cressida ends up squeezing my arm affectionately. She's desperately looking for some support to chivvy Cary along but that's not a role I can take on, so I maintain my silence.

'Oh,' she sighs, 'I'm so looking forward to chatting with you properly as I appreciate how tired you are. Breakfast is at ten to allow you both to get a good few hours' sleep. I am sorry your own holiday plans will be delayed, my dear. However, your company is much appreciated, and I want you to know that. It's a pity it took a snowstorm to engineer it, but everything happens for a reason! Maybe it was just the prompt that my darling Cary needed. I'm sure my grandson will seek you out to apologise for my behaviour. He thinks I'm a rather scandalous embarrassment because he doesn't talk about emotions and I do. One day I will succeed in making him realise it's not a weakness.' She winks at me. 'And I don't intend to give up until that day has arrived.'

5

A Startling Revelation

Cressida is right and before I can even begin to unpack, there's a tap on the door. I shout out 'come in', half-wondering if Cressida has an entourage of servants and she's sent someone to help me. But I needn't have worried, because when the door swings open its only Cary. He looks shamefaced.

'Look, I'm really sorry about that and the awkward bedroom arrangement thing. My grandma means well and she's very liberal. But sometimes she doesn't really listen, or let people explain. The moment she set eyes on you I could see that she immediately jumped to the wrong conclusion. I wasn't quite sure how to get out of it. I... um... well, I didn't have the heart to disillusion her after that as she was clearly delighted. Particularly as I've been away for quite a while and I don't want to start off my visit by upsetting her.'

'It's fine. I understand it was awkward. I tried too, but I blame the tiredness; I'm surprised either of us can string a sentence together, let alone cope with that level of conversation.'

He looks relieved, although his body language is awkward. The fact that I've seen another side to him has dented his armour.

'Do you fancy a nightcap? I need something alcoholic, I don't know about you.' Cary's offer implies he'd like some company.

I give him a little smile.

'It was an onslaught, wasn't it?' he admits. 'It's part of the reason I wasn't keen to bring you here. Grandma is a gem, just a little unusual let's say. Quirky, is probably the kindest word to use. And she dotes on me. When I'm here I feel like a small boy again and it's partly because I admire her; she's one strong woman for sure. But also because… ugh… a part of me is desperate to please her. Right, I think everyone else is in bed, so it's safe to sneak down.'

That makes me smile. No one has to sneak anywhere in a house this size.

I follow Cary out onto the landing and we lower our voices, although I'm not quite sure why we're bothering. It reminds me of being a kid and sneaking downstairs to check if Santa has been.

'Anyway, you're stuck with us until I have transport tomorrow, I'm afraid. Do you think you can cope?' he asks, as we wend our way down the beautifully curved staircase.

'It's fine, but I've just realised I forgot to thank Cressida for accommodating me. I feel like a zombie at the moment but that's no excuse to forget my manners.'

'I don't think she noticed, Leesa, her thoughts were – unfortunately – going off in another direction, entirely.'

He shakes his head, indicating that I shouldn't worry myself about it, as we head across the vast open-plan area and past the enormous tree, in front of which I'd love to linger in awe. He leads me through into a rather cosy room, given that the proportions are still magnificent. But it feels less formal, somehow.

He immediately taps a panel on the wall to turn on two table lamps and some twinkly lights on yet another Christmas tree, which nestles – not so inconspicuously – in the corner. The embers of what's left of a log fire are still glowing in the fire grate and instinctively I make my way over to it. Who can ignore even the dying heat from a real fire. That satisfying smell of woodsmoke, combined with the woodiness of cut logs sitting in the basket ready for tomorrow's fire, is magnificent.

'Brandy, whisky – what's your preference? We have most things here,' Cary asks.

'I'll have a small one of whatever you're having, thank you.' I'd prefer a good old Southern Comfort, but I know that's a blend and Cary is talking about aged, malt whiskies and the finest of brandies. I wouldn't have a clue what to ask for.

'When I can get a quiet moment alone with her I will explain, so please accept my apologies for not handling this better. It's rather embarrassing for me, actually, as that's the biggest welcome home I've had in years.' Is that a hint of amusement I detect in his voice now?

I laugh softly. Then disparate thoughts whirling around inside my head begin to slot together and my mouth falls open as I turn away from the fire to face Cary.

'Your grandmother is *the* Cressida Anderson, isn't she? I thought she looked familiar. She must think I'm a total idiot not recognising her instantly. Why on earth didn't you warn me?'

He hunches his shoulders as he walks towards me, proffering a glass.

'I rather hoped it wouldn't come up.'

'What? The fact that I'm staying in the home of an *internationally bestselling, award-winning* author? Your grandmother is beyond famous; she is the Grande Dame of contemporary romance.'

He looks suitably ashamed of himself as he raises his glass in a mock toast and takes a slug. Now this is all beginning to make a lot more sense. Romance runs through her veins and she's ended up with a grandson who apparently won't even give it a passing nod. It's like they live in two very different worlds.

'Having never read any of her books it doesn't really do anything for me, although I am very proud of what she has achieved, of course. And she is also one astute businesswoman, but Grandma can't separate fiction from real life and that's why the men in her life end up disappointing her. And maybe why my mother became so disillusioned with her own marriage.'

Now I'm shocked. That's quite a statement to make about a loved one when you are talking to someone you don't know that well. Cressida isn't just his grandmother, she's an institution.

'What do you mean?'

'Well, placing an unrealistic expectation on anyone is bound to end in disaster.'

'Hoping you will one day find someone to settle down with is an unrealistic expectation? I'd say every mother and grandmother in the world has that aspiration for their offspring.'

'It's not that simple. We are a dysfunctional family. All I can do is apologise in advance for anything further she says before I can deliver you back into the hands of normal people. Which I will do, as soon as my brother, Laurence, arrives tomorrow. He has a four-wheel drive and it shouldn't be a problem. In the meantime, if you can just play along with whatever happens, in case I can't sideline her, I'd be very grateful. I'd rather not kick off my arrival by putting a dampener on her Christmas spirit.'

He can be nice when he wants something but that sounds like one *big* favour, to me. Time to change the subject maybe, so I scan the room. It's stunningly beautiful, as old, expensively furnished houses tend to be.

'The decorations are beyond wonderful,' I comment, reaching out to touch the shiny silver stars nestling in the festive garland gracing the mantlepiece. There are also little silver stags and I'm surprised when I touch one to feel how heavy it is, until I see the hallmark and realise that it's solid silver.

'Family traditions abound here, but Grandma isn't averse to changing it up every year. I bought the stags for her as part of last year's Christmas present. It's one of her favourite animals and she was delighted with them.'

Ah, that was rather thoughtful of him. 'Well, they are beautiful. As are the lights.'

We saunter over to the tree in the corner.

'This is unusual.' I reach out and run my fingers over the springy, dark, glossy green needles. At home we haven't had a real tree for years and I never bother too much at my place, as it's a pain taking the trimmings down afterwards. But here, all this attention to detail just warms the heart in a way that is touching. Meaningful. Wonderful. Magical.

'It's a Nordmann fir. They originated from the Caucus mountains in Russia. They tend not to drop their needles and have that perfect pyramid shape, which is great for a smaller room like this. Because the pines are waxy, though, you only get a subtle hint of the smell.'

The room is huge by most people's standards and so is the tree.

'I love the fact that the needles aren't sharp but rather blunt on the ends. It's not the same as the one in the hallway, though, is it?'

'No. Grandma always orders a blue spruce for the big tree, because it fills the air with an evocative Christmas smell. It takes me back to my childhood, as that's one of the hallowed traditions from her own childhood.'

Cary cradles his whisky glass in his hands, reflectively. I pretend not to notice his moment of reflection and instead focus on the tree. The myriad of tiny, sparkling little white lights is perfect and Cressida's silver and white theme is carried throughout. A lot of time and attention has gone into the planning; this isn't something someone has thrown together, or simply pulled out of the attic to have someone else assemble. Her love of nature shines through, from the care and attention to the types of trees she chooses, the real pine cones, to the 3D white snowflakes and the beautiful little wooden stars with the tiny tartan bows.

The surprise is that you get a real sense of tradition, but not a strict adherence to the past. Her roots are firmly in the present.

'Do you mind if we go and look at the main tree? I didn't like to stand and stare at it when we arrived. But it is, beyond a shadow of a doubt, the most awesome tree I've ever seen up close.'

'Of course. Lead the way.'

My initial impression was wrong, this isn't like a film set at all. I've simply stepped into the most magical of Christmas settings, one most people can only ever dream about.

As we stand, gazing up at the twenty-foot-tall blue spruce I take in a deep breath, savouring the smell. It's pine cones and leaves and mossy earth. I close my eyes for a few moments, imagining that I'm walking through a forest and all that is missing is the sound of birdsong.

'The smell is much more pungent at night, for some reason,' Cary says, watching my reaction with interest. 'This majestic tree is native to the Rocky Mountains. It's the thick scaly bark that produces most of the scent. It's regarded as a medicinal plant, too. An infusion of the needles was used to treat colds, settle the stomach, and for rheumatic pains. In many of their traditional ceremonies, Native Americans used branches of the blue spruce as gifts to bring good fortune.'

Even fully trimmed, what stands out is the natural beauty of the tree itself. 'I love that grey-green sheen and those pointy, waxy needles. They are rather sharp though,' I admit, tentatively reaching out and wincing on contact.

'It's not the easiest of trees to install, but it's worth the hassle. The star on the top is older than I am. It's one thing we won't let Grandma change.'

A woman who adheres to old traditions but seems keen not to get bogged down by them. Cressida is a complex woman, for sure.

I finish the last of my whisky and turn to Cary, thinking what a perfect end to the day, but how totally unexpected. I envisaged him spending Christmas in a spacious, contemporary home – probably one he had built. That may well be the sort of property he owns, but instead he has returned to the place that truly represents home to him. Despite bemoaning the hard time his grandmother gives him and being under her constant scrutiny, there is nowhere else he'd rather be. And now I understand why he was a little reluctant to bring me here – because this is the place where he feels safe, but also vulnerable.

'Thank you, Cary, for rescuing me from the snow. I really appreciate it. Right, I'll pop this glass into the kitchen and head off to bed if you don't mind.'

He reaches out to take it from me. 'I'll sort it. You look done in.'

'It's been quite a day,' I remark, speaking as much to myself, as Cary.

'It certainly has. I'll get rid of these and then I'm off to grab a shower and a little rest before the quizzing begins in the morning. Hopefully, once Grandma has said her usual spiel she will back off a little. But prepare yourself to witness a bit of a showdown. She'll no doubt be organising her plan of attack between now and dawn, as she survives on merely a couple of hours' sleep, unfortunately.'

He shrugs his shoulders, clearly anxious at the thought of what's to come. The sheepish look he gives me makes me choke down a merciless laugh, which I suppose is a little mean given the circumstances. He isn't afraid of her, he's simply afraid of his own reaction.

As he heads off to dispense with the glasses, I climb the stairs to return to unpacking my suitcase. I can't help musing over this very unexpected turn of events. As soon as Cary is out of sight, I stop halfway up the staircase and turn to gaze down at the decorations.

From here that perfect ball of mistletoe beckons to me, suspended so loftily, it's clearly ready and waiting to inspire some very magical, Christmas kisses.

A flutter in my chest turns into more of an ache. I try to imagine myself standing beneath it, eyes closed and waiting in eager anticipation as the man of my dreams folds me into his arms. Sadly, I'm not seeing it with any conviction. But it is worthy of the tenderest of moments and I cast around in my head for inspiration – one screen kiss that would make any romantic swoon. Ah! The moment when Mark Darcy kisses Bridget Jones as the snowflakes fall around them. Except that was in a street in London and not inside a wonderful old country house, of course, and if I recall correctly, she was in her underwear. I sigh. One day I hope I'll find someone with whom I'll make a memory like that, standing under the mistletoe.

Also hanging from the ceiling are the most beautiful, elongated cascades of white snowflakes and small silver bells. I've only ever seen decorations as amazing as these in posh shopping malls. I can't imagine how much work goes into installing them, given the height involved.

In truth, this is beyond surreal: I'm standing here in the home of the Queen of romance and experiencing the trappings of a Christmas that is almost unbelievably glamorous. Almost as glamorous as the woman herself. But what shines out so very clearly is the love that has been put into the planning. Tomorrow is Christmas Eve and it's obvious that she can't wait to get her family together under one roof again.

Cressida doesn't do this for show, or for herself, but because the festive season is all about giving, not receiving. But even in what could be considered as a picture-perfect life, who knows what heartache that hides? I have a feeling still waters really do run deep.

'I hope your trip was enjoyable and productive,' Cressida asks Cary, as I dig into the bowl of muesli in front of me.

'Yes. There was a lot of interest and all the demonstrations were well attended. I'm expecting it to generate a lot of good leads to progress in the new year once the local sales reps process the information collected.'

Cary's right and from what I saw, SPS's sales pitch created quite a buzz. People are usually looking to save money so it's hard to attract their attention when some will only break even. But with the headline 'make some real money while you make clean energy' it was a big draw.

'And what sort of a subject was he when it came to capturing that on video, Leesa?'

With my mouth still half-full of nuts and oats, it's a few moments before I can respond.

'It was very successful. There were a few changes to the original creative brief which slowed down our progress but we're almost there.'

I can see that Cary is frowning.

'There is quite a long list of changes I've requested which still require your attention, Leesa.' His tone is clipped and his gaze doesn't waver from my face. Suddenly his business head is back in play.

'You're right, there are. But changes always involve a little *easing* to help sync it all together. Especially when we have veered so far away from the initial video concept. I am 100 per cent confident you're going to be delighted with the end result, I can assure you of that, Cary.'

I begin eating again, knowing it would be impolite of him to continue grilling me during what is meant to be a relaxing meal. Cressida doesn't give him a chance and jumps straight in.

'I'm sure Leesa and her company will do a great job, Cary. Sometimes you need to place your trust in people and let them do what they do best. Too much control can be a negative if you won't even give any consideration to other people's suggestions.'

Now she's putting him in his place and I really don't want to be sitting here witnessing this. She's prickling with exasperation as she watches Cary clear his plate, making light work of scrambled eggs and bacon. I notice she's hardly touched her scrambled eggs and I'm eking out the last morsels in my dish as a reason to avoid joining in with the conflict.

'In my experience it pays to never take anything, or anyone, for granted.' His comment sounds rather accusing to my ears and Cressida picks up on that immediately.

'Cary, have you ever listened to yourself? Honestly, sometimes your words border on the insulting. And you have this bizarre need to micromanage everything to an extent where you are in danger of losing your overall perspective.' She leans back in her chair looking across at him with something akin to disbelief written all over her face.

Cary seems rather taken aback by her reaction and I don't think he realises how damning his statement sounded.

She's right, though. He's so... ultra-serious all the time. As if he's afraid of what might happen if he strays outside of his very confined comfort zone. If only he could relax a little, he would be much more approachable. Although, I wonder if Cressida has realised the assumption she made about us is incorrect and now she's a little disappointed.

'I didn't mean to be rude, Leesa, that wasn't my intention at all. I apologise if I sounded a little abrupt. Grandma, please let's not do this now in front of our guest. I am who I am, and I doubt I'll ever change.'

As I move my eyes away from studying Cary's face to steal a look at Cressida, she appears to be a little tearful.

'You're just so worryingly black and white in your approach to life, Cary. I'm fearful of where it's all going to lead. Life is full of greys, my dear boy. Life is about subtlety, and sometimes you wade in with such force people almost... recoil.'

She turns to face me, desperately seeking some assistance. In fairness, I can sort of agree with what she's saying, but

Cary is right. This is no conversation to be having in the company of someone they don't really know, anyway.

I lift the untouched glass of apple juice in front of me to my mouth, feeling that there's no way I can contribute to this particular dialogue. However, realising that it might be a good idea to change the subject quickly, I wrack my brains to think of a diversion and grab the moment.

'By the way, I owe you a huge apology Cressida, for not instantly recognising you. And I did tell Cary off for not warning me in advance. I've been an avid reader of yours for many years, ever since, as a teen, I plucked one of your books off a shelf at the library. It's a real pleasure to meet you in person and so kind of you to offer me a bed for the night. I slept like a log.'

As I finish speaking, they both burst out laughing.

'You need to update your author photo, Grandma,' Cary interjects.

Ooh, is that a tad unkind? But Cressida hasn't taken offence and I think that's probably always been the nature of their very close relationship. Neither of them is afraid to say their piece but any tension it creates is fleeting. However, between Cressida's emotionally-driven concerns and Cary's desire to shirk away from home truths, they are at an impasse. And they probably have been for years.

'He's right, of course, the photograph on the back of my books is probably a good ten years out of date. And no apology necessary, whatsoever. In fact, we should be apologising to you for spoiling breakfast.'

A glance in Cary's direction leads me to suspect that he, too, noticed her eyes were filling up. His apology to me was a real attempt to demonstrate he was listening to what she had to say. He obviously loves his grandmother, but they seem to have totally different agendas and, clearly, that's a real stumbling block.

'Every family has their own difficulties. Did you always want to write, Cressida?'

She dabs at her mouth with the white linen napkin as a young woman approaches.

'We'll take coffee in the sitting room, Fran, thank you. Cary will fetch the tray.'

Cary stands, eager to follow Fran out of earshot. Thanks for nothing, Cary. Some gentleman you turned out to be.

I wait as Cressida rises from her chair and then she leads me into the adjoining room, where Cary and I had our late-night drink, and indicates for me to take a seat.

In daylight, the view from the window looks out over a formal garden to the rear of the house. It's mostly a white landscape, speckled with little bursts of green as some of the larger shrubs begin to lose their covering of snow.

Gravity is already beginning to take over. It's beautiful. How wonderful to have a family home that is passed down from generation to generation. Although a financial drain and a constraint at times, I'm sure. But I suppose that when you are born into a monied family it's something you simply accept as a part of your heritage.

'Where were we? Oh, yes, I longed to write from an early age and that's why everyone referred to me as *the scribbler*. I was always making observations about people and jotting things down. I knew that someday it would all come in useful. But being a wife, bringing up my daughter, organising the renovations on this house while my husband, Matthew, was away working… well, my days were full.

'I eventually began writing in my fiftieth year, it was a birthday present to myself and I haven't stopped since. Well, aside from the period after we lost our darling daughter. Matthew and I had to be strong for the boys and we were determined to face each day with optimism, for their sakes. Cary was eight years old, and Laurence had just celebrated his fifth birthday when she died. Eventually, my writing became the only way to escape the sadness.'

That's such a tragedy and the last thing I expected to hear.

'I'm so sorry for your loss. It must have taken a huge toll on you, having to remain strong and support your loved ones through such an awful time.'

'You do what you have to do. But you can't hide from grief and it still catches me unawares even after all this time, although you're the first person to whom I've admitted that.'

Now I feel awful and if Cary walks in on this conversation he is not going to be happy.

'Have you always written under your real name?'

She nods her head, settling back against the cushions.

'Yes. With the benefit of hindsight it was a big mistake not using a pen name, though. My husband did warn me at the time. But I wanted to see my name on a book, to hold it in my hands and know that at last my dream had come true. But who knew I would end up having such a long career? Or that my growing grandsons would be teased when their friends discovered my books.' Her face breaks into a little smile, as if she's enjoying a private joke.

The door opens, and Cary appears carrying a tray.

'It's a wonderful thing to have a passion that fires you up. Loving what you do is half the battle, isn't it?' I add, gently.

Cressida nods and the eye contact between us is empathetic. She turns to watch Cary as he depresses the plunger on the cafetière slowly, then pours the coffee.

'Obviously you love what you do, too. I can tell.' Cressida turns back to look at me.

It would be wrong of me not to say something about myself when I've been privy to such a revealing conversation. And I almost need to pinch myself when I remember to whom I'm speaking. I mean, *the* Cressida Anderson.

'I've always needed an outlet for my creativity. I had dreams of getting into the film industry and becoming a producer at one point. But that was before I understood how hard it is to get a foot on the ladder. It soon became obvious that working for someone else wasn't going to cut it for me. So, I set up the business, which turned out to be a bit of a rollercoaster ride. But I did it. Five years on and it's thriving, and we've won a few awards so I'm not complaining.'

Cary looks across at me. 'I didn't know that. I have been impressed, though. You and Jeff work very well together.'

Cressida switches her attention from Cary, to me, a look of surprise on her face.

'Jeff?' she enquires, meeting my gaze.

'My cameraman. He only joined me two years ago but we've been friends a long time and we spark off each other creatively. He's more like family, really. We were at university together and he studied cinematography and digital editing. I was studying screenwriting and production. We did a few projects together in the summer holidays and he spent a lot of time with me and my family.'

Cressida's expression relaxes as she takes the coffee cup Cary carries across to her. I wonder if he's switched off and thinking of something else, as he doesn't try to change the subject.

'He didn't fly back with you?'

I take the coffee cup Cary is holding out to me and decline the small pot of sugar cubes in his other hand.

'No. He met a rather nice lady at the convention and he's spending Christmas with her.'

Cressida leans back in her chair. 'Ah, love is alive and kicking. That puts a smile on my face.'

'Yes, well, that might just end up being a fleeting one, Grandma. What's the percentage rate for failed relationships these days?' Cary joins in as he takes the seat opposite me.

No wonder Cressida is a little worried about him. That's a rather jaded remark to make and she is quick to retort. Is he purposely baiting her? Falling in love has nothing to do with statistics, anyway.

'And how many businesses fail? But that doesn't stop people taking their dream forward and giving it a shot. If we let failure define us, then we're quitters and you know better than that, Cary.'

'It's a big step to take, Grandma. When people rush into making a commitment it can all go painfully wrong.'

'I'm not suggesting you *rush* into anything, Cary, but sometimes your general attitude can be off-putting. The way to a woman's heart is to show how much you care and actually put that into words.'

I find myself holding my breath, hoping she doesn't drag me into this bit of the conversation. What could I possibly say?

He shakes his head, reaching for the coffee cup on a small table next to him, taking a leisurely sip before answering.

When he lowers his cup, his expression is prosaic and he must know it will annoy her.

'We're going to have to agree to disagree, once more, Grandma. We simply look at it from two very different angles.'

She makes a half-turn to look in my direction.

'Ignore his words, Leesa, he's just trying to wind me up. Relationships need time to mature, of course they do. But the point I'm trying to make is that if he waits too long—' and she turns her head to stare directly at Cary '—then he might lose the very thing that could seal his happiness for the future.'

He sits there glowering.

Cressida is partly right, though, from what I've seen so far. I can't imagine that Cary would ever allow his heart to rule his head. But I wish she could have seen the way he was with little Hayden. Okay, so there was no real emotional interaction, but he treated the little lad like an equal. He saw that he was simply bored and needed a distraction. Making an effort to do that was, whether Cary would admit that to himself or not, a generous gesture. One that shows he doesn't have a totally hardened heart. Whether he did it to help out Hayden, or his parents, is immaterial because it was thoughtful.

Maybe he isn't a totally lost cause if Cressida could just modify her approach. There's more than one way to achieve something. In this case, she needs to try some subtlety, I think, if she wants him to stop and seriously think about his future.

Well, after one disastrous meal I'm sure Cary will be very eager to get me to my final destination the moment his brother arrives, and he can grab those keys. I do feel awkward on his behalf, though. I can draw a comparison between his grandmother and my ex-mother-in-law, Gwen, in many ways. That's another dysfunctional family story that isn't going to be easy to deal with. Who would have thought we had so much in common?

6

The Contract

As we're finishing our coffee Robert arrives to let Cressida know the lane is clear and fully accessible. She invites him to join us and Fran brings some fresh coffee.

When Cary introduced Robert as simply his grandmother's neighbour, for some reason I assumed he was married. It turns out he's a widower and reading between the lines I think Cressida and Robert spend a great deal of time in each other's company. He's a soft-spoken, gentle and kind man, very supportive of Cressida and aware of the ongoing tension between her and Cary. It's obvious he's a wealthy landowner but his hands show he likes to get stuck in and rub shoulders with his workforce. They are the hands of a man who isn't content to sit at a desk and merely oversee things.

I enjoy the stories he has to tell and it's good to hear laughter echoing around the room instead of discord. After two cups of coffee, to my surprise Cressida suggests that Cary and I go for a walk.

'The rest of the family won't arrive until late morning so why don't you take a wander down to the viaduct and show Leesa the views? I'm sure there will be some footwear to fit her in the boot room.'

Having glanced out of the window when I awoke at six this morning, it was clear that it had stopped snowing sometime during the night. The wind, too, has dropped. The drifts are very deep in places and it's going to take a long time for it to melt. But a walk would be fun and the fresh air will help to clear our heads.

'I'd love that. If it's not too much trouble,' I add.

I doubt Cary would have suggested it, but he doesn't seem fazed and we head off to find some wellies.

'Robert is a rather quiet, yet charming man, isn't he?' I comment as we walk side by side through the entrance hall. Really, I'm simply trying to fill a few moments of the silence with something uncontentious.

'Yes. My grandmother is very fond of him. Perhaps a little *too* fond.'

My sharp intake of breath, thankfully, goes unnoticed. I don't even want to consider what he means by that remark. I am curious, though, as to why his granddad hasn't put in an appearance yet.

'Here we are.' He leans forward to swing open a door and we enter a small room lined with cupboards. There's a large Belfast sink set in a beautiful, rustic wooden worktop.

'This is why houses like this should keep as many of the original features as possible. I mean, how indulgent having a boot room!'

'Originally the dogs slept in here overnight but when her second golden retriever died, Grandma lost heart and couldn't bear to replace her. That dog was like a child to her and was a great comfort after Granddad left. Maybe, as time goes on she'll get a pup again, who knows? Right, let's find a smallish pair to fit you.'

Cressida's husband *left*? Does that mean he walked out and might return at some point, or are they getting a divorce, I wonder.

Rooting through, Cary grabs a pair of new-looking boots and when I slip them on, if I wear a double pair of socks, I know they'll keep my feet both warm and dry.

'Sorted!'

'Right. I'll wait for you outside. My coat's in the hallway but take your time.'

Before I pile on the layers ready for our walk, I check my phone and sure enough there are a string of missed calls from Gwen. I can't face talking to her at the moment and instead I text to say I hope to get there by late afternoon. I figure it would be unfair of me to expect Cary to ask his brother for the keys to his car the moment they arrive.

I throw the phone down on the bed without looking at it, knowing she'll respond almost instantly. Instead, I grab my coat and seconds later I'm heading down to the front door.

'Oh, Leesa. I noticed you didn't have any gloves when you arrived. How about these? It's still very nippy out there.'

Ah, bless her! Cressida walks towards me carrying some rather smart, and no doubt expensive, soft leather gloves.

'Thank you, that's so thoughtful.'

'Well, enjoy your walk. And I just wanted to say that I'm not trying to bully Cary, but I'm afraid none of us have been a sterling role model for love's dream. That saddens me as it has hardened him, and I don't like to think of my darling

Cary paying the price for the way we've all messed up our lives and his.'

As I take the gloves I feel awful that she's trying to take me into her confidence when she's labouring under the wrong impression. I'm just passing through and while I am growing very curious, it's none of my business.

'I don't think you should worry so much about him. He'll be fine, I'm sure.'

I quickly pull on the gloves and give her a little wave. 'I hope it's not as cold as it looks.' I grimace, and she gives me a twinkling smile.

Outside, Cary is staring up at the guttering at the front of the house.

'Problems?'

'No. It all seems good for the time being, but there's a lot of snow on that roof to come down at some point. Okay. Do you know the area at all?'

I shake my head and we set off in tandem. It's good to gulp in the crisp, fresh air. The wind has abated, and the snow has been ploughed into tall banks either side of the lane. The rock salt crunches satisfyingly beneath our feet as we walk, already beginning to do its job.

Overhead, a loud roar signals a plane just taking off. We stop to watch as it flies over the roof of the house and immediately begins to veer off to the right a little, as it heads towards the Bristol Channel.

'Gosh, that's really something. It's the first plane I've heard since I arrived.'

'Yes, you only really notice it when you're in the garden. I love flying but then I get that from my grandfather. Being an aviation lover, it was the only thing he liked about the house. We spent many an hour over the years sitting out in the garden with a drink, watching the planes flying over the roof.'

'It's hard to believe how close to the airport we are.' Chatting away to Cary like this it's the most relaxed I've seen him so far.

'The number of flights has increased over time, but you get used to it. If you're a plane–lover, then you never tire of watching a metal beast climb as it heads off into the distance. There aren't any night flights, even though there are only a few properties directly in the flight path when the planes take off. As they head out over the Bristol Channel it's quite a sight when you're looking down on all of this.'

'Does your granddad miss it now he no longer lives here?' I'm not even sure that's a question I should ask, given our respective roles and that I'm an unexpected guest here. But I can't help feeling curious, as clearly his grandparents had been together for a very long time.

'If he does he wouldn't share that fact. Granddad plays everything very close to his chest. He's an interesting man and Grandma is right when she complains that he never was very demonstrative. Old-school, is the correct term to use, I think. He used to refer to her as that darned woman, would you believe?'

I laugh, and he does, too.

'So why doesn't he live here any more?' The minute I ask the question I regret it. A couple of hours and I'm out of here. Cary's manner is changing by the second and I'm warming to him in a way I didn't think was possible. But nothing has changed – he's a client, not a friend.

'He lives only a few miles away in a small hunting lodge. Granddad told me he'd always hated this house as it was a burden that came between the two of them. It was Grandma's family home going way back and when she inherited it the place was in a sorry state of neglect.

'She funded the renovation work from the stocks and shares that were also a part of her inheritance and, later, from the fruits of her writing. Her determination to rescue it annoyed him for some reason. At the time I couldn't understand it but now I wonder if it was because he could see there was a connection between her and Robert. I often wondered if their involvement began before my grandfather left. Robert's wife died nine years ago, and my grandfather eventually moved out four years after that.'

I decide it's best if I say nothing. If Cary wants to offload that's entirely up to him and I'm a good listener but it isn't really my place. Besides, I don't think I should pry out of blatant curiosity.

'Porthkerry farm is over there, adjacent to the main road. Grandma's place was the old vicarage before her family purchased it. We're heading down towards the viaduct and beyond that is the beach, which offers wonderful views of the channel.'

Cary raises his arm and points in the direction ahead, although at the moment all I can see is the next bend, where the lane curves. The snow-topped hedges that flank us either side are at head height. Rare glimpses, whenever there's a break in the hedge, confirm we're surrounded by seemingly endless fields, with no sign of human habitation at all. In summer I assume this is a mixture of crops and pasture land.

'Most of what you can see belongs to Robert's family. The old vicarage has a couple of acres but that is leased to Robert and farmed.'

It's a downhill slope now and the lane widens a little as we round the next corner. Two huge metal gates set back in the hedgerow herald the drive up to an enormous house, probably twice the size of the old vicarage. Even stopping to peer through the gates to get a closer look, the house is way in the distance. A dog comes bounding up and begins barking.

'Don't pay any attention to Dixon. He sounds like a guard dog but he's a real pussy. Jason Montague is a stockbroker. His wife Caroline is a lovely lady, very down-to-earth and heavily involved with several charities. Two kids at boarding school. Grandma refers to them as the perfect little family. You should see the size of the swimming pool at the rear of the property. There's nothing little when it comes to describing this family, but they do seem to be sticking together.'

I don't make a comment and we set off again. It isn't long before I get my first glimpse of the viaduct.

'Impressive, isn't it?' Cary reflects, noting my surprise.

'Awesome.' It's a true feat of engineering, rising up out of the landscape and dwarfing everything with its towering, sturdy pillars.

The downhill gradient steepens. It's fairly easy walking, though, with only a slight crunch underfoot now as the gravel is trodden into about an inch of increasingly slushy snow. In the fields either side it's still probably at least eight inches deep.

The setting is breathtaking and eerily quiet until the roar of another plane engine reminds us how close we are to the airport. It's impossible not to stop and watch as the huge, glinting, metallic arrow slices through the air with ease.

'If the airport's open then the main roads have been cleared. I could call a taxi, you know. I expect you have a lot of catching up to do when your brother and his family arrive.'

We continue walking and Cary turns to look at me.

'We'll have plenty of time to do that. I'd feel better seeing you safely to the door. After all, it's my fault we were running so behind on the schedule and were affected by the snow. I feel bad about that as it wasn't the easiest of flights. I didn't mean to sound as if I didn't trust or value your opinion with regard to the video, but I'm up against it at the moment.

'Only half of my board of directors are on-side with pricing the product to attract volume sales, because it's a risk. If we don't hit the numbers, then the pricepoint needed to label it as affordable will seriously hit our profit levels.'

I think I'm beginning to understand the pressure he's under both at home and at work. That can't be easy. Talking to him casually like this, he's a different man to the one who previously had me gritting my teeth whenever I heard his voice.

'But from a shareholder's point of view isn't business mainly about profit? It will still be a green initiative on which you've significantly improved, won't it, so it all helps to save the planet.'

He kicks out at a mound of powdery snow that Robert, or one of his men, has bulldozed to the side.

'If we end up going for the higher price then it means everything I've worked for will have been for nothing. Anyone could have seen this project through from the drawing board to fruition. There are lots of companies out there with enough money to develop technological advances but this new design gives us a head start. And we have the funding to roll this out. This project is as much about reaching the huge number of people who simply don't realise the options open to them, as it is selling a product.

'If we fail to get across the message that they can expect an immediate, and significant, return even for a standard two- or three-bed home, then we will miss the mark. We're talking grassroots changes here for working families used to paying large energy companies to provide their services. This will eventually become the new norm but it won't happen overnight. However, we need a significant take up to really get the ball rolling. In truth, the solar panel industry has only made a small dent in the lower end of the domestic market.'

The passion in his voice tells me how much he's emotionally invested in this project.

'It's a big ask, I can't deny that.'

I wonder if he even has a chance of achieving his goal.

'The video has to deliver on so many fronts. It has to be direct, informative and easy to digest. Power is simply power, to most people. They flick on a switch and the light comes on – there's no conscious thought involved. We're asking the average man in the street who might not give clean energy much thought, to take control, realise there is money to be made and, in doing so, make a difference. Hopefully the interest generated at the conference will be enough to convince a couple more directors that there is tremendous potential in this initiative. Anyway, enough about work as Grandma would say.'

We head off across a wide swathe of open land which runs down to the viaduct. We are now ankle-deep in snow and it's a novelty. In the distance are two people walking an Alsatian and behind us an older man with two small terriers is stooping to let them off their leashes.

I squint up at the sky as the sun appears from behind a cloud, thinking that it's hard to believe it's Christmas Eve. I think back to last year and my heart sinks in my chest, but I shrug it off. As I always do whenever the memory comes back to haunt me.

'That'll help melt it,' I say, brightly, turning to look at Cary and maybe seeing him in a slightly different light for the first time.

'Hopefully, quickly,' Cary retorts, shooting me a warm smile. I think he needed to share his worries with someone and I'm kind of glad he had this opportunity.

'So, you're about to start your Christmas celebrations later today. I'm sure your family will be relieved to have you safely back under their roof.'

I can't halt the dismissive laugh that escapes my lips like a mini explosion. 'If only you knew. I will admit I'm returning with more than a little reluctance and I'm still not ruling out a chance to just take off and head in the opposite direction.'

The sun's rays are really beginning to warm the air and I slide down the zip on my coat.

'Shall we sit for a moment and enjoy the view?' Cary indicates towards a wooden bench and we begin the slow traipse over to it.

After we kick the snow off our boots, it's rather pleasant to sit and watch the dogs as they bound about in the heaps of snow that stack up against the stonework of the viaduct.

To the side of us a copse of tall trees stand proudly looking out over the landscape, wearing nature's own festive decorations. As I stare in turn at the huge number of balls of mistletoe, it makes me smile for a moment. Few people know that it grows on a range of trees including willow, apple, and oak trees like these towering sentinels.

It's food for the birds, the bees love it for the pollen, and butterflies lay their eggs on it. But it's spread in the bird poo of those who have eaten the berries. Encased in a natural fertiliser, it prospers but the sad truth is that it's a tree-killing parasite. Life is full of strange ironies, I reflect, as I gaze around.

'It's not my family I'm supposed to be spending Christmas with, but my ex in-laws. My divorce was finalised three months ago. My husband had an affair with a friend of mine. They're still together.'

Cary looks at me with something akin to incredulity written all over his face. 'And you're going to spend Christmas with his family?'

Quite rightly his tone reflects a level of scepticism.

'Yep. They are lovely people and it wasn't their fault. Even though the marriage is over, the family bond is harder to unravel. With my parents heading off to spend Christmas in the sun and my sister, Beth, off to get to know her fiancé's family – well, I was going to be home alone. Which, I might add, was actually rather appealing.'

'Hmm… that's unfortunate but couldn't you just have made your excuses?'

This time my laugh is tarnished by the thought of some very painful memories.

'Gwen and Peter are kind, generous people and for three years I was like their second daughter. It's hard to turn my back on them and the truth is I didn't have the heart to say no.'

'That was a big ask, Leesa and it's not very fair on you under the circumstances. I'm assuming he won't be there?'

I nod, thinking life isn't fair, either. Or do people end up getting what they deserve? Sometimes I find it hard not to be bitter.

'No. He's spending Christmas with *her* family. But Gwen's mother died last month, and she's asked me to stay to help her through the first Christmas without Alice. I loved Nathan's grandma, she was one of a kind. Gwen is going through the early stages in terms of the grieving process, Cary, so what could I say?'

I slip off a glove to run a hand over my face and brush away a few stray hairs that are flicking against my eyelashes. It's making my eyes water – that's why I'm tearful, I tell myself emphatically.

'It's a final goodbye for you then; you want to draw a line under the past but it's not always easy to let go. I can understand that.' Cary's words surprise me.

'You can?'

His eyes narrow as if he's mulling something over and I wait, wondering what's coming next.

'The day my brother was married it was supposed to be a double celebration. Everything was in place and then eight days before the wedding, Paige called it off. The girl I'd sat next to at school and the woman I thought I was going to marry after being together for seven years, woke up one morning and realised she wanted more out of life.'

I gasp.

'More?'

'Excitement. She didn't want to be tied down. In fact, she wanted to travel and she did just that. Paige eventually settled down when she met someone in Hong Kong a few years later. Right man, right place.'

It's difficult to know what to say to that.

'That must have been tough on you, Cary.'

He shrugs his shoulders, nonchalantly.

'The worst bit was that it was actually a relief in one way, but a total nightmare in another. I felt numb at first, then I realised that we'd slipped into this cosy relationship that wasn't a grand passion that was going to last. We were simply going through the motions. Paige did the right thing, but it took me a while to draw that line and move on. Having done that, I'm in no hurry to put myself in that sort of situation again.'

'One of those *if only* moments, for sure. And a nightmarish one to resolve, not wanting to spoil your brother's big day.'

That must have been a horrible situation to find himself in.

'Yes, it was. Paige and I were in the process of buying a house together, too, and had to pull out, upsetting a lovely couple who didn't deserve to be messed about. As for Laurence's big day, well, everyone was on edge worrying about me. Her parents clung on for a long time. She was gone and they didn't want to lose touch with me, too. They believed she would eventually come back and want to pick up where we left off. In the end I had to sever all links for my own sanity.'

Slipping the glove back over my hand, I rise up from the bench. 'I guess we'd better start heading back. It won't look very good if you're not there to greet the new arrivals.'

I put my head back and inhale slowly. It's good to savour the crisp, fresh tang that only a heavy snowfall can bring to each intake of breath.

'You're right. I know Cressida looks strong and she is quite a force, but what happened to me was a bitter blow to her. It sucked the joy out of what was supposed to be the happiest day of our lives. It lowered her both mentally and physically for a while, although she bounced back. She always does. But seeing it all unfold was heartbreaking, I can't deny it. In your case, though, you are over him – aren't you?' Cary is direct, but then that's his style.

'Yes. But it's never quite that simple, is it? I don't regret what happened. I just regret *how* it happened. But it's going to be a difficult couple of days and now I wish I'd been strong enough to say no. I need to think of a way of signaling to them that they can't expect me to be there for them in the future.' I sigh and even to my ears it sounds defeatist.

We walk back out into the lane. Almost immediately the incline starts to bite on our calf muscles, so we automatically slow our pace.

Cary suddenly shakes his head, pursing his lips. 'Families, eh?'

Who would have thought that beneath that stern, unbending exterior, Cary was a man whose emotional life must have been in constant turmoil for a very long time; that would explain a lot of things. And Cressida is right to be worried about him, because maybe he never will risk trusting someone again. But that's a decision only Cary can make for himself.

We walk in silence for quite a while, content to listen to the birds enjoying the sunshine. They are foraging about for winter bounty, flitting in and out of the trees and hedgerows as best they can. With such a heavy covering of snow all around, the thaw is going to be a slow one.

I would love to do this walk in the summer and go further, down to the beach beyond the viaduct. But the beauty of the snow-laden fields is awesome too and the fresh air is clearing my head. It's time to face up to what threatens to be a trying few days. Gwen is my main concern in all of this because I know how fragile she is right now. She deserves to get the support she needs this Christmas, despite the fact that the family has been torn apart. However, when I leave it will be another blow to her and I know she won't want to let go.

'We're both in a rather impossible situation, aren't we? When my brother and his family arrive, it will make everything worse between Grandma and me. Fortunately, he can be a little thoughtless at times and he's bound to do something that will make me look good – at least for a moment, or two. But Grandma will look at those kids and think I should be there with a wife by my side and a kid or two of my own running around.'

'I wonder if a perfect Christmas even exists?' I muse.

'You mean happy faces, no family arguments and Christmas carols sung around the tree?'

That makes me chuckle. 'I'd swap all that for a little peace and quiet. I don't think that's something Santa can deliver, though.'

Suddenly he takes a giant step forward and spins around to face me.

'Look, I know this sounds crazy but I need you. Well, I need to enlist your help and I think this could benefit us both, equally. Nothing would mean more to me this Christmas than to make my grandmother happy. No one wants someone they love and admire to be fretting at this time of the year. Especially when they don't deserve it. Life can be unjust as times, no matter how much effort we put into it. She's given everything she has to her family and she deserves a break from all the worry.'

What on earth does he mean? I study his face but he's rather hard to read, at times.

'If Santa granted you one wish this Christmas, just for you, what would you ask for?'

I stare at him intently and he looks back at me without blinking.

'I'm being serious here,' he confirms, even though I'm looking at him as if he's lost his mind.

'Well, for the holidays to be over. To come out the other side without upsetting anyone. And without digging myself into a hole. Or committing to something I know I can't deliver simply because of the guilt factor.'

He starts laughing. 'Same here. We don't ask for much, do we?'

It is refreshing to be talking to someone who really understands what it's like to feel trapped. It's ironic, though, because Cary is the last person on earth I ever thought would be able to empathise with that feeling. He's a man who, a mere twenty-four hours ago, was driving me insane.

'Okay. Let's make a pact. We'll call it "the Santa Clause", you know, with an "e" because I'm proposing a contract of sorts. And you're a woman who, like me, expects the small print to be clearly defined. And that's important if this is going to work. Cressida already thinks you're my girlfriend, so what harm can it do if it gets us all over the holidays? It's not like you'll be here anyway, and I'll be in her good books. In return, I can be the new man in your life, which sends your ex's family a clear message about the future.'

I peer at him in total disbelief now. I know he's under pressure but isn't this a little drastic?

'We pretend it's for real?'

'There's no reason why we wouldn't be dating, so I can't see the harm in it. My grandmother will be delighted I'm taking her advice and seeing someone again. I've forgotten what it's like to feel I'm putting a smile on her face that isn't simply masking her concern. And you would be doing me a huge favour.'

'Hmm. You really think it's as simple as that?' My mind is actually whirling. It's a crazy idea but he will be dropping me off at Gwen and Peter's house. All I need to do is imply we're in a relationship; they don't actually have to meet him.

'I don't know. It seems wrong even if it would make things a whole lot easier for us both.' It's a pretty sad state of affairs when your life comes down to this sort of subterfuge.

'I can handle Cressida,' he says, confidently and that worries me. He can't handle her at all and I've witnessed that with my own eyes. In fact, this is the coward's way out and his attempt to avoid confrontation.

'I'll tell her we're taking it slowly to cement our relationship before we move on to the next level. She knows how cautious I am in every aspect of my life. I think that should do it, don't you? It's obvious we've both been feeling a little awkward but, ironically, that probably makes it seem even more believable. Clearly, we are both nervous being here together and at least that bit is true.'

He makes a funny face and I laugh good-naturedly.

'And in return, you, a mystery man, drop me off at my ex in-laws' house and I take it from there?'

'Yep. I hang around just long enough to wave goodbye, so it's clear I'm not a taxi driver. You give them the support they need and then when the moment presents itself, gently break the news that you've found someone else. They will immediately make the connection. When it's time for you to head for home you can make a clean break of it and because they care about you they will understand.'

'Well, maybe so. But the longer you and I are together in front of Cressida the more likely she will sense something doesn't ring true.'

He pauses for a moment, raising one eyebrow as he considers the dilemma.

'You're heading off to spend Christmas with your family, which is only to be expected. We can text each other a bit and I'll make that obvious to her. Trust me, with the kids running around she'll have more than enough to contend with. As far as she's concerned, once the holidays are over we pick up where we left off. At some point I can ring to tell her that we've split up, amicably, of course. I think she'll just be relieved to know love isn't totally off my agenda and that will give me some breathing space. What do you think?

Is it a deal?' He slips off a glove and I stare at his hand. It takes me a few moments before I shake on our arrangement.

'I can't believe I'm doing this,' I remark as I withdraw my hand from his.

We stare into each other's eyes rather hesitantly before exchanging an affirmative nod.

'It seems desperate people do desperate things,' he says. 'So just to be clear, when we arrive back at the house nothing at all has changed but we play it up a bit.'

I jump in. 'When the rest of your family arrive you formally introduce me as your girlfriend in earshot of Cressida to seal the deal. Later on, you whisk me away to spend Christmas with my family. A few texts and then we're done, right?'

'Yep. Sounds like the perfect relationship to me,' he muses.

I'm a little shocked still by his proposal, but what have either of us got to lose? And, more importantly, just knowing we each have a temporary solution makes surviving Christmas a lot less daunting. It's a win-win situation. I think. Unless it all goes wrong, of course. But then I won't be around anyway… I'm overthinking this and Cary is wondering why I'm looking rather dumbstruck.

'Okay, then. I intend to head home to the Cotswolds the day after Boxing Day and never return again. So, keep your fingers crossed for me.'

As he turns and we start to walk back he begins speaking and I can see that he's serious.

'I love Grandma and I would never want to hurt her. But I also hate to think she worries about me constantly when there's really no need for it,' he admits.

If he was the sort of person to sit down and talk about his future plans, I'm sure Cressida would be more relaxed about it. But this 'shrug it off' attitude of his gives the impression he gets up, goes to work, comes home and goes to bed. Like Groundhog Day. I'm positive it's not as simple as that.

'You have a very special relationship with her.'

Cary nods. 'She's everything to me. Grandma is charismatic and an eternal optimist, so how could anyone fail to love her? And a live wire. But how am I supposed to do battle with that? Well, the truth is that I can't. I'm my own man and yet I also don't want to be another man in her life who constantly disappoints her. That's why I end up saying things I don't even mean when she's on my case.'

'That's some dilemma,' I agree; now I have a slightly better understanding of the situation. 'Obviously your grandmother means well but her dream for your future doesn't seem to match with yours. At some point you need to communicate that to her, Cary.'

'Is that another way of saying man up?' he remarks. 'I appreciate that you can see both sides of this argument, Leesa. With Grandma I seem to always say the wrong thing at the wrong time and I hate upsetting her. But life is a lot easier when you have total control and you don't have anyone, or anything holding you back. And that's where I am at, right now. That's good enough for me but not for her.'

I wonder if Cary believes he has seen enough broken relationships, including his own, to put him off ever trying again? Maybe Cressida fears that's the case, even before

Cary himself is aware of it. Ha! It's rather like me, really. Been there, done that and don't want to go there again.

Either way, she would be appalled if she could hear us talking now. But sometimes in life your back is up against a wall and any way out seems like a good solution. However, to understand the enormity of that statement you must experience it firsthand.

When the situation arises it's like having something hanging over you every waking moment and it sucks the joy out of life. Believe me, because I know; I often wake up at night in a cold sweat worrying about Gwen and Peter's response when eventually that awkward and inevitable moment arrives and we say a final goodbye.

7

The Countdown Has Begun

Heading up the drive towards the house, we encounter a smart-looking dark-grey Range Rover Sport parked in front of it. Nicholas and another man are ferrying bags back and forth. One glance inside the open front door indicates a state of utter chaos inside.

'Let the party begin,' Cary mumbles, casting me a sideways glance as he walks up to the guy and throws his arms around him. After hefty pats on the back they do a man shake and then Cary steps back to look in my direction.

'Laurence, let me introduce you to Leesa Oliver. She owns Dynamic Videography and I must give you her card. You never know when it might come in handy.'

Laurence looks nothing at all like Cary and it's hard to believe they're brothers. He's well over six feet tall and has the ruddy complexion of a guy who enjoys outdoor pursuits. In fact, if I'm not mistaken it looks like he's wearing a rugby jersey beneath his open jacket.

Laurence steps forward, hand outstretched and a big grin on his face. 'Lovely to meet you, Leesa. If I'm ever in need of a videographer, I'll know where to come.'

His eyes seem to be weighing me up before he turns to look across at his brother.

'Not an easy man to work with, is he, Leesa?' It's only banter, I assume, because he's still looking at Cary, but he hasn't let go of my hand. I sort of tug it away and don't quite know how to respond. Cary comes to the rescue.

'Leesa's a perfectionist, too, Laurence, so you can stop with the character assassination.'

I'm standing here watching them and wondering whether Cary will swing a punch in Laurence's direction. Suddenly they both start laughing but I can see that Cary is nervous and maybe our little plan is already faltering.

'Ah, well, I won't need to disillusion her if you've already been working together. Anyway, we arrived a bit early as ordered and here are the keys. You do know that Robert would probably have run Leesa over to Caerphilly to save her wasting half the day here with you? I mean, it is Christmas Eve.'

'The poor chap worked through the night ploughing the lane, so it was safe for you guys. Besides, as it's my fault we were a couple of days late flying back I feel duty bound to deliver Leesa to her destination personally.' He grinds to a halt and I give him an intense look, one that says *get on with it.*

A hesitant glance passes between them and I realise that Laurence is wondering what's really going on here. But it's not for me to say anything in case Cary has decided he can't do this after all.

'I don't know this area at all and Cary was kind enough to take me down to the viaduct, which is a great walk. I'm sorry that you had to change your plans to accommodate me, though.'

Laurence bends to pick up the last two suitcases as Cary and I stand back to let him go ahead of us.

'It wasn't a problem. The kids have been up since the crack of dawn, anyway. Apologies in advance for the noise, they're a bit hyperactive.' He throws the words over his shoulder as we walk.

Entering the house there's a mountain of jackets, kiddies' back packs, larger suitcases and *things*. The sort of *things* that come with kids – comics, a book, a board game and several half-eaten bags of sweets – all strewn over the floor. Cressida is trying to listen to all three of the children talking at her in tandem. Watching them is a slim blonde lady who is obviously Laurence's wife. She's also busy sorting out a pile of little shoes so Cressida has to fend for herself.

'Kids, stop!' Laurence's command seems to echo around the hallway as the chatter instantly halts. Catching sight of Cary, they turn and run towards him.

'Uncle Cary!' More high-pitched screeching ensues.

'Oh, well, I tried. Leesa, this is my wife, Sally.' Laurence has already lost interest in attempting to calm his brood.

The littlest one clasps onto Cary's leg, the middle one throws her arms around his waist and the boy quietly awaits his turn. Cary notices he's standing there looking rather left out and he bends to scoop him into a group hug.

'Is this your girlfriend, Uncle Cary?' The older of the two girls asks, looking in my direction and both Cary and I freeze.

'Well, Daisy, as a matter of fact it is.' He peers up at me trying hard to disguise a rather mischievous smile. It keeps tweaking at the corners of his mouth and I rather think he's enjoying this moment. 'Here we have Jackson, Daisy and Chloe. I'm just about to run Leesa home as we've been stranded here in the snow and her family are expecting her.'

Cressida steps forward to peel the girls away from Cary and steer the children in the direction of the sitting room. 'Come on, lovelies, let's get some music going. It is Christmas, after all!' She flashes me the widest smile I've seen so far.

Sally turns to walk in our direction.

'Hello, Leesa. Sorry about the noise and welcome to the mad house. Or maybe I should say, the mad family.' She throws her arms around me, giving a genuinely welcoming hug and I'm touched.

I glance over her shoulder as Laurence joins in, 'Well, this is a lovely surprise. It's so like Cary, though, keeping us all in the dark.'

As she draws back, Sally turns to survey the heap on the floor, which Nicholas is now trying to assemble into some sort of order.

'Shall I take the suitcases up first, Sally?' he asks, and she nods.

'Thank you, Nicholas, that would be great. Once they calm down I'll get them to take their own backpacks and toys upstairs. Don't let them run you ragged while we're here, will you?'

He gives her a warm little smile, which she returns.

'It's fine. It's nice to have a bit of noise going on for a change and the house really comes alive at Christmas.'

I think that's the first thing I've heard Nicholas say. Clearly, he isn't just a formal butler, but regarded as one of the family. It's obvious from the way I've seen him hovering around Cressida that he hangs on her every word and I wonder if he, too, is captivated by such a warm, caring woman. Robert, Nicholas... and yet Cressida chose as a husband a man, it seems, she never succeeded in charming.

Suddenly, the strains of 'Santa Claus is Coming to Town' filter out from the sitting room.

'That will be down to Daisy.' Sally turns to look at me. 'She's on YouTube checking out the Justin Bieber videos. The arguments are about to begin.'

I look at her, rather puzzled.

'Jackson might be the eldest, but he'll jump on his iPad and leave the girls to it. Chloe will very shortly start clamouring for 'Gangnam Style', as she loves to dance. Pity they didn't record a Christmas one with the same moves—'

'I don't want this one, I don't want this one,' a not-so-little voice pipes up, loud enough to be heard over the music and carry out into the hallway.

'I'd better go and rescue Cressida. Chloe has problems handling the word no at the moment. Please excuse me.' With that Sally turns and hurries away.

'Here you go, bro,' Laurence hands Cary the keys, jingling them in front of him.

As Cary takes them from him, Laurence turns to me.

'Are you staying for lunch, or do you need to shoot straight off?'

Cary looks like he's already had enough and needs a breather. If we leave now, I figure that at least he'll be walking back in a little more prepared, ready to face an onslaught of questions.

'I ought to go as I'm already a day late. If we leave now, Cary, you will make it back in time for a relaxing family lunch. My bag is packed so it will only take me a few minutes to grab my things and thank Cressida for her hospitality.'

Cary looks relieved, although Laurence looks rather disappointed. I head off to say a quick goodbye to Cressida and the kids. Of course, I wasn't going to be allowed to leave before promising that I would be back very soon for a *real* visit. It was probably the most uncomfortable few minutes of my stay, and that's saying something.

They all seemed so genuinely happy for Cary. But as he shuts the front door behind us and we head for the car, we both breathe out a huge sigh of relief. Obviously, actors do a lot of rehearsing for a very good reason.

'Oh well,' Cary says as he lifts my luggage into the boot. 'It could have been worse.'

Maybe.

'Well, we timed that right, skipping out before the questioning begins in earnest. Well played, Leesa. At least I can give some thought to what I'm going to say when I get back.'

Cary cranes his neck to look both ways before pulling out of the lane. 'By the time I get back the kids will have calmed down a bit before they begin vying for my attention again. They're easier to handle one at a time but it seldom works out like that.'

I'm beginning to understand now, why Cary knew exactly what to do to keep Hayden quiet on the plane.

'Is that why you don't go back there very often?'

I turn to study Cary's profile as he keeps his eyes firmly fixed on the road ahead. Thankfully the gritter lorries have been out in force and the motorway is just a slushy mess. It's simply a case of making sure we don't drift into the mounds of snow piled high on the verges.

'Not at all. I probably make it as often as the rest of the family. Laurence and the crew turn up three or four times a year, at most. But then, every trip away is a major exercise for them. Well, for Sally, who runs the whole operation as if it's a military campaign. But Grandma has deadlines, anyway, and quite a busy social life.'

He turns his head slightly to check the rear-view mirror.

'Laurence runs, and part-owns, a health spa. Have you heard of the Downey House Retreat?'

The name isn't familiar to me but then I only find myself this side of the Severn whenever I'm visiting Gwen and Peter.

'Can't say I have. Looking at him it's obvious he loves sport.'

Cary chuckles.

'He likes to keep himself fit. Which is a part of the problem.'

'Problem?'

Cary nods. 'Between Sally and Laurence. Sally is home with the kids all the time and if Laurence isn't working he's organising sporting events. It is a part of his job, but it eats into their quality time as a family.'

Sally certainly looked drained, but I suppose having three young children to look after pretty much on her own, as it sounds, means her hands are full.

'Poor Sally. Looking after kids isn't easy. Give me work, any day.' I remark.

'You don't like kids?' Cary turns his head for a second, sounding surprised by my reaction.

I chew my lip pensively for a moment as emotion wells up inside me, unbidden. 'It's not that I don't like them, it's more that I don't think I have that nurturing instinct in me.' You have to be chosen to cherish a little life coming into this world, and apparently I haven't been. This isn't a subject I care to discuss at the best of times, let alone with someone I hardly know. My future is now mapped out and having kids isn't a part of it, but that's my business.

'I'm sure a lot of women feel the same way but that doesn't seem to put them off,' Cary adds.

I don't think a man can quite understand that having babies isn't necessarily a given and why would he? It isn't for everyone. But I so wish I hadn't made that careless remark, when I was simply trying to be empathetic.

'Maybe I wouldn't have the patience. Who knows? I've never really spent much time with young children. I think my sister Beth might have put me off a little, if I'm being honest. She's spoilt and always has been, being the youngest.'

Cary's face lights up with a huge grin. 'Sibling rivalry, eh?'

My attempt at going off on a slight tangent doesn't quite work, as now he's amused.

But I'm offended, which is crazy as he knows virtually nothing about me. 'Not at all. It was a textbook case of being afraid of making a mistake with the first-born, due to lack of experience. My parents were quite strict in many respects, but it made me the person I am. By the time Beth came along, nine years later, they were so overjoyed that the rule book went out the window. Once a child learns that shedding a few tears will get them whatever they want, every little thing becomes a drama. Eventually it was easier for my parents to simply give in to her.'

'You mentioned she'd recently become engaged?' He sounds genuinely interested, although I can't imagine why as our relationship is destined to be very short-lived. Then I realise that the more he knows about me, the more convincing he'll be answering those questions.

'Yes. On her twenty-first birthday last August. Planning is in progress for the wedding of the decade and the panic is on because it's going to be held on her twenty-second birthday.'

Cary glances in my direction again and I incline my head, encouraging him to keep looking straight ahead. In fairness there aren't many vehicles on the road but having come this far I want to get there in one piece.

'You sound as if you don't approve.'

I sigh. I love my baby sister Beth, but all that spoiling means she turned out to be high-maintenance.

'I suppose I feel a bit sorry for Will. Beth is the bride from hell when it comes to wanting every single little thing to be perfect. Don't get me wrong, she's budget-conscious but just half an hour listening to her going on and on about the arrangements and my head feels like it's going to explode. It's not rocket science. Pick a venue, buy a dress, a few flowers, a cake and a photographer if you must. What's the big deal?'

After my little admission he doesn't turn to look at me, but I can see that he's raised his eyebrows in surprise, I suppose.

'You're not big on weddings, either?' he asks, a hint of almost disbelief in his voice.

'No. I find them rather boring, to be honest. Beth's will be the same. All that hanging around for zillions of photos when all the guests want to do is eat and dance.'

'Cressida hosted Laurence and Sally's wedding at the house. A huge marquee was erected in the garden and the champagne flowed late into the night. I prefer to remember them both on that day when their relationship was so much simpler. They used to gaze into each other's eyes and that made Cressida very happy. In fact, the happiest she'd been for a long time. But then, after my big upset, she didn't think she'd have to wait quite so long for a repeat event.'

'But you have dated people since then, I assume.' There's an awkward pause.

'If I'm in need of company then I take someone out to dinner. But I've learnt that after a couple of dates a woman tends to think it's turning into something more. That requires effort and time, which I don't have. So, I tend to spend my weekends getting my sorry ass to the gym in between perfecting the art of avoiding people. I spend much of my working week talking, so it works for me.'

Well, at least he's honest but he's living to work, not working to live.

'Just a little tip. Don't ever enlighten Cressida about that, will you?'

'A full-blown relationship is way down on my agenda. So far down, in fact, it might have dropped off the bottom of the page.'

I burst out laughing and he joins me. 'And now we've given her false hope! I feel awful about that.'

'Don't,' he says, sounding fine about it. 'You've made her Christmas. I'll let her down gently when the time is right.

Does this look familiar to you? The satnav is saying it's the next left.'

I gaze out and sure enough I know where I am. Suddenly my stomach turns over. But I'm grateful to Cary for keeping the conversation going because it's taken my mind off the inevitable.

'Yes. Next left and there's a little cul-de-sac off to the right-hand side. Here, turn here. It's the one with the pale blue door.'

Cary pulls up outside a typical five-bedroom executive home on this pretty little estate.

'Well, all that's left to say is thanks for stepping up. I hope it goes well for you, and text or call me to say Merry Christmas. I doubt our stories will hold up if we don't have even a brief exchange at some point tomorrow. I'll hang around by the car to wave you inside so I can make a thing of being the mystery man.'

He looks across at me playfully.

'Having a new man in my life is the last thing I need, so I only hope when the moment comes I can at least sound convincing.'

He raises his eyebrows, wrinkling his brow.

'Oh. Right. Well, if you flounder give me a call and I'll be over to whisk you away. A contract is a contract, after all. I know enough about you now to keep it going when I get back and answer most of the questions,' he adds confidently. 'Wish I could say I think it will be as easy for you. Personally, I think you're making a big mistake even getting out of the car, given the circumstances.'

I'm angry with myself because I know he's right, but it's mean-spirited of him to point that out. I should have stood my ground in the first place, and I'm well aware of that. The harsh reality is that it's hard to cut ties with people who have embraced you as family, when they reach out to you.

'Why don't you put your money where your mouth is?'

Suddenly I'm in a fighting mood because his comment has annoyed me. I've just put up with his family saga, so where's his empathetic compassion?

I swing open the passenger door and head round to the rear of the car where Cary is now lifting out my suitcase and hand luggage.

'Okay. Fifty pounds says you'll regret your decision and you won't last until Boxing Day.' His eyes flash with amusement and anger rises up within me. How dare he stand in judgement of my situation. Who the hell does he think he is?

'Make that a hundred. There's no doubt in my mind you won't get off as lightly as you think. I'm going to be the one called upon to rescue you when the cracks in your plan start to show up. There's no way Cressida will let you spend the entire holiday period apart from the new woman in your life.'

It's a bold statement but I like a challenge. Having met her, I know I'm right and it does wipe that stupid, amused look off his face. We shake hands, firmly, and it occurs to me that maybe we're both nervous about what's to come and playing it down. Being single and totally unattached at Christmas seems sad to many people.

'Merry Christmas, Leesa,' Cary says, his voice suddenly warmer and sincere this time. 'Thanks for putting up with me and my family. And if we both manage to get through the festive period safely, we'll catch up in the New Year.'

I nod. 'You'll have the video by the first of February as agreed.'

'Great. Good luck.'

We're both hovering, which is embarrassing, and then suddenly he leans in to plant a kiss on my cheek. I know he's only doing this in case anyone is watching but it's still a little weird. I focus on lifting my luggage with seeming ease, as this won't work if he has to help out and follow me to the front door.

As I walk away I call over my shoulder, 'Thank you for getting me here safely, Santa. Love the upgraded sleigh.'

Before I reach the end of the path the door swings open and both Gwen and Peter welcome me into their arms. Peter immediately grabs my case and bag, turning as he does so to look at the car.

'Peter thought he heard a car pull up. I can't believe you're here at last!' Gwen says, sounding emotional.

I make a thing of leaning back a little to return Cary's embarrassingly over the top wave. Oh well, it's a start.

Now for the tough bit.

8

The Holiday Spirit is Flowing

'At last! Christmas can finally begin!' Gwen declares. But I can hear a sob as it catches in her throat and I feel like the worst ex-daughter-in-law in the world. Here I am thinking only about myself and poor Gwen is facing the first Christmas without her lovely mum. Just thinking about Alice brings a tear to my eye, too, and before I know it we're sobbing on each other's shoulders. Peter is hastily trying to work his way around us as we're part-blocking the doorway.

When I glance over Gwen's shoulder, Rachel, Nathan's sister, is standing there watching us. We exchange sad half-smiles and I can sense her own relief now that I've arrived. They're all looking to me to lift everyone's spirits. Nathan was always prone to mood swings so it inevitably fell to me to keep things jolly.

'Gwen, let's move into the sitting room where it's warmer. This poor girl is probably in need of a fortifying drink. I know I am.' Peter, bless, is so thoughtful.

Gwen releases me, looking up into my eyes with very real affection. 'You're safe and that's all that matters to me. Lunch is nearly ready. I bet you're famished.'

As I follow Gwen and Rachel through the small hallway into the cosy sitting room, I want to let out a sigh and fight hard to hold it in. There are too many memories here for me and one that I simply can't allow myself to dwell upon.

Rachel picks up the TV remote control and starts channel hopping until she finds one playing Christmas carols. The opening chords of 'O Come All Ye Faithful' fill the room and she turns down the volume a little so it's a gentle background noise. But it reminds me of so many Christmases past. Those before, and after my marriage. Feeling maudlin, I have to somehow get my act together and bring some lighthearted joy to the occasion.

'You've redecorated this room, it looks lovely.'

Both Peter and Gwen glance at each other, then look in my direction. Clearly, they are delighted I've noticed. The Christmas tree standing in the corner is a bit of an odd shape. Huge at the bottom, in fact it looks like Peter has had to cut it back because it projected too far into the room. At the top it's rather spindly and for some weird reason it tugs on my heartstrings. The baubles are rather haphazardly placed and yet it's perfect in its own imperfect, lopsided way.

'Gorgeous tree this year, Peter,' I comment, and he shifts from foot to foot, looking pleased.

'It took a bit of cutting to fit it in, but we got there in the end. Gwen, come and help me organise some drinks. It is Christmas Eve, after all!'

Moments later it's just Rachel and me. At twenty-five she's just five years younger than me, and six years younger than Nathan.

'How has it been?' I ask in a half-whisper.

'Awful,' she grimaces. 'Nan's last few days nearly did us all in. It broke Mum's heart to see her suffering. At one point, Nan cried out and asked us to let her go. There was nothing we could do and it was horrible. Truly horrible.'

Rachel's eyes begin to fill with tears. I walk over to drape my arms around her shoulders and give her a supportive hug.

'I can't even begin to imagine what you've all been through. I'm so sorry, Rachel. How are you coping?'

I gently release her, and she pulls a tissue from her sleeve to dab at her eyes.

'Okay, I suppose. I know I need to be here but I'm seeing someone now and... well, it would have been nice to have spent our first Christmas under the same roof. But I was needed at home, of course, as Nathan isn't coming. I didn't think it was fair on Mum, Dad, or Dan to invite him over given how tense things are at the moment.'

'You're a good daughter, Rachel. Nathan should have been here to help you all through this.'

'But then you wouldn't have come and Mum needs you. There are things she won't share with me, or Dad.'

'Look, this was always going to be a tough Christmas. Let's just get through it, hopefully with some smiles. Life goes on no matter what happens and all we can do is try not to let grief blot everything else out. Talking about Alice will help and when Gwen wants to reminisce I'll be here to listen.'

'Thank you, Leesa. I feared you'd say no and I'm so glad you made it. Mum's been worried sick about you,' she adds, giving me a watery smile. 'You know, being *that* time of the year.'

I will admit my tears weren't solely for Alice just now. When you lose someone at Christmas time it's hard to push the memories away because they are inextricably linked.

I smile at Rachel, willing myself to be strong. She looks back at me, hanging her head slightly as a hint of guilt flashes over her face and her eyes stray away to avoid mine. Her pale cheeks begin to blaze, and it isn't from the heat of the open coal fire in the hearth behind us.

'Mum lit a candle for—'

'Let's not dwell on that, now. It's up to us to make the best we can of this Christmas. But when I leave it will be my final goodbye.'

'We'll all miss you, Leesa. It isn't solely Mum and Dad – you've been like a sister to me.'

'I know; change is hard to handle but next year will be very different for all of us. Come on, let's plaster on a smile. Alice wouldn't want us all to be maudlin. She loved Christmas, so we need to make an effort for all our sakes.'

At that precise moment Gwen pushes open the door to the sitting room. She calls over her shoulder at Peter, who follows her through the open door carrying a tray of bottles and glasses. 'Merry Christmas. Let's get in the spirit, shall we? Sherry, or Prosecco?'

After two glasses of Prosecco my head is buzzing slightly but at least the alcohol has taken the edge off my anxiety. Several times over the last couple of hours I've found myself on the verge of opening my mouth and letting it all out. I know that would be very wrong of me. There are occasions when it could be a huge mistake to say out loud the thoughts that run through your head, without due consideration. I came here for a reason. If I let my own sorrow take over then it's going to be impossible to make a clean break because that will unite us.

'Is everyone full?' Gwen asks.

It was a lovely lunch, but in all honesty we were simply eating to please her. Nothing makes her happier than catering for the people she loves, and that includes me.

'Shall we take a little walk and grab some fresh air?' I suggest. Judging by the expressions around the table I don't know who is the most eager to head for the door.

When we leave the house Peter immediately falls in beside me, as we walk double-file across the cul-de-sac and along the path leading to the common. Rachel and Gwen are behind us, deep in conversation.

'It's a beautiful day, even if it is a little chilly,' Peter comments, sounding very relaxed.

He's really happy I'm here and that makes me feel sad.

'Yes, beautiful.'

The blue sky is now almost cloudless and as we continue walking, the snow covering the grass beneath our feet is satisfyingly crisp. It's such a pity that once it's trampled the beauty of it is lost.

'It's been a few years since we've had so much snow. It's a pity you were delayed, you would have arrived before the chaos began.'

I know he's only making polite conversation because we both know it's Gwen I've come to support.

'Yes, it was a pity and the landing was horrendous, due to crosswinds. The job over-ran by a couple of days and we were lucky to be able to change the booking.'

'You flew back with Jeff?'

'No. Jeff stayed in Australia to do some sightseeing.'

Isn't it funny how out of politeness, or maybe fear, we avoid saying the things that are going around and around inside our heads?

'It's great to be back in the UK. Christmas at the beach isn't my thing.'

He nods, taking a moment to look around before answering.

'Well, we're very glad you came. I'm grateful, Leesa. You have no idea how much you being here has brightened Gwen up. The last twelve months have turned our lives upside down and nothing will ever be the same again. Our thoughts are with you always, though. How are you doing, beneath that brave face you're showing the world?'

I glance sideways at him and I can feel the empathy.

'I'm throwing all of my energy into work. It's all I can do.' The look we exchange is tinged with sadness and regret.

Gwen and Rachel have caught up with us now and we continue in silence, walking in a straggly line across the white expanse. There are people with dogs on leads, couples walking and talking, and families with kids jumping about in the snow drifts. For the UK it's an unusual sight and everyone seems to want to get out and experience this winter wonderland setting.

After a couple of minutes Rachel holds back, saying she's dropped one of her gloves.

'You two go on, we'll catch up when we've found it,' Peter says, sounding very matter-of-fact, as if they aren't deliberately giving Gwen and me a chance for some time alone.

We walk on, linking arms.

'Nathan did a terrible thing and we'll never forgive him for that, Leesa. It's one thing when a relationship breaks down but another to cheat on your spouse. And hide it from them for such a long time given the situation; it's unbelievable our son could do that, but he did. It was wrong and there is no excuse whatsoever. I wanted to tell you how sorry we are because we've never really had the chance to talk openly, have we? The fact that you care enough to be here for us says everything. The fact that he isn't, tells you that we are having a hard time coming to terms with it all.'

I wonder if Nathan was glad he wasn't forced to choose between the family who have supported him all these years and my cheating friend, Sheryl? It has probably worked out perfectly for them. But are Gwen and Peter trying to hang on to me because they fear they are going to lose him, too?

'I'm over what happened and you have to do what's best for you all, Gwen. I came because I miss Alice and I wanted you to know that. But life goes on and she would be the first one to point that out.'

Just the thought of Alice's kindly eyes and the soft voice that had a little lilt to it is enough to have me blinking as my eyes tear up.

'She's with our little girl, Leesa. And that's something to hang onto.'

I turn away unwilling to meet her eyes. If that's what Gwen believes, then it must be a comfort, but no one knows for sure. Swiping away at a solitary tear before it's noticed makes me steel myself. Today was always going to be a tough one for so many different reasons.

Dinner isn't much better. I try to be as jolly as I can, and Peter asks me about my trip. At least talking about Australia is a safe topic. Gwen's mood swings from moment to moment and at one point I can see she's forcing herself to eat to be sociable. She'd expected all six seats around the table to be taken this year, but the empty chairs seem to dominate the room.

Fortunately, shortly after the meal is over the doorbell signals the arrival of two sets of neighbours and their offspring, who have been invited over for Christmas Eve drinks. With an extra seven bodies filling the room almost to capacity, it at least takes the pressure off. My phone pings, and I discreetly look down to see a text from Cary.

How's it going?

Awkward. You?

I survived the questioning, just. Laurence and Sally had an argument at the dinner table. Cressida is looking decidedly put out.

He doesn't need rescuing, so I suppose that's a plus. It's also a shame it isn't going well, though. There goes Cressida's attempt to make it a perfect Christmas for them all.

Another message pops onto the screen.

Boredom is a terrible thing.

I can't stop myself laughing out loud. I quickly look around to see if anyone has noticed above the din of chatter and background music. Every single person in the room has a smile on their face and it's heartwarming to see. Maybe Christmas is a time for pushing our worries firmly to one side. It's a time to literally make merry and that's infectious. The greatest gift has no price tag at all, because it's laughter. And Cary just made me laugh.

Time to make an early New Year's resolution and promise myself one thing. Next Christmas will be different. So, fate be warned – I'm talking about a Christmas miracle, no less. Now, let's spread some joy and ramp the laughter up a notch.

I sidle up to Rachel and whisper, 'It's time to break out the karaoke!'

Her eyes widen and she grins. 'I'm on it!'

9

'Tis The Season to be Jolly

It's Christmas morning and as I open one eye a sharp pain ricochets through my skull, making me wince. It wasn't so much about the wine I imbibed – I want to congratulate myself on being so restrained given the circumstances – but the fact that I didn't drink any water. Jetlag and dehydration are knocking the stuffing out of me. I slip out of bed to slink down to the kitchen and grab the largest glass I can find.

The house is silent until I approach the kitchen and I stand outside the closed door listening. There it is again, clink. Easing the door open I cautiously pop my head around the side to see Gwen in her PJs in front of the kitchen sink. Streaks of pain keep flashing across my forehead, while a sharp pain stabs at my left eye.

'Morning, Gwen. Sorry, but I'm in desperate need of some water. Actually, lots of water.'

She turns as I gently shut the door behind me.

'Aww, Merry Christmas, lovely. Take a seat. I should have checked you were matching the wine, glass for glass, with water. All that singing makes you dry. It was a great evening, though.'

She runs the cold tap for a few seconds before filling a tall glass with water and carrying it across to me. Easing herself into the adjacent seat, she reaches out to squeeze my hand.

'Merry Christmas, Gwen. I think we made Alice proud last night.'

'I do too and that was down to you. Drink this and I'll get you another one. Alice thought the world of you and she was so disappointed in Nathan. Well, that goes without saying for Peter and me, too. You will always be a part of our family, no matter what.'

She wipes a hand across her eyes and I can't bring myself to look at her tears. I take my time to swallow down half of the glass of water, giving her a chance to compose herself.

This is exactly what I feared would happen. All links between us can be severed… except one. And that will tie us together forever.

'Having you here means so much, Leesa, more than you can know. I just wish it was different because I know your emotions, like ours, would have been in total turmoil yesterday.'

She bows her head, staring down at the table and my heart constricts inside my chest for her pain; and for the pain I keep trying to push away. Gwen must feel like her little world is falling apart and, somehow, she needs to piece it back together. How can I tell her that it's unrealistic to think that I can be a part of it still?

I know that neither Gwen nor Peter will be able to turn their backs on Nathan. Eventually they have to forgive him and, like it or not, welcome Sheryl into their family – or risk losing their son. Gwen thinks that's the main problem facing her now. But that's only one half of it and she seems to be oblivious to the fact that I can't continue to be a part of the family.

I drain the glass and stand up to refill it, but she bids me to sit back down. Gwen begins talking as she turns away from me to walk across to the sink unit.

'You see, Leesa, when you have children and they grow up the hurts become bigger. It's easy to mop up the tears from a scraped knee but impossible to mend the damage done when a loved one makes a mistake that seriously affects someone else's life. It's tough to be a bystander watching things go from bad to worse. Even if you can forgive them, nothing will ever be the same again, will it?'

Oh dear. The water has eased the pain in my head a little but now I have a pain in my heart. The pain of knowing that I must begin to unravel the relationship between Gwen and me. It fills me with an uncomfortably cold chill, as she's still in denial about so many things.

'We were happy in the beginning, Gwen. But we started to grow apart quite quickly and that's why Nathan strayed. You know that I've always said it takes two to break up a marriage. Yes, it hurt to cut off a friend I'd known since school but, in my heart, I knew that my love for Nathan had dissipated. We'd slipped into a strange sort of friendship up to that point and from there on even that was ripped apart. Now, none of that bothers me because I've moved on. It stopped hurting a while ago and that's the truth.'

A light begins to shine in her eyes.

'But that's a good sign, isn't it? We don't need to lose touch, do we – after all we've been through?'

As she sits back it's clear she's trying to convince herself there's another solution; anything other than accept the inevitable truth of the situation.

'I'm seeing someone else and it wouldn't be fair on him.'

Her face falls and that happy glow extinguishes as quickly as if a light switch has been flicked off. Instinctively her hands fly up to cup her cheeks and she lets out a little sigh of breath from between her fingers.

'That's what moving on means, Gwen,' I add, gently. 'Nathan has moved on and if he's happy now, then that's a positive thing. You have to be with the right someone, not just anyone. What he has to learn is that only he is accountable for his actions.'

Gwen stares back at me looking completely stunned as my words slowly sink in, resurrecting her worst fears. I wish I could take back those words, but it's too late now. Better to say them sooner rather than later. There's no point in raising false hopes, as it only serves to prolong the pain.

Her head flops forward and she looks down into her lap. 'You're right and it's my fault. I'm always there to sort out his problems for him and now he needs to stand on his own two feet. I can't fix everything that goes wrong in his life and I also can't condone some of the things he's done. But how do I tell him that without alienating him?'

I take a hefty slug from the glass in front of me, wiping my mouth with the back of my hand.

'You'll know when he's ready to hear the truth because he'll seek you out. He has nowhere else to turn now that Alice is gone. It will have hit him hard, too. I wanted to be here for you for one last Christmas, but I can see now that it would have been kinder to make a clean break. The least I can do is to handle this in the best way I can. But it's down to me, not you.'

She begins to sob as the reality hits home. 'I'm not sure I can cope with the thought of losing someone who is like a daughter to me on top of everything else. Love isn't something you can switch off, Leesa.'

I pull my chair closer to her and place an arm around her shoulders, resting my head against hers.

'I know, Gwen. You and Peter took me into your hearts and became my second set of parents. It hurts us all. But Nathan will need to know that this is the place he can come when things aren't going right. And that's why when I leave I can't ever come back. The reality of divorce is that it impacts the whole family. He's starting over afresh. At some point you will welcome Sheryl into the place you made for me, because that's the future and I'm the past.'

We remain sitting at the table and talk about Alice for a while. Gwen shares some memories from her early childhood and it helps, I think. Somehow, we will get through Christmas day as lightheartedly as we can – what choice do we have? It will require a real effort, but there are Peter and Rachel to consider.

As I'm leaving the kitchen to go back up to my room, Gwen calls out. 'Leesa, no one will ever replace you; you do know that?'

I nod and pull the door shut behind me, then head for the ensuite.

Even under the shower I can hear my phone pinging; clearly everyone is sending out Christmas Day greetings.

Ping. Ping. Ping. It's relentless. I wish I could close my eyes and when I opened them again it would be the second of January and I'd be back at work.

Wrapping a towel around me I collapse onto the bed and start flicking through the messages. Naturally, I respond to Mum and Dad's, hoping they're having fun in the sun and to Beth, who sounds like she might just be missing my company. Getting to know the future in-laws by staying with them for the first time is quite a daunting experience and you never quite know for sure how it will go. I lucked out with Peter and Gwen, we hit it off from the start and it grew from there. You can't choose who touches your heart, it just happens.

Sighing, I trawl through another raft of seasonal greetings, sending a smiley Santa emoticon and a kiss to each one. Friends and colleagues alike – what the heck! There's no message from Jeff, just a photo of Bondi beach in blazing sunshine.

Cary has sent a string of emoticons. As I look at each one it's like a little story and a smile begins to grow on my face. It begins with a Christmas tree, then a face with rolling eyes, then a zipper–mouthed face and finally ends with a Christmas tree lying on its side. My thumbs get clicking.

> I'd say 'Merry Christmas' but any man who kills a fully-loaded Christmas tree is clearly not having fun!

He sends back a green zombie man. I reply with a woman face-palming. Wish there was one with a woman face-planting.

I've been up since four this morning. Try telling kids to go back to bed when Santa has already left a stocking on their beds!

Despite the way I'm feeling I can't help chuckling.

I'd swap. The deed is done and there isn't one warm, fuzzy, Christmassy vibe in my entire body.

He sends back a fist pump. I shake my head. No one wins in a situation like this and I'm sure Cary is well aware of that. Besides, I still have to survive until the morning, when Peter is going to drive me back to my cosy little house in Nailsworth, in the Cotswolds.

Having told Gwen I'm seeing someone, it feels like a huge weight has been lifted from my shoulders. The healing can begin for her because it has to – she can't continue to cling onto the past and what might have been. As for me, well, I don't know what the future will hold because there are things for which I can never forgive myself. How can I ever share that with a new person coming into my life?

Buzz. Buzz. Buzz.

Keep your phone to hand – I might need rescuing after all!

Cary's response doesn't surprise me at all. Cressida will, I'm sure, be wracking her brains for a reason to get us together under her roof again, as soon as possible. But I have to say that Cary's problems seem minor compared to what I'm facing here. If he knew, he'd be horrified, so all I can do is keep this light and cheerful.

I'll take any denomination in notes.

It's time to get dressed and head downstairs. Everyone will be gathering in the kitchen, which in this house is the hub of the home. While Gwen does the cooking, she's pretty good at organising people to help out. A sudden thought flashes through my head. I hope the box of presents I sent through before the trip to Australia arrived safely and are among those lying beneath the tree.

Staring back at myself in the mirror I almost don't recognise this worried-looking young woman wearing an ugly frown. Even when I try to relax my forehead it won't take it away completely. I'm supposed to be carefree and single, having the time of my life, and yet nothing could be further from the truth. What makes me feel worse is that Mum and Dad never go away for Christmas. They did it, I'm sure, because they knew I felt obligated to accept Gwen's offer. It was their way of resolving any potential dilemma for me. Now that's love. I needed to be here, in this house, for one last goodbye.

My parents have been enormously supportive of me, but I never really shared my feelings when I knew I was falling out of love with Nathan – equally as easily as I'd fallen in love with him.

Maybe he wasn't the only one who needed to do a bit of growing up. I wonder why I ever thought we were right for each other and that comes as a bit of a shock. It's strange how I chose to ignore some things that were clearly out of order. He could be a bit of a bully at times and there were a few occasions when I felt a little intimidated. It's easy now to say that but at the time I didn't know how to handle it. I suppose that's the whole point about life experience. With age comes wisdom and I don't intend putting up with that sort of behaviour ever again.

Pushing open the kitchen door, Rachel and Peter are already sitting at the table, which Gwen has laid out with her best silverware and china.

'I'm sorry I'm a bit late. I had a stack of Christmas messages to reply to and I feel bad I wasn't here to help. I'll give a hand preparing the veggies after breakfast, promise.' My voice sounds bright and breezy and Gwen replies in a similar vein.

'Just sit yourself down. Peter, you've forgotten to pour out the Christmas morning toast!'

I take the seat next to Rachel, stooping to give her a brief hug.

Peter pops the champagne cork and begins to make up the Buck's Fizz. A little orange juice mixed with a liberal amount of fizz might put some life back into us all. My parents favour a good old-fashioned Bloody Mary but Peter is delighted when I take my first sip and pronounce it a winner.

In the centre of the table is a festive platter with a pile of hot buttered toast and a hot tray bearing a dish of fluffy scrambled eggs.

'Who wants eggs benedict?' Gwen calls across. 'And Peter, can you take the marmalade and strawberry jam over to the table, please?'

Gwen organises everything like an experienced chef. She would love nothing more than to be catering for a growing family, rather than a dwindling one. I can only hope that by next year the old wounds will have healed and they can all make a fresh start. You have to look forward with optimism because it's too depressing to think otherwise.

I am starting to relax a little though, as my rumbling stomach responds to the aromas wafting around the kitchen. We begin by raising our glasses and Gwen nods at Peter, to perform the toast.

'Merry Christmas everyone and thank you, Gwen, for being our rock. Here's to good health and happiness for all in the coming year.'

For one moment I thought he was going to mention Alice and I'm relieved he didn't. It was the perfect toast and as we raise our glasses, I think of the last time I saw her, sitting at this table drinking a cup of tea.

'I'll second that!' I add, wanting Peter and Gwen to know that even though this is a painful time, I appreciate the heartfelt reasons behind them wanting to include me in their celebrations.

For today at least, I continue to be a part of their family. But after tomorrow there will be another vacant seat around the table until they make their peace with Nathan. Once that happens, now that Rachel has a boyfriend and with Gwen and Peter going strong still after thirty-plus years, there are blessings to be counted. This is real life reflected around this table, I tell myself. It's not that I've given up on love, but I think love has given up on me.

10

The Calm Before the Storm

Things are going much better than I could possibly have hoped. A quick smear of lipstick and I'm ready to tackle those Christmas veggies. As I close the bedroom door behind me and step out onto the landing, I hear a click. Looking down over the banister rail the front door opens and to my horror, Nathan is staring up at me.

'Merry Christmas, Leesa.' His voice filters up to me like something out of a bad dream. His tone is gentle for him and he hesitates for a moment before depositing his holdall on the floor.

As the final strains of 'Jingle Bell Rock' percolate through from the sitting room, the front door suddenly swings shut behind him with a bit of a bang.

Without any warning my stomach lurches at the sound and my lungs struggle to expand quickly enough to take in air. I just stand here, staring down at him. Within moments Gwen and Peter rush out into the hallway, wondering where the noise came from. Gwen pales at the sight of Nathan. Fortunately, Peter has his wits about him and immediately yanks Nathan's arm in the direction of the sitting room.

Rachel appears in the middle of all this action and rushes up the stairs, anxiously.

'Did you know he was coming?' I ask her, searching her face and hoping this wasn't planned.

'No. And look at Mum.' Gwen is leaning against the staircase, holding onto one of the spindles. We both rush down to steer her, gently, into the kitchen. Once Gwen is seated I grab a glass of cold water and she takes it from me, still unable to speak.

'Rachel, did you mention to him that I was going to be here?'

Her eyes open wide. 'No, of course not. I've only spoken to him once since the divorce was finalised. He's been too busy setting up house.'

As the words leave her lips she instantly regrets them, although it means nothing to me now.

'Oh, Leesa, I'm sorry. I was being sarcastic and I didn't mean to upset you.' As she speaks she lowers herself into the chair next to Gwen.

'We didn't invite him, Leesa,' Gwen is adamant and I can see how cross she is about it. 'I have no idea what he's doing turning up here unannounced. Peter rang Nathan to let him know that his nan didn't have very long to live. He chose not to visit her in hospital and that was his decision. Nathan did turn up at the funeral and he phoned here a week later to ask if he could come and visit. Peter took the phone out of my hand and told him it wasn't convenient. I was in no state to find myself face to face with either him, or that woman he's with. He hasn't been in touch since.'

'I understand and I'm sorry if I doubted you. It's just the shock of seeing him.' I can't seem to stop myself from pacing. Instinctively, I want to head for the door and run.

I glance at Gwen and she nods, acknowledging my apology.

'I'll go and find out what's going on.' Rachel disappears leaving us to exchange a look of concern.

'Are you okay?' Gwen whispers, although there's no one else in the room to overhear our conversation.

'I'm fine.'

Of course I'm not fine. My legs feel weak, as if they are about to let me down. It's so hot in here and I simply want to disappear.

'I need the bathroom,' I mutter, heading back out into the hallway and making my way upstairs.

Locking the door behind me, I perch on the edge of the bath as I remember doing last Christmas Eve. I'd been hiding away, then, but for a very different reason.

I sit for a while just thinking. The sadness comes in waves. It seems so much more real now I'm here and now *this* happens.

The phone in my pocket buzzes.

Chloe has eaten too many chocolates and has stomachache. Laurence has gone off in a huff because Sally said it was his turn to do kid duty. Want to swap places?

If only he knew.

Nathan's just turned up without any warning whatsoever and I don't know what to do.

A trap?

No. Everyone is in shock.

Sorry. My problems are nothing. I will leave you in peace. Ring if you need me. Good luck, Leesa.

I know I can't stay locked in here forever, so I run my hands through my hair and step back out onto the landing. To my dismay, Nathan and Peter are standing in the hallway, arguing. I freeze. Peter immediately looks up as I begin to descend, one step at a time as if in slow motion.

'Leesa, I've made it very clear to Nathan he can't stay. This isn't what Gwen or you need right now. You should have called first, Nathan. It's a bit late to have a crisis of conscience over how you've abandoned everyone. This was supposed to be a Christmas of healing. Not added stress.'

Peter shakes his head sadly and Nathan looks uncomfortable. Something deep inside of me wants to take charge for some reason, as if it's important who speaks first out of the two of us.

'I'm going to grab my coat and step out onto the patio for a breather. I think we should clear the air, Nathan. I'll give you five minutes.'

They both look at me, completely stunned by the cold and rather harsh tone of my voice. I turn and walk away from them, each step unwaveringly firm.

Outside, my lungs seem to work better. I focus on calming myself down and steeling myself for what's to come. Somehow, I must disconnect from my emotional pain, or risk falling apart. There are things I shouldn't say but which I fear will escape my lips, no matter how hard I try.

It isn't long before Nathan joins me. As I wrap my coat firmly around me we make our way down to the bottom end of the garden. I head in the direction of the small wooden shelter.

Making no move at all to talk, I can tell my silence is the last thing that he expected.

'I had to come. For so many reasons I can't even begin to explain.' He sounds agitated.

I concentrate on looking straight ahead. All I can think about is that this is the last time I will ever sit here, looking back on the house.

'Look, Leesa, if I could change what happened I would, but I can't.'

I shake my head, folding my arms across my body as if to shield myself.

'That's easy to say, Nathan.'

He slaps his hand down on the wooden slats next to him, making the little arbour rock unsteadily. The shock on my face is enough to quickly dissipate his display of anger.

'I'm sorry. I'm so sorry.' He flings his hands up, linking them behind his head. Rocking gently back and forth, he continues to perch on the edge of the seat. Maybe he's making sure he doesn't lash out again.

He never actually hit me. But looking back, there were a few occasions when I felt he was on the verge of losing control. For some reason everything I did ended up aggravating Nathan and it wasn't uncommon for him to lash out at things. He punched a cupboard door once, cutting his fist as the wooden panel split. Is that normal when two people begin to grow apart? The anger, I mean, not the violence. I see now that it was unacceptable behaviour, but I can only actually appreciate that with hindsight. Why was I such a fool?

'Look – I'm angry because I care. Doesn't that mean anything to you? It's an anniversary for me, too.' There's a note of desperation in his tone.

We're keeping our voices down but there's really no need. We can't be overheard.

'But you guessed I'd be here. I'm not afraid of you, Nathan.'

He unlinks his hands and leans forward so I can't see his face. Not that I had any intention of looking directly at him.

'I know you blame me, but it wasn't my fault.' His tone is flat. He turns to face me and his eyes are full of genuine remorse, by the look of it.

I glance at him in total disgust.

'You said you were happy about the baby. The day I found out you were sleeping with *her* I realised we had been living a lie for quite a while. But you felt trapped when I broke the news and it changed everything, didn't it? I hate myself for trying to keep us together and look what happened. A little life that was mine to cherish and protect... gone forever.'

'You were angry. You lost your balance and slipped. I put out my arm to steady you, that's all. It was an accident, Leesa. Fate.'

Fate? Then fate is cruel because why put me through all of that if I'm not good enough to be a mother, anyway?

I've gone over and over the events of last Christmas Eve in my head, so many times. I was distraught as I confronted him, but did I really slip? We were alone in Gwen and

Peter's sitting room. His admission had come out of the blue because, stupidly, I was feeling happier about life than I had done for quite a while. His arm was there and suddenly it was in my way, sending me reeling backwards and contact with the wall sent me crashing to the floor.

I wanted my heart to stop beating forever because that's what I believed I deserved. The only question I couldn't answer was what exactly happened. I only remember him repeatedly saying that in my distressed state I'd slipped. He kept repeating it over and over again, under his breath as Gwen and Peter rushed to my aid.

I insisted on going up to the bathroom as I wanted to lock myself away from Nathan. And then I noticed that I was bleeding. Just a little at first but it quickly increased, and I knew what was going to happen. I slumped down on the bathroom floor, hugging my little rounded belly. And then I howled like a wild animal. At eighteen weeks I knew she was too small to stand a chance.

I remember Gwen hammering on the door and when I let her in we held each other while we waited for the ambulance to arrive.

She slipped, she slipped… Over and over again, Nathan's words were relentlessly repeated inside my head that night. But did I believe it?

Had he lashed out at the precise moment I turned away from him in disgust? A dry sob makes me want to wretch. It doesn't matter any more, does it? The baby is gone because I failed to protect her and nothing will ever change that fact. I don't deserve to be a mum but that doesn't mean my heart doesn't ache at the thought of holding a full-term baby in my arms. And the tears I still shed late at night in bed are filled with the agony of loss.

I didn't just come here for the sake of Gwen, Peter and Rachel, this Christmas. I came to let my darling daughter know that in severing my links to this family I'm not saying goodbye to her. She will forever be in my heart; not in this house. But I needed to be here to tell her that because I wanted to make sure she knew.

'I want to make one thing clear, Nathan. I don't know what exactly happened that night. There was only one witness. And that was you. But don't you dare try to hold me responsible for your guilt. That's between you and your conscience. It's enough that I have to deal with the way I failed our daughter.'

He hangs his head. 'Sheryl said I needed to make my peace with you. It's coming between her and me.' As he turns to look in my direction I can smell alcohol on his breath. He was never a great drinker and I'm surprised by that.

'Did she now?' I shake my head in disbelief. 'We're done, Nathan. I don't want to listen to anything you have to say. And maybe you should focus on re-building your relationship with your family first, because at the moment they are barely hanging in there.'

I stand and walk back up to the house, leaving him alone with his thoughts. The moment I step in through the back door, Rachel and Gwen are standing there, anxiously awaiting my return. Gwen looks distraught and is wringing her hands. Behind her the beautifully laid out table shows how hard we were all trying to regain a sense of festive normality. But we were kidding ourselves. Just because it's Christmas, doesn't mean happiness can be taken for granted.

I put up a hand before either of them can begin speaking.

'I'm sorry but I'm exhausted. The jetlag has caught up with me, so I'm going to lie down. I thought I was strong enough to face my own demons, but I was fooling myself.'

Gwen rushes across to throw her arms around me.

'No. You were doing well, Leesa. This upset is down to Nathan and he's let us down once again. He'll be gone very soon. I promise. This Christmas isn't about *him* and it's time he understood that.'

11

The Modern Day Knight Drives a Range Rover

'Cary, I know it's late, but can you come and get me? I'm in a neighbour's house, the one on the right-hand side if you're looking directly at Gwen and Peter's.'

I can't keep the waver out of my voice and my trembling hand can barely hold the phone to my ear.

'You sound like you're in shock. I'm on my way.'

I close my eyes for a brief second, steeling myself against that horrible faint feeling that keeps trying to wash over me. Not only has Nathan caused an unforgiveable scene, but in his drunken state he's ravaged the downstairs of Peter and Gwen's lovely home. And now the police are in there trying to sort out what happened after a passerby dialled 999.

The policewoman sitting next to me closes her notebook.

'How long will it take your friend to get here?' She's been very patient, giving me time to think before I answered each of her questions.

'About forty minutes.'

Behind us a voice I don't recognise informs us that the kettle is on.

'A nice cup of tea will help calm your nerves,' the policewoman confirms, sounding genuinely sympathetic. She's used to handling people who are in shock and I expect she's seen it all before, many times. She did tell me her name, but I can't remember it.

'Are you sure you're alright? It is only that bruise on your arm, isn't it? You didn't knock your head or anything?'

I nod, unable to speak as I try to recall what happened. As Nathan struck out, one of his flailing arms hit a shelf off the wall and books flew off like missiles. I don't want to get him into any more trouble than he's already made for himself and his family.

'He wasn't trying to hit anyone, really he wasn't. It was a horrible mistake and he will be sorry once he sobers up. Nathan doesn't usually drink to excess, and this isn't like him at all.'

'Don't worry about that now. My colleague is taking a statement from Mr and Mrs Hughes as we speak. If we need any further information from you, we'll be in touch within the next few days.'

'Where is Nathan, now?'

'He's on his way to the station. The Hughes' daughter is gathering your things together.'

For some reason my teeth are beginning to chatter.

'Is Rachel alright? She didn't get hurt?'

Before she can answer me, a man appears with a tray of drinks and the policewoman grabs a mug, placing it in front of me.

'Take a few deep breaths, then sip some tea. It will help. And you're sure your friend can find alternative accommodation for you tonight?'

I nod. 'Yes. It will be fine.'

I need to distance myself from here and I really don't care where Cary takes me. I'm conscious that it's probably a 120-mile round trip to Nailsworth and it is very late on Christmas Day. I have no idea what reason he will give for having to suddenly rush off, but I know he'll think of something.

I reach forward and grab the hot mug in both hands. The contrast of the heat against my clammy skin does help to ease that awful wobbly faintness that has been so difficult to shake off. Every sip seems to fortify me a little more and I'm beginning to regain control. But it's hard to believe what happened tonight and how frightening it was for everyone.

Another police officer enters the room and nods in the direction of the woman sitting next to me. She follows him into the hallway and they talk for a while, their voices too low for me to hear what they're saying. After a few minutes I lie back against the sofa and close my eyes, for how long I don't know, but suddenly I hear Cary's voice.

As he enters the room he's escorted by the policewoman and she hands him a card, which he immediately slips into his inside jacket pocket.

Cary approaches hesitantly, kneeling down in front of me as you would with a child.

'Leesa, what on earth—' He takes one look at my desolate expression and suddenly he's taking charge.

'Your bags are in the hallway, Leesa. Stay where you are for the moment while I put them in the car. Don't move until I get back – that's an order.'

I guess I must look as awful as I feel. If I'm being honest with myself I'm not even sure I'm able to stand up and walk right now. I can't get Gwen's face out of my mind. She was ashen and distraught, her legs giving way beneath her as Peter stepped forward just in time before she fell to the floor.

It seems like Cary is gone for quite a long time. When he returns he thanks the couple whose names suddenly pop into my head; they were at the party just last night. They watch as he scoops me up in his arms to help lift me off the sofa and surprisingly my legs are a lot firmer than I expected them to be.

'Thank you for opening your home to me and I'm so very sorry for the disruption.' The eye contact between us all is charged with sadness and regret for what Peter, Gwen and Nathan will have to face in the cold light of day.

'You're welcome. It was no problem at all, really.' Alan and Silvia look as if they could both do with a strong cup of tea themselves. It's been a shocking evening for everyone who unwittingly ended up getting pulled into this.

Cary's arm is firmly around my shoulders now and we walk steadily out towards to the car.

In the darkness I have no idea what's going on inside the house next door, but it looks like all of the lights are on and a police car is still parked on the drive. So many questions whirl around inside my head, but they come and go in no particular order.

Suddenly, the front door opens, and someone steps out. It's mere seconds before they are close enough for me to see that it's Peter. He hurries over to us as if he's scared we'll turn and walk away.

'Leesa, I wanted to catch you before you left. Gwen and I, we... we're so sorry for everything that's happened. Gwen is in a state of shock, as you must be, too. Rachel can't stop crying. Nathan went too far this time and we both hope that sobering up in a police cell overnight will bring him to his senses. You are okay, aren't you?'

'Yes, really. Please don't worry about me, Peter. Give Gwen my love. I just need to…'

Peter's glance hones in on Cary. 'Is this your—'

'Yes, this is Cary.'

Cary gently retracts his arm from around me and the two men shake hands.

'Nice to meet you, Cary. Sorry about the appalling circumstances. This really has shocked us all to the core. We had no idea our son had a violent streak and we've seen a side of him that has horrified us. You will look after Leesa, won't you?'

He sounds choked and with that he leans forward, throwing his arms around me and hugging me fiercely.

'Take care, darling girl.'

Immediately I find myself being steered towards the car, so I don't have to watch Peter walk away.

Cary keeps glancing down at me as he helps me slide into the passenger seat. I settle myself in and gratefully let the headrest do its job. He doesn't say a word but fusses over doing up my seatbelt as if I'm incapable. Strangely enough, I'm more than content to have him take charge.

'I'm good. Really. It's all been a bit of a shock, that's all.' I owe him an explanation, but I don't quite know where to start to explain what happened. Sucking in a deep breath, I wait for Cary to walk around to the driver's side. When he's sitting next to me and we begin to pull away from the kerb, I feel an overwhelming sense of relief. Of finality. A line has now been drawn and there is no going back.

'You're safe now, so relax. I'm just going to make a quick call.'

He presses a button on the dashboard and the console lights up, then a dialling tone fills the car. It rings for only a few seconds before a voice looms up out of the darkness.

'Cary?'

'Yes, Granddad, it's me.'

'Twice in one day; you must be bored at the big gathering.'

'Look, I have a friend who needs a quiet room for the night and there are too many distractions back at the house. I know it's late but—'

'No problem at all. My guest bed is always made up, you know that.'

'Great, thank you. We're about twenty minutes away. See you in a bit.'

The light fades to nothing as the caller disconnects.

'I don't mean to be trouble, really I don't, and this wasn't at all what I was—'

'Hey, it's me you're talking to. I understand drama, my life is full of it. You need a warm bed and you need peace and quiet with no prying eyes. Granddad's place is perfect and if you need anything at all… well, at least someone will be within earshot. I think that's important right now. He doesn't say much, and he won't require an explanation. Let's just focus on getting you settled there for the night and in the morning I'll drive over and we can talk, okay?'

'Okay. And thank you, Cary. I know this is more than you bargained for – than either of us bargained for. I owe you and I won't forget that.'

'As I said, we'll talk in the morning. Now lie back and try to unwind. As long as you're in one piece, after a good night's sleep you'll feel a whole lot better than you look right now.'

I'm too shattered to pick up on the way he's trying to lighten the moment, but it's appreciated. There was no one else I could call, given the situation. Cary Anderson has, quite simply, rescued me as surely as any hero from one of Cressida's novels.

Opening my eyes with a start as the engine dies, I stare across at Cary, feeling a little disorientated.

'You fell into a deep sleep and I didn't like to wake you. We're here. I'll get you settled in for the night. Granddad's a bit of a loner, but he's someone you can count on in times of need. He doesn't poke his nose into other people's business.'

Before I have time to even think about the fact that I don't really know anything at all about this man whose home I'm about to enter, Cary is helping me out of the car. We seem to have parked at the rear of a property and there's no lighting here. In the pitch-black I can make out the outline of an old stone lodge. As we walk around it, I can see that it could probably fit inside a third of the ground-floor footprint of Cressida's house. Cary searches in his pocket for a key to the front door and moments later we're stepping inside.

The interior is warm, and a welcoming light glows in the small, enclosed entrance porch. From there we walk directly into a sitting room with a big open fireplace, where embers still glow and then a right turn takes us into a small passageway. Cary leans in front of me to swing open an old-style latched door.

It's not an exceptionally large room but it feels very cosy and countryfied. I don't know what I was expecting but it's beautifully furnished with some lovely traditional pieces and a sleigh bed made of solid oak.

'Very Christmassy,' I find myself saying, rather bizarrely.

'And comfortable,' Cary adds.

He returns to the car to get my things and I slip off my coat and see that there's a bottle of mineral water on the table next to the bed. I notice that the curtains have been drawn, too.

'Here you go. The door between the two wardrobes leads into the ensuite. There's no bath, just a shower, I'm afraid.'

I turn to look at Cary, struggling to muster even a weak smile.

'I'm tired, that's all.'

'That will be the shock hitting your system. Get some rest and I'll drive over in the morning as soon as I can get away.'

He takes two paces forward to wrap his arms around me and I wonder how he knew what I wanted most, at this exact moment, was to be held. We stand, motionless, for almost a minute before he releases me.

'The worst is over. Sleep well.' And with that he's gone.

I hate Christmas. I really hate it.

12

A Little Oasis

I'm awake long before Cary's text lights up my phone.

How did you sleep?

Good, as soon as my head sunk into the pillow.

This morning I'm feeling embarrassed about causing so much trouble to so many people. It feels like it was all my fault and yet I'm not even sure what happened. When Gwen knocked on my bedroom door to give me the full story about Nathan's sudden appearance, I understood her dilemma. He'd had a huge row with Sheryl. Nathan was always fiery and I bet her parents were there expecting a cosy family Christmas dinner. Gwen wasn't sure if he simply walked out or was asked to leave.

We agreed that Peter would drive me home and I began packing my things. I walked into Gwen and Peter's sitting room after it had all kicked off and for one moment fear hit my stomach with an insidious chill. I saw the large, almost empty, glass on the coffee table next to a bottle of whisky. Who thought that was a good idea, I wondered. Then I realised that while Nathan was probably drunk and had lost control, he was still only lashing out at things, not people. Maybe he was only a risk to himself. But I wasn't the only one in shock at what I was witnessing and one thing is very clear to all of us now. He needs help.

I can't get across for about an hour. Granddad is up, and he said when you're ready, wander out through to the kitchen at the back of the lodge. He'll make you some tea and toast.

My fingers instantly start clicking.

Okay. See you later. And sorry for pulling you into my nightmare.

He replies with a smiley face. Guess there's not an emoticon to express pity.

The shower is hot and when I'm dressed I pull my hair up into a ponytail as it feels straggly, but I couldn't face washing and blow drying it. I don't look too bad, just a little tired but I'm hungry and that, I suppose, is a good sign.

Walking out into the tiny passageway I notice two wonderfully worn oak steps in the far corner. Sticking my head around the curved wall, there's a staircase leading up to the first floor. It's narrow and dark as the only window is a small one in the adjacent wall. But a little vase sits on the sill with some fresh white roses and the radiator below it wafts the perfume up into the air.

I'm intrigued now as I filter out into the sitting room, noting that the fire hasn't been cleared of the ashes from yesterday. I make my way out through a door which is directly opposite the one we entered through last night. It leads into a dining room big enough to accommodate a large wooden armoire and a table to seat six people quite comfortably. There's a window seat looking out over what I assume is the side garden and as I turn to open the only other door in the room, I can hear the low sound of music. Easing the latch up as noiselessly as I can, I peer inside.

'I wondered if you were awake, so I texted Cary. Thought you might be hungry.'

The man buttering toast at the butcher's block island has a full head of grey hair and when he turns to face me, he raises one eyebrow.

'Leesa, isn't it?'

'Yes. And you're Matthew.'

He smiles. 'You've heard a bit about me then. I hope it wasn't from Cressida.'

His eyes sparkle with amusement and he's not at all what I was expecting. Nothing I'd heard had prepared me for the relaxed, smiling man in front of me. He's wearing a baggy sweater, and corduroy trousers, and for some reason he reminds me of a gardener.

'Do you mind laying the table? Everything you need will be in the dresser over there. Tea or coffee?'

I pull out a drawer and grab some teaspoons and knives, then hunt for some plates.

'Coffee, please, would be amazing. And that toast smells divine.'

'Nothing hits the spot like a slice of hot, buttered toast after the world has caved in.'

'Hmm. Isn't that the truth,' I reply, surprising myself. Cary said he keeps himself to himself but Matthew is going out of his way to make me feel comfortable and I appreciate that.

When the table is laid, and we take our seats opposite each other, all Matthew talks about, in between munching on toast, is the lodge and the garden. Then it occurs to me that he's simply keeping me occupied. Whether that's because Cary told him to do so, or he's worried I'll launch into some grand explanation about my circumstances, I have no idea. But I feel very at ease.

'The darned snow fell before I could tie up my palm and I'm going to have to do a lot of hacking to rescue it. The weight of it blighted some of the new growth, so it will mean stripping back the damaged leaves to allow it to renew itself from the heart again.'

Ironically, that description hits home with me. This is day one of my own fresh start, I suppose, as all of my links with Nathan's family have to be cut. It's time for me to nurture my own heart again.

After a second cup of coffee and three pieces of toast, I feel pleasantly full.

'Fancy a tour?' Matthew asks, nodding in the direction of the window that overlooks the side garden.

'I'd love that, thank you.'

'It's not huge but the garden surrounds the lodge on all four sides so it's very private.'

We clear the dishes and Matthew washes while I dry them. Then we head off to grab our coats.

The back door is in the traditional stable-style, the top half has a glass panel and opens independently to the bottom half. While I wait for Matthew to unlock it, I let my gaze take in the detail of the kitchen. It has a large sloping roof towering above us, which indicates it's an extension on the side of the original building. Once we're outside it all becomes clear.

Two huge chimney stacks grace the hand-hewn, tiled roof which branches off in three directions.

'Originally it was more or less two rooms up and down. It was a place for the riders to gather before the hunt. Over the years it had been extended but for the most part it's over 250 years old. The newest addition, the kitchen extension, was built in the late 1800s.'

Matthew doesn't stop to take in my look of fascination, as if he's oblivious and I sense he's quite a shy person at heart. I wonder if people sometimes misinterpret that as him being a little aloof, or reserved.

'It's delightful. I love the mullioned windows set in the buff stone. And you tend this garden alone?'

Ahead of us is a circular area abutted by a greenhouse and two sheds. In the middle is a large tree and around that are raised beds. Snow still covers much of it but there's enough greenery poking through to show it's both a winter and summer garden, with plenty of evergreen plants.

'Yes. In summer it's a blaze of colour and I simply work with what was originally here. But I gather the seeds each year and plant out the seedlings every spring to keep the flowers coming. The rest is mainly pruning and weeding. It keeps me out of mischief, as they say.'

We trudge along the path that wraps around the lodge and Matthew talks me through the planting as if I'm a trainee, but it's actually very interesting.

'Hey, he's not boring you with all those Latin names, is he?'

Cary's appearance has us both spinning around on our heels. A warm, fuzzy feeling begins to glow in the pit of my stomach. How is it that I suddenly feel safe whenever Cary is around? I guess he's more like his granddad than he realises.

'I only do that when I feel the need to show off. And I do it precisely because I know it bores people. Well, I guess I'll leave you to it, then.'

To my surprise Matthew turns and walks away without even a glance in my direction. Retracing my steps, I walk over to stand beside Cary.

'You scared him away. We were having a nice chat.'

I feel a tad awkward standing here facing Cary after last night. Should I hug him by way of thanks, or pretend everything is normal? Which it isn't. As if sensing my hesitation, he leans in to kiss my cheek.

'Glad to see you looking so much better. I guess we need to come up with an action plan for today. Boxing Day is a weird one, isn't it? Nothing happening because everyone is flaked out after over-indulging yesterday.'

'Almost everyone,' I mutter under my breath.

We saunter along the gravelled path towards the rear of the lodge, but in a way, I would have liked to have continued with Matthew's tour. Instead, Cary leads me back the way we came and then across to a large, single-storey building built of similar, although much newer, stone.

'This is Granddad's work-in-progress. It's probably unlocked.'

The handle turns, and we walk inside. It's an open-plan shell at the moment but large enough to be divided into two separate rooms and accommodate a good-sized bathroom.

'What's it for?'

'I have no idea, but it keeps him busy. He was an architect and it's in his nature to design things. A local builder is giving him a hand. It's big enough to be a little country retreat, so perhaps he intends to rent it out. Who knows? Now the shell is complete it will probably only take a couple of months to fit out the interior.'

Cary leads me across to an old wooden settle being used as a workbench and moves a couple of tools scattered on the top. Then he sweeps his glove over it to clear most of the dust and indicates for me to take a seat. Lowering himself down next to me, we both let out weary sighs.

'What a mess!' I declare, and Cary shakes his head in a sorry way.

'It's even worse than you think. When I joked about winning the bet I wasn't being entirely truthful.'

'No!' My disbelief is hard to hide.

'Yes. But I used you in name only, so technically it isn't a draw, although I will admit timing-wise I might have beaten you to it.'

I'm relieved, which sounds awful, but it helps a little to know this isn't one-sided.

'The Christmas Day meal is stressful, what can I say? Sitting around the table with one's family for a dinner that stretches out over a painfully prolonged period is, quite frankly, traumatic. It's the creeping death as one by one the questioning moves around the table. Okay, so the kids took up a big part of that because they ramble when they tell you their news. Little Chloe still can't quite fathom out what's real from what's a story, so hers always ends up resembling some sort of a fairytale. I'm pretty sure she didn't really bump into a wolf one day in the garden.'

This time I burst out laughing.

'And when it was your turn?'

'No wolves, but I can only talk about work for so long. Cressida said she's relieved I'm finally getting some balance in my life. That's where you came into it. I managed to conjure up a few convincing facts. I mean, I know how you like your coffee and some of your favourite foods.' He looks at me with a rueful smile. 'It seems there was quite a bit I took note of in our time together. I even impressed Laurence, although he did say that he didn't know what you saw in me. Usually my trump card is that he thinks I'm one lucky man as I only get nagged during the holidays. Guess he envies me for something else now.'

Hmm. 'Well, that doesn't sound too bad.'

'It wasn't, until Chloe piped up again.'

I look at him askance. Chloe is, what – three, I think? Rather young to say anything untoward.

'This time she asked if she could marry me. I started laughing, of course. But she was serious, as they tend to be at that age. Then Laurence joined in, saying that I wasn't free any longer.'

'Ah, she wants to marry you, that's sweet!' I smirk, mercilessly.

'It would have been, but the kids ran off to play and left the subject on the table, so to speak. Cressida began talking about it being time to put her affairs in order and start decluttering her life. In her will the house is left to me as the eldest and her investments and rights to her books are left to Laurence. She said she was growing tired of having to run the house and grounds and it was time to re-think her future.'

I swallow hard. Isn't that what people do when they know they're ill and preparing for the inevitable? Cressida certainly looks like she's in good health to me. Cary continues, but his frown is deepening by the second.

'It was weird and we all looked at her aghast. She loves that house, it's been a large part of her life's work, aside from raising us and writing her novels. When we tried to draw her out and get some sort of indication of what was really behind this she was evasive. The conclusion we came to is that Grandma is ill but has no intention of sharing the details. Laurence and I spoke privately, afterwards. He thinks she made the announcement because she believes it won't be long until I tie the knot. With you. I know it must sound like I complain about her a lot but she's the most important person in my life, Leesa. I couldn't even begin to think about life without her.'

I'm astounded, and I can see how moved Cary is, even considering the unthinkable. Death is the only inevitable thing about life, but it still comes as a shock when we are forced to stare it in the face.

'I will admit that it brought a lump to all our throats and my brain went into overdrive. She said something about wanting her family to be settled and with all the worries it was getting too much for her. Laurence looked directly at me, raising his eyebrows as if to imply she only ever worries about me, which isn't true. But suddenly I opened my mouth and out it came. The look of joy that passed over her face when I said that you and I were making plans for the future, made me instantly realise what I'd done. Given her hope.'

Seconds pass and I swallow down the growing lump in my own throat.

'It seems we're officially moving forward at speed.' He gives me a sheepish look.

'I can't believe you didn't come clean! It's one thing to fib to get through Christmas, but to lie to a lady who is trying to put her affairs in order is—'

'Wrong, or kind? It changes nothing with regard to her will, which we've always tried to brush off but about which Cressida, being Cressida, has always been firm. She says when she goes she wants it to be fair and for everyone to know exactly what her wishes are.'

I don't know whose situation is worse – mine, or Cary's. On balance I think he wins. Poor Cressida: she's such a vibrant lady and it's hard to believe.

'So did my late-night call come at the wrong or the right time? I can't fathom this out.'

'Well, they have no idea at all what it was about, and I sort of indicated all would become clear when I take you back with me.'

'You said what?'

'Oh, um, did you want me to drive you home today, instead? I mean, I can do that, of course.'

I shake my head, wanting to make him feel that wasn't my expectation at all, even though it was. After all, we have a deal and he's more than honoured his end of the bargain. Now I must honour my commitment. What I wasn't prepared for was the fact that this, it seems, is only just the beginning of a little journey we're about to make together. Apparently, a hero comes at quite a price these days. But I was in dire need and I'm grateful to him.

A part of me also acknowledges that there is no point whatsoever in wallowing in my own misery. When I get home, Mum and Dad will want to Skype to find out what went wrong, in case there is anything they can do to help. But I'm not sure I'm ready to share it with them quite yet. This was always going to be the Christmas from hell and I knew that from the start.

13

Quid Pro Quo

On the drive back to Cressida's I tell Cary all about the incident with Nathan. Well, as much as I wanted to share. What happened last year is my problem. My guilt and my pain are firmly locked away deep inside of me.

'Instead of beginning the healing process for us all, Nathan turned it into a total disaster.'

'Hey, you can't beat yourself up over what happened. You have to let it go.' Cary insists.

It's surprisingly easy talking to him, as he doesn't have that knee-jerk emotional response that Mum will have, for instance. He looks at things in a very practical way and that's precisely what I need right now.

'I'm glad Peter caught us before we left as it felt like an ending, a final goodbye. And having met you, I'm sure he will talk about it to Gwen. It's a relief, but I regret the way things have turned out for them.'

'Why do you keep putting the blame back on yourself? Nothing you've just shared with me has been your fault. I'm horrified to think that I was the one who dropped you off and put you in danger.'

'Danger?'

'Nathan is a bully and a violent one at that, Leesa.'

'He was just angry with himself and he'd had a few drinks which didn't help.'

'Listen to yourself, Leesa. You are an astute and very successful businesswoman who evaluates situations and people all the time. And yet, here you are, making excuses for a man who needs professional help. It might be normal behaviour for him, but he's obviously out of control.'

I've always thought of Nathan as moody because that's how he was but even his parents were shocked by this latest turn of events. Did Sheryl ask Nathan to leave because she's seen a side of him she doesn't like and isn't prepared to put up with it? Or was it really about her own guilt and that's why she wanted him to make his peace with me?

My phone pings, and it's a text from Mum.

You've gone very quiet, honey. Is everything alright? How is Gwen doing? Love Ma x

The sound that escapes my lips is one of sheer exasperation and for a brief second Cary turns his head to look at me.

'What's wrong now?'

'It's my mum. She's just asked about Gwen.'

Cary lets out an expletive, then apologises for cursing.

It hasn't gone quite as well as I'd hoped, I'm afraid. Off to a friend's for Boxing Day and will ring you when I can. Your errant daughter. Lx

Her response is instant.

Oh, that's not good. This was supposed to heal wounds for you, too, Leesa. I knew we should have stayed at home. Look, as soon as you're ready to talk, we're here for you. You did what you could, honey and I'm gutted it seems to have gone wrong. You put other people before yourself and look what happens! Sending a hug. Please ring soon. Mum x

'You're not sharing what happened with her by text, are you?' Cary's voice is tinged with empathy.

'No, of course not but I have to say something. I've told Mum that I'm off to a friend's house for Boxing Day, so I probably have twenty-four hours before I have to share the sorry details. I'll need to psych myself up before they see me on camera, though.'

'Look, would you rather I took you straight home? We can say you didn't feel well. It doesn't seem fair inflicting yet another stressful situation on you.'

I can see his concern is genuine and that's rather touching.

What I can't tell him is that right now I'm in desperate need of a knight in shining armour. Someone strong enough to come to my rescue. Who would have thought that person would be Cary? But, for the time being, he's the only person who understands both sides of this horrible saga.

'To be honest with you I really don't want to be on my own. I'm not usually a needy sort of person, but the last two days have shaken me, I will admit.'

One thing I simply can't admit, is that if I am left on my own I'm scared of where my thoughts might take me. This was always going to be a tough Christmas, I knew that – but this could take me over the edge if I start dwelling on it.

He nods, shooting me a glance. 'That's perfectly understandable given the situation.'

Suddenly I feel embarrassed. I hardly know him and I'm not usually all me, me, me. *Pull yourself together lady*, I admonish myself. Thinking about someone else's problems will help – it always does because self-pity is such a wasted emotion. That I suddenly feel so safe with Cary is unexpected, but I do. We both have supportive families but sometimes... well, that's not what you need to get you through a tough situation. I don't want to talk about it in detail, yet – living it was bad enough for now.

'I guess you and I had better talk about the plan to rescue you, then. What do you want me to say when Cressida begins questioning me?'

Cary shrugs his shoulders. 'Her writer's instinct gives her that constant quest for detail, unfortunately. She tends to see a story in everything.'

'Well, life is made up of a series of little stories, really. Look, I know this was your idea but I will find it easier if we keep it as close to the truth as possible. That's if we're going to have a chance of convincing her this thing between us is real. What do you think?'

He nods his head, his eyes not straying from the road.

'I think you're right. In fact, I feel uncomfortable saying this but your unplanned return works in our favour. We could say that we were missing each other and that adds weight to our... little story.'

Staring out at the snow-covered fields as they flash by, I examine my conscience. After what I've just been through it rather puts this into perspective. I owe Cary and he owes his grandmother. My head continues to mull over the pros and cons. Not least the fact that, personally, this could be a welcome distraction for me. It will end all thoughts about Nathan and the Hughes because I will need to be on my toes.

We lapse into an easy silence, but I steal a few sly glances at Cary as he drives. He's an attractive man and his presence is commanding. I can't think of anyone better, or more believable, to have as my partner in crime.

Oh heck, what possible harm can it do? I need this for my own sanity and in the process I'll be repaying Cary for rescuing me.

'If Cressida is putting her affairs in order then I can understand why you want to avoid her having to worry about you. I am also very grateful to you, Cary, for honouring your side of the bargain. I don't intend to renege on my side of things. But how do we *play* this?'

'The truth is that I don't know. Let's see how it goes and hopefully we can keep it low-key. Grandma is aware we've only known each other for a short while and won't be expecting us to jump into things too quickly. It would set off alarm bells if I suddenly informed her we were planning an engagement party. So you and I keep in touch and I'll talk about you to her whenever I can. How does that sound to you?'

'Perfect. But what about Matthew?'

'Granddad and Grandma don't talk very often. Besides, it's not his style to share information and he doesn't really know anything, anyway. Grandma calls him a closed book and that was another part of their problem over the years.'

I'm beginning to think that maybe Cressida's view of Matthew has coloured Cary's judgement of him, too. While

Matthew didn't ask any personal questions, he did mention Cressida's name and I wonder what would have happened if I'd started chatting to him about her? Maybe no one ever gives him the opportunity to get the past off his chest, as it were. Sometimes having someone to listen is cathartic and good for the soul.

'So, are you really ready for this?'

I swallow hard. 'Yep.' I sound a lot more confident than I feel.

Cary pulls the car to a halt on the drive, alongside another vehicle.

'I see Robert is here and that means he's probably staying for lunch. He's almost family, so I guess we're in luck. We are only going to have to say this once so no fears of getting the story wrong.'

I shrug my shoulders. It's too late to back out now. Cary turns to face me, hesitation momentarily reflected in his eyes. Impulsively, I lean forward and plant a kiss on his mouth; he pulls back, looking surprised.

But my own surprise outweighs his by a long shot. He responded and I found myself hesitating before pulling away. Awkward. Recovering quickly, it's obvious Cary is still struggling to regain his composure.

'What? You don't kiss your girlfriends? That was a test run in case we need to become demonstrative. First kisses are awkward and now it's no big deal because we've done it before.'

As we get out of the car and walk around to the rear to grab my bags, we both have resigned, yet determined looks on our faces. He opens the boot and turns to look at me.

'You're a real surprise, Leesa,' he remarks, and I can see how nervous he is about this.

The front door swings open and our heads turn to see Cressida, framed in the doorway, her eyes sparkling.

'What doesn't kill you, makes you stronger,' I reply, hoping the old adage is truthful.

Cary inclines his head, almost touching mine as he grabs my suitcase and I grab my bag. 'Here we go, then.' His voice is low, and my stomach immediately begins to flutter with nerves.

As we approach the house Cary hangs back so that I can step inside and into Cressida's arms.

'Oh my dear Leesa, welcome back. I'm so delighted your lovely family were willing to spare you so that you could spend a little quality time with us. It means so much, it really does.'

Releasing me, she turns to hug Cary and lingers with her arms around him for several seconds longer than he seems comfortable about.

'You've made me very happy, dear boy. Ooh, Christmas is such a magical time! And the best gifts aren't always the ones wrapped up in shiny paper under the tree.' Pulling back, she winks at me as she finally releases Cary.

Thankfully, as we filter into the dining room Cressida insists I sit next to her and opposite Cary. It's a relief as at least I won't have constant eye contact with her when the questioning begins. It's a full table with Robert, Laurence, Sally and the kids. There's a little squabbling over who sits where but after a minute or two everyone settles down and Cressida proposes a toast.

'Wishing everyone a wonderful Boxing Day and officially welcoming Leesa into our fold.' Even the children clink glasses, albeit theirs are full of what little Chloe refers to as bean juice. Given the colour, I think she means blackcurrant juice.

'So, how old are you, Chloe?' I figure if I start off the conversation by talking to the kids then it will delay the questioning.

'Eight,' she declares, solemnly.

'No, you're not!' Daisy jumps in, giving Chloe a serious frown. 'Jackson is eight. You're three.'

Chloe doesn't look very pleased to have been overruled.

'I'm free,' she replies, rather grumpily.

I try my best to rein in my smile. 'Okay, so three, eight and remind me how old you are, Daisy?'

'I'm six. My birthday is in November.'

I turn to look at Jackson, who is sitting there looking extremely bored.

'What's it like being a big brother, Jackson?'

He gives me a grimace. 'Annoying,' he says and immediately begins fiddling with his watch, killing my attempt to converse with him.

Cressida is flashing Cary a *don't leave her to struggle* look that's so overt everyone is now staring at him. He clears his throat but can't think of anything to say, so I have no choice other than to jump in again.

'I'm sorry I couldn't stay, but I'm thrilled to be back today. Cary and I have only known each other a few weeks but he's an amazing man.' It's all true, of course, now that I've seen another side of him. The one when he isn't wearing his work hat.

'Well, it's hard to believe anyone would put up with him, but...' Laurence pauses for effect. 'It's about time my big brother started sorting out his life. Goodness knows what you see in him, Leesa, but I'm damn sure he knows he's one lucky guy.'

Cressida is quick to join in. 'I'm delighted for you both, that goes without saying. It's so important to have things in common and you share the same work ethic, so that is wonderful. Although, I do hope you'll learn to relax a little and enjoy more quality time together. Do you travel much, Leesa?'

I cast a quick glance at Cary, but I can't read his expression.

'I'm afraid so. It's mostly in the UK, though.'

'That's a pity but I'm sure the two of you will work it out.' Her face is radiant and in a way I'm glad the kids are here because I'm sure she's holding back. The real questions will come later.

At last Cary manages to find his voice.

'We had a great time together in Australia. But this is also a bonus.'

I almost splutter with exasperation at Cary's rather uninspired delivery. If he expects this to work, he's going to have to at least sound a little more enthusiastic about the new love of his life.

Cressida raises her glass, and tips it in his direction. 'Well, it's deserving of a very special toast. What a way to end the year... another addition to our table. I can't wait for the family New Year's Eve party.' Cressida looks at Cary with a purposeful glint in her eye and then turns to look at me.

'Cary has mentioned it to you, hasn't he, Leesa?'

My glass is still raised in the air and I take a quick sip before lowering my arm.

'Of course, and I'd be delighted to join in with the celebrations.'

This time the look on Cary's face is one of sheer relief and I can see that he's full of anxiety. Cressida is not just his grandma, but his second mother. Having lost his own mother at such a tender age no wonder the thought of losing Cressida has sent him into a panic. Guess I won't be seeing my parents at New Year's, either. This is going to take some explaining though. But, as it was for Cressida, I know they will regard it as the perfect Christmas present.

'Hey, Mum. How's the weather?'

'Hi, honey, lovely to hear your voice! You sound much brighter this morning and that's such a relief. We're really missing you. This seemed like a good idea when we booked it, but it doesn't feel like Christmas at all. It's blisteringly hot here and even in the shade I'm having to plaster on the sun-tan lotion.'

Staring out from the well-appointed bedroom window at fields still deep in snow, despite the gentle thaw, it's hard to imagine walking around in a bikini.

'Hey, you guys needed to get away from it all for a little while. Besides, we'll work on making next Christmas the best one ever – for us all. I bet Dad's loving the heat.'

'He's in the sea most of the time. We spent the morning snorkelling. It's hard to believe it's Boxing Day. And you're at a friend's, you said? That's a rather unexpected turn of events. I'm sorry things didn't go as planned.'

I can hear the concern in her voice. I know Mum would rather be at home than on a sunbed but that was the sacrifice they made for me.

Mum and Dad are quite laid-back by nature, but I suppose it's only natural to want to see your offspring settled. People like Gwen and Cressida take it a little too far in my opinion, because some things simply can't be forced. I know that must be so hard to accept for people who often make things happen based on sheer determination and the strength of their own willpower. I can't decide whether to be in awe of that fact or feel sorry for them, because there will be successes, but the failures will be devastating.

'It's time to cut ties with Peter and Gwen, Mum. That door is now firmly shut and I'm moving on.'

A few seconds of silence tell me that Mum wasn't expecting such a seemingly positive and straightforward result.

'Well, that's great news. Dad and I simply wanted to do what was best for you this Christmas, Leesa. It's been a rough time for you, honey, and we rather hoped you'd eventually find the strength to cut the ties. But it's usually best to let them unravel gradually. We just don't want you walking away with any regrets, that's all.'

She sounds a little hesitant, as if it's too good to be true. I know Gwen will get in touch with her very soon and I need Mum to say the right thing, convincingly.

Lifting the corners of my mouth to help give my voice a little lift, I say the words I know she's longing to hear. 'There's someone new in my life,' I announce, sounding surprisingly positive and much brighter than I feel right now.

There's a brief pause.

'Well, that's an unexpected surprise! Why on earth didn't you tell us before we left?'

Oh no, now she sounds really excited. In my haste to make it sound real, it came out as more of a confession. Mum might think this is something I've been sitting on for a while.

'It's early days, Mum. It's the man I've been working for in Australia. His name is Cary. Cary Anderson.'

'Really?' A note of caution is creeping in. 'Both you *and* Jeff have to travel thousands of miles to find that interesting *someone*? What a coincidence. It must be something in the water.'

She gives a nervous laugh and I know that's not a good sign.

'You'll like Cary, Mum. He's a great guy and I'm staying at his grandma's house at the moment.'

That – of course – is a game-changer.

'Really? Oh, that's truly wonderful news,' she gushes and my heart sinks forlornly. Telling someone I love what they want to hear instead of the truth isn't my defining moment as a dutiful daughter.

'I can't believe Dad and I are so far away and missing all of the excitement! Perhaps you can bring him to our house for New Year,' Mum adds.

My palms are beginning to sweat.

'Well, I've been invited back here to a family New Year's Eve party, but we'll work something out, I promise.'

'I can't wait to tell Dad!'

This is a quick fix and at some point I will be breaking bad news again. But I refuse to spoil their entire Christmas and I want their last few days in the sun to be fun.

'I must go. Someone just knocked on my bedroom door. Love to you both and happy Boxing Day!'

I don't think I could have kept up that conversation for much longer without blurting out the truth and I grimace. However, a second tap on the door sees me plastering on a smile.

'Come in,' I call out and Cary's head appears around the door. 'Is it okay to come in?' He looks uncomfortable for some reason.

'Of course. I was just speaking to my mum and broke the news about New Year's Eve.' I inform him, holding up my phone. 'Smile!'

It's a good shot of him, the hint of surprise tinged with amusement means it looks very natural.

'What's this all about?'

'Every self-respecting couple have photos of each other on their phones. You'd better take one of me, while we remember.'

He pulls his phone from his pocket and I toss my hair back, turning my head to give him a teasing look over my shoulder. It's supposed to be vampish, but he's laughing at me. 'Keep it going, I need to get at least one good shot!'

I stop messing around and give him a half-smile.

'Great, that will do. Now to break the news... we've been summoned to Cressida's office.'

He raises his eyebrows towards the heavens.

'Office? That's ominous, isn't it?'

'Yep. The inner sanctum. There's no escaping once we're inside.'

I take a deep breath then push my hands together, in prayer-mode.

'We can do this! She's a powerful, determined woman but now it's time for her to relax a little. You owe it to her to make things as smooth as possible.' And I'm going to be doing the exact same thing.

'Amen to that,' Cary replies, with a firm resolve.

As our eyes meet, the telling look I receive in return bears no resemblance at all to the exacting man I've been working for these past few weeks. I'm seeing the person beneath that professional exterior and what I see is vulnerability. I wonder what exactly Cary sees as he stares back at me?

14

A Glimpse Inside an Ivory Tower

I had no idea the old vicarage even had a third floor disappearing up into the eaves of the building. In fact, I'd assumed that the line of three doors on the landing were, in fact, storage cupboards. It turns out that the one in the middle is the understated entrance to a flight of stairs. With no natural light and a wall either side, the glow from the floor-level lighting on each step is soft, but perfectly adequate.

'Surprised?' Cary calls out over his shoulder as I follow a couple of paces behind him.

'Very.'

When we reach the landing at the top there are two doors directly in front of us and one on the returning walls either side. The overhead inset lighting mimics daylight, although it's a little muted. Between the doors are floor to ceiling mirrored panels and it's a little unsettling being faced with numerous reflections of yourself at every angle.

'Clever, isn't it? As kids, Laurence and I loved coming up here to explore. It was off-limits most of the time and I must admit we were a handful at times; boisterous, always playfighting and not very careful when it came to ensuring we didn't end up breaking things.'

'Four rooms?'

Cary indicates to our right. 'That's a bathroom, next to it is a bedroom then Cressida's office, which adjoins a separate sitting room.'

He strides forward, placing his hand on one of the door handles and swinging it open, watching for my reaction as he does so.

We step into a room that faces the rear of the house. The entire back wall is made up of glass doors which concertina back, leading out onto a roof terrace. The views are far-reaching, looking out over the fields and the tops of trees, to the Channel beyond. Cressida's desk faces outwards and as I spin around I see that the wall behind me is lined with bookshelves. I can't even begin to imagine how many books there are here, but it's a huge collection. However, the lady herself is nowhere to be seen.

'Come and have a look at the view,' he encourages, turning and heading away from me.

I follow Cary as he walks across to the far side of the room, gazing out beyond the contemporary styling of the terrace with it's dark-grey, slate paving and central water feature. A white marble ball, some three feet high, is covered in a shimmering layer of gently cascading water, rippling downwards and disappearing into the pebbles below. All the materials are natural and it's very Zen and tranquil.

While Cary remains focused on the view, I grab the opportunity to scan around the room, taking in the precise neatness of everything within it. The Georgian-style desk has been hand painted in silver-grey and distressed. On it sit two separate monitors and keyboards, set side by side. A small stack of files nestles between them. There are several framed photos, I suspect of Cary and Laurence, but I don't feel I can sidle over to take a better look. Suddenly, a panel in the wall swings open and Cressida is standing there, grinning from ear to ear.

'I never thought I'd see this day. My eldest grandson and his girlfriend standing in my office. This has made one ageing romance writer very, very happy, you do know that?'

She walks across to stand between us, sliding an arm around our respective waists and giving a little satisfied hug.

'A special moment, indeed,' she almost whispers to herself.

'It's beautiful,' I remark, feeling the need to say something but not quite sure what. It's not just the view that is a surprise but the way the space has been used to create a separate little world up here.

'Thank you, Leesa. It's rather indulgent as I can write just as easily from anywhere in the house, but over the years it has been a sanctuary during some very difficult times. Up here it's easy to forget my troubles for a while and disappear into a world surrounded by characters who whisk me away from it all. Now, I look at it and think it's under-used and I feel isolated at times. In fact, the whole house only comes to life when the family gather here and that's a waste. This house deserves to be filled with people and love again. I didn't expend all that time and money preserving it, for it to become a dusty old place with no life inside its walls.'

Withdrawing her arms, she spins around to gaze upon her desk. There's a hint of sadness in her eyes and yet this is where she has created so many novels that have enriched and enthralled readers' lives over the years.

'You can't seriously be thinking of turning your back on the house, Grandma? You belong here. We all gravitate around you.'

Is Cary trying to convince himself that things will continue as normal – *can* continue as normal, despite Cressida's blatant attempt to forewarn him that there are changes to come? Even if it's simply about her taking some time for herself.

'He's like his father and his grandfather, Leesa. They don't like change. But nothing in life stands still forever. If it did then life would be boring. We all have to move on and consider our next steps with an open mind.'

Is she talking about Cary and me, or herself, I wonder?

'It's time for you to embrace my wishes, Cary. You have considerably more energy than I have, enough to oversee this house. But you can't live here alone. It's time to put down roots, dear boy, and that's why your news has delighted me.'

'My life isn't here, Grandma. This house is your domain.'

He seems annoyed by her comment, unwilling to enter into a conversation when he could so easily ask her what's really going on here.

'I sincerely hope he opens up to you a little more than he does to me, Leesa. It's that stiff-upper-lip mentality he's inherited. Where's the hint of the modern man in him? Showing one's emotions is not a weakness and I have no idea why he's so repressed. My lovely daughter didn't teach him that and as he and his brother were with me from quite a tender age, it certainly wasn't me. I simply want to know what's going on inside that head of his sometimes – as would anyone who is a part of his life.'

Cary turns to face her, his exasperation very visible.

'Grandma, when every man in your virtual book life is a knight on a white horse, doing the noble thing and never getting it wrong, your expectations are unreasonable. Granddad couldn't cope with the pressure, neither could my father. Okay, Laurence is doing quite well considering he's an Anderson. As for me, well, how could I ever measure up to my namesake, the one and only Cary Grant? Suave, smooth-talking and enigmatic simply isn't me. I can't pretend to Leesa that I'm someone I'm not because I'll simply fail to deliver.'

Cressida presses her hands together, her stance firm.

'You're missing the point, Cary. You aren't supposed to be someone else, you're supposed to be you. But a gentler, kinder and more-in-touch-with-your-feelings type of you. If not for me, do it for Leesa and for the sake of your own future. I wanted to see you both in private because the beginning of a relationship is a crucial time. It's where you set the ground rules and from here you either grow closer together, or you grow apart. It means a lot to me to think of you having someone by your side who will be a partner in both life and love. And I hope that this house will be a part of your future too, Cary.'

I can see that he's starting to get rattled and from where I'm standing, rightly so. But I can also hear the love inherent in her words and reflected in her eyes whenever she gazes at him. Cressida idolises him and she's fearful, by the sound of it – unable to accept that history could repeat itself again if Cary doesn't make an effort to change. It isn't only about this house and his inheritance but him realising that Cressida won't be around forever. His response is swift.

'Even the great man himself admitted during an interview that he, too, wanted to be Cary Grant. Instead, in real life he was Archibald Alexander Leach and his personal life was far from fulfilling as we later came to discover. Sad, but true.'

I know people do name their children after their idols. But the dashing, sophisticated icon of the silver screen is impossible to live up to for anyone, let alone someone who doesn't appear to have a single romantic bone in his body. Cary is right to be irked by it, although I do find the irony rather amusing.

Cressida smiles across at him benevolently. Her voice is calm and gentle.

'My dear boy, life is what we choose to make it. You're prepared to try when it comes to anything work-related. When it comes to affairs of the heart you look around at the failures and make that your excuse for keeping your emotions in check and being cautious. I want you to celebrate what you have with Leesa and nurture it. That's all I'm asking.'

'Well, I didn't have far to look to see how badly things can go wrong, did I?'

Eek! Now I wish I could just dematerialise and whisk myself away somewhere else. This is way too personal and it's as if they've forgotten I'm here. This harks back to old family wounds and that's none of my business.

Cressida frowns and lets out a lingering sigh that is poignantly heartfelt.

'Cary, I have never stopped loving your grandfather in the same way that your mother never stopped loving your father. But they were both stubborn men. I can't speak about your father now, because that would be unfair of me. It's been many years since I've seen him, and he may have changed his ways and found happiness. Although I am disappointed he has never reached out to you and appears to have disowned us all.

'That doesn't mean I would turn my back on him if he appeared at the door. Regrets tend to rear their head when we least expect them; what's important is that we take the time out to do something about it. Even if it's only to acknowledge that we're sorry. But as for your grandfather, I never measured him against anything or anyone; all he ever had to do to keep me by his side was to return the love I gave him. The only time he has ever been the least bit romantic, or emotionally thoughtful, was when he appeared in my novels. Then I made him the man he was inside; the man he was too afraid to be. And now he's old and he's alone.'

Oh no, Cary don't say it!

'I know and you're right. He doesn't reach out to anyone and neither does my father.'

At last I can let out the breath I've been holding in. I thought he was going to throw the same words back at her. This could be a turning point for them if Cressida handles it correctly.

'This isn't about romance or sweeping a woman off her feet. It's about being man enough to say something simple like "I love you," or noticing when the person you live with is in need of something, maybe a healing hug. There's a reason a mother reminds her children constantly of how dear they are to her. It builds their self-esteem to know they are wanted and loved. But as wives, mothers and grandmothers we, too, long to hear the sentiment returned. In truth, I don't know if your grandfather even really loved me in the beginning. Or whether he married me because it was expected of him. I guess I'll never know that for sure now, because he's too old to change.'

I feel tearful watching them facing each other and saying things that are hard to listen to but, I imagine, even harder to admit.

The atmosphere is growing tense and I feel it's the right thing to at least try to change the subject. I think that would be quite a relief to them both but what can I say?

'People often mellow.' I throw the thought out there and they both turn to look at me, slightly puzzled.

'Mellow?' Cary queries, a frown forming on his forehead. By comparison, Cressida looks a little relieved.

'It's just an observation, but is it possible that sometimes we don't notice the little changes occurring in the people around us? Matthew struck me as a shy man; very private. But he wasn't uncommunicative. Maybe he's not sure how to broach a conversation about the past and any regrets he might have.'

'You've met Matthew?' Cressida sounds a little put out.

I didn't realise Cary hadn't told Cressida about last night.

I nod and Cressida smiles at me with her eyes, knowing now is not the moment to halt this conversation. Cary looks puzzled.

'Granddad talking about the past? That's hard to imagine.'

I turn to face Cary full-on. 'Have you ever let him know you're there to listen if he wants to talk to you?'

Cary's head tips back in surprise. 'Well, no. Why would I?'

It's hard not to roll my eyes at Cary's curt response.

'Because it didn't look like he gets a lot of company and there are things you can't discuss with a total stranger, anyway. You might be the only person he ever sees, and in whom he could confide. If he wanted to, that is.'

Cressida remains silent.

'So, I what... ask him if he needs to offload? Isn't that something you do with a trained counsellor?'

Cressida reaches out to put her hand on Cary's arm.

'It's not offloading, Cary, it's sharing. A problem shared is a problem halved, as the old saying goes. Matthew has a few friends but none he'd feel comfortable enough with to really talk to and that's rather sad, isn't it?'

Cary's expression shows that he, too, wishes he was somewhere else, anywhere rather than here.

'Okay. I get the message, loud and clear. Don't end up like Granddad. Although from what I've seen he's not exactly unhappy with his life as it is now.'

Cressida glances in my direction and we exchange disbelieving shakes of the head.

'And how would you know that, Cary, if you've never asked the question?' I level at him. Then I realise I probably took the words out of Cressida's mouth.

'So how did you get to meet my rather retiring, estranged husband?'

'It's a long story,' I admit rather reluctantly.

'Well, maybe Cary could go off and sort out a nice pot of tea while we have a chat in my sitting room?'

Cressida immediately links arms and steers me in the direction of the half-open, hidden doorway, leaving Cary with no option but to do as she bid him.

I keep it simple and tell her that, following on from my divorce, saying goodbye to Nathan's family is allowing me to begin the next chapter of my life. She seemed to understand that it was a dilemma, but also something I had to do.

'That says a lot about you, Leesa, as it must have been a very difficult visit. I'm just a little surprised… I mean, Cary is such a closed person. Very black and white. Right or wrong.'

'And you think I'm ruled by my heart, rather than my head?'

She takes a moment to consider that statement.

'No. I think you might have been like that at one time but now I think you're veering in the other direction. It's called self-preservation. I know it's annoying when people insist on giving you advice when you haven't asked for it; the person offering it, though, often has a genuinely good reason for doing so. Sharing one's own experiences, painful lessons that are never forgotten, is a way of trying to avoid someone else going through the exact same thing.

'Don't veer too far in the other direction, will you? And don't let Cary convince you his way is the right way to conduct a relationship. The safest option is always in the middle, rarely to one extreme or the other.'

15

The Perfect End to the Christmas from Hell

'Jeff? Why aren't you down on the beach sharing a cold beer with Tania?'

He's certainly the last person I expected to be ringing me as I'm getting ready to go down for a cosy, adults-only dinner this evening. And I've been told to dress up which, given the contents of my suitcase, means wearing a black jersey knit dress and draping a scarf around the neckline to add some colour.

'Your mum's been texting me. What's this about you and Cary Anderson? She seems to think the two of you have hit it off and is asking questions.'

My stomach does an involuntary lurch.

'What sort of questions?'

'The name of his company and a casual "what's he like", which wasn't casual at all. What's going on?'

I can't tell Mum one story and Jeff another.

'Cary and I are dating. How's Tania?'

'What do you mean, dating? He was a bloody nuisance and he was driving you insane wanting to tweak every single little thing. And I haven't even looked at the last few emails you sent me with further updates. Every change he makes impacts on something else. It's beyond crazy.'

I agree with him but somehow we must pull it all together cohesively.

'It was a long trip back and Cary is quite different when he's not in work mode.'

'Your mum said you were staying with his family?'

I don't believe it! This means Mum is concerned about me, as she's usually very discreet and gives nothing away.

'Oh, and I'm not supposed to mention it to you but she's worried. I guess it all went off okay with the ex-in-laws, then.'

I bet none of this makes any sense to him; he knows me only too well. Besides, I'm still coming to terms with it all myself.

But my gut instincts are screaming at me because there's something else going on here. Jeff isn't a gossip and I've always known he's Mum's little fallback when she doesn't want to bother me. But he thinks it's their little secret and suddenly he's not concerned whether I know they talk. So, the fact that he wants to get to the bottom of it means something else is up.

'No, it didn't. Jeff, what aren't you telling me?'

Silence.

More silence. I wait, patiently.

'You were right,' he confirms. 'Tania is a great girl.'

That's it? Another wait. A little less patiently this time… three, four, five—

'Tania is off travelling in the New Year. She's asked me to go with her.'

I try to keep myself calm.

'Travelling? What, around Australia?'

Okay, so he's going to want some time off and that means juggling the work schedule.

'No. Thailand and then on to Malaysia for starters.'

For starters?

'I know this is all very sudden, Leesa,' he continues, 'and I hate doing it to you. But I guess I've been waiting all my life for something like this to happen to me. It's like I've suddenly woken up and realised there's more to life than living and working in the town in which you were born. I feel bad about it but I'm handing in my notice. The timing is awful, it being Christmas and all, but I wanted to give you fair warning. I'll fly back to the UK for the second of January as originally planned, to wrap everything up. I also need to sort out what I'm going to do with the house. I appreciate that it puts you in an awkward position. But I know someone I think could step in and take my place. You could give him a try.'

I can't quite take this in.

'Jeff, you aren't leaving the UK for good, are you?'

I hear a sharp intake of breath. 'The truth is, I just don't know for sure where I'm going to end up, Leesa. It would be wrong of me to pretend otherwise. Tania is quite a live wire and she doesn't let anything hold her back. I've never felt this way about anyone before and suddenly nothing else in my life is important any more.'

Jeff has lost his mind! He's throwing away everything he's worked for – his whole career.

'But how will you manage for money? And what about your family?' I hope I don't sound like I'm being negative when he sounds so happy. But bubbles burst and if—

'Look, don't worry about me. You need to focus on recruiting someone to replace me. I appreciate that the last thing you need right now is work stress when you've finally found someone you actually want to get into a relationship with. That's a huge deal for you and I don't want my news to throw you off course. I'm just a tad surprised that someone turned out to be Cary Anderson, though. I found him bordering on rude at times and I wondered if he was born into money. You know the sort; they take everything and everyone for granted. I don't want to seem negative, here, Leesa but this isn't a rebound thing, is it? I'd hate for you to get hurt again so soon.'

This is hard because now I want to defend Cary, even though I can totally understand why Jeff would think that.

'No, I'm being careful and it might not go anywhere, anyway. He's a nice man underneath that cool, professional veneer and he's been under a lot of pressure, that's all. But Tania, well… she is lovely but I didn't see this coming. I mean, backpacking is a very different lifestyle choice. But all that matters is that you're happy.'

I mean that and besides, Jeff doesn't owe me anything, other than to finish off the work in progress. And his concern for me is touching.

'Guess we're both a little apprehensive about the next step,' he jokes.

'I am excited for you, Jeff. Email me that guy's details and I'll make contact. It's just that I'm going to miss having you around.' My voice creaks to an uncertain halt.

'I know, and Leesa, please know that this is the last thing I ever thought would happen. When I get back we'll focus on finishing off Cary's precious little project. And don't worry, it will come together and he'll be delighted with the end result. It's going to be my number one priority. Besides, I can't really allow myself to relax about the future until I know you're sorted – business-wise as well as personally.'

'I knew you wouldn't let me down, Jeff.'

I try hard not to let my voice wobble. Jeff isn't only my best friend and employee, but he knows me better than anyone. He's like a brother to me and here I am, unwilling to let him go when I should be celebrating his good news. But I'm also worried because it's clear he has his doubts about Cary and me. And no wonder. This is the first time I've ever lied to Jeff and it doesn't sit well with me.

Mum's going to miss him, too, because he's like a surrogate son and he's always been her comfort zone. Someone to keep an eye on me, she's always said. But now she'll be worried because if Jeff didn't know very much about my relationship with Cary, then she'll wonder what I'm hiding.

What on earth am I going to do? One problem has turned into two and they couldn't be more different but both mean that my whole life is now in turmoil.

'I'm happy for you, Jeff, really I am. But nothing is going to be the same without you, bro.'

'I can't pretend it isn't a little scary, Leesa. But when I'm with Tania she gives me a sort of confidence I didn't have before. I'll do that email now and don't tell your mum I blabbed. She's just a bit anxious given everything you've been through in this last year. I didn't say very much, only that Cary seemed like a sound bloke. Speak soon and remember, I'm always only a phone call away. I'll still have your back when you need me.'

As the line disconnects I hate the fact that everyone is still worrying about me. Well, I'm strong and determined. It's a huge dent losing Jeff, I will admit, and finding the right person to fill his shoes isn't going to be easy.

Ironically, it seems that Cary is the perfect person to have in my life right now; he isn't overly emotional, he's a strong individual and we seem to fit together quite well. After all, isn't a relationship a bit like any contract between two willing parties? And without Jeff, the go-to man in my life, I'm probably going to be in need of a listening ear.

Jeff is giving up a lot to please Tania, but on the reverse side of that she seems to have given him a new lease of life and a fresh perspective. I can't begrudge him that because I want him to be happy and if this is what it takes then I should suck it up and be happy for him. I wonder if Cary is, unwittingly, about to give me a new lease of life?

The first think I do is to send Mum that photo I took of Cary.

Thought you might like to see the man your daughter is dating. Did I mention that his grandmother is Cressida Anderson, the famous author? Dressing for dinner now but I'll tell you more tomorrow, promise! Lx

That should at least reassure her. Obviously, Jeff hasn't broken his own news to her yet and when he does she will be reeling. The timing of this is unfortunate but then life is often like that. When change happens, you have no choice but to accept it and go with the flow.

As for developments with Cary, it's just as well we are sticking to the truth as closely as we can. Otherwise this would be a nightmare situation to handle on top of everything else. And the more I witness of the discussions between Cressida and Cary, the more I'm beginning to wish I knew the whole story. But I also think they aren't being very fair to Matthew and I'd quite like to do something about that. What exactly, I have no idea, but that doesn't mean an opportunity won't present itself.

An email notification pops up on my phone and I open it, scrolling through it until I see the name Jeff is putting forward. I don't recognise it at all and a part of me feels anxious about having to start again with someone new. I hope we can build that perfect working relationship but it won't happen overnight.

Right, Zack Ward, let's see how keen you are to grab an exciting, new opportunity. If you look at your emails on Boxing Day, then you're serious about work.

My fingers fly over the keyboard as I introduce myself and explain that Jeff passed on his details. I tell him a little bit about the company and what we do. I hit send, push my phone into the top of my bag and take one last look in the mirror.

Earrings. I need earrings. I dive into the side-pocket of my carry-on holdall and pull out a pair of rather elegant, silver leaf earrings. Considering it's basically a plain, little black dress, I do look like I've made a bit of an effort.

Walking along the landing, I arrive at Cary's bedroom door and tap nervously. Within seconds it's flung open.

'I was just about to wander along to see how you were doing. Come in.' He closes the door behind me. 'Thanks for earlier on, you know, reassuring Cressida – being open about the divorce thing meant a lot to her.'

It's rather nice that he's prepared to acknowledge that, and I give him a warm smile. Looking at the effort he's made, I must say he wears an evening suit well. I'm guessing that didn't come out of his suitcase. His white shirt doesn't have a single crease in it and the open neck lends an air of casualness he carries off to perfection.

'Will I do? There's nothing really inspiring in my suitcase,' I admit, regretfully. But then Gwen and Peter weren't big on formalwear.

Cary glances over me with a quizzical eye, taking his time and I start laughing. He's kidding around with me.

'You'll do. I know it's all still a little awkward, but we've sort of slipped into this quite well, haven't we?'

I give him a cautious glance. Is he still kidding? He looks serious.

'That's weird because I was thinking the exact same thing. I just sent that photo I took of you to my mum. I feel bad because she wanted me to take you to meet her and Dad at New Year. If you really do want me to come to the family party, I have to appease her somehow.'

After checking his watch, he opens the door for me and we begin to make our way downstairs.

'Let me put it this way, it would sound warning bells if you weren't there so that was a good move. It's important your parents are included in this, obviously, and we will remedy that. Hopefully, tonight will be more relaxed than this afternoon and I can promise you that the meal will be well worth the hassle. The chef, Marcel, is amazing and he's a long-time friend of Grandma's. She's famous for her very entertaining dinner parties and delightful food accompanied by superb wines, although these days they are few and far between.

'Marcel also runs a busy restaurant, but he rarely sends one of his trainees when Grandma reaches out to him. He's yet another Cressida devotee but then she's known him for years and helped him financially when he started out. She's a nurturer and people whose lives she touches tend to become devoted friends. Anyway, hopefully you'll feel less in the spotlight and will be able to sit back, enjoy the food and join in as and when you want to.'

I give him a sideways glance.

'Um… holding hands would be a nice touch, Cary.'

He hesitates for a moment, forgetting our ruse. 'Ah, yes.' Then immediately reaches out.

The feel of his hand as it closes over mine is comforting. Everything around me feels like a constant battle these days and just having someone here who understands is a bonus, a gift even. My head is still reeling from Jeff's news and the thought of what's to come. But Cary is right and tonight I'm going to try to relax. After all, who would have thought I'd be here, dining at the same table as a famous author and my… boyfriend. I bite my lip to stop myself breaking into a ridiculous grin. What's not to enjoy? I could do a lot worse, I muse, than walking hand-in-hand with an attractive, intelligent and successful man like Cary.

'Ah, perfect timing!'

Turning around in unison as if we rehearsed it, we glance back up to the landing where Cressida stands peering down at us.

'What a handsome couple you make.' She sounds delighted.

I slip my hand out of Cary's by way of a hint and he duly walks back up the stairs to escort his grandmother down. She's wearing a beautiful, floor-length dress in a rich purple taffeta.

I continue down and wait for them at the bottom of the stairs. With Christmas music playing softly in the background, the stately tree dripping with tinsel and the prettiest of baubles reflecting the twinkling fairy lights, this could be a scene from a Christmas card. I'm beginning to feel comfortable here, as if I fit in. However, this isn't real and I have to keep reminding myself that it's merely a matter of convenience. Like hiring an escort for an evening, except our deal is on a quid pro quo basis.

When they descend into the hallway Cressida's face gleams with pride, as Cary offers me his other arm and escorts us into the formal dining room.

Lit only by candles, the crystal glassware on the table glints, sending shards of rainbow light across the pale-grey, linen tablecloth. Robert, Sally and Laurence all stop talking when we enter.

'Stay there, I need to capture this moment,' Sally says as she jumps up out of her seat with her phone in her hand.

I steal a glance at Cary, thinking maybe he'll be rolling his eyes but his smile matches Cressida's. Me? The enormity of what we're doing is beginning to sink in and as we take our seats I find myself hoping I don't regret this at some point in the not-too-distant future.

'It's weird getting used to seeing someone sitting next to Cary,' Laurence muses and Sally gives him a little shove. He looks at her, his eyes flaring. 'What? It's true. The last one was, what, three years ago? Monica, wasn't it?'

Nicholas stoops to place the first course in front of me. The scallops look like they've been cooked to perfection – nut brown on the top and a translucent white beneath. A drizzle of something green that's probably a pea puree and a few carefully placed strands of wild rocket leaves make it picture-perfect. I wait while everyone else is served, anxious to hear Cary's response.

'Yes, I did bring Monica here once. Easter, I believe. That particular experience taught me another lesson. There's no point at all in introducing you to a passing acquaintance; you lot are a daunting prospect for anyone to face. Ignore my brother, Leesa.'

Cary's eyes are fixed on Laurence, who seems delighted to have him on the defensive.

'There you go, Grandma. You knew that one day he'd bring home the right one.'

I daren't even glance in Cary's direction after that comment.

It's like eye tennis and Robert, clearly feeling a little uncomfortable, rescues me.

'Well, I'm seriously hungry and think we should stop talking and start eating.'

I give him a grateful little smile, picking up my knife and fork to place the first sliver of scallop into my mouth. It's meltingly divine and Cary was right. Marcel is an exquisite chef. He must feel very indebted to Cressida to be in her home, cooking for us all tonight. But then she's a person with connections and I suspect she's very good at putting the right people together to their mutual benefit.

Robert doesn't give Laurence and Cary a chance to pick up on their conversation after the first course is done. Instead he asks Sally whether Chloe is at nursery yet and it's a relief to be able to sit and listen to her talk about each of her children in turn.

Once the first course plates are cleared, the waitress returns and silence reigns for a while as we focus on the meltingly divine fillet steak with champagne sauce.

It's hard to believe that twenty-four hours ago I was sitting on a sofa with a policewoman next to me, taking a statement. Suddenly something occurs to me that I hadn't quite grasped before. Maybe one's personal life needs to be planned as carefully as you plan your career. I don't simply take on any client, I take on clients whose products or services I believe in, and for whom I think I can deliver exactly what they need, and, in the process, exceed their expectations.

Fate made my path collide with Nathan's and look how that ended. Cary and I are growing very comfortable around each other and that's not only unexpected, but increasingly welcomed after Jeff's news. I know my acquaintance with Cary is temporary, but it feels like a lifeline at the moment. A way to turn around people's sympathy for me and reassure them I'm okay. The reality might be a little different but I'm still standing, as they say. And who knows what the future might bring, anyway?

16

The Makings of a Plan

I will admit that saying goodbye to everyone is hard as both Sally and Cressida are visibly upset, which is touching.

Sally gives me a genuinely warm hug.

'Oh, I so wish you didn't have to go home today. But just knowing you are going to be around for the party next week is marvellous! For the first time ever, I have someone I can talk to who can empathise about being involved with an Anderson. It's little short of a Christmas miracle!'

Everyone begins laughing and it does help to ease an awkward moment. But it's time for me to leave, as I promised Mum and Dad this morning that I'd call round to check on their place. They'll be home the day after tomorrow and given the amount of snow we've had I don't want them walking back into any surprises, like a burst pipe or a leak.

Cary finally takes control and bundles me into the Range Rover after one more hug from Cressida.

'This is the last trip for me in this,' he adds as he starts the engine. 'I think the thaw is sufficient to be able to use Grandma's car for the rest of my stay.'

'Will Laurence and Sally be here until the New Year?'

Cary chuckles. 'Yep. We're all prisoners until after the big party.'

'That's mean, Cary. Cressida's Christmas preparations represent hours of work.'

His face drops a little. 'I'm half-joking. Would I rather be somewhere hot, not surrounded by family? Well, before this little episode with Grandma about putting her affairs in order, I would have said most definitely. But you're right and I'm starting to see that what I take for granted is actually rather special.'

Oh. I didn't mean to make him maudlin.

'Your presence has made all the difference, though,' he adds, glancing at me rather meaningfully for a brief second. 'Grandma is like a totally different person around me suddenly. It's a huge relief not having that constant pressure of teetering on the edge of a cutting retort because she's pushing me too hard. I could get used to this easier existence. I rather like the thought of being in her good books when I'm here.'

Wow. There's my answer, right there and I didn't even have to prompt him.

'Well, I wasn't going to say anything but seeing as you've more or less said what I was thinking, then maybe we've inadvertently hit on a brilliant solution. Being free and single can be a drawback sometimes. All that effort in getting to know someone new, only to discover you have very little in common. Or worse, they don't even realise it's a non-starter and it's stressful letting them down easy. Then you begin all over again. In between these traumatic interludes, family and friends' matchmaking unwittingly keeps the pressure on. You begin to feel as if something is broken that needs a quick fix to make it right.

'I'm happy enough with my life as it is but there are times, I will admit, that it would be handy having someone supportive by my side. Like the holidays, for instance. But as for the rest of my time, well, I want to grow the business and reap the rewards. There's no point in working hard unless you set yourself goals and from here on in mine are going to be increasingly ambitious.'

Suddenly, Cary pulls the car into a layby, switches off the engine and turns to look at me with interest in his eyes.

'I think we're both on the same page here and I need to check that you're serious. I mean, this would signal some sort of longer-term commitment. But you're an attractive woman, Leesa, and are you prepared to settle for this—'

'… mutual arrangement? Hell, yes! I've been through one awful divorce and I have no intention of getting myself into another situation like that. I'm not looking for marriage, Cary, I'm looking for a companion of convenience. A relationship that doesn't come with all of the usual complications because, like yourself, it doesn't suit my plans.'

I can feel my cheeks beginning to glow a little. So, he thinks I'm attractive, does he? Well, he's certainly someone I'm thrilled to take home to my parents because I know they will definitely approve of him. Who wouldn't?

'Snap. Where do we draw the line?'

I gulp. Here we go – he's a man who likes to thrash out the small print and so do I, but this is a potentially sensitive area.

'As far as is necessary, on the proviso that we're both comfortable with whatever happens. We're consenting adults who know our own minds, and this is a mutually beneficial deal. I'm done with letting fate take control and now I'm taking back control of every aspect of my life.'

That sounded a tad on the dismissive side; I mean, he is a client even if he also happens to be a very attractive and intelligent guy. I cast around for something suitable to add to acknowledge that fact, but he jumps straight in.

'Amen to that! My sentiments, exactly. Okay, so you attend the big party at the house and let me know when and where with regards to meeting your parents and putting their minds at rest. After that we go our separate ways and reconvene at Easter?'

I give him a wink.

'Nailed it! I have a bit of an uphill climb once I'm back at work and this simply takes away so many annoying little ankle-biting problems for me.'

Cary kicks the engine into life and we head back out onto the road.

'It's a deal, then. It sounds pretty damn perfect to me. It's a wonder more people haven't thought about a practical alternative to fill the gap between being single and being married. Maybe less marriages would fail if couples spent less time together and not more.'

Oh, Cressida, I'm so glad you can't hear this conversation. But your grandson is happy, and I think that's really all you're looking for, so you can be at peace. I need Cary, as much as he needs me and that's a great basis on which to have an understanding. I know you wouldn't want him to go through a rocky marriage like I've had to because it makes life a total misery. I think that as an unmarried, part-time couple we have a real chance of making this work to our mutual advantage.

'And how's the video coming along? Jeff won't get distracted and fall behind on those final changes, will he? It's important he hits that February first deadline.'

Cary is one cool character. His work hat is back on for a moment and he sounds exactly like the man who was driving me mad in Australia. I can see why Jeff was a little disbelieving of my news.

'You have my word on it.'

I know Jeff won't let me down, but the worry over replacing him is a problem I don't want to share with anyone right now. How ironic that one area of my life is now shaping up rather nicely and I've swapped that for another equally pressing one. All of my plans for expansion in the spring were based on the assumption that I would only have one new recruit to sort out, not two. I have a real challenge ahead of me now, so it's going to be time to roll up my sleeves and attack it head-on.

Mum and Dad's return sees them bursting with questions, not least because it's obvious they now know about Jeff's plans. Naturally, they are very happy for him, but anxious, too, about how it will impact upon me. However, it's easy to allay their concerns because I have a plan and a potential new recruit. And after whizzing through a few photos of Cary on my phone, they are clearly delighted, which does prick my conscience a little. But I don't want them to feel they have to constantly worry about me because it's not fair on them.

Although they've never interfered or passed comment on my decisions, I often see the concern reflected in their eyes.

It makes me realise what a huge commitment it is to have a child and they chose to have two.

Wouldn't life be so much easier if you simply fell in love with someone and spent your life looking after each other? Huh! Even getting that bit right is difficult, I've found. And maybe my miscarriage was a sign that I'm not destined to be a mother at all. It ended up breaking my heart and I can't ever put myself through that again. I'm thirty years old and I still feel I have so much to learn, and to prove. If I can't sort myself out, how can I take responsibility for bringing another new life into this world, no matter who I'm with?

'It seems this trip to Australia was a major turning point for both you and Jeff,' Dad remarks quite casually.

'Yes, and so unexpected. The new guy is starting on the eighteenth of January. Jeff will have finished off the Australian project and probably be several thousand miles away by then. But judging by his CV, Zack Ward is a good candidate. I do hope so, because I need him to settle in quickly.'

Mum frowns at me. 'You sound hesitant. It takes time to get to know someone and understand how they operate. I know it's difficult when it's such a small team, but every relationship requires work.'

I wonder if Mum is only talking about Zack, or whether she has concerns about Cary suddenly coming into my life. Do they think I grabbed the first available guy in desperation because now that I'm single again and Jeff is leaving, suddenly I feel very alone? Because they couldn't be more wrong.

Dad nods in agreement and I look from one to the other of them.

'Zack's been working as a self-employed consultant for the last few years and I just wonder how he'll cope as an employee working to someone else's timetable. It's going to be an adjustment all round and we'll have to see how it goes.'

I hate seeing that look on Mum's face, the one where she crinkles her brow. I wonder what her gut instinct is telling her. She's a great believer in that and it's rubbed off on me.

Employing Jeff when the previous incumbent left was a no-brainer. I clicked with Jeff immediately that day when we walked into our first lecture at university and happened to find ourselves sitting next to each other. He's good at what he does but when I started up the business I couldn't afford to employ anyone. So I drafted in help as and when I needed it. When the day came to expand, Jeff wasn't available and I ended up taking on a guy who was okay, but eventually he moved on. Jeff was looking around for a new challenge and offered to take his place. We were a dream team but now the end is in sight.

I wasn't able to sit across a table to interview Zack, as he's working in France at the moment. However, we've chatted several times via Skype. I'm hoping that when he arrives I can run through everything once and leave him to get on with it. The meetings I have diarised won't affect his workload for probably six weeks, but it also means I won't have much free time to do any handholding.

'And you promise we'll meet Cary in person on New Year's Day?'

'I promise, and he can't wait to meet you both. We will only be able to stay a couple of hours because we'll be tired from the party at Cressida's. Plus, he's heading off to London in the evening as he's back to work the following day. And, of course, I'll need to be at work bright and early, as Jeff will be back. We're going to have a lot to cover before his official last day.'

'Maybe we can all catch up at Easter for a more leisurely get together, Leesa. We can take you and Cary out for a special meal. You'll be feeling more relaxed about work by then and hopefully the pressure will be off. What do you think?'

Dad, no doubt, simply wants to have time to vet Cary and check that I'm not making another huge mistake. He never took to Nathan. Dad did make an effort to be sociable, but it was very obvious to me. Mum is trying to step back a little into her usual encouraging role, happy to trust that I've learnt a few lessons and Cary is different. Which he is, of course, given our arrangement. But Dad is going to need a little reassurance and I know Cary will deliver.

'So, tell us all about *the* Cressida Anderson! What's she like? The woman is an icon of her generation. Does Cary write?'

I smile to myself, 'No, Mum. He doesn't write.' I can see her interest is really piqued. As for Cary, well, I'm sure he would have said if he did. 'She's as glamorous and sophisticated as you probably imagine. And she dotes on Cary and his brother, Laurence.'

My phone kicks into life and it's a text.

'Sorry, I have to respond to this. It's from Jeff.'

I walk out to the kitchen, leaning against the countertop as I scroll down.

It's only me. Slight change of plan. I've been working flat-out to process all those changes Cary wanted ahead of our session on the second of January. I've just downloaded the penultimate version of the 'Solar Powered Solutions – The Future Starts Here' video to the system. I know you will probably want me to tweak a couple of things but it's polished and it presents well. I've emailed you about two things you told me to change but with the other amendments I think that would be a mistake now. Let me know what you think. Must go, we're off to a party on the beach. Laters.

Laters?

Switching to my inbox I open Jeff's email and my face falls. The reason he's been working on finalising the video is that Tania has managed to find them a good deal on tickets. They fly out on the first leg of their journey on the tenth of January. Now I'm concerned that he's been rushing it and I really need to get online and check it out for myself. I slip the phone back into my pocket with a sigh.

'Sorry guys,' I say as I walk back in, interrupting Mum and Dad. 'I have to go. Work calls. Jeff wants me to review Cary's video and time is running out for him to make any final changes.'

They both look disappointed.

'We feel like we've hardly seen you. And you'll miss Beth's news about Christmas with Will's family. I bet you haven't even spoken to her while we've been away.'

I try not to hang my head. 'We texted on Christmas morning. She said she was having a lovely time. Please tell her I'm sorry to have missed her. If she wants to ring for a chat I'll try my best to listen patiently to the tedious details about colour plans, flowers and seating arrangements for the wedding. Seriously, I can't be the only one avoiding her right now.'

Mum's face looks a picture as she tries not to laugh and gives me a look of stern indignation instead.

'That's a little unkind. One day soon that could be you, Leesa. I will, of course, encourage her to ring you and you will, of course, politely listen.'

Me it will most definitely not be – ever again. I did it once and that was enough. I don't need a man in my life to complete me, all I need is a good team to help me realise my dreams. But I don't have to point that out and I do love my baby sister, even though she was a nightmare to live with.

'I must go, but it's great just knowing you're back safe and sound.'

Mum throws her arms around me, giving me a grateful hug. 'Love you, darling and we're here if you need anything. Anything at all.'

I escape as quickly as I can, mindful that Beth is on her way. But I'm really concerned because Jeff is usually a perfectionist and he never rushes anything. In fact, my concern is so consuming that I'm home before I know it. I pull up on the drive, a little shocked to realise that I can't remember a significant chunk of the journey. I only hope I didn't go through any red traffic lights while the whirling thoughts filling my head blocked everything else out.

Climbing the stairs to my office two at a time, my stomach begins to flutter with nerves. It's obviously important to get this right because Cary is a prestigious client. But now we have established this more personal arrangement, for some reason I'm even more on edge as I log in.

As I sit watching the opening and middle scenes that are already etched on my brain, I have to admit it is pretty damn good but to my dismay, the last ninety seconds are off. It lacks impact after a pretty sharp, and concise, portrayal of Cary's seminar.

The tagline nails the marketing strategy, sending a clear message that people who own their own homes do have a choice and will make money from it day one. Comparing a house powered by the traditional means to one with the new system, Cary's delivery of the overall message is persuasive. We can all choose to make a difference to the negative effects of modern living on the environment. Once the initial costs are paid off, the return will continue to grow. It's a win-win situation.

However, the finale is simply too cumbersome and needs to be slicker. Short, sharp and focused is what's called for, whereas it feels like information is coming at you from all angles.

What worries me is why Jeff couldn't see that. Normally he'd be on the phone telling me it isn't right, and it needs a lot more work. My fear is that if Cary sees this as it stands now, he'll start pulling the entire thing apart, rather than addressing the last remaining issue. It has to be as near to perfect as we can make it before I hand it over for Cary's approval. But the amount of time we have left to complete this is fast running out.

I'm confident we can sort this when Jeff is back. Between us we'll deliver.

A sudden feeling of intense sadness hits me out of nowhere. I'm about to lose yet another person from my daily life whom I regarded as family. Jeff is my best friend and my sounding board; I've always valued his advice, even if he was a little too cautious for my liking. But to whom can I turn in the future when he isn't around?

17

New Year, Old Wounds

Cressida's party is every bit as flamboyant as I expected it to be. The house is packed and the buffet is lavish. With creative cocktails named after some of the heroes from her bestselling novels, it's a huge hit. Cary has remained glued to my side more or less the entire evening. I recognise a few faces from the literary world but most of the names go over my head and, in the end, Cary gives up on his running commentary.

Eventually we filter out into the hallway, where one of the large walls in this impressively grand heart of the house has become a theatre screen. It's been showing back-to-back black and white Christmas films all evening.

Heart-warming, feel-good nostalgia at its best.

'Can we sit and watch for a little while?' I ask, knowing he won't be exactly happy with my request.

He grimaces. 'If you insist.' But his tone is one of amusement, I note.

There are several rows of chairs and we head towards the back.

'Cary, it would really help me if I understood a little more about your childhood. Cressida assumes I know everything but all I have is disparate bits and pieces. I don't want to unwittingly end up saying the wrong thing.'

Cary and I stare up at the flickering images of *It's A Wonderful Life* as he begins speaking in a hushed tone.

'My mother's childhood was filled with my grandmother's idealistic, romantic nonsense. I think she believed that everyone has a soul mate. Grandma's extensive library of old black and white films fired her imagination and a firm belief that the perfect man for her was out there, somewhere. As a consequence, my mother ended up naming both myself and my younger brother after film stars from the thirties. Sadly, I fear we have both let her down on that front.'

'Laurence… Olivier?'

He nods his head and my lips twitch, but I manage to keep a straight face.

'Great choice. I'm partial to a black and white movie, myself. Particularly at Christmas.'

It was meant to make him feel better and lighten the moment. However, he doesn't look amused and rolls his eyes.

'Oh, not you as well! Grandma has spent her entire life being in love with love and trying to spread her mantra. I'm all for keeping it real. Anyway, I'm more of a James Stewart than a Cary Grant,' Cary muses, shooting me a smug grin.

'What makes you say that? I thought you hated that whole iconic screen hero premise.'

He finishes off the last of his cocktail in one, placing the empty glass on the tray of a passing waitress. I notice that she rewards him with a beaming smile as if he's doing her a favour.

'He portrayed more ordinary characters, I feel. Cary Grant was the ultimate charmer and enigmatic in a way that James, and most other men, simply can't pull off.'

I look around for somewhere to deposit my own, now empty, glass to no avail and Cary whisks it out of my hand. Magically, the same waitress appears from seemingly nowhere.

'Hmm… I think there's a little more Cary Grant in you than you think. A large part of his appeal was his wicked sense of humour. Women always fall for that.'

It raises a short, sharp laugh. Suddenly his mood changes as he continues.

'My mother ended up trapped in a loveless marriage until one day my father lashed out at her. She fled with us two boys in tow and that was the beginning of the end. Her health went downhill very quickly and it was later discovered that she had a hole in her heart.'

He sounds very matter of fact, but I can tell by the look on his face it pains him to think about it.

'I still have memories of my mum; she was a very loving, selfless person. Grandma was distraught to think of her daughter's last months filled with the turmoil of a painful divorce. My father cut all ties, so Mum had our surnames changed by deed poll and after that we lived as Andersons.'

'And you haven't seen him since?'

Cary shakes his head, turning to look at me.

'No. The truth is that Granddad is the only man who was ever there for Laurence and me. Okay, he had a somewhat stern disposition on occasions, but he often came home from work drained and we were rather boisterous. When the weekends came around, though, he always made time for us and we would go off exploring together. Obviously, it was Grandma who was there with us the most and naturally we turned to her first and foremost.'

I try to imagine what it must have been like suddenly having to look after two small boys while mourning the loss of a daughter. And at a time in their lives when grandparents expect to be able to focus a little more on each other. It's like having a second family. I wonder if Matthew felt excluded at times?

'I don't know about you but I could do with some fresh air. It's another hour until the firework display begins at a quarter past twelve and I'm already beginning to wane.'

Cary does look tired and a little drawn, but then I probably don't look any better.

'Great idea. Lead on.'

I've had some very late nights lately, but none of it has been fun. I can't tell Cary that, of course, because most of it is due to the pressure I'm feeling over his video.

We head back into the sitting room and step out through the French doors to make our way down the path, which leads us to a seating area in the orchard. Suddenly, Cressida appears behind us looking rather agitated.

'Cary, I need a little assistance. I'm so sorry to interrupt, Leesa, this won't take long.'

She disappears back inside, and I wave Cary off in the same direction.

'Go. It's fine. You know where to find me.'

There's a chill in the air but it's a very pleasant night and I amble down towards the cluster of wooden seats beneath the leafless apple trees. Low-level lighting has turned the night-time garden into a very tranquil place. There's enough light to follow the path and catch glimpses of the shrubs which flank either side of it, but beyond that the shadows from a waning moon mask everything.

'This is a pleasant surprise.' A solitary voice wells up out of the dark nothingness. Then a shape steps forward and I'm shocked to see that it's Matthew.

'Same here. I didn't see you inside and Cary never mentioned that you were here.'

Matthew extends his hand and I take it, carefully stepping off the path in my high heels and onto the mossy lawn.

'Take it steady; it's a bit slippery. There's a lot of clay on this land and with all that snow it takes a while to drain. The benches are dry, though.'

I shrug my evening jacket tight up against my neck and once we're seated it's a lovely sheltered spot.

'Not bad, is it? The trees break the wind and here we're in a bit of a dip. The added advantage is that we can't be seen from the house.'

'You're hiding?' I speak without thinking and then feel a little awkward because it sounded challenging.

'No. Or yes, maybe a little. I always get invited and if I don't turn up then Cressida starts to worry something is up. But I'm not a part of her world any more and she forgets that. I don't want to step back into this and besides, it's awkward when Robert's around.'

Matthew leans forward, stretching out his back.

I know I should let his comment pass as it isn't an invitation to talk, but I can't help myself.

'Old wounds.' My tone reflects the sadness I feel for a difficult situation.

'It's tough when something isn't really over but it's also not salvageable.'

I'm shocked by his words. I find it rather hard to believe Cressida is insensitive enough to insist on Matthew being here. It must hurt him to see Robert and Cressida socialising, almost as if they are a couple.

'Oh, the anger is gone because it was years ago now,' he's quick to assure me. 'It feels like another lifetime, to be honest. I was a fool and so was Eve.'

I frown. 'Who's Eve?'

Matthew turns to look at me with sadness in his eyes.

'Robert's wife. It was just one of those things. Robert worked long hours on the farm and Cressida was always busy. If she wasn't looking after the boys then she was poring over plans for renovating what I refer to as this *mausoleum*.'

'You mean this house?'

He nods.

'It was too much to take on because it was falling apart. I know it's worth a fair bit now and it is a beautiful house once more. But it killed our marriage. That still doesn't excuse my affair and both Eve and I were horrified afterwards, realising what we'd done. We were just two very lonely people at the time. It was the one thing we had in common. Like me, Eve wasn't into all this dramatic, emotional stuff. We were simply two people desperately in need of feeling something, anything, to justify our existence. It was a momentary lapse and we both knew it was a big mistake. But the damage had been done and we had to live with the consequences of a moment of pure madness.'

I can't believe it. Cary thinks Cressida was the one who had an affair.

'I thought—' I stop myself in time. It's not for me to voice Cary's suspicions.

'It wasn't planned, if that's what you think. We simply found ourselves alone together and one thing led to another. Robert forgave her but, of course, he never forgave me. He stayed with her until the end and he was devoted. But I knew he didn't love her and Eve herself told me it wasn't a love match but an arranged marriage. Two significant landowning families joining forces by encouraging their offspring to wed. No, he never loved Eve, but he's always been in love with Cressida.'

I struggle to keep my face composed and not to reveal how horrified I am by Matthew's revelation. Cary has absolutely no idea of the truth and this is almost incomprehensible.

'But Robert knows that I've always loved her and that she loves me. The stumbling block is this house and what it represents. And that's why I'm willing to be here, but not in there. Does that make any sort of sense to you?'

'It makes perfect sense, although I can't pretend it isn't the last thing I suspected.' Cary's voice appears out of the darkness and both mine and Matthew's heads pivot in his direction.

Matthew remains silent and I don't know what to say. After a few moments Cary walks across the springy turf to sit on the bench opposite Matthew and me.

'All these years I've been cold to Robert. Since you left all he's ever shown is support for Grandma and I never once saw him do anything out of place. That's why I didn't just tolerate him being around. I had to be grateful because he was – whether I liked it or not – Grandma's tower of strength. But it hurt and I watched him, waiting for the moment he let down his guard and showed his true nature. I thought that Grandma's head was so full of romantic nonsense that she'd brought all of this on herself. And no one ever thought to tell Laurence and me the truth.'

'Would it have changed anything?' Matthew peers across at Cary, his voice full of sadness. But I also sense a little relief as if he never was happy about burying the secrets of the past.

'Robert is a good man and yet I've always felt uncomfortable around him because I blamed him for Grandma's unhappiness; I can't speak for Laurence. I even struggled with my own conscience because I didn't want to like or admire the man, but that's exactly what I ended up doing. You can only judge someone by their actions and he never put a foot wrong. Once you upped and left, he was the one Grandma rang whenever she needed something, and I hated that it was him and not you. You should have told us, Granddad.'

Matthew's head is bent forward. 'I know this sounds like an excuse, but we're talking about something that happened almost thirty years ago. We all moved on from it, although in hindsight not very successfully.'

Cary looks agitated. 'So why did you suddenly decide to walk away five years ago? Now that doesn't make any sense at all. If you weren't happy why didn't you leave long before that? Was it your choice, or Grandma's?'

Matthew's head tips back and he faces Cary's stare with steely determination.

'I left because I wanted a divorce. I thought that four years on from Eve's death Robert might finally grab the opportunity to tell Cressida how he feels about her. None of us are getting any younger and I owed him. And Cressida.'

Cary shakes his head as if it's too much to take in. 'But you aren't divorced.'

'No, because Cressida refused to entertain the idea as she doesn't want to address the financial issues, as she puts it. She says we're *estranged*, which is sufficient. It's a term I absolutely loathe because who uses that these days? Only novelists, I suspect, because it smacks of drama. She knows I'll never push it, even though I don't want anything from her. I'm ticking over just fine as I am. But unless she changes her mind, that's the way we stay. Look, I'm sorry as it was never my intention to share this with you, Cary, because that's not what she wanted.'

'Oh, but you were quite happy to share it with Leesa.'

A guilty look fleetingly passes over Matthew's face.

'Yes, because sometimes even I need to confide in someone. I needed to hear myself say it... own it, if you like. Whatever happens, don't mention this to your grandma. I've caused her enough heartache over the years and there's no point in dragging all of this up again now.'

With that Matthew stands, placing one hand on my shoulder.

'Thanks for listening, Leesa. It helps to share on a night like this when the past is taunting me. I only put in an appearance because of her, but it's hard.'

With that he turns to walk back over to the path. I stare after him until he's consumed in darkness.

'Look, I'm really sorry about that, Cary. I wasn't prying, that wasn't my intention at all. It was obvious Matthew needed to talk and I just happened to be here.'

Cary stands and strides across to sit next to me, the bench shifting a little as he lowers himself down onto it.

'Poor Grandma. Her hero turned out to be the villain of the story. Do you think she's punishing him by using his guilt to stop them cutting all ties?'

I ponder over his words. 'No. She's not a vindictive woman. Cressida will have witnessed pretty much most of life's harsher events in her life and these things happen; people make mistakes and regret them, all the time. But one thing I don't understand is that I clearly remember Cressida saying that she didn't think Matthew had ever loved her, as if they had never sat down and talked about it.'

I turn my head and Cary and I stare at each other, a rather tragic thought occurring to us both.

'You think she has no idea he's in love with her?' He's not really looking for my endorsement, because his heart is telling him the answer.

'Yes, and that's so sad, Cary. Clearly, she has always loved him. I find it hard to believe she chose this house over the chance to embrace their love, though. And now she's content to hand it over to you? Just like that, as if she was only ever a temporary custodian, when it seems to have blighted her life in one way. Was she simply being a dutiful daughter? If so, that's bizarre, like something out of a Victorian novel.'

The cold is beginning to consume me now and I shiver, involuntarily.

'We should head back inside.'

'Sorry, I meant to ask if everything is okay with Cressida?'

He nods, smiling at me for a second or two, lifting the mood. 'One of Grandma's guests had a little too much to drink and it required two of us to help her into the back seat of her limousine.'

'Oh. I see. By contrast I feel decidedly sober and I can't believe it's New Year's Eve. Christmas feels like a very long time ago.'

As we stand, Cary edges closer and for some stupid reason my heart begins to race. *None of this is real, Leesa,* I chide myself.

'People do a great job of messing up their lives, don't they?'

For a split-second I think he's going to lean in to kiss me but instead he offers me his arm. But he wanted to kiss me at that precise moment. I could see it in his eyes. There is a growing sense of chemistry between us, but do we need that sort of complication to throw into the mix?

'Will you mention any of this to Cressida, despite what Matthew said?' I query, as we begin the walk back up to the house.

'Not yet. I'm going to talk to Robert, though, and see if he knows what's going on with her and why she suddenly wants to make big changes in her life. Someone must know something, and I don't want to do the wrong thing and upset her. At least Granddad was right about that.'

*

After what turned out to be a rather sombre end to the old year, this morning the sun is shining, as if joyfully announcing the arrival of the first of January. Even the chilly north-easterly wind has abated.

Consensus of opinion around the breakfast table is that the party was a huge success and Cressida seems content. Cary is rather withdrawn this morning, but the kids are in high spirits and no one really notices except me.

He excuses himself from the table and disappears, I assume to have some quiet time alone to think about what's happened. He doesn't seem to look for me to follow him. Sally immediately engages me in conversation, so it would be awkward to excuse myself to go check he's okay. To my slight dismay, when everyone eventually decides it's time to move, little Chloe clamours for my attention and insists I accompany them on their walk down to the beach.

'Please come.' Chloe's little upturned face is pouty. 'Please.'

'Of course, but I have to keep an eye on the time. I'm going to take Uncle Cary to visit my mummy and daddy later this morning.'

She considers that for a moment. 'Can I be a bridesmaid when you get married?'

I gaze at her expectant face, stunned for a moment and totally lost for words as an awkward silence settles around me. I look up to see both Sally and Cressida waiting to hear my response with amused interest.

'Ah, what little girl doesn't love a big, frothy dress? Maybe Uncle Cary and I could buy you a princess dress from the Disney shop for Easter. It's fun dressing up, isn't it?'

Focus deflected, rather cleverly I think, but then Daisy chimes in.

'It's rude to ask for things, Chloe. Mummy, she's being naughty, isn't she?'

Sally puts her hand on Chloe's shoulder to steer her out into the hallway and turns her head to reply to Daisy over her shoulder.

'We don't ask for things, girls, and you both know that. Chloe, what's all this about?'

Cressida answers Sally's question.

'It's my fault, Sally. Chloe came up to the office and was looking at my photos. I was telling Chloe all about your wedding day and how wonderful the marquee looked in the garden. Seeing everyone all dressed up she thought it was rather magical.'

All eyes turn in my direction and I'm so glad Cary isn't here. 'Sounds lovely,' I reply to the unspoken question and with a fleeting smile I head off upstairs.

I go in search of Cary. He isn't in his room and I walk over to the window on the landing to see if he's outside. Scanning around, I can't see him and then, suddenly, I notice a solitary figure walking down the lane and just about to turn the bend to disappear out of sight. It might be him but where's he going? Then I realise he's on his way to see Robert and I panic.

Grabbing my things, I rush downstairs.

'Guys, head out when you're ready and I'll catch up with you in a bit. I won't be long.'

I don't give anyone a chance to ask where I'm going, as I set off at speed. Pulling on my knitted bobble hat it isn't long before I'm pulling it off again and undoing the zipper on my jacket. As I round that first bend I catch sight of Cary and call out to him. He turns, surprised to see me and slows his pace until I catch up.

'Is this a good idea?' I level the words at him, knowing it's none of my business and he could say as much.

'I don't know. But it's a conversation I need to have. You can either come with me or head back.'

Grr. Why does Cary have to be so... correct? A little knowledge can be a dangerous thing and I think it would be better not to wade in but to wait and see what happens.

He begins walking again and I have to trot to keep up with him.

'Wouldn't it be safer not to address this head-on? At least now you know the truth you can feel more relaxed around Robert. That might be a better way of handling it. A gradual acceptance.'

He shakes his head, unwilling now to slow his pace and delay any longer. I run on ahead and then turn to stop in front of him, my hands on my hips. He comes to an abrupt halt.

'Leesa, this is a wrong I have to put right. End of story.'

And with that he steps around me. I reluctantly follow a pace or two behind him. The farm is in sight now and one of the tractors is blocking the entrance. There appears to be a problem because there are three guys next to it, one of whom is lying on the floor with only his legs clearly visible. Robert immediately looks up, says something to the man next to him and walks over to shake Cary's hand.

'It's a fine morning. Getting some air after all the excitement of last night's party?' He grins at us both and then leans in to give me a brief hug.

We're out of earshot of the two men working on the tractor and Cary launches straight in.

'Robert, this is awkward because I owe you a huge apology. I've always been grateful to you for being there for Grandma, but I had jumped to an embarrassing conclusion. In doing so I wronged you and I should have known better than that. You are a good man who has always been very supportive towards me and that makes my assumption even more ludicrous in hindsight. You are always straight with me and fair in your dealings. I just simply didn't have the courage to ask the question to allay my fears. I thought perhaps your feelings for my grandma had been too strong to resist, but now I know the truth I'm horrified by the injustice that was done to you. Armed with that knowledge your support is an even greater tribute to your strength of character in putting your own hurt second to hers.'

Robert bows his head for a second, before looking back at Cary again with sadness written all over his face.

'Your heart was telling you what your head couldn't understand. The truth is that I came to love Cressida over the years, too much to hurt her or my lovely wife, Eve, by admitting how I felt. I knew from the start that I wasn't the one for Cressida. So, I did what I could because she's special, Cary. Like a lioness protecting her cubs, she can be fearsome at times but there's always good reason and she doesn't have a selfish bone in her body. That's why she won't give up pushing you until she feels her job is done and you can see your way forward more clearly. Finally, she feels you're heading in the right direction and that means a lot to her at this point in her life.'

Cary's face isn't giving anything away, even when Robert glances in my direction before returning his gaze to Cary.

'It takes a lot of inner strength to be there for someone and not ask for anything in return. I won't refer to this again, but I have one question I need to ask. This… thing with Grandma wanting to hand over her legacy now is worrying. Do you know what's really going on?'

When Cary faltered my heart skipped a beat. Even though he's a very straight-talking kind of person he can't bring himself to ask Robert outright if she has a life-threatening illness.

Robert looks concerned, but I don't think he knows anything judging by his reaction.

'I have no idea at all, Cary. Wish I did. All I do know is that Cressida likes things to be done in the right way and she feels this immense responsibility for the whole family. She worries as much about what might happen after she's gone, as she does about what's happening now in your lives.

'I keep telling her that she raised you both well and that's all that matters. You'll make your own decisions going forward based on what you think is right at the time. She has to trust that fate will take you where you're supposed to go. I wish she could just relax and enjoy each day for what it brings. Once you hit eighty I believe you need to look at every day as a bonus.'

Cary glances my way and I give him a sympathetic smile. I know how bitterly disappointed he is that even Robert doesn't have the answer he seeks.

He turns back to offer his hand once more.

'I appreciate your honesty, Robert. Sorry to have interrupted you. Problems with the tractor?'

Robert half-turns to look at the two men who are now crouched down, one holding a spanner and tightening something.

'Nothing three heads can't solve. On a day like this it's easy to shirk off life's little annoyances. I might head out for a walk myself in a bit. You off to the beach?'

Cary's still embroiled in his disappointment and I answer for him.

'Yes. Laurence, Sally and the kids are already heading down there and we're off to catch up with them.'

'Well, if I don't see you before you both head for home, travel safely.'

With a wave, I steer Cary back out into the lane and down towards the viaduct and beyond. Maybe Cressida isn't the only one who has to remember that some things are what they are and one of life's greatest challenges is acceptance.

18

Back to Work with a Vengeance

Another day, another dollar – or pound, in my case. It's the first day back at work and it's all change. I feel like I've been away from my desk for months.

What makes it even worse is that we were supposed to start work on those amendments today but Jeff texted to ask if we could pick it up tomorrow instead. Every time we communicate now it's a brief call, or by text. I already feel that I'm a part of his past and it hurts.

I head into the kitchen for an injection of caffeine. Popping the kettle on to boil I look around for my bag and begin searching through it until I find the little white card.

With coffee in one hand, and the card in the other, I head back upstairs.

'Is that George? This is Leesa Oliver. We sat next to each other on the plane from Sydney.'

'Ah, hello Leesa. Of course, I remember! Happy New Year to you. Did your festivities go well?'

'It was great, thank you. I hope you don't mind me phoning you, but we talked briefly about your grandson and a possible career change. I don't have a permanent vacancy at the moment for someone at his level. But I am in need of a little temporary help between now and the eighteenth of February. It's short notice, though, and even if he has the know-how, he might not have the time to take it on. Even so, I'd still like to have a chat with him to find out a little more about his work.'

It's a long shot, but I need a simple demo put together to showcase the company's most recent work. Annoyingly it's something I could do myself but I just don't have the time. With a lot of new clients booked in for pitch meetings, I need something up-to-date to show them and I need it produced quickly.

'Tim would jump at the chance, I can tell you that without hesitation. He's desperate for any experience he can get to add to his CV. I'll text him your number as he's at work at the moment but as soon as he's free you can expect a call. If you give him a shot he won't let you down. And I'm not just saying that because he's my grandson. He's hard-working and passionate about his hobby. He's spent every penny he's earnt on getting everything he needs to pursue it professionally. It's just a case of waiting for that break to prove he's more than a casual YouTuber. Thank you, Leesa. Guess it's little Hayden we have to thank for putting us together.'

He ends the call on a chuckle. Less than five minutes later I get a text message.

Thanks for getting in touch. I'll ring you the moment I leave work. Tim Richardson

A little smile tugs at the corners of my mouth. None of my usual go-to people are likely to be able to take on a rush job, as most will have their own post-holiday backlogs to cope with. I've checked Tim out on YouTube and I must admit I'm impressed. But there's an element of risk taking on someone who doesn't have a track record in the business. This could be a good way of testing him because if only half of the meetings I have this month result in some new business, then there could just be a job offer on the table.

It's time to settle down and start working on some video concept boards so I'm geared up to pitch and get those contracts signed and sealed.

After a tiring day I'm in need of a stiff drink, but on investigation I find that there's nothing at all in the house. I'm cold and dejected so it's hot chocolate with marshmallows and hello to a big, satisfying sugar spike. I'm stretched out on the sofa with my shoes kicked off and blissfully sipping gingerly from my steaming mug, when the phone rings. Reluctantly putting down my hand-warmer, I answer and a rather deep voice with a distinctly warm vibe echoes down the line.

'Is that Leesa?'

'Yes, speaking.'

'I'm Tim, George's grandson.'

'Oh, hi Tim, thank you so much for getting back to me. I run a company called Dynamic Videography and we are an agency who make promotional videos for a wide range of products and services. I'm looking for some additional help on a project-by-project basis. George told me you post a lot of videos to YouTube and you're keen to get some hands-on experience to add to your CV?'

'Absolutely! It's not easy to get people to take you seriously unless you have a solid platform to prove your skills. That's why I set up my YouTube account. Mostly it's stuff I've put together and submitted as coursework for the Diploma in Creative Media Production I'm studying. But there's some fun, experimental stuff on there, too. I can send you the link if you want to take a look.'

I'm a little surprised, as George didn't mention that Tim was taking a formal qualification. And he doesn't sound quite as young as I'd expected, but then George is in his eighties at a guess and Tim is clearly not a teenager, that's for sure. His voice has a wonderful gravelly quality to it and I can't help thinking he would be the perfect candidate for a voiceover.

'I will admit to being ahead of you there. I've already checked you out and I like what I see. I was wondering if we could meet up for a chat? I have no idea where you're based.'

'Swindon. Where are you?'

'Nailsworth, near Stroud. What if we meet up at a halfway point as soon as possible? George mentioned you work in finance.'

Suddenly his voice loses a little of that lighthearted quality.

'Yes, I'm a manager of a debt recovery section. It pays the bills, but I need to do something that fires me up. It would have to be an evening meet-up. Is that okay?'

I grab my mug of hot chocolate with my free hand and take a quick slurp. An 'mmm…' slips out. 'Oh, sorry about that. Um, how quickly could we get together?'

He pauses for a second or two. 'Did you have something urgent in mind?'

I think it's best to be honest as I've run out of options.

'Well, it's not a huge job in itself, but it's important and I needed it done yesterday.'

'Great. How about tomorrow night?'

I can't say I feel relief as such until I know more about him, but I feel a little glimmer of hope.

'Text me where and what time and I'll be there. Thanks, Tim. I'm looking forward to meeting you in person.'

Even before I finish speaking my phone starts bleeping and as I switch calls, Beth's high-pitched, excitable voice assaults my hearing.

'Well, go you!'

I have to stifle a sigh. I'm really not in the mood for a convoluted chat with my baby sister.

'What have I done now?'

'D'oh! Cary Anderson! Mum and Dad are clearly impressed. If he wasn't simply trying to get on their good side, then he sounds like a dream.'

I know the meal with Mum and Dad went well and Cary was both charming and attentive; so much so that on several occasions I almost burst out laughing. He was acting, of course, but only we knew that. Mum and Dad were enthralled. I know it's ridiculous given the real situation. But I felt good on seeing their reaction. Proud, actually, as he did a great job. I'm sick of being the one they worry about all the time. It was never like that before Nathan came into my life and I don't ever intend subjecting them to that again.

'He's a charming man, what can I say?'

'Yeees! And he's *Cressida Anderson's* grandson. Why on earth am I having to hear this backstory from Mum and Dad? You never tell me anything, Leesa.'

I try not to groan. All Beth usually talks about is the wedding, so this is a bit of a surprise diversion for her.

'And he is coming, isn't he? I mean, he's put the third of August in his diary? Do you think it would be too cheeky to invite Cressida?'

OMG – it's official, she is the sister from hell!

'No, it would not be appropriate to invite Cressida Anderson as I hardly know her.'

I hope my tone is clipped enough to convey the message that I'm not even going to consider that as a serious question.

'But you will bring Cary as your plus one, won't you? I mean, you won't do anything silly like break up with him between now and the wedding, will you? He sounds like the first decent date you've had in a long time. Some of the others have been a bit… weird.'

Now she's pressing my buttons.

'Weird? I recall at least two blind dates you insisted on fixing me up on and bizarre came to mind. Since when did you consider that a sports fanatic, or a *Star Trek* lookalike who attended every convention around the world, were likely to have anything in common with me?'

Sadly, it's a true statement and yes, I did suffer through a date with each of them. The only upside is that I learnt a little about rugby, which sounded terrifyingly violent and I did go home and watch the first ten minutes of a *Star Trek* film. In fact, I kind of enjoyed it and vowed when I had time I'd sit and watch the whole film. But that was several months ago now, so I guess I didn't catch the bug.

'Which is why I'm appealing to you not to mess this up. I want my maid of honour to have a suitable escort to act as one of the ushers. I'm ringing to suggest that the four of us get together, so we can discuss what role Cary can play on the day.'

Typical! Cary is supposed to be my love interest and all Beth can think about is his potential role in her wedding. Bridezilla extraordinaire, or what?

'He's very busy, Beth. He's a chief executive of a large company and I seriously doubt he'll have time to do any more than attend on the day. Anyway, it's still a long way off and anything could happen.'

There's a squeak down the line. 'No! Mum says he's very photogenic and I want the photos to be magazine-worthy. I'll text you a couple of different dates and you arrange something. I mean, this is important, Leesa. My big sister has found a man worthy of her, at last, and Will and I want to meet him. Promise me you won't throw one of your wobbles and break up with him on a whim.'

She makes it sound depressingly like a last-ditch attempt to escape a life as a single woman.

'Okay. I'll see what I can do but I don't want you bothering Cary every five minutes. It wouldn't be fair on him because he's so busy.'

'Yes, but isn't it exciting, Leesa? I mean, you'll be marrying into publishing royalty!'

I gasp and quickly excuse myself, saying someone is at the door. Placing the phone down on the table, I sink the rest of my now lukewarm, hot chocolate in one. A sugar high is quite a nice thing and minutes later I'm heading towards the fridge. Now I'm craving carbs.

A ping has me scrambling for the phone once more and it's Tim with a location, a postcode, and a firm date for tomorrow at seven o'clock. I look up at the ceiling, 'Thank you!' I mutter at whoever is looking after me and deciding after a phone call with Beth I could do with a little good news.

If Jeff isn't on my doorstep bright and early tomorrow morning and raring to go, then this meeting with Tim might turn out to be even more vital.

19

Love, Life and Reality

'I can't believe you're really here,' I almost squeal in Jeff's ear as I hug him close to me.

'Hey, I'm a day later than planned so I was expecting you to be mad with me but I was like a zombie yesterday. I slept for twelve hours straight.'

I give him a look and he smirks back at me. 'We have some work to do, haven't we? At least there are no distractions here.'

I usher him inside and shut the front door behind him.

'I know. Let's grab a coffee to take up with us. Is it weird being back?'

He dumps his backpack on the floor in the hallway and eases off his jacket.

'Well, actually what's strange is not having Tania around. It feels like something is missing.'

I pop the mugs down on the worktop and begin shovelling the coffee granules. When I turn to glance at him our eyes meet – and suddenly what I'm seeing is not the old Jeff, he's different somehow. Yes, he has a great tan and he's a little trimmer, but he also looks energised. Is that solely down to a long sleep after an even longer flight, I wonder?

'Why are you staring at me? Have I grown a third eye or something?' he jokes.

Turning back around to pour out the boiling water, I give a quick stir and hand him a mug.

'Here, follow me up to the office. I guess I missed seeing that rugged old face of yours. Great haircut.'

He snorts as he follows behind me.

'A lot of the surfers have braids and Tania did it for me. For a kook I'm not doing too badly. I've learnt how to handle myself when I get caught in a rip. She's pretty good but then she's got a couple of years' experience under her belt.'

'Kook?'

We settle ourselves down in front of the desk and it's just like old times. But different.

'New guy on the beach. It's exhilarating, Leesa, and if it wasn't for Tania I doubt I'd ever have thought about jumping on a board.'

Even as he talks his hands are moving over the keyboard and he's pulling up files on the multi screens.

'I feel bad now I'm back here. I took another look at the video early this morning and I was kidding myself. Somehow nothing seems to matter quite so much when the sun is so hot and the water is so inviting. Who wants to stay inside punching away on a keyboard when you could be out there having fun?'

I start laughing. Jeff a surfer dude. And Jeff not taking work seriously. His happiness is infectious, though.

'Why are you laughing at me?'

'Because this is a you I have never seen before. Wow – stop there. That's the point after which you seriously got it wrong.'

He grimaces. 'Okay boss, start trawling through for some replacement shots and we'll do a little cutting and pasting.'

I fire up the screen in front of me and in unison we're back in business.

'So it's the real thing with Tania, then?'

He stops for a moment, his fingers hovering over the keys.

'Well, I've said the words. So I guess it is.'

I turn to look at him, unable to hide my surprise.

'You've told her that you love her?'

He nods. 'Yes. This isn't a whim, Leesa. I don't care where I end up as long as Tania is with me. She wants to surf and travel, so hey, so be it. Now highlight at least six stills because I'm wiping this whole bit from here, to here.'

I nod in agreement. It's so easy working with Jeff, we have always sparked off each other. Once I've made my selection, he focuses on pulling it together as he turns my vision into reality. We don't talk as he begins to smooth out the bumps.

Before we know it, it's lunchtime and we head downstairs. In the kitchen I make a pile of sandwiches and he attacks them with gusto.

'So, I need to know what's going on in your life and I don't mean work. You survived Christmas but I know it was a tough one. And this Cary thing. I still can't get over it.'

Suddenly my mouth feels dry. I have to keep up the pretence in case he talks to Mum and lets something slip.

'It wasn't the best Christmas but that's all done now…' I grind to a halt, unable to think of anything else I can add.

'I always thought you deserved someone better than Nathan. If you ask me, which you didn't, that guy is a disaster waiting to happen. But now it seems that Cary is your future. That's quite something.'

I force my face into smiley mode. 'I spent some time with his family. His grandmother is Cressida Anderson, the novelist.'

'Blimey. Even I've heard of her. Romance, isn't it? She's been around for years. I thought Cary came from money. Wasn't her grandfather a banker?'

It hasn't occurred to me to check online but that's interesting.

'I don't know. She's lovely and they were all very welcoming.'

'Sounds cosy. Big house, was it?'

'Yes. They aren't any different from the rest of us, though. Everyone has problems.'

'And you saw another side to the man himself, then?'

He stops eating and sits back, watching my reaction.

'It was a long trip home and we talked about a lot of things. The more we shared, the more we realised we had in common. We've both had a rough time personally and it was actually nice being with someone who understood. I think you have to go through a similar experience in order to be able to comprehend how it affects you.'

'You told him about the baby?' Jeff's reaction is one of shock.

'No. Not that. Just Nathan and the Christmas from hell.'

He begins eating again.

'Early days, then. But you really think it's going somewhere if you're getting to know his family?'

I pause, as if I'm thinking about it but the answer is already imprinted on my brain.

'We're taking it one day at a time but when I went back to stay at New Year I received a very warm welcome back.'

To my complete and utter relief that seems to make a difference and Jeff's smile returns.

'You know, Leesa, I'm proud of you. I can't believe what you've had to contend with and yet you've continued to put other people first. People, I have to tell you, who I don't think deserved your loyalty because they were a part of the problem. But, hey, you're one strong woman and Cary must be rather special if you've connected with him. Good for you.'

I hike my smile up a little and hopefully he'll put my growing pink glow down to something other than embarrassment for not being straight with him.

'And once this job is finished and we've made the business side of Cary happy, I can head off back to sunnier climes knowing you are in safe hands. And he's a guy who will most definitely understand your ambitions, but don't forget to stop and have some fun, will you? It's more liberating than you might think when you find the right someone to enjoy it with. Trust me, because I know.'

Jeff heads off mid-afternoon, confident that another day and a half, at most, and he'll have the soundtrack fully synched. We'll then have a final version to show Cary.

He has plenty of time to finish off other loose ends before he flies back, but today will probably be the last time we work together. It leaves me in a sombre mood and yet I need to gear myself up ready to meet Tim this evening.

I should be getting some serious work done but my mind keeps drifting. Eventually I give up trying, opting for an indulgent soak in the tub and some essential oils. It certainly lifts my mood, in general, until about an hour later when the phone rings.

'Hello?'

The screen tells me that it's an unidentified number.

'Leesa, it's Sheryl. Please, please don't hang up on me.'

I can tell from the wobble in her voice that she's upset.

'I don't want to talk to you and I'm going to cut you off.'

'Please, Leesa, I understand. But this is important.'

Her voice grates on my ear. However, I'm so shocked by her desperate tone that I know I can't simply ignore her.

'I'm listening.'

She clears her throat then sniffs, and it's obvious she's been crying.

'When you were with Nathan, did he ever hit you?'

'No.'

She sniffs again, struggling to compose herself.

'You didn't lose the baby because of anything he did? It really was an accident? At Christmas we had a row, a big one. He threw some things and it scared me.'

I close my eyes momentarily, torn between feeling anger and then pity.

'I was upset after he admitted the two of you were sleeping together. I turned and slipped. That's what Nathan told me. If you want to know more then you must ask him yourself. Or speak to his parents if he hasn't already told you what happened on Christmas Day. There's nothing more that I can tell you.'

'I'm sorry. I'm so sorry. It's just that—'

'Please don't ever call me again, Sheryl. Friends don't do what you did to me. I hope no one ever does the same to you.'

I click end call and slump down onto the bed.

How can I accuse Nathan of something I only suspect and might well have been an accident for all I know? I've given her the only warning I can. It sickens me to think that I put up with his moods and everyone around him did the same. I guess that now his parents' attitudes have changed, too, there's no one to pander to him. Sheryl is already seeing a side of him that is getting worse and not better, by the sound of it. What turns a man who used to be quite even-tempered into a bully?

Suddenly my fingers are dialling.

'Cary Anderson.' His voice is in work mode and I instantly regret calling him. He hasn't even looked to see who it is.

'It's Leesa, Cary. Is now a bad time?'

'Hey, of course not. Problems?'

'No, the video is going well and we'll have the final version to show you in the next couple of days.' It comes out a little too bright and breezy.

'I didn't mean with the video.'

'Oh, thanks, um… I wanted to ask your opinion about something to do with Nathan.'

An image of Cary flashes into my head and I see him at his desk, leaning back in the chair as he pulls away from the keyboard. I wonder if he minds that I'm interrupting him?

'Sheryl has just phoned to ask whether Nathan ever hit me. All I could say was no, although there was one occasion when we collided. Well, I was upset and my vision was obscured by tears. Nathan was next to me and put out his arm to stop me from falling… well, that's what he kept telling me. But hand on heart I can't say for sure because I was sobbing hysterically at the time.'

I can't bring myself to share the whole story but it's enough for him to understand my dilemma. He takes a few moments and I wait, anxiously.

'Hmm. You can't accuse someone of something unless you are 100 per cent sure of the facts. Clearly you have your suspicions, but given the circumstances it's a tough one. Did you give her a general warning, though? And does she know about what happened at his parents' home?'

'Yes. I suggested she talk to them about it as clearly his behaviour is concerning her. And I told her never to phone me again,' I admit.

'Well, you've done all that you can reasonably be expected to, given the situation. She shouldn't have called you.'

'I know and it shows how worried she is but I don't want to get involved. He was so different when we first met, nothing at all like the man he has turned into.'

I hoist myself further up the bed, sinking into the pillows for comfort.

'So what changed?'

It's a fair enough question and I take a few seconds to consider it before replying.

'Ironically, when I think back, things began to go wrong for us shortly after I set up the business. He was happy when I had to live from month to month, always worrying about my income and he was very supportive. Maybe my determination to succeed changed me.'

I let out a sigh. Was it all my fault? Did I unwittingly push him away?

'Or did it change something in him?' Cary's voice sounds accusing. 'Some men feel threatened by a successful woman and you're going from strength to strength. Maybe that threw up his own insecurities. It's pretty pathetic if his anger stems from jealousy, but it happens.'

The thought sends a chill to my stomach. What if he meant to hit me because he didn't want the responsibility of a baby? When I'd initially broken the news to him, he was surprised but said he was pleased. Well, he wasn't the only one who was surprised and I freely admit that. Sadly, it had been the result of make-up sex after yet another row. But that day, for some reason, he was in a mood. It seemed to annoy him that I was so happy, as were his parents. Suddenly, he let rip and admitted he'd been seeing Sheryl for several months. The reality hit me that it was over and it had been since well before I became pregnant.

'I'm sorry to cut this short, Leesa, but I'm about to leave the office. I have a work function to attend this evening. If you want to talk some more I'll be home around eleven, okay?'

'Thanks, Cary, but I'm fine now. I've done all I can. It's good to have someone else's opinion, though, and I'm grateful. Enjoy your evening.'

It's almost time to get ready to go out but I find myself clicking onto Google and typing in *marital bullying*. I'm horrified by what I read. Not least because I never saw myself as a victim but that, it seems, is the classic pattern. I was too focused on building my business to see what was happening. That's why I put up with his increasingly bizarre behaviour.

I copy the link and text it to Sheryl. Then I block her number. Cary is right – I've done all I can. One thing is for sure, no one is *ever* going to put me in a situation like that again.

20

A Glimmer of Hope

I'm totally reliant upon the satnav to negotiate the dark and twisty country lanes. Pulling off the main Cirencester road, I head towards North Cerney. It's probably taken me no more than half an hour by the time I pull into the car park and I'm surprised to see that it's quite full, considering it's mid-week. After a day of torrential rain at least it's dry now. But the wind quickly whisks my hair in all directions, sticking strands to my lip gloss like a manic blow dry.

Walking across the car park to The Wayfair Inn, I wonder why I've never been here before, as it's almost on my doorstep. Still battling to hold my hair away from my eyes, I lose my balance as my left foot stumbles into a water-filled pothole and my upper body begins to topple forwards. I brace myself for a fall before I'm suddenly scooped upright and find myself looking into the shadowy face of a young man.

'Are you okay?'

The gravelly voice takes me back to last night's phone call.

'Tim?'

He peers at me, checking both of my feet are firmly on the ground before he removes his arms from around me.

'Leesa?'

Composing myself, I hold out my hand and his returning handshake is a firm one, I'm pleased to note.

'Come on, let's get out of this wind before it sweeps you off your feet again.' With that he gives me a wink.

'Well, thanks for saving me. The drinks are definitely on me.' I return his wink with a genuinely grateful smile. The surface of the car park is loose gravel and if I'd gone down it would most certainly have hurt.

'Let's head into the snug where there's a log burner. It's quieter in there.'

I follow him inside this majestic old building with its low ceilings and original beams. He has to duck a little here and there, but he is obviously very familiar with the interior layout.

'This is my cousin's local, so I come here quite a bit.' With that he waves out to the guy behind the bar, before steering me through into a long corridor with natural stone walls and on into a second, smaller bar called The Posset.

'Great timing. This will fill up quickly once the early bird diners have finished their meals. It's the warmest place to sit in this draughty old building. How about the table in the corner?'

I nod and a couple of strides and he's pulling out a chair for me. As I gradually smooth down my wayward hair and the heat begins to warm me up, I can see that he's a little nervous. Tim has quite a beard going on there and longish dark brown hair I should imagine, but it's very neatly tied back. In fact, I'd say he's quite meticulous with his presentation; he's trying to look older than he really is, and I wonder why. Age? Hmm, around twenty-two or twenty-three I think, which is quite young to be a manager in something as testing as a debt recovery section. Maybe that explains it.

As he slips off his coat and takes the seat opposite me at the cosy little table for two, it all feels a little bit, well, intimate. More like a date than an informal interview. Aside from a couple standing at the bar waiting to be served it's just us.

'I can't believe I didn't see that pothole, it really was very opportune, thank you,' I admit, looking down at my left boot and rocking it back and forth to check the stability of the heel.

'Near miss. Nice to know that sometimes I'm capable of being in the right place at the right time.'

Hmm… do I sense a little general discontent coming through in his tone, there?

I grab the purse out of my bag. 'What would you like to drink?'

'I should get these.' He half–rises from his chair.

'No, I insist.' I wave my hand to stop him going any further.

'I don't do alcohol. A cappuccino would be great, thanks.'

Well, that's a first for me when I'm buying but it's nice to hear. By the time I get to the bar the couple have walked past me to take a seat at the table directly in front of the log burner. I order two coffees, hoping what they serve isn't that weak stuff and has some guts to it. I'm still a little tense after my near-fall.

'Haven't seen you in here before?' the young barman enquires in a friendly manner.

'No. First time. Nice old building and lovely ambience.'

'It certainly is. Good to see Tim here with a lady; makes a nice change.' Then he winks at me.

Ah, I take it that they know each other. But I'm beginning to feel like some sort of cougar, as clearly the guy behind the bar doesn't realise this isn't a blind date. I'm checking out Tim's skills, not his charming persona. Perhaps a business meeting shouldn't really be held in a pub.

'I'll bring the coffees over when they're ready.'

I swipe my card over the machine and he smiles, running his eyes over me in a most unprofessional manner.

As I spin back around I catch Tim watching my every movement. At least, I think that's what he's doing but maybe he's trying to catch his friend's eye, to stop him. For one moment he reminds me of a young Jeff. The same slightly awkward, sort of embarrassed persona that comes with being extremely shy.

Settling myself back down into the carver chair, I look directly at Tim. It's time to get down to business. 'So, you're a manager in what I should imagine is a very stressful job.'

He fiddles nervously with the placemat on the table in front of him.

'I work for my uncle's finance company. Don't get me wrong, I wasn't granted any favours, and I had to start at the bottom. I spent a couple of years working there part-time on telesales while I was at college. Eventually I joined the admin team after gaining my diploma in Business Management, three years ago.'

Doing the maths, he's probably around twenty-three then so I was right.

'You sound as if you have regrets.'

The barman arrives with a tray. 'Hey, Tim. Loved the parkour video, by the way. Great stuff!'

Suddenly, there's a little frantic eye contact going on between them. Tim nods in acknowledgement, grabbing the coffees off the tray as if to indicate he's interrupting.

The young guy shoots him a puzzled look, then turns on his heels without further comment.

'Parkour?'

'Sorry. It's one of the experimental videos. A mate of mine does this mad running, climbing and jumping stuff.'

'Oh, I know what parkour is but it's interesting that you tackle all sorts of subject matter. How did it all start?'

He's nervous, unsure where to begin but I need to understand why he wants to make this huge change in his working life.

'Look, it might sound like I dabble but I've just gained a level one award in Mixed Media Techniques and I've attended countless workshops – everything from the use of various software editing programmes, to adding titles, visual effects and soundtracks.'

I stop him there.

'As I said, your YouTube channel is impressive and a great showcase for your work. The initial project I have in mind, as I mentioned, is an urgent one. If you want to take a look at it, I can give you online access to our system and talk you through what I need. But as this is a bit of a risk I need it done without delay, because if it doesn't work out then I will have to look elsewhere for some temporary help. I hope you don't mind me being frank with you, but I have a diary full of pitch meetings in January and early February. Unfortunately, I'm losing a key member of staff and his replacement doesn't start until the eighteenth of January.'

I stop to sip my coffee and realise he hasn't taken his eyes off me the entire time we've been talking. He looks keen, that's for sure.

'I can do it. Really I can.'

'But the day job?'

'Is a day job. I'm on the PC most evenings anyway. I'll give it my best shot. Just tell me exactly what you need and I'll do it. If I think I'm going to be out of my depth and I can't, then I'll be upfront and admit it.'

'Okay. It's a big ask, I know, but I think you might enjoy the challenge. We haven't discussed money.'

He sits back a little, raising his cup to his mouth and taking a sip. My phone starts to skitter across the table and a quick glance tells me it's Beth. I switch it off, cross with myself that I've forgotten to ask Cary about a convenient date to meet up.

'Sorry about that, Tim.'

'Pay me whatever is the going rate if you're happy with my work. After that we can talk about future projects if I succeed in impressing you.'

There's a resolve in his voice that is impressive, and I might just have found the right person for the job. Result. Well, it will be a result if he can follow instructions to the letter and work quickly.

Naturally, Tim asks about the history of the company and seems content to sit back and listen. There's a little nervous tick that keeps tugging away at the side of his eye. He's trying so hard to keep his cool but I can see he's excited by this proposal.

'My company is well-established but small. I have major changes planned for this year and hope it will provide me with an opportunity to expand quite quickly. But before I can do that I have to produce several thirty second video concepts for the meetings I have booked. If I succeed in converting just 25 per cent of the pitches into contracts, then I will be looking to expand the team.'

I talk about some of the projects we've handled in the past. Then I touch on the new direction in which I'd like to go, and he nods enthusiastically. Tim is desperate to prove himself and he realises this is a real opportunity. He doesn't want to mess up and is trying a little too hard to impress me. What he might lack in experience, though, he makes up for with his desire to change his future and that is impressive. Suddenly, my gut instincts are telling me that he won't let me down and maybe I've found another Jeff in the making.

Walking out together, he can't hide his excitement about the opportunity I'm offering him. At the end of the day he's young and hungry; and that's exactly what I'm looking for – someone who can learn on the job.

'Hi Cary, how did it go last night?'

Beth has texted me three times since last night. If I don't come up with a date for our get-together then she'll twig something isn't quite right. But I hate bothering Cary again today and I feel distinctly awkward calling him.

'Good, thanks. I intended speaking to you this morning, anyway, to check you were okay after that call. It's not your responsibility what happens with Nathan from here on in, you do know that?'

'Yes. I sent Sheryl a link and then blocked her number on my phone.'

'Hopefully, that should put an end to it.' He pauses. 'There wasn't time to mention it yesterday, but Grandma has been asking after you. She's already making plans for Easter and I wondered if you could possibly bear another visit?'

He sounds uncomfortable about asking, and I jump straight in.

'Of course, it's no problem at all.'

When I lay my own request on him he might think I'm asking too much in return, though.

'The way things are looking I probably won't have a chance to go back for a visit before the Easter break, anyway. I know she'll be upset about that but there's nothing I can do.'

The concern in his voice is tinged with guilt.

'But she will understand,' I say, gently.

'Laurence has already been in touch voicing his own concerns, which hasn't helped. Travelling all over the country doing these presentations is going to be exhausting, but the pressure is mounting.'

He already sounds tired and maybe a little jaded, considering he's only been back at work for two days.

'But the sales figures are going in the right direction, aren't they?'

He makes a noise with his throat, like a stifled laugh.

'Slowly and the board is on my back because of that. We're entering the fourth quarter of our financial year. Our sales team are working hard now to convert the rash of leads generated by the exhibition in Australia, but the target number is tough. Ironically, though, on my return I found out that the product has just won the prestigious Innovative Energy Solutions Industry Award.'

'That's marvellous, Cary. You must be delighted about that. Surely that's proof you're on the right track.'

'Yes and no. The directors and the shareholders focus on the bottom line and we have quite a way to go.'

It strikes me as very unfair, given how hard he's worked for this, that even winning an award isn't enough to ease the pressure on him.

'When does the ceremony take place?'

He chuckles. 'The fourteenth of February, no less and they will be airing Dynamic Videography's video in public for the first time. So the pressure is on you to make sure those final amendments do the trick. And now I have a scintillating speech to add to my to-do list, too.'

Has he ever let up on reminding me I must deliver? I sigh, but at least he's poking fun at himself to lighten the moment. Cary certainly isn't the easiest client to please but I'm sure we will end up exceeding his expectations. When he sees the final cut, hopefully he will view it as a whole with a fresh set of eyes, rather than doggedly analysing every single frame.

'Sorry, I should have asked how recruitment was going first, as I can appreciate how worried you've been. Is there any news?'

'Jeff's replacement, Zack, arrives on the eighteenth. I'm confident he'll hit the ground running, as they say.'

'I'm surprised that you don't sound stressed about the delay.'

'I'm not,' I admit. 'I have someone stepping in to help out. His name is Tim. He's the grandson of the man I sat next to on the first leg of our journey back from Australia. He's young but he has a little experience behind him and he's keen.'

'I'm pleased for you. It must be a huge worry lifted in the interim.'

I know that Cary can appreciate that more than anyone else around me.

'Well, Tim will be on a steep learning curve, but I have high hopes of being able to offer him a full-time, permanent position if he delivers. I've also heard good things about Zack, who is less of an ideas man but a very experienced cameraman and a technical whizz. I am starting to feel that things could slot rather neatly into place. I really think between the three of us we could make a pretty dynamic team.'

'That's a major step for you, Leesa. You've turned one giant headache into a promising opportunity so kudos for your entrepreneurial spirit. I'm impressed. Successful people are those who keep jumping the hurdles.'

'If the pitch meetings I have planned go well, then this could be a significant turning point for the company. I can't expand unless I take a huge leap of faith with potentially two new team members. I will admit that financially it's a mega risk, though. But I'm fed up of playing it safe. Anyway, I'm sorry to hear you still don't have a clear picture about what's happening back at the old vicarage.'

He breathes out and I can feel his exasperation over the situation with his grandmother.

'It's a constant worry but my hands are tied at the moment. Still, when Grandma asked what you and I were doing for Valentine's Day it was an easy excuse. These things are usually very drawn out, black-tie affairs and definitely not a romantic setting.'

'Where is it being held?'

'The Science Museum in South Kensington, why?'

'Did I tell you I love museums?' I can't help myself, and I start laughing.

'Well, this must be one big favour you're phoning me about if an Easter visit with my family isn't enough of a fair exchange. I didn't like to ask for two favours, but if you're offering then I won't say no, Leesa. You'd better let me know what I'm in for before I get cold feet.'

I clear my throat. 'Can you earmark the third of August on your calendar as that's the day my sister gets married.' I feel myself cringe. 'And as she hasn't met you yet—'

'Ah, well, that's a fair enough swap in return for one meal at Easter and being my significant other at a dazzling award ceremony, I suppose. But I will warn you that weddings are definitely not my thing, so I'll need a sharp elbow to rouse me if I begin to look bored during the celebrations.'

Result! Bridezilla will be happy.

'Great, thank you. I love an opportunity to wear a posh frock. Besides, I'm genuinely pleased for you, Cary. Anyway, Cressida is bound to think it's rather odd if I'm not there by your side.'

There's a low 'hmm' of agreement.

'You're right. Jeez, this is just such a civilised way of getting around this awkward stuff. That's what I like about you, Leesa.'

My grip tightens on the phone.

'What?'

'You're like me. You do what you have to do to keep the people you love happy, but don't let it detract from your main focus.'

I find myself nodding but I will admit the words do have a bit of a hollow ring to them. Does that make us a pair of cold-hearted, overly ambitious people? Or two sad people who will end up alone, because we are incapable of making a romantic relationship work? It dawns on me that aside from Cary there isn't anyone else I could have asked to be my plus one.

'Well, I hate to break the bad news, but my sister is anxious that you have a role in her wedding as an usher. My parents have been gushing about you. As Cressida's grandson you've impressed her even before she's met you in person. I did say that August is a long way away, though and—'

'You don't intend breaking up with me in the interim, I hope? Of course I'll be an usher, and text me a couple of dates so that I can meet the happy couple. It's the least I can do. And I'm really delighted you are up for the awards ceremony. I will be honest and admit that I wasn't relishing going without someone on my arm. I'm staying overnight at the Knightsbridge Hotel. I could book you a room as it will be a late one. All that celebrating and drinking champagne. It's a hard life!'

His spirits have lifted, and he seems to have put his worries to one side for a moment. I am relieved that our arrangement is working out well mutually and at least I can satisfy Beth for the time being.

'That would be great, thanks.'

'How long is Jeff going to be around?'

'A week. I still can't believe he isn't simply going on an extended holiday. I will miss his friendship as much as I'll miss him at work. He's on a high and I can only hope that continues and he doesn't have any regrets. He's morphing into a different person to the one I've always known. I guess that's what falling in love does to you.'

Am I just the teensiest bit envious, I wonder? Jeff is leaving behind all of his worries and responsibilities, so he can savour each day as it comes. There are moments when I feel so anxious about the imminent future. Ploughing forward in the aftermath of my personal disasters has been tough. What if I end up taking one risk too many because I'm desperate to prove I can get at least something right in my life?

'Yeah, turns everything on its head until it's over. Then you're left to pick up the pieces, from what I've seen. Still, it might not come to that. Anyway, I'll email you the hotel booking, and you'll earmark Monday the twenty-second of April for the Anderson Easter Monday lunch? Grandma will be delighted. Send my regards to your parents, won't you?'

There's a general cheerfulness in his voice that wasn't there when he first answered the phone. Ironically, I feel like I've succeeded in lifting his spirits a little.

'I will do. And I'll find a suitable posh frock for that black-tie event. I hope someone will be videoing the occasion.'

Cary bursts out laughing. 'Of course, and I'm only sorry I don't have any sway in the company they employ. I'm afraid this is one video in which you'll be appearing as the beautiful lady on my arm, rather than the one standing behind the camera directing the action.'

As we disconnect an image of Cary's face flashes in front of me. He never seems to feel lonely. The sort of feeling that hits you when you've had a bad day and walk in through your front door wishing someone was there who could give you a reassuring hug.

Stop it, Leesa, I chide myself. You have a plan and it's moving forward – you are going to be just fine.

21

Acting Up

One thing is for sure: this is going to be the strangest Valentine's Day I've ever had. My stomach is feeling very jittery indeed, today. The best way to overcome one's nerves is to exude confidence, the article I'm reading informs me. Well, I've done just about everything I can think of to give myself a boost to achieve precisely that. My hair and nails look amazing, thanks to the local beauty salon, and my specially-purchased little black dress looks elegant and sophisticated. It follows the curves of my body with ease, magically smoothing out the little jelly belly from a spate of overly indulgent, cupcake-eating days of angst about finances.

One last glance in the mirror as I pull on the cashmere, silver-grey, cropped evening jacket and I flick my head to check my silver spiral earrings. I'm content with what I see and think I do at least look the part. Glancing around the hotel room, it's in dire need of a tidy but I'm conscious I'm running a little late, so I head straight downstairs.

There are several men standing at the bar talking and laughing, but my eyes instantly alight on Cary. There's something about the way he holds himself that sets him apart; it makes him stand out in a crowd. Like it or not, there *is* a touch of the Cary Grant about him in his general demeanor.

A warm feeling starts to fill my stomach with butterflies as I stare at his back, taking in every little detail of his well-tailored, black evening suit. Sensing my presence, he turns. Smiling at him a little nervously, I'm conscious that the men either side of him are now watching my approach with interest.

He steps forward, grabbing my left hand in an unexpected and familiar way, then stoops to kiss me on the lips. It's merely a second or two and there's a hint of amusement in his eyes as he draws back. The fizz between us is undeniable; it's like a little spark of electricity and I can see he's enjoying the moment. I realise that I've missed being around him – how weird is that?

'Leesa, you look amazing. Let me introduce you to my colleagues. This is Harry Templeton, he's my Vice President and Edward Connelly, here, is our Chief Financial Officer.'

I shake Harry's hand, noticing that his eyes narrow as he peers back at me. I feel distinctly uncomfortable but manage to flash him an easy smile. He's probably in his sixties with a receding hairline and very rotund middle, but no one would describe him as jolly. In fact, his resting face seems to favour a scowl. When I turn to shake Edward's hand it's a totally different vibe and he immediately breaks out into a welcoming smile, pumping my hand up and down.

'Lovely to meet you, Leesa. I had been wondering what was putting a spring in Cary's step lately and now I know it wasn't just the award. It's going to be quite an evening.'

Cary and I both laugh good-naturedly but Harry, I notice, doesn't make any attempt to join in. I hook my arm around Cary's and peer up at him with an adoring look on my face. The game is on.

'I wouldn't have missed it for the world, Edward. Cary has worked so hard and it's wonderful to see him garnering the recognition he deserves from the industry.'

Harry gives a dismissive nod in a begrudging endorsement of my praise. Edward's eyebrows seem to expand upwards, as if he's trying to warn me to be a little cautious and Cary, well, he's trying not to laugh. Maybe that was going a bit far.

Squeezing Cary's arm, I lean into him. 'I'm under orders to get a photo, darling.'

Cary gives a polite cough, a little hint that I'm overdoing it, before attracting the barman's attention to order me a drink. Once we both have a glass in our hands he's quick to usher me away, saying there are a few people to whom he really must introduce me. Instead we find a quiet corner in one of the smaller rooms that lead off from the bar.

'Awkward, wasn't it?' I remark as soon as we are out of earshot of anyone.

'You can say that again. Harry's up to something. When I walked in he was deep in conversation with Edward. It was clear Edward wasn't happy with whatever Harry was saying and he looked almost relieved when I turned up. Edward and I have been friends for years, so I'll get the full story later, no doubt, but it was hard not to start laughing when you made that entrance. You played the classic adoring girlfriend and it threw Harry, completely. I've never seen him lost for words before.'

I'm glad I went with my gut instincts. 'As long as I know what role you want me to play, I can play it. Edward seemed like a nice man, but I took an instant dislike to Harry. He's one to watch out for, that's for sure.'

Cary inclines his head. 'You're quite astute when it comes to weighing people up. It's no secret Harry wants to oust me as CEO but, fortunately, Edward and a few of the other directors are still backing me. It's a closely fought battle and one that rages on. Harry's only concern is the profit margin, but I believe that the company has to stand by its ethos and look at things over a longer-term. Short-term gains might look good, but we have to practise what we preach. We're serious about converting the masses to clean energy and to do that it has to be affordable.'

Cary looks at his watch.

'Are we pressed for time?' I query. He takes a large gulp of his drink and replaces the glass on the table, pushing it away.

'The taxi will be here soon, so we should make a move.'

I've hardly touched my drink, but I want to keep a clear head anyway, so I stand up to join Cary.

'You're really worried, aren't you?'

We walk side by side, out through to the hotel reception and then halt for a moment to slip into our coats.

'Harry says we're running out of time to hit the minimum targets the board set. With such a tight profit margin if there isn't a sudden spike in sales he'll call for a vote of *no confidence.* I'll lose a couple of supporters because at the end of the day we have a duty to our shareholders. Naturally, they tend to measure success by the dividends we pay out. That's business and I knew the risks when I set this project up, but I hoped I'd done enough to get the turnover we needed.'

He looks gutted and I hesitate before speaking because I feel sad for him. What can I possibly say to make him feel better, other than to put it into perspective – whether that's helpful, or not?

'You've won a prestigious award. Surely that must reassure the board and the shareholders that you're doing something right? Whatever happens, I don't think anyone could have done any more than you to get this project off the ground. It would be ridiculous for anyone to expect instant results.' I can't pretend to understand the complexities of a large company, but this is an accolade that really means something. It's not a night when Cary should feel anything other than proud of himself.

I catch his hand and give it a meaningful squeeze.

'I know that Cressida is very proud of you and Matthew, too.' I stop short of adding that I feel a sense of pride on his behalf but that's a little weird given our situation.

'Hmm. Granddad is avoiding me but that's no surprise. I haven't seen him at all since the New Year's party and his unexpected revelation.'

There's more to it, I think, but Cary doesn't really understand that. The shocking revelation about the affair overshadows everything in his eyes.

We walk out through the lobby doors and down the steps. I wait while Cary talks to the doorman, who then escorts us to a waiting taxi. As I settle back I decide I ought to say something because it's so easy for wires to become crossed. That would be a shame in this case.

'You know, it isn't easy for Matthew, walking back into a house that's full of memories.'

Cary scoffs. 'Then why doesn't he just refuse Cressida's invitation?'

Do I tread carefully here, or speak my piece?

'Maybe this is about your mother, Katherine. Have you ever stopped to consider that?'

I feel bad raising this tonight of all nights. But Cary is a man used to making big business decisions, often based on limited information. He's used to tapping into his gut feelings so he relies upon that quite heavily. But what if they aren't as reliable when it comes to taking into account one's emotions? Or other people's emotions, come to that?

'He lost a daughter. The house will remind him of so many happy times, as well as the sad ones. Perhaps for him it's more of a pilgrimage. A chance to feel close to her again and maybe that's why Cressida invites him.'

I can see a look of confusion passing over Cary's face as if he'd never considered that before. He says nothing for a few moments and I glance out the window, allowing him some quiet time in which to consider my words. I feel sad that he's being pulled in so many different directions, because it's a lot to handle.

'He chose to leave, Leesa. My mother's death was a devastating blow to us all. And life-changing from there on in. As kids I'm sure Laurence and I spent time fantasising about what life would have been like if she'd been around. Losing one parent and being rejected by another is tough on a child. We were lucky, of course, because Grandma kept us all going, but Laurence and I internalised it in different ways.

'I compartmentalised my emotions and set myself goals to keep me from dwelling on the sense of loss that has never gone away. Laurence talked about it a lot more, but it wasn't until he met Sally that his life fell into place. She filled the hole in his life. I guess that out of the two of us I was harder work. Grandma kept trying to drag me back in touch with my feelings, but I didn't see that as productive. That's why she took it so hard when Paige left me. Paige was her glimmer of hope for getting me back on track.'

'That's so sad, Cary. I can't even begin to imagine how Cressida found that strength to rise to such an enormous challenge, when inside her heart must have been breaking the whole time,' I admit.

'When Granddad left five years ago, after we'd survived so much together, it seemed a bit pointless. He wasn't going off to a better life, he just locked himself away from everything and everyone. Grandma didn't deserve to go through yet another upheaval. She'd struggled to gain a semblance of normality for the family – well, normal for us, and remarkable, given what we now know. How on earth she managed to forgive him for what must have been a bitter blow to her at the time, I don't know. But she did and when he walked away like that, without any real warning, she must have felt betrayed for a second time.'

I'm astounded to hear Cary's slant on this.

For Matthew, having suffered so much loss in his life – his beloved daughter, the respect of his wife – the toll it has taken is becoming increasingly clear. I know a little about that myself. How the pain never, ever leaves you, but it eats away deep inside of you. Insidious and making you feel a lesser person because of it. But Cary should stop to consider quite carefully what he does next, because this is a fragile situation he's dealing with. 'Have you never stopped to consider that maybe he was exiling himself because he felt that's what he deserved? Now that *you* know about what happened between him and Robert's wife, he's distancing himself once again. This time it's from you, probably because he thinks he's lost any respect you had for him. In his eyes, the mistake he made invalidates his part in your upbringing. I bet Matthew thinks he failed you, as he failed Cressida. But he loved and nurtured you like a father; never forget that because he made a lot of sacrifices on your behalf. You're going to have to reach out to him, Cary, and find a way to forgive him.'

Even in the gloom of the taxi his look is dismissive. 'Why should I?'

'Because he's your granddad, he loves you and people have affairs. It happens. He regretted it and he's punished himself over and over, by the sound of it. We all make mistakes in life and can only hope that the people we love will forgive us when we mess up. The difference between him and your biological father is that Matthew never stopped loving you. Don't turn your back on him now, Cary. Reach out and talk to him. Then take it from there.'

Whether my words hit home, I don't know. Maybe he remembers Matthew admitting that he has always loved Cressida and that at least counts for something, I have no idea, but he nods and shrugs. Oh, how I long to throw my arms around him as there is a still a vestige of that sad little boy within him, who has never come to terms with what life snatched away from him.

I return my gaze to the buildings towering above us as the traffic begins to slow.

'I thought this was a role you were playing?' Cary's voice is a mere whisper as he leans in to me. His breath is warm on the side of my cheek.

My heart stops for a second, until I whip my head back around to look at him. I can see that he's back in playful mode once more and I realise that's the only way he can deal with this. I'll give him his due – he's always prepared to listen, but he never reacts instantly. He likes to digest information and no doubt weigh up the pros and cons. That's the sign of a real businessman but when it comes to one's personal life it's rarely that straightforward.

'I'm getting into character, that's what an actress does.'

He frowns, rolling his eyes and I can see he isn't angry with me. The point I've made is valid. Sometimes with Cary it's almost as if he's playing devil's advocate, too, until he's convinced himself what he's hearing makes sense. And now he seems quite happy to mull over my words before he makes his decision. I can only hope he doesn't take too long because I'd hate to see a growing wedge pushing these two very stubborn men even further apart.

I knew this was going to be quite a prestigious affair, but I wasn't expecting the packed crowd as we filter inside the museum. Once our names are ticked off the official attendees' list we are given name badges and almost before they're pinned on, one of the assembled waiters steps forward proffering a tray of champagne flutes. Grabbing a glass in each hand, Cary indicates for me to follow him through the tightly packed throng to find somewhere a little more comfortable to stand and enjoy our drink.

As we begin to move forward, a number of people call out to him, but he doesn't stop; he simply raises the glasses he's carrying above his head, by way of acknowledgement. I follow in his wake, very grateful as he steers us forward.

The crowd is much thinner the further in we go; small groups are forming as a steady stream of newcomers filter into the large, open space. The volume of noise is rather annoying. Even though we are standing back against a wall, well out of the way so we can survey the scene, it's oppressive. The hollowness of the space seems to magnify a cacophony of sounds that don't blend together at all. It lends an air of chaos to the scene.

'Acoustics aren't that great, are they?' I comment.

Cary leans in, turning his head to look at me.

'We're only in here for the initial pre-drinks affair. Not a fan of crowds?'

I grimace. 'Not really.'

Raising my glass, Cary lifts his to chink.

'Well, congratulations, Cary. And if you need to circulate, please don't hesitate on my behalf. I'll just tag along wearing a polite smile, like the adoring girlfriend I am.'

He peers at me over the top of his glass as he takes a sip, his eyes smiling and his mouth twitching. Cary exudes a magnetic charm when he's relaxed and allows himself to let down his guard. There's a tantalisingly flirtatious edge to his demeanour tonight and I will admit I'm not complaining.

'I will need to acknowledge a few people but, to be honest, having you here with me is a great excuse. I'll keep it short and sweet, I promise. The canapés are always amazing, but I thought we'd slide out as soon as the presentations are over and grab dinner? What do you think?'

'Perfect, if you're sure you won't be missed.'

'I don't care if I am. I don't mean to sound ungrateful, but while this benefits the company in many ways, I doubt it will have much of an impact on the battle I'm caught up in at the moment.'

Cary sounds distracted and decidedly weary, but quickly replaces his increasingly sober look with a good-natured smile. 'Right, let's get the socialising out of the way. I'll introduce you to a few people who will be curious about the new woman in my life. I appreciate that it's a tad awkward, so we won't hang around, just keep on the move. The ceremony begins in thirty-five minutes so hopefully we'll be out of here by nine o'clock, at the latest.'

With that we deposit our half-empty glasses on a passing waiter's tray and Cary takes my hand in his. As our eyes meet I get a brief glimpse of the turmoil behind that impenetrable façade. He's steeling himself and with my free hand I touch his arm.

'Try to enjoy this, Cary. It's in recognition of your achievements, remember, so ignore the other stuff if only for tonight.'

Clearly, my words touch a nerve and he leans into me, placing a modest kiss on my right cheek as he squeezes my hand.

'You're quite something, Leesa Oliver. I couldn't have picked anyone better to accompany me, if I'd tried.' The look he bestows upon me makes my heart skip a beat. It's kind of nice to feel needed.

Twenty minutes later and I'm in the process of being introduced to the fourth group of Cary's associates, as we circulate among the sprawling mass of people. It's mostly hand-shaking and a few pleasantries followed by quite genuine expressions of delight about the award. Unexpectedly, a young woman suddenly appears at Cary's side.

'Sincere apologies for interrupting, Cary. We're about to take a few press photos before we start.'

Cary turns towards me. 'Leesa, my darling, I'm going to have to abandon you for a short while to head off with Gayle, who is the press officer. Gayle, this is my significant other, Leesa Oliver, who owns Dynamic Videography.'

We exchange brief smiles, although mine reflects the plug Cary just gave me so effortlessly. Gayle indicates to the guy behind her, stepping back so he can lean in to get a quick snap of Cary and me. Cary throws his arms around me, holding me close as we pose for the shot. Looking up at him, I can see he is a little uncertain about leaving me stranded with a group of total strangers. Suddenly a voice booms out above the jumble of background noise.

'I'll escort Leesa over to the presentation area. I assume that's in order, Gayle?'

As Harry Templeton thrusts himself into the midst of the cluster of people circling us, a few take a step back. One or two of the others peer at him with sudden interest. It seems the animosity between the two of them is public knowledge, by the look of it.

Cary's face is immobile, and I instantly jump in.

'Thank you, Harry, that's very kind of you. Don't worry, Cary, I'll be fine. I will see you in a little while.'

Gayle has already turned and begins to walk away. I can feel the reluctance as Cary quickly stoops to kiss my cheek. As he slowly draws back, his mouth brushes my ear and he whispers, 'He knows how we met. Stick to the truth.'

Cary spins on his heels. He walks away quickly to catch up with Gayle, who has been swallowed up by the crowd.

'This way.' Harry indicates for me to follow him and we head towards a flight of stairs.

We walk in an awkward silence while I wrack my brains, eager to make small talk. I don't want him to think Cary has said anything untoward about him if he senses my discomfort in his company. I need to hide it and appear bright and breezy, so I launch into the first thing that comes into my head.

'Is this an annual event, Harry? How many prizes will be awarded this evening?'

He doesn't look my way as we continue up the staircase.

'Yes. Three. I'm surprised Cary didn't enlighten you.'

Harry's voice is monotonous and it's almost impossible to attach any interpretation to the tone. His manner is slightly caustic, but then it wasn't any different when I was first introduced to him in the bar.

'He's modest and hasn't really said very much about the award.' It's difficult to instantly think up a response. I'm trying to be careful what I say and, to my dismay, Harry turns his head abruptly to look at me.

'He hasn't? You don't find it rather tedious having to accompany Cary to a business-related event about which you know nothing?'

His eyes narrow as we reach a large balconied area and head towards a set of double-doors. A large sign indicates this is where the ceremony is being held.

'I wasn't sure I could make it tonight, but I managed to rearrange my schedule at the last minute. I would have been so disappointed not to be here tonight to support Cary.'

Hopefully that sounds believable.

Harry holds one of the doors open for me to step through. Unfortunately, there are barely a dozen people scattered around the vast seating area. Everyone is still downstairs, happily quaffing champagne and nattering away. He heads for the front row and we sit slightly to the right of the podium.

As I settle myself down, Harry begins speaking.

'How long have you known Cary?'

Is he making small talk, I wonder? But Cary whispered that he knew how we met.

'Since last December.'

'Ah, yes. The exhibition. But you didn't know each other before that?'

Instinctively I shake my head, almost before the words are out of my mouth. 'No.'

I lapse into silence, glancing around the room nonchalantly and hoping he doesn't ask me another question.

'So, what exactly do you do?'

I turn my head back to the front, focusing on a young guy who is shuffling papers into a pile, before placing them on the lectern. At least I can avoid looking at Harry.

'I own a company which specialises in producing marketing videos. We're about to expand into the training sector.' My tone hardens a little. This isn't polite conversation; this is digging for information.

'Your face looks familiar to me, though. I feel like I've seen you before.'

I stop to think for a moment. 'I came to the offices for a meeting at the beginning of November to discuss the requirements.'

'Ah, so you had met Cary before you worked on the video.'

I frown.

'Not socially,' I reply, firmly.

'And that changed while you were away working together. I see. I'm sure Cary will be able to give you a lot of sound business advice that will come in very useful.'

Is he trying to imply that Cary and I have some sort of business connection beyond just a single contract? My hands are beginning to feel clammy. What exactly does Harry think he can prise out of me? I'm growing weary of this and turn to watch a steady stream of people suddenly entering the room.

'I think I'll pop to the cloakroom while the seats are filling up. Don't worry if someone takes mine, Harry. I'll probably stand to the side as I want to get a photo of Cary. See you later.'

With that, I make my escape without looking back.

Sidling back into the room, I work my way around to a good vantage point. Mercifully, I'm partially consumed by the shadows, as the lights have already been dimmed; all eyes are on the brightly lit stage. I'm out of Harry's direct line of sight, too, which is perfect.

After a very slick PowerPoint presentation, the lights are turned up a little and the award ceremony begins in earnest with the third prize winner. Then the second prize winner takes the stage and as his speech draws to a close even my hands are beginning to sweat a little, so I have no idea how Cary must be feeling right now. And then suddenly he's there, centre stage and looking every bit like a winner. Cool, calm and assured.

His speech is passionate; it's clear that it comes from the heart.

'If we waste energy, we fail not only ourselves and future generations, but the planet, which is temporarily in our care. We are merely custodians for the period we are here. And we aren't doing a very good job of looking after it.

'The future belongs to us all. It's time to invest in that future and that involves every single one of us. It's all about the choices we make and where we choose to invest our time and money.'

There's a solid round of applause as Cary punches a key on the laptop.

'And this is the next step forward.' The big screen behind him kicks into life, the Energy Solutions Industry Award logo being replaced by the opening shot of the video. Our video.

'I would like to acknowledge the sterling work done by Leesa Oliver and Jeff Martin from Dynamic Videography, who filmed and produced this video to an almost impossible timescale. But, as it more than amply demonstrates, the recent energy awareness convention in Sydney was buzzing.

Aside from doing numerous presentations, it was a very informative, and galvanizing, opportunity to meet up with other industry professionals. People, I believe will be instrumental in not simply rolling forward their current projects but want a stake in pushing the boundaries. This will result in speeding up what are already considered to be ambitious goals.'

As the video begins, I feel like I'm back in Sydney. But this time I see it from a slightly different perspective. Cary was buzzing the whole time – no wonder he was so focused; the nervous energy he was expending must have taken a monumental effort.

He wasn't just being a salesman, he was there to convince anyone who would listen that doing their little bit could have a real impact. It wasn't about preaching to those who were already on the bandwagon, but persuading the people who weren't already on board. And that's what I missed somehow.

How did I not really take in the solar panels on the back of Cressida's home, or the little control panels Nicholas so diligently kept flicking open every time he entered a room? Or the wind turbines at the farm?

The only move towards the future of greener energy that I, or my family have made, is to use LED light bulbs. Protecting the environment affects us all and Cary is right, it's the average man in the street who is lagging behind in the war on waste and the resulting damage it does.

When the video finishes and Cary is presented with his award, there is an outstanding round of applause that seems to go on and on. Whatever bad feeling he's experienced at work, clearly he has the respect of his peers. Sadly, he's so caught up in the constant battle he has to fight on a daily basis, that he won't allow himself to enjoy the moment in a self-satisfying way.

But Cressida is going to love watching this when I play it back to her and even I feel a little overcome to have witnessed it in person. Well done, Cary – your mother would have been so proud to see you up there on stage tonight. Passion like that can only come from a person with a genuinely good heart.

22

Happy Valentine's Day

'I hope you're prepared for one very proud grandma moment, when I email this to Cressida.' I indicate to my phone, as we head away from the museum. 'I only wish that she'd been here in person to see it.'

'Yes, well, I had to put my foot down rather firmly about that. As soon as she knew you'd be here, she was fine, of course.' He shoots me a rueful look. 'You didn't have to go to all that trouble, you know. One photo would have sufficed. It's not a part of the job.'

Was accepting that welcoming kiss when I arrived, or hanging on his arm and giving him frequent looks of admiration, a part of the job – or going too far, I wonder? But I didn't see him complaining. This is all becoming way too easy for me, though. I'm enjoying it, being perceived as Cary's love interest. Listen to me – if I can't keep my emotions in check then I'm in danger of facing yet another big upset in my life. Rejection.

'*Job*?' I query, pushing my rather worrying thoughts aside.

'Sorry, contract.' He looks bemused, but I can see that he's relieved tonight's event is over.

'Talking about jobs. Harry was grilling me about when you and I first met.'

Cary shrugs his shoulders. 'Don't fret about it. He was probably making conversation and couldn't think of anything else to say. He's not the most sociable of people. Few get on with him and many are wary of him, justifiably so from his past record. He's not averse to turning information he comes across to his advantage. Even when the source is spurious and it's tantamount to gossip. You know what people are like and sometimes a rumour can do a lot of damage.'

Knowing that, I wonder why Cary doesn't seem at all concerned. We draw to a halt outside an Italian restaurant and when we peer inside, to our dismay, it's packed solid.

I catch sight of a guy producing a single red rose from inside his jacket. Sadly, I suspect it's made of silk but at least that means it's intact.

'Oh, I keep forgetting it's Valentine's Day! It won't be easy to get a table anywhere, I should imagine.' Cary looks apologetic. And I mean *really* apologetic, as if he was looking forward to this, too. 'I should have booked somewhere. We'd better head back to the hotel, we might have better luck there.'

Cary grabs my hand, giving it a reassuring squeeze. My skin tingles at his touch and I find myself squeezing back. He deserves a lavish celebratory dinner at the very least.

As he raises his other arm to flag down a taxi, I still can't believe he doesn't want me to repeat my conversation with Harry. Maybe I'm feeling uneasy about it because I took an instant dislike to the man. Even though Cary has the measure of him, that doesn't mean he should become blasé, or lower his guard. But he does seem more concerned about not disappointing me over having a nice, relaxing dinner together. Albeit Valentine's Day appears to be little more than a nuisance to him, as it's spoiling his plans.

I fleetingly wonder what it would be like if we were really seeing each other. Would Cary be plying me with flowers and chocolates? Or is he the sort of man who would pull a little jewellery box from his inside pocket, like they do in the films? Is there a romantic buried deep inside that often stiff, and decidedly rugged, exterior?

'So, you're definitely not worried then, about Harry?'

'No. I think he stepped in because he wanted to be seen with a gorgeous-looking lady at his side. Harry and I go back a few years. He hails from Cardiff and his wife is an old friend of Grandma's. He headhunted me to fill a position that opened up a few years back. He assumed I would be his ally as time went on, but I got the job on my own merits and rose quickly. He does harbour a grudge but don't worry about it. I know all of his tricks by now.'

I feel I've overstepped my role a little and Cary shouldn't have to justify his actions to me. Despite the alarm jangling in my head I have no choice but to let it go.

'What happens to the award you were presented with? Do you get to keep it?'

'Yes, I gave it to Edward to take back to the office tomorrow. I'm off to Yorkshire in the morning.'

'That's a pity.' That he can't take it home and that he'll be heading off tomorrow, probably early. So, we only have a couple of hours left, at most, to catch up.

We sink into the back seat, finally able to relax and when we arrive at the hotel reception they confirm the restaurant is fully booked.

'Can we get room service?' Cary enquires, and my stomach rumbles a low growl of complaint.

'Of course, sir.' The man proffers a menu and Cary opens it, indicating for me to take a look. I lean into him, scanning the flowery writing for something hearty.

'How hungry are you?' Cary asks, turning to look at me.

'Very. A gourmet burger would hit the spot.'

'Make that two gourmet burgers, please. Room 601?' Cary looks at me for confirmation that I'm happy to eat it in his room and I nod.

In fact, his room is a little bigger than mine, accommodating a table with two chairs in addition to a small sofa and a coffee table.

'Take a seat. I'll raid the mini bar. Alcoholic, or soft drink?'

Having sunk a couple of glasses of champagne I think it's time to opt for water.

We slump down onto the chairs either side of the table. I immediately slip off my shoes, making an apology as I do so. Cary slips off his jacket, grinning as he stares at my wriggling toes.

'That feels so good,' I exclaim.

'Happy Valentine's Day!' We chink mini water bottles. 'I wonder what Grandma would say if she could see us now. "Not much of a romantic dinner for two, Cary", I suspect!'

I laugh, finding myself sitting here and grinning at him. And feeling extremely comfortable.

'Are you allowed to tell me what happened behind the scenes tonight? I thought it all went very smoothly. Were you nervous making your speech?'

Cary is almost finished giving me the lowdown when there's a knock on the door and he jumps up, eager to welcome in the waiter. This is no ordinary room service, though. The waiter lays the table; then the plates, covered with silver domes, are carried across with a little panache. As soon as we are seated he ceremoniously lifts the lids in tandem and wishes us 'Bon appétit' before leaving.

We're both so hungry we begin immediately, not really appreciating the perfect presentation of the tall stacks, secured with wooden skewers. The triple-cooked chips smell heavenly and this is just the food to soak up that alcohol.

Silence reigns while we wolf down a few bites to take away the urgent hunger pangs before slowing down. Then Cary begins speaking again.

'I don't get nervous in a work situation because I know I'm in control. Where I flounder is when I'm having to deal with people's emotions and hang-ups. Now, kids I can cope with because if you give them what they want they're usually happy.'

I'm making quick work of demolishing this burger, but I stop long enough to answer.

'Bribery?'

'Now I don't see it that way. Think about it; take my niece Daisy, for example. Her life is full of frustrations. Jackson is two years older and has more developed skills and a little more freedom; Chloe demands more attention as a three-year-old who is still prone to tantrums. Being the middle sibling makes it difficult for Daisy to shine, as she's rarely the first to achieve anything by way of a milestone. Chloe is the baby of the family. For some reason, I've noticed, parents tend to pander to the youngest member out of nothing more than sentimentality. There are times when Daisy doesn't feel noticed. Giving her some attention isn't spoiling her and it makes her feel good.'

I have a flashback to Hayden, when Cary began playing with him on the journey back from Australia.

'Well, you've more patience than I have; the seven-plus years' gap between Beth and myself meant she was a constant thorn in my side from the moment she began walking and talking.'

Cary gives me a knowing little grin. 'Ah, eldest child syndrome. You remembered the early years when life was simpler without a sibling to consider. Learning to share your parents, your toys maybe and your time isn't easy. Life's lessons can be hard.'

I burst out laughing. 'Well, I don't intend to have kids anyway, so it's all academic to me. I'll leave that to Beth. How about you?'

Cary frowns, putting down his knife and fork for a moment.

'The hours I work I seriously doubt there's a woman out there who would want to settle down with me. I'm not avoiding it, simply being pragmatic. I would love to have kids, but I'd rarely be around to enjoy time with them. Marriages like that tend to end up in divorce, so I might have to settle for being an uncle. Besides, I get to hand them back when they're on a sugar rush because I've been feeding them sweets.'

Cary is a constant source of surprise. Things I think will probably have gone over his head, seem to resonate with him. He has a really sensitive streak deep inside him and along with that goes the ability to get hurt, because you can't have one without the other. That's why he tries his best to contain it, I suppose. Life has taught him that you can't take anything for granted.

'There's something so satisfying when you spend time with a child on a one-to-one basis,' he continues. 'It's grounding and it doesn't hurt anyone to be reminded of life through a child's eyes again. Actually, it was Jackson who inspired the project I'm working on.'

He's eight; I look at Cary, cocking an eyebrow.

'You don't believe me? I took him on a ride to get up close to a wind turbine because he's always been fascinated by them. We parked in a little pull-in and walked up to a gated field. It was a windy day and the hum of the blades fascinated him; he was nearly six at the time. I explained that it generated electricity and he asked why everyone didn't have one in their garden, even if it would have to be a smaller version.

'We talked then about solar panels and I explained a little about green energy and the environment. I admitted it was mainly down to the cost, because many people's homes are smaller. They wouldn't be able to generate enough power for their own needs, so it might not make it worthwhile. I thought I'd lost him on that one when he piped up, "But can't the people with the extra power help them out to make it better for everyone?" And he had a point in a way, which I took on board.'

I'm looking at Cary quite stunned. 'Are you serious, or are you joking with me?'

'Do I look like I'm joking?'

'Well, what a bright kid, for starters, but a child's-eye view is simplistic, to say the very least. What you are trying to achieve is incredible, Cary, but if you fail—'

'Then I'm out of a job and the gamble didn't pay off. But if I succeed then I will have achieved something and made Granddad proud. Most of this goes over Grandma's head, but as an architect he understands the implications. I guess I inherited my passionate nature not solely from her, but from him, too. Hers was channelled into writing romantic books. It helps to keep disillusioned people hopeful that true love does exist, I presume. Mine is in convincing people every single one of us has the power to make a difference when it comes to energy consumption.'

Just when I think I'm getting to understand this very complex man, he reveals something new that makes me think I don't know him at all. I'm beginning to understand a little of what he keeps buried, unable – or unwilling – to let it come to the fore. His little story about Jackson has touched my heart and who would have guessed? And it's so good to hear that Matthew's opinion is still important to him.

'I hope you succeed, Cary, I really do. I simply hadn't considered the full impact of what you are trying to achieve.'

'Well, we'll find out whether my gamble worked, before too long. Winning the award will help because of the extra exposure and that could make all the difference.'

I sit back, my stomach full and a fluttering in my chest that might, or might not, be a touch of indigestion from eating too fast. Or is it because Cary's honesty is so endearing?

'Before I meet your sister, you are going to have to coach me on what I should, and shouldn't say.' Cary interrupts my chain of thought.

I was wondering if Cressida had any idea how vulnerable Cary is right now? Or is that precisely why she's so worried, unsure of how he'll handle it if his dream suddenly begins to fall apart. What else does he have in his life at the moment? I drag myself back into the moment with some reluctance, to answer him. What hits home is that I'm in much the same position. If I get it wrong I will lose everything and then how do you find the motivation to pick up the pieces and start over again?

'Beth's mind is much like the life of a butterfly; it seldom settles in any one place for long because it constantly flits around. Simply be your charming self and try to take the tedious wedding details seriously. You will be fine. I promise. When you turn on the charm you really are rather charismatic. But then, I suspect that you are well aware of that fact.'

Cary raises an eyebrow, looking distinctly amused as he stares back at me. His plate is empty, and he pushes it away, wiping his mouth on the napkin before screwing it up. Suddenly I'm seeing him in an entirely different light and this isn't the first time he's surprised me in this way.

'Well, I wanted to make the effort to show my sincere appreciation, as under normal circumstances I know I'm the last person you expected to be sharing your Valentine's Day dinner with,' he chuckles. 'I hope this wasn't too much of a sacrifice on your part.'

He's teasing me and I flash him an *I'm not falling for it* look. When he switches his thoughts away from work his mood lightens perceptibly and the fun side of him is never far from the surface. It's just a pity he doesn't unleash it more often. But it also sounds a little like he's fishing and I wonder how he expects me to respond. Do I admit that I'm more than happy to be in his company tonight? If this was a real date would I be fighting off the attraction between us that is growing by the second? I decide, with more than a little reluctance, it's best to play it safe.

'Not at all, far from it. In fact, it helps keep our little story going as far as my family is concerned. One thing Beth is good at is matchmaking and she's sharp when it comes to reading people. She's a recruitment consultant and I swear she goes more by gut instinct than she does the details on the database.'

A little worm of doubt begins to work its way into my mind. I wonder if when she sees Cary and me together for the first time, she'll be suspicious. Cary looks at me quizzically.

'You don't think Beth will sense what we're doing?'

Great minds think alike.

'I hope not. I mean, on paper we'd make a reasonable enough couple, wouldn't we?'

Cary holds up his left hand and begins counting off fingers. 'We're both workaholics; I'm a little older but not too old at thirty-five, I hope.'

He pauses, and I nod. 'I was thirty in October.'

'We obviously look good together to fool family and my peers tonight.' He moves on to his fourth finger. 'We're both family-oriented.'

I snort. 'Umm... want to keep them happy so we can enjoy a quiet life, you mean. You're stretching it a bit now.'

He moves on, tapping his little finger whilst wearing a blank expression.

'We both have younger siblings to put up with. That must deserve some sort of recognition!'

I raise my eyebrows and shrug my shoulders. It's pretty pathetic, to my ears.

'There you go. Five reasons to convince Beth we're made for each other. Easy.'

I make a move, conscious it's getting late and as I stand, Cary does, too.

'You made tonight bearable, Leesa, and I'm very grateful to you.'

When his tone changes the ground seems to shift beneath my feet. His look is intense and in sharp contrast to the joking around. Why is it when you find someone who ignites that spark, deep inside of you, nothing else *fits*? Well, aside from the traits that drive most other people mad, like being way too intense and being ambitious.

As soon as our eyes meet, I feel a moment's hesitation run through me. A sense of not wanting to head back to my room to spend the night alone. Reluctantly I turn and as I walk towards the door, Cary follows one pace behind. If he shows any sign of hesitation now, would I stay?

'Sleep well, Leesa. Sorry I won't be around for breakfast tomorrow, but I have to get off sharpish. Let me know how it goes with Zack and I'll keep you up to date if there are any developments with Cressida. Oh, and let me have a couple of dates for the big meet up with Beth and Will.'

I half-turn to give him a pleasant smile at the precise moment he begins to lean in, I suspect, to kiss my cheek. His lips briefly glance off the side of my face and at least it isn't a disaster and we don't collide. The moment has passed. Assuming it was a moment, of course.

'We need to work on our hellos and goodbyes if we're going to be convincing. May I?'

He looks me square in the eyes and I nod, surprised by his request. Cary raises his arms to fold them around my shoulders and pulls me gently up against him. It feels rather like time has slowed. I'm nervous as his face moves nearer, the tickle of his breath on my skin before his lips meet mine is enticing. As I sink into him the heat radiating out from his body comes as a surprise. I find myself wondering if he too is fighting an urgent sense of mounting desire?

'Happy Valentine's Day,' he whispers. But he doesn't immediately pull away and his hesitation tells me everything I need to know.

'I don't have to go back to my room,' I murmur softly.

He tilts his head to stare into my eyes.

'I'm that obvious, am I? Or dare I venture to ask if we are both thinking the same thing?' His smile is teasingly warm.

'Well, our styles might be different but maybe there is a little Cary Grant in you, after all. You whisk me off to an impressive awards ceremony, then make a speech that has people standing up to applaud you. Then, you wine and dine me in style. What more could any woman ask for?'

He bursts out laughing.

'Well, I can promise you that things will only get better from here on in. I aim to please.'

And he does. Twice over.

My phone skitters across the bedside table and I roll over rather reluctantly to reach out for it.

'You left without saying goodbye.'

There's an air of disappointment in Cary's voice.

'I knew you had an early start and I figured you needed at least a couple of hours' undisturbed sleep.'

This is every bit as awkward as I feared it might be.

'Thoughtful. But it doesn't feel right, somehow. Are we cool about what happened, I mean, no regrets?'

I'm surprised he's so concerned. I thought we had already agreed that whatever we both felt comfortable with was fine.

'It was just sex, Cary. And pretty good sex, at that.' I start giggling but he doesn't join in.

'I just wondered if it wasn't such a good idea to get caught up in the moment. You know, given our arrangement.' He's worried but I thought we were both very clear about where we stood, last night. It was just a bit of fun – well, that was the intention.

'Don't worry. Everything is fine. Now, you might have been up for an hour but I'm just about to jump in the shower. Travel safe and thanks for an entertaining evening.'

Now I get a laugh.

'Okay, I get the message. You don't want to talk about it and that's fine; I was simply checking, that's all. And you are very welcome,' he says. He's still laughing as the line disconnects.

It's not that I don't want to talk about it, but rather that I'm scared about what I might unintentionally blurt out. That I had a great time. That I wished it meant something more, but neither of us planned for this to happen and it's not Cary's fault at all. It wasn't love at first sight when we met, or anything even approaching that. This has only ever been about convenience. *Hold on a moment there, Leesa.* My inner voice brings my thoughts to an abrupt halt.

So your first reaction that day you first met Cary wasn't to run your hand through your hair to check you were looking your best? And kid yourself all you want, but those hazel-green eyes of his did a double-take and you saw that. And when he thrust out his hand and you made contact, a warmth coursed through your veins. His warmth. Admittedly, he began interrogating you, which spoilt the moment and it did go downhill from there for a while, but suddenly it's heading in a whole new direction.

You don't jump into bed with just anyone, Leesa. So why do you think Cary isn't equally as discerning? Fear. Fear of rejection. Or fear of commitment? Fear of losing control over your feelings and laying yourself bare to a man again.

Sometimes I really hate that inner voice of mine; who wants to listen to their conscience preaching away at them?

And now you're trying to pretend it wasn't the best night of your life. Or that you longed to stay but wrenched yourself away, because that darned man is such a closed book. Was he using you? No. You matched him every single step of the way and whatever happens next, you know you have no regrets at all.

Two people who can create that sort of passion aren't faking anything. But passion alone doesn't make for a solid relationship. Maybe neither of you are ready and who knows when, or if, that could ever change. So much baggage, so many disappointments that keep pulling you both back.

'Enough,' I say out loud, loath to face the facts. 'Give me a break, please.'

23

Bold and Brave, or Foolhardy?

'Hey, Leesa, how was your day?'

I watch as Tim adjusts the position of his laptop so he's in line with the centre of his screen.

'Productive, so good, thanks. Did you get the link to those files Zack sent across?'

'Yep. Working on them right now, actually and—'

There's a loud knock and suddenly the door behind Tim opens. To my surprise his granddad walks in. Realising Tim's on Skype, he immediately apologises and turns to leave.

'Hi, George. How are you?'

Tim spins around in his seat and George leans in towards the screen, smiling. 'Very well, thank you, Leesa. I didn't mean to interrupt.'

It's the first time I've spoken to him since he put me in touch with Tim and I want to let him know how grateful I am. It's working out much better than I could have expected.

'Your grandson has quickly become my right-hand man and I have some news he might want to share with you in a bit.'

George's smile grows. 'I knew he wouldn't let either of us down, that's why I had no hesitation in recommending him, Leesa. I'm really glad it turned out to be mutually beneficial.'

Tim quickly turns back to face me, his interest piqued.

'I hope it's good news,' he asks, tentatively.

'Well, I don't know if it's going to present you with a dilemma with regard to working for your uncle, but I'm finally in a position to be able to offer you a full-time job if you want it.'

He does a double-take. 'You're serious?'

'I'm just putting the formal offer together and will send it over shortly. Given your level of experience I think the package is fair. If you continue as you're going, then I'm prepared to review your salary in six months' time. By then, hopefully, some of these new contracts will have been seen through to completion, easing my cash flow situation.'

He looks stunned. 'But you said Zack had settled in quickly and there's so much he can handle that I can't, right now.'

'Are you trying to talk yourself out of this? Between the two of you everything I need to get the job done is covered. I understand it's awkward when you work for a family business and rather than lose you, of course I'm prepared to accept whatever hours you feel you can offer me.'

He places his hands on the desk and leans into the screen, a smile wiping away any doubts I have that he won't go for it.

'I'm in. I don't need to see the details. And I have a confession to make. I resigned from my job three weeks ago.'

I suck in a breath. 'I did wonder how you were getting through so much work.'

'I didn't like to say in case it put you in an awkward position, but I'd had enough. I've rented out my flat on a six-month lease and moved in with Granddad. It's helping us both out at the same time. I can keep an eye on him and do a bit of DIY, and meanwhile my mortgage gets paid and money isn't a huge worry.'

Now I feel bad, although relieved to be in a position to make our arrangement permanent.

'Sorry you had to do that, Tim, but I needed to ensure I could guarantee what I was offering. And remember, the starting salary will increase and the quicker we see a return for all our hard work, the quicker I'll be sharing the rewards. I think we three make a good team and I'm very optimistic about the future.'

He settles back in his chair, that grin now extending from ear to ear.

'Best news I've had since the first time I met you.' As soon as the words are out of his mouth, he begins to look a little flustered. 'I mean, that was a big deal for me.'

'Well, this is huge deal for me and Dynamic Videography, so welcome aboard, Tim. Let me know if there are any problems with those files. And thanks, too, for the demo of your voiceover for the first training video. I'll be presenting it to the client tomorrow, so fingers crossed! You did a great job, but then I think you already know that. Speak soon.'

I'm about to click end call when Tim adds, 'Thanks, Leesa, this means a lot to me. Sleep well.'

Almost immediately, my phone kicks into life again and it's Beth. Oh well, more wedding trivia, I suspect. I force my mouth into a smile as I greet her, hoping my tone doesn't sound as jaded as I'm feeling with her at the moment.

'Hey, Beth.'

'Can I have Cary's telephone number? I need to pass it on to Greg. He's cracking on with plans for the stag do and it's easier if he has Cary's number, so he can talk to him direct. I don't suppose he's there with you now?'

I roll my eyes. I'm sure that's the last thing Cary needs, what with work pressures and worrying about Cressida.

'No, he isn't; I'm working, actually. I'll text it to you in a bit. I'm sure he'll make it if he can, but he always has a busy schedule and it often conflicts with my own.'

She giggles. 'What a pair you are! I don't suppose you've changed your mind about suggesting Cressida is invited, too?'

'No. I haven't.' I thought I'd already made that crystal clear.

'Spoilsport. What a coup that would be. Imagine it! Sometimes I get the feeling your heart isn't in this, which is a bit mean-spirited. You aren't upset because you're only the second maid of honour, are you? I mean, I assumed you wouldn't have time to organise the hen party and get hands on with some of the arrangements.'

When I heard the 'heart isn't in this' bit my own turned over uneasily in my chest. I thought for one awful moment she had suspicions about my relationship with Cary. But her words still send a wave of guilt washing over me.

'No, of course not! I appreciate that you understand why my focus has to be firmly on work at the moment. I don't mean to be a grouch, honestly. It will be truly wonderful on the day but all the stuff that leads up to it just isn't my thing, you know that. You've been friends with Olivia since pre-school and she'll make a much better job of supporting you, anyway.'

'Okay. As long as you aren't feeling pushed out, or anything.'

Pushed out? If I had my way we wouldn't talk about it at all. I'd just turn up on the day in my floaty dress, counting the hours until it's over. But I am delighted that my little sister has found her Prince Charming and with her innate attention to detail I'm sure everything will be perfect. And Will is such a darling man: a real keeper.

'Besides,' she continues before I can respond, 'it might inspire Cary to take your relationship to the next level.'

I can't help smiling as I imagine the look on his face. 'Unlikely. Anyway, I'm not in a rush to tie myself to anyone in the foreseeable future.'

Beth makes a noise with her throat that sounds like a reprimand.

'You said you wouldn't break up with him before the wedding! He's a lovely guy but if you don't make an effort he might lose interest in you.'

Oh no, I need to be careful here.

'We're fine, I promise. And Cary wouldn't have committed to being an usher if he thought we weren't still going to be seeing each other. All I'm saying is that we're taking it slowly. Don't forget that we only get to see each other every couple of weeks because of our respective commitments.'

She sighs, sounding a little exasperated.

'And that's such a pity. When will you be seeing him next?'

'Ten days. Easter Monday, at a family dinner hosted by Cressida.'

She tuts. 'Now a good sibling would have wheedled an invite for her little sister to meet the wonderful lady in person. But as you aren't engaged or anything yet, I guess there's no point in even asking.'

'No.'

'Oh, well. I will leave you to get on with your work, then. I blame Jeff, of course. If he hadn't decided to swan off around the world you might have had some free time to have a little fun. Then things might have developed much more quickly.'

I find myself gritting my teeth at Beth's pointed comments. As usual, it's all about *her* disappointment that the timeframe for my new relationship doesn't quite fit in with *her* plans. And I was seriously considering letting her in on the secret! But this is about giving Mum and Dad a break from worrying about me. I have my doubts Beth would be capable of keeping it quiet, anyway.

I just hope we can all get through this event with no major upsets and then, hopefully, normality will reign once more. Then, Cary and I will be able to part company amicably, having survived our respective nightmarish situations. It will be a huge relief, that's for sure. Well, not the parting bit, as I'm going to miss having him to turn to – he's grown on me in a way I never expected. Hand on heart, at times I sort of wish this was real, but he made his position clear from the start. We both did. I just didn't think I'd change my mind about anything, but then I didn't really understand him in the very beginning.

'I really must go. I'm tired and I have an important email to finish before I can even think of jumping into the shower. I'll text that number across shortly, promise.'

*

I'm out of the shower, towel-drying my hair, when my phone begins to vibrate. Snatching it up and wondering what on earth Beth wants *now*, I see that it's Cary's name on the display.

'Hi Cary. How are you?'

'Good, thanks. I'm not sure if this is a silly question but Beth rang to put me in touch with the best man, Greg. She asked if aside from acting as the usher for the groom's side of the family at the church, whether I could take control of the men's buttonholes.'

I start chuckling. 'A single flower with a bit of greenery that's worn on the lapel of the jacket.'

He grunts. 'I know what a buttonhole is, but do I have to go somewhere and order them? And how do I know what to get? She didn't mention any particular colour.'

'Ha! Ha! Sorry, I know it's not funny and I do appreciate you not throwing up your hands, saying "enough already". The florist will deliver them to the church. Your job will be to ensure the guys do wear them. Men don't seem to appreciate it's important for the photographs. Each flower comes complete with a large pin, so it's easy.'

I hear a rather relieved sounding 'Ah.'

'Yes, well, they sometimes take a bit of convincing, believe me. Your task is to be dogged in your determination.'

He laughs, softly.

'I haven't been to that many weddings and I can't say I ever really took much notice. At first, I thought she was making a joke as it sounds rather weird, like performing some sort of inspection. Then I twigged and panicked, as I wondered if she meant I was supposed to source them and make sure they arrived on the day. I mean, that could mess everything up, couldn't it?'

'It most certainly could. We're talking Bridezilla here and she won't miss one little detail if something is out of place. Now I wouldn't give a damn, personally. I think it's all a bit of a chore to be honest.'

'I thought most girls grew up dreaming about being a bride?'

'Nope. That's a fallacy perpetrated by the companies who profit from the small percentage of people who can afford to throw away a huge amount of money on a wedding. Putting it into perspective it's just one day, after all. A wedding dress doesn't have to cost fifteen grand, but it can, and more. Beth can't afford to be that crazy, but the costs are mounting up. I don't know why they don't just disappear for a few days and come back when the deed is done, throw a party and everyone is happy.'

I pop Cary on speaker phone, so I can detangle my hair before it gets too dry.

'It sounds like the perfect stress-free solution to me.' He sounds amused.

'Actually, I've been meaning to call you to say thanks for making our little get-together last week with the happy couple go so smoothly. You succeeded in charming Beth, as I knew you would.'

I continue to tug at a knot that refuses to be teased out.

'My pleasure. Definitely less stressful than what I put you through with Harry.' His voice hardened the moment he mentioned that name as if he was gritting his teeth.

'Problems?'

I stop fussing with my hair and instead wrap the damp towel around it, as this might command my full attention. I perch on the edge of the bath.

'Harry is making a bit of noise at the moment, trying to imply that I don't always stick to the rules. You were right, he was questioning you. He did some digging and discovered that when I commissioned you to produce the video I didn't follow standard procedure. Normally, before a contract is agreed we obtain three quotes to benchmark the going rate for the job. That doesn't mean we necessarily go with the cheapest every time, but it's a part of our financial regime. Obviously, one-offs like the video tend to fall outside our usual purchasing protocols. That's more pertinent to big money contracts to replace or maintain the computers for instance. Anyway, there wasn't time to talk to three different providers and you met the two main requirements. You had a track record and could show relevant examples of your work. Plus, you could meet the very unrealistic timeframe, considering we were expecting you to drop everything and head off to Australia at short notice.'

He pauses and I wait for the *but*.

'But in this case Harry is being vocal because of my relationship with you. He's implying I should have declared a potential conflict of interest with Edward, as the Chief Financial Officer.'

I swear under my breath. 'That's pathetic. I told him we didn't know each other beforehand. He did try to dispute that fact, as he said I looked familiar to him. I told him I'd called to the offices when you interviewed me. He probably saw me then but that was the first time you and I had ever crossed paths, which is true.'

I don't see a problem there; it's easily explainable and hardly huge money.

'As an isolated incident it's meaningless, petty even. But it comes on the back of a major disagreement at board level. We failed to hit the three-month sales target for the new product by a whopping 38 per cent. We'll barely break even and that's a red flag. So, all he needs now is one more vote to gain the majority and we reposition the product in the marketplace.'

I'm confused. 'Which means?'

'We switch from targeting the small domestic market and upscale the product, and the price, to make inroads into the commercial property market. The target would be medium-sized businesses and organisations.'

He sounds deflated.

'Can't you do both?'

Cary draws in a deep breath and he sounds worn out.

'It's not that simple. It's a bit like getting in a small, local company who are geared up to handle redecorating the average three bed house. Two men, possibly, and let's say two weeks top to bottom and they move on to the next job; that can be replicated with as many teams as you have. When you consider working on a medium-sized office block, everything changes. The amount of men you need, the volume of materials and even the problem of guesstimating timescales. There are a number of different issues that don't arise in the domestic environment. Maybe some of the work will have to be done at evenings and weekends because of the noise generated, for example.

'We're almost at the cut-off point beyond which it will be too late to change the strategy without incurring substantial additional costs if we change the model. It's a production problem really. Volume, which reduces the cost price of each standard unit, versus a more bespoke, and therefore more costly, system. But businesses will naturally be attracted because of the increased gains on offer.

'There was a sound financial reason for not going for that market to begin with, as it requires further capital investment. That's stage two in the plan but first we need to recoup some of our initial investment. We're already working on the prototype for commercial operations and we're way ahead of the game. But it's always all about cash flow no matter how large a company is.'

I feel depressed on his behalf.

'Harry is simply grasping at anything he can to undermine you, then. You said one more vote, does that mean if he obtains that then you're out and he's in?'

'Well, no. He broke the news yesterday that he's taking early retirement in eighteen months' time and everyone was shocked. He's proposing that his niece replace him.'

'What? And he had the gall to accuse you of impropriety over a relatively small invoice? She'll be his puppet, surely?'

'No. Her credentials are impeccable, and she's learnt from the best. But she will come armed with every little bit of dirt and leverage Harry has been able to glean in his time with the company. He wants me gone, because this is personal. He felt I snatched the CEO job out from under him, but when you tread on people to get where you want to be sometimes it's payback time. And that's what happened. I won our little battle by a big majority and he will never forget that.'

'You replace one enemy with another if she replaces him, then?'

He says nothing, and I know it's because he feels the end is in sight. It's hard to believe and it makes me realise that even though I lie awake at night going over figures in my head, my problems are at least under my control.

'I wish there was some way in which I could help, Cary. Sometimes it's comforting just having someone there who understands, isn't it? I know at Christmas when you came to rescue me, you took charge and that was precisely what I needed to get me through that night. Do you want me to jump in the car and drive up? It's, what, three hours? At this time of the day the traffic is less congested.'

There's a moment's silence before he responds.

'Hey, I'm fine. I didn't mean to worry you. I'm big enough to fight my own battles, although I really do appreciate the offer. And thanks for clearing up the buttonhole thing. Oh, I'd better check that you're still on for Easter Monday? Grandma mentions you every time we speak and always sends her love.'

'Of course. I'm looking forward to it. Take care, Cary.'

It's weird flitting in and out of each other's lives like this and I find it difficult to switch off from our conversation. Everything he's worked for is on the line and I sort of know how that feels. But who will be there beside him to help pick up the pieces if it does fall apart? He'll no doubt give the outward impression that he's coping as he won't want to burden Cressida or the family. That doesn't bode well, and I have no idea if when that time comes I will still be involved in any way. Cressida is right to be worried about him, because I am, too.

Darn it Cary, I don't need this sort of complication and it's definitely not in our contract. I refuse to waste my time worrying over a man who continues to ignore the warning signs. Why hang on to the bitter end when it's clear you are fighting a losing battle?

I'm suddenly feeling irrationally angry at his blind stubbornness. Is it because in his time of need it would have been nice if he chose to reach out to me? It strikes me that he purposely pushes people away when he's feeling particularly vulnerable, the times when other people look for comfort. That's not a demonstration of his strength, but his weakness. I shake my head, sadly. Why make yourself unlovable, Cary, when there's an infinitely loveable man within?

24

It's Not What They Say, It's What They Do

The day before the Easter holidays is a busy one. Zack is archiving files and streamlining our online system. It should make life a lot easier because the original set-up was never planned, as such, it simply developed organically. There never was time to step back and consider the future needs of the business.

In between backing up the old system ready for the changeover in case anything went wrong, Zack and I had a lot of back and forth on the phone. He discovered a mass of folders that seemed to contain backups of backups. Well, that was Jeff and I will admit there's a lot to be said for someone who doesn't believe in taking risks. I laugh to myself; his lifestyle now is one big risk. Anything could happen, but I know he's never felt more alive, or happier than he does now. Maybe stepping outside your comfort zone for the first time is an eye-opener and you begin to question everything you once took for granted.

It's early evening before I realise I haven't spoken to Tim at all today, which is unusual, so I pick up the phone and call him.

'Hey, Tim, just calling to say I hope you have a lovely Easter.'

'Oh, um, thanks, Leesa.'

I lie back on the sofa, letting my body relax for the first time since I hopped out of bed at six this morning. 'It's been a bit of a nightmare day with these system changes, but—'

The doorbell chimes and I reluctantly ease myself back up into a standing position. I wonder who on earth it can be, as I'm not expecting company. I nestle the phone between my chin and my shoulder.

'Sorry, Tim, I just need to answer the d—' As I swing it open Tim is standing in front of me with a big bunch of roses and gypsophila in his hands.

I open my mouth to speak when he makes a face. It's a cross between the guilt of being caught out doing something you shouldn't do and wishing the ground would swallow you up whole. I stand here gazing at him and trying to comprehend what's going on.

'Flowers?' I ask when I finally find my voice. 'Are they for me?'

He nods, and I usher him inside.

'That's a kind gesture.'

He stands there, awkwardly gazing around and I indicate for him to walk through into the sitting room.

'Tea, coffee?'

'No thanks, I can't stay. I'm on my way to meet up with some friends. I wasn't intending to knock on your door. I was going to leave them on the doorstep and then send you a text, when you rang. Now I'm standing here in front of you I just feel like a bit of an idiot.'

Oh dear.

Tim hands them to me and I reward him with an acknowledging smile, but inwardly I'm exasperated. If I were a man he wouldn't be standing here giving me flowers, would he? I know I'm being way too nice, but stamping on someone's feelings – whether it's a gesture of thanks, or something else – is a difficult thing for me to do. This isn't appropriate and I can see he's now feeling extremely awkward about it. I take them from him, laying the bouquet down on the side table without so much as a glance.

'Well, it's very kind of you, thanks, Tim. How's George? Would you like to sit down for a few minutes?'

'He's good, thank you and no, I'd best get off. I was just wondering if you, um, had any free time over Easter to go for a drink? Or a meal if you like… to show my appreciation.'

Appreciation? Heck. Just when I was hoping the awkwardness of this moment might have taught him something, he doesn't back off.

'Actually, I'm heading off to spend some time with my parents before meeting up with my friend… umm… *boyfriend*, on Monday.' I labour the word to get the message across.

He shifts his weight from his left leg onto his right and then back again. If I'd left the front door open I swear he'd be running through it as we speak. He looks terrified.

'Oh, right. Anyway, must go. I hope you get to have some fun. Life can't be all work, can it?'

We exchange eye contact and as I try to read his face I note the slight flush. I lower my gaze, noticing the anxious way he draws the palms of his hands down over the side seams of his jeans. Now he's worried that he's overstepped the mark, so I give him a bright and reassuring smile. Or is that the wrong thing to do? Oh, hell!

'Well, have a great time, Tim, and thank you for the very kind thought. Let's hope the sun decides to grace this bank holiday so we can all have a little fun.'

I close the door and spin around, my body sagging as I lean against it. Poor Tim, that took a lot of courage. I only hope I was convincing in my attempt to make light of it so he can save face. I don't want to lose him, that's for sure, because he's a valued employee now and I'd hate for this to affect our working relationship going forward. What *was* he thinking, though?

Most of the weekend is taken up with family time. Mum insists on getting us all together for a meal, so I stay overnight at their house to help with the preparations. Beth and Will join us on Easter Sunday and after a leisurely lunch we head out for a long walk. It actually turns out to be rather relaxing after the frenetic activity of the last couple of months.

Reference is made to the fact that it's a shame Cary couldn't join us, but I simply nod and agree. Mainly, it's endless conversations concerning things like how many tiers there should be on the wedding cake. The upside is that I no longer feel that I'm the focus of attention that I was previously with all of the angst over the divorce and, well, other things that we all avoid talking about. But at least I feel at ease.

There's even time to relax and curl up with my Kindle. I'm reading Cressida's latest release. It has much more of a contemporary feel to it than most of her books that I've read in the past, and the style of the cover is very trendy. Out of curiosity I Google her author page on Amazon and am quite surprised to see that all of her titles have been rebranded.

Her next book is due out in September, I note, and is already up for pre-order. I click the button and then get back to reading. I'm hoping this story does have a happy ending, because the way Cressida writes it makes you feel that the characters are friends, not simply a figment of her imagination. I'm gripped and grateful for the sheer escapism. Tomorrow I'll be sitting next to Cary around the table with Cressida and her family. That could be a novel in the making there, if only she knew the truth.

'How are you feeling?'

Cary has led me into what Cressida refers to as the winter sitting room. It's the room where Cary and I lingered over our nightcap, before everything started to snowball. It's snug in here with the big, open fireplace, which is no doubt in use regularly throughout the cold months of the year. That lingering smell of wood smoke spirits me back to that night. I had no idea, then, how involved I'd end up becoming in Cary's life.

He walks over to the window, staring out at the gardens and avoiding eye contact.

'Good. Do you think Grandma looks tired, or am I being a little paranoid these days?'

I wish he'd turn to look at me. I know at some point we'll part ways, hopefully both in a much better place by then as our respective issues work themselves out; but I'm beginning to feel a real sense of... what? Involvement in his life, or the trappings of responsibility that come with a growing friendship? A friendship that for me, has turned into something more, something it can never be.

Or is it merely that fleeting, physical attraction that would fade over time, anyway? Am I fooling myself that it feels more real somehow because we've shared such painful truths with each other? Things that neither of us thought we'd ever voice out loud to anyone. But then I've seen and felt his passion in a very real way, too. That was real.

'No, it's not paranoia. I don't think she looks ill, though, I really don't. Maybe she isn't sleeping well at the moment.'

Finally, he turns around. 'If the opportunity presents itself and you don't feel too awkward, could you engineer some alone time with her? She's still talking about making changes and now Laurence and Sally are growing concerned, too. She's pressing me to take over the house and live here at weekends. It's all a part of this "putting her life in order" obsession. Laurence told me she's in the process of selling a significant part of her portfolio of shares. She told him the funds will be his, because it's his "inheritance." Obviously, he's rather uncomfortable with that, in the same way that I don't want her transferring this house into my name. It's unnecessarily morbid, if you ask me, because there's a lot of life left in her yet.'

I don't see how I can refuse his request, especially given the way she's acting at the moment.

'This isn't a purely financial decision on her part, is it? I mean, maybe her accountant has advised her to do this sooner, rather than later. I don't know anything at all about the tax implications when someone dies, but maybe this is simply forward planning. Hopefully well in advance of anything happening.'

He frowns. 'It's depressing, is what it is. Anyway, when someone dies all gifts made in the last seven years of their life have to be declared and will count as part of their estate for tax purposes. She will have sought advice because there's Granddad to consider as they are estranged, not divorced.'

'Well, I'll do my best to create an opportunity, but I doubt she'll mention any of this as it wouldn't be appropriate, surely? After all, it's none of my business.'

'Hmm, she might not see it that way. Granddad has been in touch with me recently and we finally had a good chat. I voiced my concerns about Grandma and he admitted it was the worst thing he ever did walking away from her.'

'That's so sad, Cary.'

'How close do any of us come to making a bad decision and something unexpected happens to save us from ourselves? It's hard not to believe that fate has a hand, but when it goes badly wrong, isn't that fate, too?'

He pauses, no doubt replaying the conversation with Matthew in his head.

'He said that he thinks of her all the time. Of what she gave up and the sacrifices she made for us all. He said that his moment of madness brought him back to his senses. But I sort of understood him when he said something had been missing.

'Grandma had put Laurence and me first, because of the situation. On top of that her work was necessary and demanding, so there must have been times he felt maybe a little unseen. Unheard. Unappreciated, even, for what he'd given up and considering all that he gave of himself, too.'

I think that's the singular, most sensitive thing I've heard Cary say and it tugs at my core.

'I think you're right,' I add, unable to keep the waver out of my voice as I swallow hard.

'I wonder if I should try to convince her to give him one more chance.'

It's such a difficult situation for him to be in. Old hurts still strong enough to create fresh wounds. Pain that keeps on giving.

'You would be taking quite a risk getting involved, Cary. Cressida might see it as taking sides against her because she was the innocent party; have you considered that?'

Cary shrugs his shoulders. 'Well, it's a risk I have to take. As for talking to you, she might be glad to share whatever is worrying her at the moment. You're a listener, Leesa, and I've appreciated that fact. I think she will, too.'

He saunters over to the sofa, lowering himself down into the cushions and letting out a satisfied sigh.

Then he pats the space next to him and I walk across, grinning.

'Well, we're both surviving, Cary, despite the problems we're juggling, so I guess that's a positive.'

'How is it turning out with Zack and Tim? Is it all coming together?'

I lie back, glancing up at the ornate plasterwork around the small chandelier above our heads.

'Great, actually. Although, there might be one awkward little blip on the horizon. I hope I nipped it in the bud, though.'

I tell him about the incident with the flowers and he frowns.

'I had the impression he still has a lot to learn and that was totally out of order.'

Annoyingly, I feel my cheeks begin to get warm. 'He does in many respects but not in others. We have a professional relationship only and I certainly haven't encouraged this in any way. I just don't want there to be any awkwardness between us when we get back to work after the holidays. Do you think I dented his pride?'

Cary nods his head. 'Probably, but he'll get over it. Just act as if it didn't happen. But if he continues you have to be firm as it could be construed as harassment.'

'My thoughts, entirely. Thanks. I'd hate to lose him. The work is stacking up and I'm already relying upon him quite heavily. In a year or two, at most, I hope to be able to consider further expansion. Being internet-based is so much easier than having to cope with the expenses and problems associated with working out of an office.

'I also want to look at expanding the list of services on offer. Zack and I have talked about offering a custom-designed website package to clients. It dovetails nicely with our corporate branding and mission statement promo videos. We would contract out the work and he would manage the projects. The bonus is that he has the skills and also the contacts. Anyone he recruited would be of the right calibre to deliver a good product to a deadline.'

Cary looks impressed. 'I like your way of thinking. Keep the overheads low and take a profit off the top. You thrive on it, don't you? There are some really golden opportunities out there for those brave enough to grab them. But you can only do that if you are prepared to take a risk and diversify when you see an opening.'

Coming from such an astute businessman, that means a lot. 'Thank you, Cary. I'm not rushing ahead without due regard, but I'm not afraid of straying outside my comfort zone, either. It's merely a case of getting the timing right and this is the time.'

Nothing is going to stop me now.

'Success only comes off the back of hard work. People who can't comprehend how tough it is put it down to luck, but we each make our own luck.'

I can see that came from the heart. Cary didn't get to where he is without a lot of sacrifice and dogged determination.

'The irony is that being with Nathan and going through a messy divorce sucked energy that should have gone into my business. But it could also have inflated the value of it. Then I would have ended up being even worse off. If I'd had to hand over a lump sum I would most certainly have been angry, but instead I gave away my share of the equity in our former house. And yes, Sheryl did move straight in. The place I rent now is comfortable and it suits my current needs. So, I'm not unhappy as I value my newfound freedom. I simply got a little lost there for a while but now I'm back on track.'

'What's that saying? "Actions prove who someone is, words just prove who they want to be." You're determined, Leesa, and that's half the battle.'

His eyes flick over me and I can feel the increasing heat as it radiates upwards from my neck. I'm embarrassed now, and he can see that.

'Sorry, that didn't sound the least bit patronising in here.' He taps his temple. 'What I meant to say is that I admire your entrepreneurial spirit. And the fact that you don't complain when the unexpected happens, you simply look for solutions. That shows real grit and that's admirable. I didn't mean to make you feel uncomfortable; it was simply my inept attempt at a compliment.'

'I forgive you.' I sit upright. 'I'd better make a move if I'm going to find time to chat with Cressida today. I need to make myself visible and available.'

We stand, eyeing each other with a little uncertainty for some reason. We've grown accustomed to greeting each other with a genuine hug and a kiss on the cheek. But I still get flashbacks from Valentine's night in the hotel.

We never refer to it, of course, but the memory lingers on inside my head. Somehow it doesn't feel real, as if it was a dream. For one night only, Cary became the man I've always dreamt of being with and the cruel truth is that he wouldn't understand that. He's turned himself into someone else in order to survive, but I glimpsed the man he could have been.

'Rather than being cooped up in here with me. Point taken but I enjoy our chats, Leesa, I want you to know that.'

I smile at him warmly.

Cary knows how to honour a contract, that's for sure. But I wonder whether he ever stops to think back to that evening? He never seems to feel lonely and if he does, it's not me he reaches out to. And why would he? We are two very different people when it comes to facing up to our emotions.

25

Cressida's Master Plan

I spend a little time in conversation with Sally – well, in between constant interruptions from Jackson, Daisy and Chloe. It's Mum this or Mum that every couple of minutes and I feel like saying 'Stop! You do have a dad, too – go bother him for a change!'

Of course, Laurence and Cary have disappeared, and I suspect they are in the kids' playroom grabbing a quiet game of pool.

When Cressida suddenly appears in the doorway, she looks across and immediately heads in our direction. This is my chance to get her on her own, but I need to divert her before she sits down. I jump up, muttering an excuse to Sally and walk double-time to waylay Cressida.

'Are you busy? I've nearly finished reading *In the Mind's Eye* and I'm loving it. I noticed that all your covers have been updated recently. I don't suppose you have copies of any of the originals from your very early publications you could show me? I love the new contemporary look, but I'd be fascinated to see how they compare.'

'I do, indeed. Let's head upstairs. Yes, it's given my old titles a new lease of life. But with that comes new obligations. In the old days, publishers handled everything for you; the author only had to write the stories. Now I have a Twitter account and a Facebook page, aside from a website, but I have nothing at all to do with that, thankfully. But every day I wake up and I'm supposed to post something interesting.'

She screws up her face as we walk side by side up the staircase.

'Oh dear, I can imagine that's a bit daunting.'

'It is.' She nods, taking my arm and I wonder if it's to be genial, or for support. She seems a little breathless and it isn't the first time I've noticed that.

'So, what do you find to say?'

Her soft laughter is quite girlish at times. 'I began by looking out of the window and talking about the weather but I soon tired of that. Now I Tweet as a different character for the entire day. If someone guesses who I am by the end of the day, they win a signed copy of one of my titles. It takes seconds to get into character mode; people actually spend all day trying to figure it out. Imagine! And it's nice because I do get to engage with my readers.'

We circumnavigate her desk and stand in front of the wall of books. It extends from the floor to the ceiling. Letting go of my arm she places her fingers lightly on one of the spines, pulling it out and handing it to me.

'*His Warm Embrace* was the first book I wrote. I still remember the thrill of signing that contract. The cover was quite typical in its day. The raven-haired heroine reclining and the impossibly handsome, dark-haired Adonis staring down at her with his eyes flashing in indignation. The cover has changed a couple of times over the years. But this latest revamp is a bit of a re-launch, and the pressure is on to put out two books a year, again.'

I stare down at it, careful not to let it drop. It has that old book smell and the colours on the cover are muted, not simply from design but also from age. It's been read a number of times, and the spine is proof of that.

'An old story is like an old friend. I re-read them whenever I'm in need of a little comfort. That might sound vain, but it isn't about vanity. Each time I settle down to read, old memories come flooding back. The years after Katherine died, when Cary and Laurence had finally adjusted to their loss. I'd sit and write, keeping one eye on them whenever they were home from school.'

She seeks out another novel and hands it to me, then another. Five in total and I lay them out on the desk.

'There's something instantly recognisable about the original covers but not really representative of the words inside, if you get my drift. I know at least three of these stories and they aren't bodice-ripping romances full of domineering men and subservient women, as the covers might imply. But I'm also drawn to pick them up as there's that hint of instant attraction and surrendering to one's emotions. I was probably a young teen when I discovered them on the library shelves and maybe it is all about memories, in my case of early freedoms. What your characters taught me was that life is full of problems, not all of which can be overcome. But some can, and I guess there's always a moral, or two, lurking in the background.'

She smiles, her eyes lowered to scan the familiar graphics, probably remembering the first time she was shown the original proof.

'Like a fairytale, I like that thought. I suppose the message is not to give up but to find something, or someone you believe in and stick with it.'

She indicates for us to move over to the comfy chairs looking out over the rooftop terrace.

'Your latest book is different,' I admit. 'I'm fearful of reaching the end because I know what I want to happen, but I'm not sure it will.'

We sit facing each other across the small coffee table.

'Ah, well, times change and the way we live our lives has changed. Some people give up too easily in my opinion and my characters, well, they must be believable, above all else. Life's journey is one long, bumpy road but the message is to look at life's disappointments as simply a gateway to a new opportunity. And sometimes we look back and are grateful for that. I won't say any more as I don't want to spoil it for you. I do have readers who tell me they read the last chapter first, before page one. It puzzled me for many years. Then one lady explained it to me. She said that if she didn't do that she would race through the story, anxious on behalf of the characters about what would happen in the end. It didn't dull her enjoyment in any way at all but allowed her to savour the words on every page. I found it rather humbling. We all think the way we do things is the right, or the best, way. But we are all different and what works for one, doesn't necessarily work for another.'

It's time to nudge the conversation in another direction. However, I can't simply change the subject. Especially as

I'm finding our little chat fascinating and would love to hear more. But I am here on a mission.

'It must be wonderful to be surrounded by so many books and so many memories. Having your collection around you must be a comfort when you're writing.'

She rubs her hands together absentmindedly and I can see she's deep in thought. Then she turns her head to look directly at me.

'I'm tired, Leesa. Tired in spirit more than body. The words aren't flowing as they always have and it's because my head is full of worries. Things that once brought me joy now seem like encumbrances. Take this house, for instance. It requires a lot of effort just to run it, even with the sterling assistance of Nicholas. He's been with me for such a long time that it feels like forever. The man wears so many different hats, effortlessly, that he is irreplaceable. Sadly, his time here is running out because next year he intends to retire.'

She doesn't look upset about that, but I can imagine it will be a big upheaval.

'It's no wonder you're having trouble focusing, Cressida. But you'll get it sorted and then things will settle down again.'

Even sitting on a soft couch, the way she holds herself and her demeanour is disciplined. Sit straight, look presentable and smile politely – it's an old-school doctrine that is like a cloak, hiding anything untoward beneath it.

'They would settle down an awful lot quicker if Cary accepted he's losing the battle and began to put his own future first. My biggest fear is that these years will fly by all too quickly and one day he will realise so much life has passed him by. I don't want it to be too late, or for him to have regrets and I'm beginning to run out of patience.

'Saving the planet is all well and good, but there are times when he's too altruistic and it clouds his judgement. This house represents so much that is dear to me. Why it's important that Cary makes this his home is because he's a man who needs roots, whether he appreciates that fact, or not. His roots are here and at the moment that is all he has; taking over control will, I hope, trigger a big change in his approach to life. In doing so he will set me free. Free to travel, spend time in the sunshine and write to my heart's content, knowing he's settled. What means equally as much to me now, is that you have joined him, but I'm weary of waiting for him to see the truth of his situation. You can fool your head, but you can't fool your heart.'

I'm shocked and my head is spinning. Does Cressida know our relationship is a sham but is hoping that something comes of it?

'The truth?'

'This has to be in strictest confidence, Leesa, but I feel you understand and I trust your intentions are good. Cary is beginning to care for you in a way he didn't expect. His Vice President is an awful man, whose wife isn't much better *and* she's a gossip. Unfortunately, our paths cross from time to time because we have a lot of friends in common. At a party recently, I overheard her boasting that her niece was going to slot into Harry's place when he retires.'

'Oh, yes, Cary is aware of that because he's already mentioned it.'

She shakes her head, sadly. 'Felicity didn't stop there. She said that it wouldn't be long before the CEO's chair had a new incumbent. Which means Harry has been up to his usual tricks and, I suspect, is calling in favours owed.'

'Are you going to tell Cary?'

Cressida shakes her head, once more.

'Cary is astute: he will have worked that out for himself, but he doesn't know when to give up. He can't seem to let go of his dream and it's making him miserable. I'm praying that having you in his life, and taking on this house, will fill the void that is coming. Hopefully, it will allow him to finally focus on a future without the horrendous pressures he's been under. I've been so worried about him, but he is his own man and I can't tell him what to do.'

I swallow hard before responding.

'I'm afraid you overestimate my influence on Cary, Cressida. And my own wounds are still quite raw when it comes to trusting someone again. I understand how frustrating it is when someone refuses to listen, but we both know that Cary isn't ready to accept defeat. That's why he won't walk away.'

The way she turns her head towards the window for a moment, before returning her gaze to me, reveals a sense of inner torment. Why did I ever doubt she had a firm grasp on what Cary's been going through, I wonder.

However, the look in her eyes reflects hope. The very least she deserves is my respect and honesty, but I can't betray Cary. Or divulge the fact that what we are doing is, in his eyes anyway, supposed to ease her mind. My spirits sink, forlornly, as I'm torn between two people I've come to care about.

'But you are here now and everything is different.'

The words are like a dagger to my heart.

'You know there are no guarantees, Cressida, don't you?' What else can I say? I can hardly dismiss what she regards as a gut feeling that this might *work out*.

Her smile is one of a loving grandmother who won't give up hope.

'I know him inside and out, Leesa. I firmly believe that what he thought he wanted isn't what is going to make him happy in the long-term. Please, just be there for him and let's see where fate ends up taking you both.'

She does know, but she is trying to convince herself that I'm the solution to all of Cary's problems.

'I fear you are going to be disappointed, Cressida.'

How far should I go, given that this is a conversation in which Cary should be taking part, I wonder.

'You feel nothing at all for my grandson?'

I can hardly face her anxious stare.

'I'm not sure what I feel. I think you are right in one respect about him and maybe he simply needs time to accept his fate. But I'm at a crossroads, too. Domesticity isn't on the horizon for me and may never be.'

Cressida leans across to place her hand over mine.

'Let's trust that we will all end up where we are supposed to be. All I'm asking is that when the going gets tough you are there for him if he needs you. Can you promise me that, at least?'

'Of course.'

My own emotions are in freefall now. I can't pretend the thought of Cary doesn't stir a sense of something deeper within me. It felt so good to be in someone's arms again but one night of passion doesn't change anything; it's like a one-night stand with someone you sort of know. Well enough to understand you can relax about it because you both know it won't happen again. Sadly, I have my own agenda, which makes it virtually impossible to get sidetracked on what could very well turn out to be a one-sided attraction. Too much is at stake and I must divorce my head from my heart, even if I suspect that I'm simply making excuses because I'm scared.

She squeezes my hand encouragingly and I remain silent, managing only to raise a weak smile as guilt consumes me.

The Anderson family lunch is a chaotic affair; everyone talking over each other, interspersed with the kids' antics. Jackson is a very sensible, rather serious boy for his age and it's easy to talk to him when you get him on his own. Daisy is quite pouty today, little Chloe wanting to dominate everything and, as Daisy put it, giving her a headache.

'Mummy, why do I have to eat all of my vegetables when Chloe can leave hers?'

Sally looks at Daisy, pointedly. 'Because you are shooting up and need all of those vitamins, darling. You know that Chloe is going through a phase, as you did at her age. The rule is that she has to at least take a bite of everything on the plate in front of her. I'm counting on you to show her what big girls do.'

Daisy rolls her eyes as Chloe pipes up.

'Don't like carrots. Don't like parsnips. I like chips.'

Sally looks across the table at Laurence, who simply shrugs his shoulders.

'Well, Chloe,' Cary jumps in, 'if you want to grow big and strong, like Daisy, I'm afraid chips won't do it. I love chips too, but as a treat. Did you know carrots are good for your eyes?'

'Benji loves carrots but I don't like the taste, Uncle Cary.'

'Well, rabbits are clever animals, Chloe, and eating carrots helps them to see in the dark.'

Chloe frowns, wrinkling up her nose as she considers that statement. 'If I eat all of my carrots maybe I will be able to read in the dark, then?'

Sally masks a chuckle. Chloe always has a book in her hand, it seems, and I can imagine bedtimes are difficult. I remember the 'just one more' syndrome I used to practise when I was a child, after being told it was time for lights out.

'Well, let's both give it a try and see if it works. We might have to eat quite a lot, though.'

Chloe spears a small piece and I look away for fear I will burst out laughing. She chews doggedly before swallowing, as if she put a whole carrot in her mouth in one go.

'Bet I finish before you do.' Cary eggs her on and she picks up the pace.

Laurence laughs, then turns to look at his wife with a growing smile.

'I think it's time we shared the news, Sally, don't you?'

All eyes are now on Sally, who immediately goes bright pink. 'I thought we were going to tell the children first?' she quizzes Laurence.

'Oh. I forgot.'

Sally looks a little exasperated, but I notice that her eyes are shining.

'Jackson, Daisy and Chloe – what do you think about having a little brother or sister sometime in November?

Wouldn't that make it a very special Christmas for us all this year?'

Jackson grins, Daisy claps her hands to her face with joy and Chloe frowns.

'I don't want to share my bedroom,' Chloe blurts out, looking appalled.

'Oh no, darling, the baby will sleep in Mummy and Daddy's room for a few weeks before moving into a new nursery. And Daddy is going to change his working hours so he can do the morning school run in future. And—' she gazes across at Laurence, beaming from ear-to-ear '—Daddy has a new assistant, so weekends will be quality family time in future.'

It's making me tear up a little seeing the delighted look on everyone's faces. Aside from Chloe, whose face is still scrunched up, her arms firmly crossed to demonstrate her disapproval. It's quite comical, actually.

Cressida stands and both Laurence and Sally approach her for a congratulatory hug.

'I'm thrilled for you all, lovelies. Am I assuming you will be extending the house to accommodate the nursery?'

'Yes, the plans are being drawn up already. And thank you, Grandma – your generosity allowed that to happen and a few other adjustments in our lifestyle.'

It appears that Cressida has finally persuaded Laurence to take his inheritance, but that only serves to increase the pressure on Cary. I glance in his direction and he seems genuinely happy to hear their news. However, I can see the tiredness written all over his face. If anyone looks unwell, it's him – not Cressida, who is now glowing with happiness.

26

Shocking News

I felt uncomfortable walking away from Cary at Easter, unable to share much of the private conversation I'd had with Cressida. Aside from the fact that she was overloaded, not ill, as he'd feared. I suggested that maybe she was looking to him to take some of the pressure away and left it at that.

Knowing that Cressida had already guessed what was really going on between us is something I left out of the conversation. And the fact that she was choosing to pin her hopes on the impossible happening. She would, no doubt, reveal that information when she was ready. It's crazy thinking that the friendship developing between Cary and me might grow into something else. How can it? We would both have to want the same things, at the same time. It would be foolhardy to move forward simply to give her peace of mind and it wouldn't be doing any of us a favour.

I do dream about a nice little detached house in a leafy suburb, with a dog and two cats and maybe a man who understands how I tick. But he's the optional extra and I'm thinking along the lines of someone who could dip in and out of my life, as necessary. Work is now the number one priority because I need to secure my future financially. I've wasted too much time already over one man who wasn't worthy, to risk that happening all over again. And when it comes to Cary, aside from all the other potential problems, our backgrounds are so very different. And that's something I can't do anything about.

'Time for a coffee break, boss?' Tim suggests.

Today I've hired a room as Zack, Tim and I are videoing a series of tutorials for the first telesales training contract. I'm on the laptop controlling the PowerPoint presentation on the screen behind Tim, as he reads from the prompt cards Zack is holding up. We've arrived at a natural point to break and I nod, so Zack walks over to turn off the camera. Tim is a natural and I guess his confidence comes from his dealings as a credit controller. He once told me that sometimes people would turn up at the offices and on one occasion he was assaulted. A guy grabbed him by the throat after Tim informed him the debt was now in the hands of the high court.

As Zack heads out to call his wife, who has taken the day off work because their four-year-old, Tilly, has tonsillitis, Tim makes use of the espresso machine in the corner.

'Cappuccino?'

I nod.

Working with Tim is fine, but since the flower incident it's obvious he feels a little awkward being around me.

I stand, arching my back a little and glad to stretch out my legs. We've been at it for just over three hours now and it's quite intense.

'If we keep up this pace we'll only need another day to wrap it up,' I comment, as I saunter over to grab the cup Tim is holding out to me.

He hands it over, giving me that familiar cheeky little grin of his.

'Leesa, I owe you a formal apology. I didn't mean to cause offence with the flowers, you know that – right? I think you're an amazing woman and I wanted you to know how grateful I am for this opportunity to prove myself. It means a lot to me.'

I admire his courage because it was obvious something was troubling him; I just hope he hasn't finally spat it out just to say he's leaving.

'I realised afterwards that it the wrong way to express my gratitude. It could have been misinterpreted and I'd hate to upset the person you've been seeing. If he found out and thought I'd overstepped—'

I put up my hand to stop him.

'It's fine. Really. My *friend*—' I labour the word '—is actually a client – ex-client – so no harm done.'

I've made a mess of this, having said Cary was my boyfriend to discourage Tim. If I don't play it down a little now, implying it's not common knowledge, the risk is in Tim fielding a phone call from Cary and saying something. I don't want Cary to think I've been talking about him to Tim. Oh, this is going from bad to worse!

However, the look of relief on Tim's face is immense. Maybe I'm overthinking this and it doesn't really matter.

'I was worried sick you might sack me,' he admits.

'Just keep up the good work and everything will be fine. I'm glad to have you on the team, so relax. You more than pull your weight and you're a real asset,'

Youthful exuberance – oh, how I remember that in my dim and distant past.

The pace doesn't slow at work and the next three months whizz by with tremendous results. I have a little over two weeks until I'm off work for ten days, having decided that not only am I due for a break, but Beth deserves my undivided attention in the run-up to the wedding.

Lately she's been jittery. That's probably to be expected in the aftermath of the recent hen party, which reminded us all we're on countdown. Cary survived the more raucous stag do, but I think alcohol played a big part and they at least saw Will safely through it.

Now I'm already working down my list of tasks I need to wrap up before I hand over to Zack and Tim. In preparation, I've diverted the work number to Tim, to whom it was no big deal. He even offered to add that function to his role, seemingly delighted when I took him up on it. Most approaches come via the website, anyway, so calls are usually only from clients whose work we're currently handling. He will act as a filter and only pass on anything he can't handle.

My phone vibrates and it's Tim.

'Sorry to trouble you, Leesa. A moment ago, I answered the phone to a sobbing woman who didn't give her name. When she realised it wasn't you on the end of the line, she hung up. Shall I try to trace her from the call log?'

My head goes into panic mode. 'No. But thanks for flagging it up.'

I dial Mum's number. 'Is everything alright?'

'No. You'd better phone Beth, she's in a bit of a state. Can you ring her straight away, honey? Let me know how it goes.'

Click. Dial.

Beth answers immediately, but all I hear is sobbing.

'It's me. You rang my work number by mistake and it doesn't come through to me any more. Take your time.'

I sit for several minutes and the sobbing gradually lessens. She blows her nose, making a concerted effort, only to start all over again.

'Give me a moment.' Her voice is almost unrecognisable.

Eventually she pulls herself together.

'Take a few deep breaths before you begin, Beth. Whatever it is, I'm here for you.'

She sniffs, then blows her nose. Noisily drawing in a huge breath, she holds it for a few moments before expelling the air.

'I made a big mistake, Leesa. I've broken up with Will. It's over.'

I'm gob-smacked. My jaw drops as I search around for something suitable to say. I can't find any words and I snap my mouth shut, my fingers tightening on the phone.

'He was just going along with everything but not really getting involved. Like, I'd have conversations with him and I swear he agreed with everything I suggested. I thought at first that was because he loved me. Hah! I thought we were so in tune nothing could go wrong. How stupid was I?'

The bitterness in her voice horrifies me. This is Will she's talking about and I agree, he is a bit of a yes man. But only because he wants her to be happy. Isn't that what you do when you love someone?

'The bakery sent the invoice for the wedding cake and Will went berserk. It's not as if it wasn't in the budget and we chose it together.'

'You broke up because of a cake?'

She sniffs and there's another round of nose-blowing.

'Yes. No. He said he was sick of it. "Sick of what?" I asked him. And he said… *everything*. I threw the engagement ring back at him and told him I never want to set eyes on him ever again.'

I draw in a sharp breath. First of all, I can't believe this. It makes no sense. Secondly, they will be throwing away thousands of pounds. Most things have already been paid for upfront and, ironically, it's probably only the cake itself that can be cancelled at this late stage. My head is whirling, so what must it be like for Beth? And Mum? And Will?

'It's the pressure, Beth. A wedding is one of the most stressful events in anyone's life. I'm sure Will didn't—'

'Maybe he didn't, but I meant it. Why didn't anyone stop me? I was out of control, more in love with the idea of realising my dream than with Will.'

I sit down, before I fall down. I'm trembling all over.

'You. Don't. Love. Will?'

It comes out staccato fashion.

She sniffs again, loudly. 'Maybe the Will I love doesn't exist, because he turned into a raging monster before my eyes. I just want it all to be over now.' She begins sobbing once more. 'It's the waste, Leesa, and what will people think?'

Wow. 'Who cares what they think, Beth. If you are doing the right thing then that's all that matters.'

More nose-blowing. 'My head is cracking so I need to go and take some tablets. I'll ring you later when I'm calmer. Thanks, sis, for being so understanding and kind. I know I've been a royal pain in the ass, and maybe I deserve this.'

'No one deserves this, Beth. Love you, little sister. You will get through it. We'll speak later.'

The line disconnects, and I sit back in my chair. Staring at the phone in sheer disbelief, I feel as if I've just dreamt the whole thing up.

Seconds later I dial Cary's number, thinking the guys probably exchanged numbers on their weekend away and forewarned is forearmed.

I simply blurt it all out – probably verbatim, as Beth's words are still going around and around inside my head.

'That must have been some expensive cake!' he remarks, but I can tell from his tone he's saying the first thing that comes into his head. He certainly isn't taking this lightly. 'Obviously the pressure has been building for some time but, heck, Leesa – they complement each other so well. This is sheer madness. They stand to waste a ton of money if they pull out now. I can see them regretting this once they have both calmed down. Is it going to be possible to encourage them to take a day or two to think it through? It's so eleventh-hour anyway. What difference would it make other than to allow them to pick things back up if this is just the result of pre-wedding stress?'

'I don't know. It was hard enough for Beth to tell me what happened, let alone have a meaningful conversation with her. Beth was adamant that she just wants it all to be over now, as she put it. She sounded pretty convinced she'd made a huge mistake, so I don't know, Cary. She's going to phone me later but it's not looking good.'

Many of the guests will have already bought their outfits and wedding gifts… it makes me go hot and cold all over. What a mess!

'No one else is involved, I suppose?'

Strangely enough, that thought hadn't even occurred to me. That's how convinced I was that it was a veritable match made in heaven.

'I doubt Beth would have held that back if it were the case. And it would be out of character for either of them, which makes this all the more difficult to understand. Anyway, sorry to go on about it but I thought I should warn you. How are things going at your end?'

There's a loud *harrumph*.

'Falling apart faster than I can pull it back together again. And I hate to ask another favour when you have a major crisis to deal with, but Grandma has invited the two of us to dinner. At our earliest convenience.'

I can hear a lift in his voice as if he's smiling at the inference.

'Ah, like an audience with the Queen – who can refuse?' I join in with his attempt to lighten the mood.

'Having worked on Laurence, she's now turned her attention back to me. And by implication, I'm afraid, *you*. Not having seen you since Easter I think she just wants to make sure things are still good between us.'

I'm so tempted to tell him she knows what we're doing, and she longs for me to be a solution. The solution, I suppose.

'In fairness I haven't seen much of her. She's been busy doing a book signing tour and I've been fighting the longest battle of my career. I've been putting off getting in touch with you about it because it raises another little issue. I still haven't broached the subject of Granddad and I was hoping to do so and give her time to think about it before our next visit. But now she's pressing me on this.'

Why is life so full of little issues?

'Is your granddad chasing you, too?' What an awkward situation for him to be in.

'Fortunately, he's still busy getting his little guest suite in the garden completed. I was going to ask if there was any chance you can get away this weekend for an overnight stay at my grandma's. But now this upset over the wedding has happened maybe that's not going to be possible.'

'I'll know more when I talk to Beth later today. She sounded adamant it was over, in which case she'll probably go to Mum and Dad's for some TLC. She will want to keep a low profile as this is going to take some unpicking and that's going to be a painful process. I'll text you with a simple yes or no, as soon as I've spoken to her. It might be best to have a third party there if you are going to broach the subject of Matthew, anyway.'

The anxiety must be building for him and that's the last thing he needs.

'Thanks, Leesa. How's work?'

'Ironically, everything is going just fine. Busy, of course, but I like it that way.'

'And is your protégé behaving himself?'

Ooh, that's out of the blue. Do I detect a note of annoyance creeping into his tone?

'He's young. I spelt it out to him and he now understands how easy it is to cross the line. It might have taught him a useful lesson for the future, but I felt bad '

'Yes, well, he should know better. It's highly unprofessional. As his boss, you would have been well within your rights to give him a formal warning.'

I know where Cary is coming from, but this is Tim, grandson of George, who I happened to sit next to on a plane as a mere fluke. And we aren't talking about some mega company here; just a small team where I'm the boss, but both Zack and Tim are working as hard as they can because they're committed. One for all and all for one. I might be a canny businesswoman but I have a soft heart, or so it seems.

'Oh, while I think of it, I don't have the work number any more – it goes straight through to Tim. So always ring me on this number. Anyway, I'll text you later. Bye for now.'

27

Decisions

I swing open the door of the taxi and Cary appears moments later. He leans in to give me a hug and plant a kiss firmly on my cheek, clearly very pleased to see me. Why does it feel so natural when it ought to feel strange? We aren't doing this merely to keep up appearances because there's no one else around.

'Any further developments with Beth?' he asks, taking my overnight bag from me and leading me upstairs. 'Ironically, Grandma is at a function and won't be back until around seven.'

He talks over his shoulder as I follow behind.

'No, she's adamant. It's been a frantic time phoning around to make sure everyone is aware. I have visions of forgetting someone and they turn up at the church to find the doors locked. Dad talked to Will, who took on the task of making sure all of the arrangements were cancelled. Everyone is treating Beth like she's ill, which is driving her mad, but she does need time alone to think. Mum is fielding her calls and you can imagine how difficult that is!'

'What a total nightmare.' His voice is full of sympathy.

'And some. Dad and Will are working out the final cost, less anything that can be returned or refunded, and will split it in two. Unfortunately, the wedding dress has been tailored to fit and I have no idea what Beth will do with it. For the time being Mum has shoved everything in the spare room and firmly shut the door on it all. It's turning into a real saga.'

I'm in the same room as before; it's directly below Cressida's roof terrace and has far-reaching views, out over the Bristol Channel.

Cary and I stand side by side, staring out.

'Sort of puts you off the idea of marriage, doesn't it?' he half-mumbles to himself.

'I was never into it in the first place but I still did it. And look how that turned out,' I declare vehemently.

He turns to look at me and studies my face.

'What if it was a more civilised arrangement? An extension of the agreement we already have?'

'To placate Cressida?'

He nods. 'You'd save on rent and there's plenty of room here. It's just a thought.'

'Cary, it's nearly noon and I need a drink before we tackle this topic.'

'Come on, Nicholas is out shopping but he has organised a buffet lunch. He's fussing over tonight's dinner for the three of us because Grandma told him she's celebrating a new book deal. Plus she's keen to catch up with us both, of course.'

I grimace. 'I didn't bring anything very dressy. Is that a faux pas?' I turn my head and look at him, walking one pace behind me as we head out onto the landing.

Suddenly, Cary catches my hand and spins me around.

'You always look good no matter what you wear.'

My hand is still in his and the feel of his skin on mine sends a little quiver up my spine. If this was just about us then, heck, my mouth would be on his right now, leaving him in no uncertainty that I'm up for throwing caution to the wind. But this is about deceiving a woman by implying Cary and I really do have a long-term future together, which isn't the case. She deserves to be treated with more respect than that. Not just because she's famous, affluent, or even his grandmother – but because she loves him with all her heart.

'As tempting as that offer is, Cary,' I try not to sound a tad sarcastic, 'there comes a point when you have to decide whether it's kinder to be truthful, rather than to give false hope. Doing what we've done for a short time is one thing; it gave us both a reprieve, a little breathing space when the pressure became too much. This house and you installed here, happily married and filling it with a brood of little ones, is Cressida's dream for you. To let her believe it's going to come true isn't just placating her, it's sidestepping the issue.'

I wish he would let go of my hand.

'I'm not in a good place at the moment, Leesa. I can't give her what she wants right this minute. I know there is chemistry building between you and me, it's obvious but neither of us is in a position to rush into anything. We're both trying to ignore it, because it complicates things that are already difficult to contend with. I'm trying to find a way around it that would allow my grandma to go off and do what she wants to do. It would give us time to get to know each other, without pressure. Just to see where it leads.'

I laugh, and it sounds jaded. 'Like housemates?'

I disentangle my hand from his.

'How many people could have made our arrangement work? Few, if any, I suspect. We understand each other, Leesa, and that's a good basis on which to build.'

Not in my little world, Cary, that voice in my head silently retorts. I'm never, ever going to settle for anything ever again. If it's not the real thing then I'm not prepared to expose myself. No matter what my gut instincts might be telling me, because they've been wrong before.

We saunter downstairs in a sombre mood and head for the kitchen. The house feels so empty with just the two of us here. Such a contrast to the family gatherings when it's full of noise and laughter. I briefly picture Cary and I rattling around, avoiding each other on the bad days after realising we made a mistake and I don't fit in here – I shudder, before dismissing the vision.

'Red or white?' Cary asks over his shoulder as he plucks two wine glasses from a cupboard.

'Red, please. Can I help?'

He's deep in thought, no doubt contemplating the next step in his ill-conceived little plan.

'Or should I just stand around looking decorative?'

'Sorry, my mind was elsewhere. There are two platters in the fridge, that large double-door unit over there. They need to go on the tray that Nicholas left out for us.'

Everything is so neat and pristine. Even the tray is covered with a white linen cloth. What would it be like to live here? I'm not a linen cloth person, that's for sure. It was once a permanent family home, in the real sense of the word. It can be so again, I'm sure. But this isn't the lifestyle for me.

Cary pours a little wine into each glass and hands them to me.

'I'll carry the tray. After you.'

When the cover comes off the platters I seriously doubt it was Nicholas who assembled them. This isn't robust, Jamie Oliver food but a selection of delicate bites with a whole host of different flavours. Fish, meat and vegetarian. It sure beats a sandwich from the local supermarket.

'You've gone very quiet,' Cary observes as he raises his glass and holds it aloft.

What to toast? It certainly isn't success.

'To solutions,' I jump in quickly.

Is my heart beating just a little bit faster as I scan his face? I remember his lips on mine and how good it felt. Physical desire and love are two different things, I remind myself. And if it's not mutual then it's a non-starter. Stick to the plan, Leesa, and don't get sidetracked.

'I'm really sorry. It's all a bit screwed up and that was very unfair of me. Of course, you are right. But maybe I need to stand back a little and come at this from a different angle.' His response is unexpected.

'Angle?'

'Grandma hasn't been happy since Granddad left and I wonder if that's at the root of her desire to make sweeping changes. I know Granddad hasn't been happy since he left here, either. Maybe this house isn't waiting for me at all, but for them to get back together.'

The thinnest sliver of beef on a little bed of horseradish and dill, topped with a small square of Stilton, sends my taste buds into rapture. So much so, that I take my time to savour it before answering. I can see he's watching intently for my reaction, although I'm loath to get drawn in. It's becoming an increasingly difficult scenario now, as he's ignoring how volatile the situation could become.

'I understand why you think that's a good idea, Cary. But it's a delicate matter, given what we now know.'

'You don't agree it's the right thing to do, given that I'm all out of options?'

'Cressida is worried about *you*, not Matthew.'

He shrugs, nonchalantly and this time takes a long swig from his wine glass.

'As I said, I'm out of options, Leesa.'

I'm beginning to lose patience with him. Some problems can't be fixed so why doesn't he focus on what he can control?

'Cary, I've seen the reaction you get from women when you're in a room full of people. Their eyes seek you out. The married females wistfully, the unattached females thinking of ways to catch your attention. Isn't it time you brushed off those insecurities and opened yourself up a little? Why fake it when you have everything going for you to make it happen for real?'

He stops eating, leaning back in his chair to stare blankly at me for a few seconds.

'As much as I downplay it, for obvious reasons, every date I've ever had is a potential opportunity to find someone special. But they never are and that's the problem. Paige knew me, the man I am inside and I felt comfortable with her. I could be myself.'

He sounds so vulnerable at this moment and I'm surprised he's admitted that to me.

'Maybe you're expecting too much, too soon. Attraction is instant, but love grows. What exactly are you looking for, or rather, what type of person are you looking for?'

He shifts uncomfortably in his chair, no doubt wishing I'd just stop talking.

'Sally. Well, not *Laurence's* Sally, obviously, but someone like her. She sacrifices a lot for Laurence and the kids, accepting that it will be a few more years before she can think about her own ambitions…'

Why couldn't he just have said 'You'?

He continues as I brush aside a sense of gutting disappointment. 'Everything she does is out of love for them and it's honest. Real. No one could ask for more than that.'

And I thought he was a man who wasn't tapped into his emotions. But at least I know where I stand. He's made me feel emotional now. Cary clears his throat, nervously.

'Time to change the subject, I think. After lunch shall we take a walk down to the farm? Robert made me promise I'd swing by, so he could say hello. You've made quite an impression on him.'

'Because he thinks we're a couple and he's taking an interest out of concern for you, Cary. Doesn't that make you feel bad?' I know it's stupid feeling angry, but I do. Cary has no idea at all that he's hurt me, so how can I hold that against him?

Our eyes meet, and he at least has the decency to look slightly abashed, although I'm not sure why. Maybe he didn't mean to be so honest and now he's regretting it.

'Hmm. Let me pose a question, it isn't a trick one. How many men are you seeing outside of work, aside from me?'

'None.'

'Not even that young guy at work?'

He knows his name.

'No.'

'I rang and asked you to come and spend the weekend. You agreed. Isn't that technically a date?'

Now he's playing with me and I'm not falling for his little strategy to enlist my help. That *what harm can it do* mentality is dangerous and cavalier. For me, now, it has to be all about self-preservation.

'I like you, Cary, and I will be honest and say that wasn't the case when we first met. I know so much about you, your family and your life now, that I feel involved. As I would for any friend going through a hard time. But I'm not prepared to be anyone's long-term, *temporary* solution. Even that is a form of commitment.'

A look of nervous disappointment causes him to frown.

'Point taken. But do you know what? You're good for me, Leesa; you make me stop and think about what I'm doing. That makes me a better person, more *grounded* as Grandma would probably say. Plus, you aren't impressed by all this.' He flicks his wrist, gesturing with an outstretched hand at the building around us. 'You don't sulk, and you never complain. So, what do you want out of life, Leesa?'

I need to keep this simple, as I have no intention of revealing my true feelings to him. I'm done with heartbreak and there's no point in self-inflicting even more pain than I already have to cope with.

'To make a success of my business and live in a cosy three-bedroom house somewhere green and leafy, with two cats and a dog. And lots of peace and quiet.'

'Isn't there something missing?'

'If you mean a man, then no. Sex, well, that's a maybe.'

Cary sits back in his chair and sighs.

'Why does it have to be so complicated?'

'It's only complicated when you tie yourself to the wrong person, as I can confirm from bitter experience.'

'So it's still a no, then? But you won't walk away now and leave me stranded, will you?' He looks at me intently.

This situation we find ourselves in has to be unpicked carefully and I'm more aware of that than ever, now.

'You focus on trying to get Cressida and Matthew talking, rather than fooling her into believing she's going to acquire another granddaughter-in-law, and I'm still in.' In truth, I don't have a choice.

'You're a tough negotiator, Leesa and one hard woman,' he declares but it's an offer he can't refuse.

The truth makes my stomach churn. My parents and my sister think Cary is perfect and now that's a major headache for me.

And your mouth is very kissable, Cary Anderson, ignoring the fact that I've just turned down the worst proposal ever to move in with a man. But you weren't offering me your heart, just a revised contract full of small print.

That little voice is screaming in my ear, *Why couldn't it have been a genuine proposal?* The fact is that Cary isn't looking for a long-term relationship and commitment. He's looking for an easy way out when it comes to solving his problems.

'How is life treating you, Leesa?'

Robert offered to walk me down to a small brook that filters across one of the fields, while Cary is engaged in conversation with his nephew,

'Um, well, let's just say it's a little testing right now.'

I know Robert's interest is real, but life has become so complicated I can't even begin to explain it. Besides, he'd be horrified if I told him the truth, and disappointed in both Cary, and me.

'Ah. I did wonder. Something Cressida hinted at before we decided to spend less time together.'

I turn, and I can see that wasn't a slip, he wanted me to know.

'Is Cary aware?'

He shakes his head. 'I doubt Cressida would have shared our decision. It's for the best. She never was going to be mine, but it does hurt. She said she was setting me free although there was no arrangement between us. Just an unspoken, mutual respect, I suppose, and that's where it ended for her.'

He looks away and we continue for a while in silence.

'It hurts to love someone when they don't return that love in the same way,' he admits.

'Loneliness is an awful thing, Robert. I do hope you can move on.'

'Everything changes with time. I'm going to be doing a bit of travelling and I can't wait to cross some of those destinations off my bucket list.'

He smiles and there's no bitterness, just acceptance tinged with sadness. But there's a little gleam I see in his eyes.

'An old friend has recently returned to the UK. Gina is an artist and she's been living in France for a while; she's a lovely lady with a very outgoing personality. We've decided to head off on a bit of a holiday together, starting with a couple of months touring Europe. Well, she's pulled me into her plans, is the truth of it. But you know, maybe that's just what I need. She doesn't want to frighten me off.' He lowers his voice conspiratorially, giving me a wink.

'And the farm?'

'My nephew will manage it. He's still learning the ropes but the men I employ have been with me for a long time. They'll soon learn to work together as a team. I've done my bit and now it's time to kick back.'

'That's wonderful to hear, Robert, you deserve it.'

He glances behind us for a moment, his eyes alighting on Cary.

'You're an important part of Cressida's plan, you know. She believes you're the right person for Cary.'

Hearing those words crushes my heart as if someone has just stomped on it.

'That hasn't escaped my attention. This life isn't for me, Robert. If I'm being honest the house is more suited to Laurence and Sally. Cressida must accept that and amend her plans accordingly, because Cary isn't ready to commit to anyone.'

He slows to a halt, and we stare down at the little ribbon of babbling water as it swirls around a bend at the edge of the field. The sound is calming.

'I'm really sorry to hear that, but there's no telling her, Leesa. She's at her wits' end and if something doesn't change soon, then I worry about the effect on her. She usually writes every single day, but she hasn't written a word now in over two months.'

That's incredible. And sad.

'I knew she was struggling but now I understand her need to get away from it all. One assumes that as you get older, life gets easier. She has spent her life looking after everyone and, like yourself, it's time for her to stand back. Writing is her joy and I'm so sorry to hear she's being robbed of it. Cary would be devastated if he knew that.'

Robert kicks out idly at a tuft of grass with his work boot.

'That's why he mustn't find out, but I wanted you to know what was driving this and it isn't simply Cressida laying down the law. She's a wonderful woman, but a troubled one at the moment. This stays just between us, right?'

For some reason I turn and instinctively throw my arms around Robert's shoulders to give him a hug. He hugs back, much to my surprise.

'Do what's right for you, Leesa, then you can't really go wrong. I'm about to do the same and what I've learnt is that forcing things for the wrong reason simply creates an even bigger problem.'

Unwittingly, Robert has just endorsed what feels like the biggest decision I've ever had to make – and that's to accept there is nothing more I can do to help Cary. He is the only one who can seal his own destiny. Cressida has no choice but to accept that and I wonder if she will ever forgive me for giving up on him?

We stand here for a minute or so before turning to head back. Change is never easy, but it's coming. For all of us.

28

Time to Face Facts

'My darling, Leesa, it's so wonderful to see you. Thank you for taking the time to come and visit, I know you're busy at work. I keep badgering Cary for updates. It sounds like you are turning that business of yours on its head and that shows great courage.'

Cressida and I link arms as we walk into the dining room. Cary is distracted, probably rehearsing the little speech he has planned for later, in his head.

Nicholas is in the kitchen supervising the chef and it's obvious Cressida has something special to share with us. Cary looks charming in his charcoal grey suit and white shirt, and one of my usual little black dresses looks chic, if a little boring. Cressida, on the other hand, arrived only an hour ago and has transformed herself into a vision of shimmering glory. Her black, floor-length dress has a cascade of gold beading raining down over one shoulder and I can't help but think of the elegant starlets from her much adored black and white films.

While I tell Cressida about my future plans for the business, and then break the news about my sister's wedding coming unglued, Cary becomes the wine waiter. Sounds from the kitchen indicate that there's a lot going on and anyway, it gives him something to do.

Half an hour later, we get the signal to take our seats.

The table looks beautiful. The light from the silver candelabra creates a relaxing ambience which, it seems, is lost on us all. Cary is on edge; Cressida is warily watching him wondering what's coming and I'm… I'm in the middle. I'm hoping my fears are unfounded and it doesn't deteriorate quickly once Cary raises the topic of Matthew.

'This is delicious, Cressida. I adore smoked salmon. Did you choose the menu?'

Well, it's lame but someone needs to kick off the conversation.

'I did. The trouble with hiring a chef is that he, or she, is out to impress. That often means keeping up with trends. The popularity of smoked salmon waxes and wanes. Tonight's dinner is a facsimile of the first formal dinner party I hosted. The main course is chicken in red wine, but of course these days it has another name. Poor Chef, but some dishes are too good to be cast aside. Of course, in my original menu the dessert was Black Forest Gateau, something I never liked anyway. Chef will be creating a special chocolate dessert for us as a surprise.'

Cressida is happy to chatter away but Cary isn't even listening, by the look of it.

'Anything to report, Cary?'

He must realise that his behaviour so far will strike her as a little distant, to say the least.

'No. No change for the moment.'

Cressida pushes her plate away to focus her full attention on her grandson.

'There's something bothering you, it's obvious. Would you care to share it before it spoils the entire meal and my little announcement?'

Eek.

Nicholas appears to begin clearing the plates and Cressida extends her arm to put her hand gently on his as he draws near.

'Slight change of plan, Nicholas, and do please apologise to Chef. Can you hold off serving the main course for a short while? I will give you the nod when we are ready. I know it will send the kitchen into panic mode but a little silver foil and a reheat in the microwave is a small price to pay.'

She begins laughing and Nicholas follows suit.

'Whatever you wish, Cressida. I'll pour him a large glass of wine and I know he can't resist a game of cards.'

For all the formality that is a part of her life, and Nicholas' in service to her, there is a sound understanding and friendship between them. No wonder she's anxious about his impending retirement, as he is irreplaceable to her.

'Right, Cary, it's time to speak from the heart. Even if it's something I don't want to hear.'

I wonder if Cary will back out, but he wipes his mouth on his napkin and sits tall in his chair.

'I know about the affair, Grandma.'

As the seconds tick by she looks at him impassively.

'Well, I'm shocked Matthew finally decided to speak up about it after all this time. And disappointed he chose to burden you with it now, Cary.' Her look is one of bitter disapproval. The tone is icy.

'He needed to get it off his chest and, ironically, it was Leesa he told. I simply gatecrashed the conversation. What we learnt was that Granddad has never stopped loving you. It was you he really wanted to talk to that night, but you've shut him out.'

Cressida shakes her head, sadly.

'Despite what Matthew might believe now, he really wasn't hopelessly in love with me when we were first married. I was the one who was besotted with him, but he – well, let's say that the physical attraction between us was stronger than his resolve. We had many differences of opinion and a great many rows in those early years, although I will admit a part of the problem was due to my fiery temperament. It was a long time ago, though, and the mind plays tricks.'

Cary shifts uneasily in his seat. He doesn't want to go too far, but he can't stop there.

'You were young and with age comes wisdom, you're always saying that. If you didn't think he would eventually come to return your love in the same way, why did you marry him?'

It's a fair question but I wish Cary's tone wasn't quite so challenging. He's in danger of losing any goodwill his intervention might generate.

'I was quite the party girl in those days. I fell in love with Matthew because he was different. I refused to listen to what my head was saying, and my parents encouraged me because they were relieved, I think. I know my father hoped that marriage would be a calming influence.' She looks away, old memories making her eyes twinkle for a moment or two.

Cary glances at me and I shake my head discreetly, indicating that he shouldn't interrupt her flow.

'My mind was always chock-full of words. My imagination seemed to constantly pick up the little threads that make up our lives and weave them into little daydreams. Of course, there was always a happy ending in here—' she taps her temple '—because I was an eternal optimist. Well, that was when I was young and inexperienced. Before reality set in.'

Cary is looking at her intently, maybe seeing a glimpse of the young Cressida for the very first time. What is a little worrying, is that suddenly Cressida has an air of... tiredness, or defeat, about her. Even in the short time I've known her it seems strangely out of character for this naturally bubbly, glass-half-full, lady.

'But he came to understand what loving someone means and that's why he left because he wanted what was best for you.'

She turns to look at Cary, reluctantly letting go of the memories for a moment to focus on his words.

'Matthew packed his bags and walked away without so much as a word of explanation. That hurt almost as much as his infidelity, all those years before. Eve was a good-looking woman with a frailty that made the men she came into contact with want to protect her. I always felt she thought I was overly exuberant, as if the energy spilling out of me was in some way almost indecent. Have you heard of the term rude health? I was strong and vibrant, ready to grab life and run with it – I didn't realise men needed to feel *needed*.

'Here was this gentle, fragile woman, like a lily; a delicate flower in strong contrast to me – the robust daisy. Eve understood that in order to endear a man to you, you had to learn to rely upon him, even when you were perfectly capable of doing something for yourself. Everyone needs to feel needed. I saw that as total nonsense and, quite frankly, demeaning – to him, I might add. I refused to contain my passion for life. I never was going to be a softly-spoken, retiring lady who settled, or languished, simply to satisfy someone's ego.'

Actually, I'm in awe of that statement as I watch this incredibly strong and brave woman raking over the past.

'My life ended up being a battle of willpower versus fate, if you like. I wanted Matthew to love me as I was and see me as his soul mate, but sadly his affair proved that was never going to happen.'

Cary's facial expression is strained; emotionally Cressida is showing him her pain and my heart aches for the disappointments she's had to endure. Each one along the way must have felt like a huge slap in the face. She didn't let anything erode that fierce determination of hers; however, I wonder when exactly she decided to give up on Matthew. After all, she still hasn't agreed to a divorce, and I would hate to think that was her way of punishing him. In fact, I refuse to believe that, so there must be another reason.

'Isn't it time to give Granddad a chance to explain? The fact that he's facing up to what he did after all these years surely means something?' Cary's voice is even, but what he's restraining can't be hidden and is reflected in his tone. It's one of regret and anguish, mirroring my own sentiments at hearing her poignant words.

'Merely that he's getting old. It's too late and I'm done. He can have the divorce, although unless one of us is going to enter into another relationship it seems like a waste of time and solicitors' fees to me. Fate is a real force to be reckoned with and I'm tired.

'Besides, it's easier to live my life through my characters now. They feel the pain of life, but there's always a happy ending because they have the sense to know when to give up on something. That's what I always lacked, and my father knew that. He hoped that in marrying Matthew I would eventually learn that very valuable lesson in life and settle for what I had; what he felt was real. He didn't realise quite how stubborn I could be when I wanted something.' She half-laughs, as if it's some private joke and I could cheerfully let open the floodgates and sob my heart out for her.

'I let go of my dream to write and settled into the role of wife, homemaker and, a little later, a mother. That's when everything in my world changed, because the love I felt for my children gave my life purpose. Later, of course, my grandchildren were to become a reason to keep on going after your darling mother died. But when, finally, I became a published author it gave me back something I feared I had lost. A belief in myself, I suppose and the realisation that my dreams weren't simply empty promises to fill a void within me. I became loved for what I do and that was humbling.

'I truly believe that it is only love that makes this life bearable. Money, possessions and all the trappings don't make for happiness. So, I write about people who aren't afraid of saying "I love you" to someone, because we all need to hear those words. Your granddad has never once told me that he loved me, and I believe it's because I never really succeeded in touching his heart in that way. And that's the truth of it.'

Neither Cary nor I know what to say, because there's no doubt in our minds that when Matthew was talking about Cressida that night in the garden, he *was* speaking the truth. How had he never found the courage to tell her how he felt? Or at least admit the affair was a momentary lapse he bitterly regretted. Had Cressida unwittingly been her own worst enemy, so full of energy and so capable that Matthew felt he was... dispensable? Somehow not good enough to match the heroes in her head?

'You must listen to what he has to say, Grandma. It isn't over, it never will be. You owe him that.'

'Do I? Because that isn't how I see it, at all. It's too little, too late, Cary. He's too old to change his ways now and I don't intend wasting what time I have left listening to his excuses.'

Is that what this is all about? Time is running out and Cressida has made up her mind to draw a line under the past as far as Matthew is concerned, to focus on Cary? In which case, I fear that there's nothing Cary can say that will make a difference.

He stands, wandering over to the window and taking a moment to glance out. I doubt he's taking in the scenery. Suddenly, he turns back to face Cressida.

'Whose life hasn't been touched by love in some way, shape, or form – even if they find it difficult talking about it? He showed his love by working hard all those years to keep us all together. Did you never stop to consider that maybe your sudden success somehow eroded his self-confidence when he was at a low ebb? I never saw him shed a tear, even at Mum's funeral. He held it all in while we fell apart.

'Granddad isn't so very different from a lot of men of his generation who were brought up not to show their feelings. After a while maybe it's so ingrained, even if they want to let it out they don't quite know where to start. Jeez, even I struggle sometimes to talk about the things I bottle up inside for fear of letting it out and losing control. What I'm trying to say is that we're all different, but no one finds it easy to show their vulnerability.'

Cressida frowns. 'And I want to end my days with someone who isn't afraid to face up to his feelings. Or alone, because my characters can give me everything I need and are a darned sight easier to contend with! That's my entitlement, Cary.' The angle of her head is a telltale sign that Cary needs to choose his words carefully.

'You're a natural-born writer because you can put words together in a way that brings a fictional story to life. The reader is able to step into that world for a while and away from their worries. That's your God-given gift. Granddad's skills allowed him to create some very beautiful buildings that will remain standing long after he's gone. He's not perfect, Grandma, no one is and perhaps it's not too late for him to redeem himself, if he can face his demons and share the truth with you. He was your rock for a long time, even if you don't quite see it in that way.'

Cressida's frown tells me Cary's words have made her stop and think.

'The world would be a very dark place to live, indeed, if we couldn't find it in our hearts to forgive. I forgave

Matthew years ago because the alternative was to end up hating him and I could never do that. I always believed he was the one for me and there could be no other. It broke my heart when he shattered my trust and hearts aren't easily mended I'm afraid, Cary. I don't think mine is strong enough to relive those painful memories now, even if I have misjudged him. I can't give you an answer, Cary, but I will think about what you've said.'

'It was never my intention to upset you, Grandma. But I couldn't let this go because I saw the truth in his eyes.'

Cressida bows her head, her eyes closed as she begins speaking once more.

'What I find touching, Cary, is your belief in him and clearly whatever he said to you convinced you to fight his cause. I want you two to be close because you are right, he spent his entire life being a decent, hard-working man who provided for his family during difficult times. Nothing can take that away from him. If I'd known that following my dream would have widened the rift between the two of us, then that is something I would have been more than willing to sacrifice. *If* I had believed he truly loved me. Now leave me to my thoughts and trust that whatever I decide will be for the best. This is one old wound that has never healed. I know you mean well, but some damage can't be undone.'

With that Cressida rises from her chair and makes her way to the door. Neither of us move a muscle until we can no longer see her and then Cary expels the breath he's been holding in. As he does, his shoulders hunch slightly and he looks like he's been on the receiving end of a vicious blow to the chest. He looks defeated. I hurry over and throw my arms around him. I know we're both hoping we haven't done more harm than good.

Nicholas appears in the doorway, checking to see if we are ready for him to wait on us.

'I'm so sorry, Nicholas. Cressida isn't feeling well. Can you explain to the chef? I think we're done for tonight,' I say, gently.

One glance at Cary and I can see his face is ashen. He thinks he handled it all wrong and this is exactly what I feared might happen.

'Some coffee might be a good idea.'

Nicholas blinks in acknowledgement, concern etched on his face. I can't believe how terse the conversation became between Cressida and Cary. Something is going on with her and that's very clear, but tonight Cary also touched a raw nerve.

And we didn't get to celebrate her new contract, the good news she wanted to share solely with us. She put so much thought into this evening, hoping it would be a bonding experience for us all. A wonderful memory to look back on.

What a nightmare this has turned into and I have no idea what will happen next.

Being woken by the buzzing as my phone skitters around on the bedside table is annoying, to say the least. I groan as I roll over, extending my arm so that my hand can locate it by feel alone, reluctant to open my eyes. Then I realise it isn't the alarm going off but a text, and pull it close to me, squinting.

My grandma has gone.

I gasp. What?

What do you mean?

I couldn't sleep so I went down to make a coffee. I bumped into Nicholas and he said she left well over an hour ago. Robert picked her up; apparently, she had two suitcases with her.

I look at the time and it's not quite 7 a.m.

That's crazy. Why didn't she mention that, last night? Are you saying she's run off with Robert?

I wait. Seconds tick by.

I don't know.

I'll quickly shower and get dressed. Meet you in the kitchen in twenty minutes.

By the time I make my way downstairs Cary has had enough time to get over the initial shock and he's in the middle of sending Cressida a text.

'Hi. I'm nearly done. I need to find out what's going on because this is really out of character for her.'

I pour myself a coffee and join him at the table. He's staring down at his phone.

'She won't respond, Cary. The fact that she left means she needs some time alone.'

'Does it?' he blurts out, sounding distraught. 'Or does it mean she's decided Robert is her future after all and I've unwittingly pushed her into that?'

I know he's only thinking of Matthew, but I'm sure he's reading this all wrong. Should I share the things Robert told me in confidence?

'You think she's at the farm?'

'Let's walk down and find out.'

He's out of his seat and striding towards the hallway before I'm even on my feet and I hurry to catch up. Grabbing my coat, I struggle to pull it on as I follow him out through the front door. We leave Nicholas standing in the doorway of the sitting room wondering what on earth is going on.

'You won't get angry, will you, Cary? Cressida has to make up her own mind and there's no point in trying to interfere. If she's there, then you'll know she won't come to any harm and you are going to have to wait until she's ready to return.'

'But I made Granddad a promise that I'd persuade her to at least listen to him. If she is about to cut him out of her life for good, then it's even more important she hears him out.'

He's agitated and there's nothing I can say to calm him down. I'm having to break into a trot beside him in order to keep up. It's probably coming up to 7.30 a.m. now. While there is the occasional sound of a vehicle up on the top road, it seems to be just us and the birds enjoying the fresh air in this quiet little community. However, as we draw closer to the farm there is quite a bit of movement and Cary heads, purposefully, towards an open barn door. As he walks past Robert's old Land Rover he glances inside. I do the same, but I can't see any sign of suitcases.

Inside the barn a young man stands at a long workbench, pouring animal feed into metal buckets.

'Is Robert here?' Cary fires off the question without introduction.

'He's around somewhere, probably in the brick building next to the stables. There's a problem with the generator this morning. Do you want me to fetch him?'

Cary shakes his head, already turning to retrace his steps. 'No. I'll find him. Thanks.'

I catch up to him, my voice a half-whisper. 'Cary, it's not Robert's fault. You will stay calm, won't you?'

He seems to dismiss my words without a thought and doesn't glance over his shoulder at me, even though I'm a whole stride behind him.

I hear a noise and up ahead I spot Robert, so I wave out. He immediately begins walking towards us.

Speeding up to overtake Cary, I intercept him. 'Is Cressida here?' I ask, but he shakes his head.

'No. And I don't know what's going on.' He looks concerned and I believe him.

Cary has caught up with us. 'You picked her up. Where did you take her?'

'To the station. When I woke up at five this morning I had a text from her. She'd sent it during the night, asking if I could pick her up at six o'clock, as she needed a lift. I assumed you had a problem with the car, or something.'

Cary looks bewildered. 'She didn't say where she was going, or what train she was catching?'

Robert's frown deepens. 'No. It fleetingly entered my head that something wasn't quite right as she wasn't her usual talkative self. She insisted I pull up outside the station and told me she was meeting up with someone who would help with her suitcases. Cressida was a little abrupt if I'm being honest and in no mood for silly questions. I assumed she was off on some writing jaunt or other. You look worried, Cary, and now you're worrying me, too. Did something happen at the house last night?'

Cary shakes his head, raising his hand to lay it on Robert's shoulder reassuringly.

'Not really. You know what she's like when she gets an idea in her head. Can I just ask you whether she said anything at all that might indicate what her intentions were?'

Robert's head tips back as he pauses for thought. 'No, damn it! Doesn't she know how worrying this is, with no clues at all as to her whereabouts? She knew I wouldn't question her, but she also knows I wouldn't have given her a lift if I hadn't been labouring under the impression it was a planned trip.' His eyes search Cary's face, clearly feeling he's let him down.

'Let's hope a little time away will allow her to recharge those batteries. Hopefully, she'll ring in a day or two, asking me to fetch her back. It's my fault,' Cary admits, seeing Robert's very real concern. 'I tried to convince her to meet up with Granddad. There's so much that has been left unsaid and it's bloody silly at their age. They need to sit down together and sort it all out once and for all.'

Robert sighs. 'Good luck with that, Cary. They are two stubborn, strong personalities and that's always been the problem. Cressida can be quite formidable at times and Matthew, well, he has a habit of digging in his heels and switching off. When you know what's going on, can you let me know? Just that's she's alright, if you don't mind.'

Cary squeezes Robert's shoulder before removing his hand.

'Of course. And thanks for being there for her this morning. I regret that the words we had last night meant she wanted to get away without further discussion and felt she had to call on you. It means I went too far.'

I watch as they exchange a telling glance and it just serves to demonstrate how loved Cressida is by those around her. That love has grown because of the kindnesses she's shown to everyone who has touched her life in some way. It's humbling.

When it's time for me to leave there's still no news and Cressida isn't answering her mobile, or texts.

We head off to the station in silence, neither feeling able to make an effort to lighten the mood that has settled over us.

However, Cary suddenly decides to park the car and walk over to the station with me. At the entrance, though, he takes a diversion around the far side of the building to the taxi rank.

A couple of the drivers are standing in a group in front of one of the cars, chatting.

'I don't suppose any of you were around early this morning. Around six-thirty, maybe?'

There a little head-shaking going on but one guy nods. 'I've been here since first thing.'

'Do you recall seeing an older woman with two suitcases being dropped off outside the station?'

'I do. It was a bit odd, actually.'

Cary glances at me briefly before looking back at the driver. 'Why?'

'Well, I was second in the queue. She waited until the Range Rover that she arrived in was out of sight and then jumped in the first taxi-cab. She wasn't catching a train at all.'

'Is the driver here, now?'

'No. Pete only does a three-hour stint in the morning. He heads off around eight and doesn't put in an appearance again until his evening shift.'

Cary thanks him and we walk back to the front entrance.

'She doesn't want to be found, Cary, so there's nothing you can do about it. I wish I didn't have to leave.'

Despite my firm intentions to step back, like it or not, we are wrapped up in each other's lives to a degree and I feel that I owe Cressida something, even if Cary has brought this on himself.

When we hug goodbye I can feel the tension in his body and the seconds pass before eventually he pulls away. I steel myself, knowing that I must be strong and not waver. If he needed me he wouldn't let me go.

'Take care of yourself, Leesa. And thanks. I'll be in touch as soon as I hear something.'

I nod, unable to speak. The thought of Cressida going off on her own is a real worry and I know Cary won't rest until he finds her.

The next day Cary forwards on an email from Cressida.

My dear Cary,

It pained me to walk away like that, but it has all become a little overwhelming. I knew that if I had told you what I was about to do you would have tried to talk me out of it.

I'm staying in temporary accommodation until I have finished the book I'm working on. For that to happen I need to distance myself from you all for a few months. Contractual obligations aside, a team of people are relying upon me to deliver and yet I'm beginning to fear that my writing muse has deserted me forever.

It's my happy place, you see. The little world into which I escape. And it's coming up to yet another anniversary of the day I lost my beautiful daughter and your wonderful mother. This year, for some reason, it's hitting me even harder. So, I know you will all forgive me for putting myself first on this one occasion. I'll come back stronger for it and that's what's important.

I have no idea how long it will take. Today the page remains blank still, but the words are beginning to swirl around inside my head once more and I'm hoping that's a good sign.

Please express my sincere apologies to Leesa; it was rude of me to leave without saying goodbye, but I know she will understand. As for you, my lovely, darling man – you are constantly in my heart and my thoughts until I'm in a position to return. Do, please, tell Laurence and Sally not to worry and I will return before the baby arrives. And, of course, I'll check in by email from time to time.

Maybe it's time for you to do some serious thinking, too. I believe and trust that your instincts will take you in the direction you are supposed to go, if you let them.

Until we meet again, my love always.

Grandma

I reply, feeling a little relieved, saying that at least she's safe. There is nothing at all he can do about it, except give her the time she needs.

Cary informs me that he will be staying at the house and commuting daily, so he can keep an eye on things. He promises he'll ring the moment she returns. Or, worryingly, when he has succeeded in finding her.

Oh, Cary. It's time to sort yourself out and not worry about Cressida.

There's nothing more I can do, so it's head down and back to work. Even though my mind can't switch off from a problem that isn't even mine to influence.

29

The Final Straw

Later in the day I text Mum, asking how Beth is doing but rather ominously, she doesn't instantly respond. About twenty minutes later Dad is knocking on my door.

'Well, this is a nice surprise,' I remark, as he literally stomps into the hallway. 'Oh, what's up?'

I follow him into the sitting room and he opens his mouth; like a dam bursting open, there's a flood of words.

'She's driving us mad, Leesa. We're walking around afraid to talk in our own house for fear of saying the wrong thing. Everything is an issue and nothing we do or say is right. The atmosphere is making us all feel depressed. I know it's awful and a huge waste of money, but no one died. We can't send her packing and Mum and I were wondering if, well, if you still intend to take some time off even though the wedding has been cancelled?'

Oh no.

'I hadn't made up my mind, Dad. I have a full day's work planned for today, anyway, as I'm not officially on holiday until tomorrow. But something else has come up, so while I haven't cancelled my time off, I might end up getting pulled into that.'

He looks totally crestfallen. 'Oh. I understand. Don't worry, we'll get through this somehow.'

Guilt descends over me, reminding me that I'm putting Cary and his family first and that's wrong; Beth is my sister and maybe what she needs now isn't the company of fretting, anxious parents.

'What did you have in mind? Beth is welcome to come here, of course.'

A little smile starts to creep over Dad's face.

'I've pulled the old camper van out of storage and dusted him off. He's fuelled up and the fridge is fully stocked.'

'You would let *me* drive your beloved Victor the Volkswagen? I've waited since the day I passed my driving test to get behind the wheel. Dad, I'm ashamed of you – this is blatant bribery and the answer is *yes*.'

'Beth, can you check the satnav again? I think we've taken a wrong turn. Why is it that campsites are always in the most obscure of places?' I mutter, exasperated.

'D'oh! Because people like to stay in the heart of the countryside and the Lake District is no exception. Stop fretting, we'll stumble across it eventually.'

My phone begins to buzz in my pocket.

'Can you see who that is, please, just in case it's important. I'm going to turn left here and I will pull in if I can find a spot.'

'You have a string of missed calls; we must have been out of signal for a while. Hello? Sorry, can you speak up a bit. The engine is rather noisy. Oh, right. Hang on a second.'

Beth lowers the phone, and her voice.

'It's Tim, from work? He says he needs to talk to you urgently. He wants to warn you about your friend. I'll put it on speakerphone.'

Great! Day three of the trip and already there's a problem.

'Hold on Tim, I'm pulling over. Beth, this spot isn't ideal as there are a few big potholes, so brace yourself for a series of bumps.' Nursing Dad's baby as gently as I can, it takes a few moments to bring Victor to a safe halt.

'Right, Tim, what's up?'

'A guy rang asking to speak to you urgently. I said you weren't available at the moment and asked if he wanted to leave a message. He said no, then demanded that I put him through to you immediately.'

My mouth goes dry. That can only be Cary and the missed calls must have been from him. He's assuming I'm at work. Great.

I bet Tim did the whole 'Good morning, this is Tim speaking, how can I help?' thing. Perfect when it's a client, but I can see now that it will have annoyed Cary not to be instantly put through to me.

I'd admitted to Tim that he was an ex-client, after having recklessly blurted out that Cary was my boyfriend. I had to correct that, while leaving it rather vague. If Cary thought I'd been discussing him with Tim, he'd be livid, so I thought it was the wisest thing to do.

Tim ploughs on.

'He was being cagey, well, rude even. I've dealt with his sort before. They often turn out to be unscrupulous salespeople. Anyway, *then* he said he was your boyfriend and it was a family matter. That made alarm bells ring in my head, as you'd made it clear he was just a client now. I thought that maybe, given his brusque attitude, he was hoping to find out where you are. So I told him I knew that information was incorrect, because you'd told me so yourself. Then he slammed the phone down on me. You are safe, aren't you?'

Nightmare! Tim thinks we were involved and now we're not. This mix up isn't Tim's fault and he sounds genuinely concerned. Ironically, he thought he was protecting me. I should have texted Cary to let him know I was travelling. If Cary has news it must be important.

'I'll deal with it, don't worry. Thanks for your help and for letting me know.'

I click end call. What else could I say? Beth is staring at me.

'You and Cary broke up?'

My chin flops down onto my chest. What have I done?

I immediately redial Cary's number, but it goes straight to answerphone. I'm conscious we have a campsite to find and it could take a while, so I text him.

So sorry I missed your calls. Patchy signal. Touring Lake District in camper van with Beth. Last-minute change of plan. I will call you later. Hope you were phoning with good news.

'I'm your sister, Leesa and I demand to know what's going on.'

'Not now, Beth.' The growl in my voice is enough to have her sinking back in her seat. If I get one of Victor's wheels stuck in a pothole we're stuffed, and Dad would never forgive me if there's so much as the tiniest mark on Victor.

Cary won't answer my calls, or the two explanatory emails I've written, begging him to get in touch. The only contact we've had since is one short response he did via text.

Tim does a good job of shielding you from unwanted intrusions. I received the message loud and clear.

My mind continues to conjure up a dozen different scenarios about what might have gone wrong – but if Cary won't speak to me, now, it all ends here. Jealousy is an ugly emotion and I didn't think he was like that – but clearly, he is. Even if Cary was understandably upset when I didn't immediately return his calls, my emails explained everything in great detail. Cary's treatment of Tim was little short of harassment and I think he owes Tim an apology at the very least. The man is infuriating and he simply can't treat people that way. The world doesn't exist to serve him.

By day five of our trip anger sets in. If Cary has had an accident, surely he could have asked someone close to him to let me know? Sally maybe. If he's annoyed about Tim's questioning that's one thing, but he knows I'm anxious to hear news of Cressida. Is he now trying to punish me with his silence? If Beth wasn't with me I would jump in the van and drive straight to Porthkerry without stopping, just so I can put an end to my misery.

I continue to text every morning and every night, but even when we arrive back home there's still no word. And, rather dejectedly, I see there's no letter of apology waiting on the mat and no messages on the answerphone.

We unload my things and then I drive Victor and Beth back to Mum and Dad's.

'Was it a good break?' Mum asks, tentatively, as if she hasn't been in touch daily to check on us.

'Lovely,' I confirm, giving Beth a meaningful look to remind her to say nothing. Not that I've enlightened her, and she's dying to know what's really been going on. But taking her away for a break means she's in my debt and I can only hope she doesn't blurt it out. I decide to make a quick exit, though, before Mum or Dad ask about Cary.

'I'm going to head back. It's been a long drive and I'm tired.'

We all exchange hugs and Dad follows me out to my car.

'I started her up every day and she has a full tank.'

Dad's cars have names. Mine don't. Why is it a *she*, I wonder?

'Something's up. What is it? Was Beth hard work?' Dad asks, sympathetically.

'Not really. This mood is down to me and it's something I have to sort out for myself. But thanks, Dad. Can I ask you a really odd question?'

'Fire away.'

'When you met Mum, was it love at first sight?'

His eyes widen, and he grins back at me. 'Good Lord, no. We shared the same circle of friends for a long while before I decided to ask her out on a date.'

I've heard Mum's side of the story, but never Dad's.

'Which was because…?'

He runs his hand along his chin, in thinking mode.

'Nothing major. I don't think either of us were ready, if I'm honest. Mum was the serious type, always studying and making excuses not to come out with the crowd. And then, one day I looked at her and something was different. If I remember rightly, I'd caught her looking at my mate, Ian, with what I thought was interest. It made me realise I was wasting time and if I didn't get a move on someone else would snap her up.'

'And Mum?'

I smile to myself as I know this bit, but I am curious to hear Dad's version.

'She said I grew on her, which was a good job as first impressions aren't always correct. She thought I was a bit reckless way back then. I couldn't handle alcohol and I made a bit of a fool of myself on a few occasions. But getting with your mum was the best thing I ever did, and I changed. We changed each other. And here we are with two lovely, if sometimes troublesome, daughters who are a constant worry and a constant source of delight. When it's meant to be, things have a way of falling into place but sometimes you need to be patient.'

'That's good to hear, Dad. Sorry about the worry… and constantly adding to it.'

'I assume this is about Cary?'

I nod. 'Time to part company. He's ignoring all contact from me. Maybe I read more into it than was actually there. It hurts admitting that, but I refuse to chase after someone who won't commit and throws a tantrum when I'm not instantly available.'

'Ah, we did wonder. I'll tell Mum. Best to find out now, love. Less painful than further on down the road.'

He shrugs and smiles, leaning in to scoop me into his arms.

'Any man who doesn't worship the ground you stand on isn't good enough for my daughter. But I didn't take Cary for that kind of a fool and I admit, I am disappointed in him.' He whispers the words into my hair and I half-wonder if he didn't mean to say that out loud.

I'm disappointed, too, as much as I'm trying to rationalise it. How can you get angry when someone rejects you, when you never wanted them in the first place? Unless, of course, you did. And you were only fooling yourself because you didn't want to get hurt again.

On the drive back home I decide I have no choice other than to accept the fact that Cary has taken umbrage and isn't even prepared to give me a chance to explain. Our contract is done. What I told Tim wasn't meant to be repeated, it was simply the truth and correcting his observation. If Cary talked to him with an abrasive attitude, then he was the one at fault. And if he can ignore me for so long after a string of missed calls, then it's blatantly obviously he is able to handle whatever he's dealing with without any further help from me. I have no choice but to accept that and move on; or risk looking like a desperately clingy woman who refuses to let go when something is done. Well, that's never been my style and Cary shouldn't flatter himself that he's so much of a catch I'll take whatever he dishes out.

I'm back at work on Monday, and with no spurious boyfriend and no Bridezilla to contend with, maybe it's time to grab some me-time in between building my little empire.

Zumba here I come! This is going to be the year I get myself fit and stop letting other people's problems drag me down. Woo-hoo!

Woo-hoo, indeed.

Whoop.

Gulp.

Not feeling it.

A single tear trickles down my cheek. Don't be so ridiculous, Leesa, I mumble to myself as I focus on the road ahead. It's pretty pathetic to discover at this point that you have genuine feelings for someone who can cast you aside so easily.

What rams it home is something that Dad said. One day he looked at Mum and something was different. Looking back, I thought Cary and I might have had a moment like that on Valentine's Day, although it sent me into a bit of a spin. So, I put it down to sexual chemistry, at the time. But try as I might I couldn't get it out of my head afterwards. Was it the same for him? Well, obviously not.

Besides, he's looking for the type of person I can never be. I'm not the hostess and domestic goddess he needs in order to make his life complete. Dedicating my life to running a large country house and looking after a growing family simply isn't for me after what I've been through. Cressida would understand, I'm sure.

However, she is a lady who set aside her own ambitions, and her dream, because nature had given her the necessary nurturing skills in abundance. I have the compassion, I suppose, but not the aptitude. As for being a sick nurse and mopping fevered brows – just the thought of it makes me feel faint. And I'd rather order in than slave over a cookbook.

At the precise moment that an innate sense of connection – for want of a better word – registered with me, I swear I thought I saw something similar reflected on Cary's face. As Dad said, if it's meant to be, everything will fall into place. If it isn't, then it falls apart and tears won't change anything.

Wrong time, wrong place and maybe that was the point – wrong guy, yet again! I would rather stay single forever than go through yet another relationship disaster because I don't think my heart can take any more pain.

5TH DECEMBER

30

A Call for Help

Christmas is looming and finally the pace at work is slowing down after a bumper autumn. Zack, Tim and I are off on our first official office party tomorrow and I'm going to present them with a cash Christmas bonus. I think it's generous enough to put a big smile on their faces and thank them for demonstrating more commitment than I could have reasonably expected. That old saying is true. Treat people the way you want to be treated. Talk to people the way you want to be talked to, because respect is earned, not given. They have both earned my respect and, in return, I do believe I've earned theirs.

With the forward schedule already promising an even better start for the first two quarters of the new year, I can at last breathe a huge sigh of relief. The salaries are getting paid and the profit margin will allow for further expansion.

Dynamic Videography has jumped up to the next level and it's energising. In fact, if I could skip the obligatory Christmas season celebrations altogether, I'd happily work through it. My dream is finally coming true and it's energising. But with Zack and Tim both owed a lot of holiday, the sensible thing to do was to close for business for what is, usually, the quietest period of the year.

I will be grabbing online time but focusing on business planning, in between trying to convince everyone I also feel seasonably jolly, which I don't. Yet again. Even though I've made an uneasy pact with myself about the mistakes I've made and leaving them *all* firmly in the past.

I'm feeling decidedly 'bah humbug' because success, I've found, isn't everything. Oh, I'm over the Cary thing, because there's no point in wanting what you can't have. I'm a lot of things, but I'm no fool. It hurt a lot more than I could have dreamt; more than every other disappointment I've ever felt. And that was a shock.

What doesn't help this year is that Beth is rarely around these days. She seems to be avoiding all of us, so Christmas plans are thin on the ground. She won't give Mum and Dad a straight answer about what she wants to do over the holidays, which is a real headache. They don't want to force her to join in if she isn't in the mood, but also can't bear to think of her home alone in a depressive funk.

The upside is that as long as I turn up for Christmas dinner at the very minimum, then I'll look good. Poor Mum and Dad are probably well and truly fed up with the two of us by now. If I were them I'd book a flight somewhere sunny again and say to hell with trying to get a festive vibe going. Last year they did it to accommodate us; this year they should do it to get away from two unappreciative daughters who have no festive motivation whatsoever. What is it with my family? One bad year is down to an unfortunate set of circumstances; two, actually three, consecutive bad years means that neither Beth nor I have taken control of our lives.

'I really don't know for sure what I'm going to be doing because things are a bit in limbo right now,' Beth admitted, last time we spoke. 'I'm not trying to be a pain, Leesa, but you're in the same position. I bet you'll be grinning and bearing it, wishing you could retire to your office and do something productive.'

She still doesn't know what happened with Cary, but I'm sure she has a rough picture in her head.

These days I have no idea what's going on with her because where once I couldn't shut her up, now she's very reluctant to talk. She's hardly ever at home and rarely visits Mum and Dad. Which is why they are trying so hard to pin her down, as they feel her first Christmas after the wedding disaster might be difficult. It hasn't occurred to them that is true for me, too, because the success of the business has been a cause to celebrate. So, I have no choice other than to fall in with everyone's plans, once it's all thrashed out, and make the best of it. Or risk drawing attention to myself about a subject I don't intend discussing with anyone.

An email alert pops up on the screen and I click on it.

Hey Leesa

I know you are busy tying up some loose ends before the break, but I texted you a name and telephone number about half an hour ago and I notice you haven't seen it yet? It's from someone named Matthew and it sounded important. He asked if you would be kind enough to give him a call as soon as you are free. He said he'd be around for about an hour.

Have you heard from Zack yet? I wondered how Abbie was doing.

Tim

Matthew? The only Matthew I know is Matthew Anderson.

Hi Tim

Thanks for the prompt, I'll return that call now. Zack rang about an hour ago to say he's taken his wife to A&E but there's a long wait. No doubt they will X-ray her ankle and he said he would phone later in the day to let me know what's happening.

Our office party might have to be postponed, I'm afraid, but we'll sort something out.

I'll be in touch later when I know more.

Leesa

Picking up my phone I stare at Tim's text. The last person on earth I ever expected to have contact with was Matthew. I click on the highlighted number and wait, rather puzzled, to say the least.

'Matthew speaking.'

'It's Leesa, Matthew. How are you?'

My stomach begins to churn. Don't let this be bad news; please don't let this be bad news.

'Ticking over. Thank you for getting back to me and I expect you are a little surprised by my call.'

'Surprised and delighted, Matthew. You have been in my thoughts and I do hope that things are going well.'

Do I mention Cressida's name, or would that be the wrong thing to do?

'I can't pretend it hasn't been a traumatic time,' he admits.

My stomach does an unexpected somersault as I prepare myself for the worst.

'I don't really know where to start. I suppose the detail now is superfluous and I should begin with my biggest concern.'

A lump rises up in my throat and my fingers tighten around the phone, poised and waiting.

'Is it possible to jump in and rescue someone who is too stubborn to admit they have made a mistake?' Matthew sounds likes he's about to break down.

Is he talking about Cressida, Cary, or himself?

'I'm sorry, Matthew, but I don't understand.'

'And I'm not surprised, Leesa. It's such a long story… so much has happened… but I can't digress. There is a question I need to ask you, but I will fully understand if it's one you don't want to answer.'

Now I'm starting to feel queasy. 'I think it's best you just say what's on your mind, Matthew.'

'How close were you to Cary?'

Considering I haven't seen or heard from Cary for a little over four months now, I'd say not very.

'We understood each other, at the time.'

Oh dear, that sounds awful.

'I know you haven't seen each other in a while, but forgive me, I don't have the full story. I haven't seen him since the third week of July, myself.'

That's just before the weekend I stayed over at Cressida's.

'Is there a problem?'

'Yes, but it's complicated. Look, I will level with you. I think he's been in the house alone for much of that time and I'm worried about him.'

My head begins to spin.

'Alone? What about Nicholas? And isn't Cressida back there with him now?'

A muffled sound of movement, like the phone almost being dropped or something, stops him. When he resumes, his tone is anxious.

'I've just found out that he let Nicholas go.'

What? I'm stunned. 'That's awful! I can't believe Cressida has allowed it.'

'She doesn't know, Leesa, and neither of them know I'm turning to you for help. There isn't time to explain everything in detail as I only have a couple of minutes, but there's a big favour I need to ask of you. I have nowhere else to turn. I can't inflict this worry on Laurence and Sally as she's in hospital at the moment. The baby could come at any time and Laurence has his hands full. I rang Robert, who recently returned from a trip abroad, because I still can't get any reply from Cary at all. Robert has walked up to the house several times over the past two days but can't get a response, either. This morning Robert even waylaid the postman, who confirmed Cary has been there, as he signed for a letter one day last week. I just need to know he's alright. I wondered if you might elicit some sort of response from him. I'm indisposed at the moment, or I'd be round there battering on his door, myself.'

Clearly, Matthew thinks there was more between Cary and I than was the case.

'Matthew, I seriously doubt Cary will respond to any contact from me after all this time. He cut me off after a misunderstanding without giving me a chance to explain. Perhaps he needs some time alone. I doubt he will ignore you for long.'

Matthew clears his throat, nervously. 'I'm waiting for the doctor to arrive and it might involve some running around afterwards, or a little trip to the hospital. Leesa, I wouldn't ask unless I was really worried about him and I am.'

Matthew can't hide the anxiety in his voice and it sounds like he has problems of his own to contend with.

'I'm sorry to hear that, Matthew, and I do hope you get well quickly. Of course, I'll try to get hold of him and I will report back. But I really do think that Cressida is probably the only person he will respond to.'

He exhales slowly, as if I've just taken a huge weight off his shoulders. 'Let's hope that's not the case. Thank you, Leesa, you have no idea what this means to me. I'm being pulled in all directions and even though I'm terribly worried about Cary, I'm virtually stuck here, unable to travel very far.'

Ironically, Cary was worried about Cressida's health, when maybe it was Matthew he should have been watching more closely. That's so sad to hear and obviously Cary is totally unaware of the situation.

*

After leaving two messages and several texts with no sign of a response, my annoyance is growing. How selfish is Cary, cutting everyone off like this, fully aware that his family will be worrying about what's going on with him? I do the only other thing I can think of to force his hand: I jump in the car and head to Porthkerry.

Halfway there, the Bluetooth suddenly kicks in and it's Zack.

'Hi Leesa. We're waiting for Abbie's ankle to be plastered up. She's fine, but it's quite a bad fracture and she's totally immobile at present.'

'I'm so sorry to hear that, Zack. Is there anything I can do?'

'No. There will be more waiting around and then when we get home we'll figure out how we're going to cope. It's a bit of a nightmare and we're lucky that Abbie's parents could step in and are looking after Tilly overnight.'

'Well, don't even think about work. You have a nice run of time off now until after Christmas. I was going to hand you a cheque at our festive lunch tomorrow. It's a Christmas bonus and it comes with my grateful thanks. I'll do a bank transfer instead and I hope it will give some cheer after what you've been through today.'

'Leesa, that's really nice of you and much appreciated, believe me. I feel bad as there are a few things I wanted to wrap up before the hols began. I thought I had another two days to get it done and now this happens. I assure you that I will be jumping online as soon as I can, to get that sorted. Have a great Christmas, Leesa, and I'll see you in the New Year, then.'

A little windfall is always handy, especially at this time of the year. It feels good to be able to recognise hard work in a financial way.

I turn off the main road and begin travelling along the narrow lane. Even before I catch sight of the extended porch, with the impressive stone lions standing guard, my stomach begins to flutter nervously.

In the gloom of the early evening I'm surprised there is no welcoming light to guide visitors to the front door. Suddenly, the anger I've been carrying around with me over Cary's ambivalent attitude towards other people, rises with a vengeance. Matthew is worried sick about him but does he care? No.

Okay, I know why Cary has been avoiding *me*: because he's egotistical, self-obsessed and a coward when it comes to facing up to his feelings. So instead of admitting that he's afraid to commit, he picks on something ridiculous, like thinking there's something going on between Tim and me. And rather than admit that, he accuses me of using Tim as a... what did Cary say? Shield? But the more I think about the situation, the odder it becomes and I know that's part of the reason I'm here. I need to hear him say there is no *us* and it never was real because I'm done with being dragged back into his life when he messes up.

It's obvious that someone is home, as I can see a solitary light coming from the winter sitting room. Pulling onto the gravelled drive, I notice Cary's car isn't here. Then, I wonder if leaving the light on is an added security measure and he isn't here at all, but travelling abroad on either work or pleasure. How am I supposed to know what's going on?

When I get out of the car, I stand for a few moments looking up at the façade of this beautiful old building, grand even in the darkness. One I never thought I'd see up close, ever again. How can I feel nostalgic for a life that was never mine?

I ring the bell and stand back, but nothing happens. After a few minutes I ring again. Then I hammer on the door with my fist. Still nothing. The jacket I'm wearing isn't very thick and I shiver as the cold night air starts to permeate through. Why none of the garden lights are switched on, I don't know, but I figure my best bet is to walk around to the back door. In the dark it's not quite as easy as I thought it would be, and once or twice I stumble, having to save myself from ending up sprawled across the frozen dirt.

There are no lights on at the rear of the house at all. It's beginning to feel a little creepy if I'm honest and the last thing I want is to be wandering around in the dark if I'm here all alone. Even if I cried out for help, there are no neighbours within earshot. Instinctively, I keep going, using the wall as my guide and testing one step ahead rather gingerly with my foot before advancing. Eventually, I can reach out to grab the backdoor handle to check it and, rather shockingly, it turns. With much trepidation, I step inside. I have absolutely no idea where the light switch is located. All I can do is call out and hope someone is home. Someone who belongs here.

'Cary? It's Leesa. You didn't hear the doorbell.' I call out in the shadowy darkness, as loudly as I can.

Suddenly, a quiet voice rears up out of the gloom, making me jump.

'I heard the doorbell. I didn't want to answer it.'

Well, hello to you, too.

'Matthew asked me to drop by to see if you are alright. Is there a reason you're walking around in the dark? Is there a problem with the electrics?'

The downstairs switches must be working, as there is a slight glimmer of light seeping in around the edge of the partially open kitchen door. It's not enough to lighten the room and my eyes are still adjusting after the pitch-black darkness. I have no idea where he's standing. Without warning I hear a click and suddenly everything is bathed in light.

'No. Drop by?'

I squint at him, trying not to look shocked at what I see. Cary is unshaven and has been for a couple of weeks by the look of it. It's strange seeing him with facial hair and he has quite a defined beard and moustache now. Overall, he looks haggard; wearing a crumpled shirt and jeans, most unlike him. Has he been sleeping in his clothes?

He's staring back at me, a blank expression on his face.

'Robert called around, too. You haven't been answering your phone and Matthew was worried. Is your phone working?'

Now he looks back at me, rather confused. 'I didn't know.'

It's obvious something is wrong here. It's not simply the state he's in, or the state the kitchen is in now I'm able to look around. But Cary's reactions are slow and I catch sight of a collection of empty wine bottles.

'You'd better sit down before you fall down. How much alcohol have you had? I'll put the kettle on and start clearing up this mess.' The smell isn't at all pleasant and I'm shocked he would let things deteriorate to this point. 'Have you eaten anything other than takeaways since you've been staying here?'

I slip off my jacket, fill the kettle and begin binning the rubbish that has been abandoned on virtually every available work surface. And this is a big kitchen. Some of the pizza boxes are empty but there's also a lot of wasted food here. It's as if he ordered in, then changed his mind when it arrived.

Fifteen minutes and one large mug of coffee later, Cary is still sitting at the island and continues to watch me, not a word having passed his lips. I've disposed of three black sacks full of rubbish and the worktops have been cleaned with an antibacterial spray and buffed.

'Have you eaten today?' I ask him and after an inordinate pause he answers.

'No.' There's another pause, then a good couple of minutes later, 'I don't think so.'

What's even more worrying is that he needs to stop and consider what I'm saying as if the words aren't making any sense to him.

There's little point in questioning Cary while he's in his alcohol-induced haze. Instead I dive into the freezer, pull out some bread to defrost in the microwave and then grab some butter and cheese from the fridge.

'Cheese on toast coming up,' I inform him.

'I think I ate yesterday,' he adds.

He doesn't seem aware that his behaviour is odd and I hope the caffeine and some food in his stomach will rally him. I'm wondering now whether this is the result of having sunk into some sort of depressive state. His face is thinner and his skin has a sort of pallor to it. I wish I was more clued up but the truth is that inside I'm panicking. I'm the last person anyone would call in when someone is ill. As I gaze at him, he seems unaware of my concerns and I wonder if he even knows what day it is.

When I place the plate in front of him he automatically picks up the knife and fork to begin eating. His movements are slow and methodical. It's as if he's simply going through the motions because that's what you do when someone puts food in front of you. I tell him I'm popping to the cloakroom, but instead I head out into the hallway, turning on lights as I go. Just inside the front door I locate the switches for the outside lights and flick them on, dialling Matthew's number as I walk. What if I've misjudged the situation? His speech isn't slurred, so maybe alcohol isn't at fault here. A cold chill begins to work its way around my body and what I feel is a real sense of fear.

'It's Leesa. I'm here with Cary and there's something wrong with him. Can you come over, right now? I'm not sure if he needs a doctor.'

'I have a bit of a situation going on here and I'm waiting for a nurse to arrive. I'll give Robert a call and tell him it's urgent. He'll get there quicker than I can, anyway. Just keep Cary talking, Leesa. And thank you, my dear. This is so unlike him that I feared something was wrong. I'm more grateful than you can know.'

I hurry back to check on Cary, but he's still eating and hasn't seemed to notice my absence at all. The seconds tick by until eventually the sound of the doorbell makes me physically jump; my nerves are on edge and my hands are trembling.

'Robert, thank you for coming over so promptly. I'm really scared. At first, I thought he was simply hungover, so I made him drink some coffee and eat something. Now I'm wondering if that was a huge mistake. Most of the takeaway food hanging around was almost untouched, so he hasn't been eating. What if he's taken an overdose? I've been here probably half an hour, though, and he wouldn't still be conscious if that was the case – would he?'

'I doubt it. Sounds like we should phone for a doctor, though, just in case. Let's take a look at him first.'

Robert's presence is calming and the sensation of panic subsides a little. I hadn't realised how fast I was breathing and I try to control it, gradually slowing down my pounding heartbeat.

As we walk into the kitchen Cary slowly turns his head in our direction.

'Cary, my friend, how are you doing?' Robert greets him, cheerily.

Cary frowns and the long pause causes Robert to shoot me a look of concern.

'Robert. Why are you here?'

I'm already dialling the emergency number as Robert leans in to me and whispers, 'Doctor it is, then.'

'I was passing by,' Robert explains. He walks over to Cary, taking the seat next to him.

I turn and head out into the hallway as a voice answers and the questioning begins. A few minutes later Robert joins me just as I'm about to hang up. The man on the other end asks if there is anyone here with me who can look out for the vehicle. I confirm, grateful for the way he has drawn information out of me when my head is all over the place.

'Someone's on their way. Robert, do you know what's been going on here?'

He turns to look at me.

'I haven't a clue, Leesa. Wish I did, but I only flew back from Italy a couple of days ago. Matthew rang me yesterday and asked me to pop in and check on Cary. I walked up three times during the day and twice again this morning, but there was no answer. And no sign of any movement inside the house when I peered through the windows. Cary's car wasn't parked up, so naturally I assumed he wasn't here. It must be in the garage. You stay with Cary, I'll have a quick check around upstairs before I head up to the top road. If it's not just alcohol, there might be pill bottles or something we can show the doctor when he arrives. I don't think for one moment it's an overdose but best keep him talking if you can.'

It seems like I wait forever, as I sit next to Cary. Having convinced him that he was better off lying on the bed, he said he couldn't stand having the light on and we're sitting in the gloomy darkness.

He fell into a troubled sleep within minutes, so deep that twice I've leant over him to check that he's still breathing. Suddenly, his voice shatters the eerie silence.

'It's all wrong,' he yells. 'It wasn't my fault... I screwed up...' His words tail off, but he lashes out with his left arm, as if pushing someone away. 'I didn't tell her,' he half-sobs. 'I wanted to, but I couldn't. I was scared and now I'm so cold.'

I jump up as Cary twists and turns, trying to avoid his flailing arms while I tuck the duvet in around him for comfort and warmth. This is beyond painful to watch. I wonder if he thinks I'm Cressida?

'I love her, Grandma,' he adds, softly, confirming my suspicions. 'I love her and that scares me because she's hurting. What if I hurt her too? What if I hurt her... too?'

He lapses into silence and I brush away a solitary tear that trickles down my cheek, as I throw my arms around his body to keep him warm.

31

The Rescue Remedy… is Me

'You have no idea what you've put me through in the last two days, Cary Anderson,' I admonish. 'And now you wake up demanding a bacon sandwich! What do you think I am – your personal nurse, general dogsbody and now a chef, rolled into one?'

'Be grateful it's only a short-term position,' Cary laughs, pressing down on the bed to lever himself into a sitting position. 'However, I know what I am and that is a very lucky man.'

I place a bottle of mineral water in his hands, an empty glass and a sachet from the tray, and instruct him to drink it before I return.

'Well, I'm deadly serious when I say that if there was anyone else who could sit with you I would be driving up that lane right now. This is definitely *not* my calling.' My voice softens. 'But I am relieved you aren't rambling any more. You are hard enough work when you're being your usual, stubborn self but that was something else.'

I'm also thankful the doctor didn't whisk him off to hospital but trusted me to look after him. Who would have thought that would happen? It was scary but I didn't want to leave his side for one single moment. I turn my back on Cary as he begins to pour water into the glass, and head downstairs.

Cooking in someone else's kitchen is a nightmare, especially one as grand as this. But having taken delivery of a large online order to put a stop to the takeaway meals, I'm the official chef by default. But it does feel surreal. I remember watching Cary preparing lunch and not being able to visualise myself ever feeling at ease here. And certainly not finding myself in charge of the cooker, but here I am. Hopefully, tomorrow Cary will be fully rested and back on his feet; my nursing stint will have come to an end, thankfully, and I will have survived. Miraculously, so will have the patient. But this has been my worst nightmare come to life.

The doorbell rings and I head off to answer it. Robert is standing there with a carrier bag in his hand and a warm smile on his face. He enters and we hug, both relieved that our worst fears were unfounded.

'I Googled it after you rang. Some energy drinks for the patient. How is he doing?'

'Much better; there can't be an awful lot wrong with him now if he can face a bacon sandwich. The results of the blood tests came back this morning pretty much in line with what the doctor expected. Low levels of potassium and sodium due to a moderate case of dehydration after a bad case of the flu.'

Robert raises his eyebrows to the heavens.

'I just wish I hadn't been away – the timing was unfortunate, to say the least. I saw him briefly before he flew off to the States on an important work trip but I assumed he'd be staying in London on his return. It was a big mistake Cary coming back here alone – what was he thinking?'

I nod in agreement. 'To be honest with you, Robert, he was probably exhausted, and I had no idea he'd even been away. With no one around to stop him, it sounds to me like he was working all hours. No wonder the flu hit him so hard. Stress can be a killer.'

'Did he say why he let Nicholas go? If he'd been here this could all have been avoided.'

Guilt is like a knife slowly turning in my gut. I feel the exact same way – I let Cary down when he needed me the most and it was only my pride that held me back.

'No. He hasn't said anything about that, Cressida, or Matthew, either. He slept on and off all day yesterday and in between I concentrated on getting those fluids into him, as ordered. I spent the first night in a chair next to the bed and in the early hours of the morning he was ready to talk, so I simply listened. But it was a bit rambly, to be honest. Finally, as the hours passed, the confusion, muscle cramps and general weakness left him. Last night was easier and we both managed some sleep.'

'You look remarkable under the circumstances. You must be shattered.'

'I am. I borrowed a dressing gown and washed my clothes to help perk me up. I ran the iron over them earlier on and then grabbed a quick shower. I feel almost human again.'

'Has he spoken about what happened in London?'

'He was forced out, albeit with a golden handshake. He's awake and sitting up, he'll no doubt tell you all about it. I thought he'd be devastated but, in the end, he was glad to walk away. However, I think the stress of that on top of worrying about Cressida meant the flu hit him hard. He said he could barely make it to the bathroom and back, let alone think about eating or drinking. Can I interest you in a sandwich?'

Robert shakes his head. 'Tempting but I can't stay long, so I'd best pay my regards upstairs.'

As Robert heads to the door he suddenly spins back around. 'Leesa, fate has a funny way of making paths cross when the time is right, doesn't it? Then suddenly everything falls into place. I'd called round and was convinced he wasn't even here, and then you came along at precisely the right moment. Thank God he switched on that light. They do say there is no such thing as a coincidence and maybe that bears some thinking about.'

He disappears out of view, leaving me with a spatula hovering above the frying pan and an astonished look on my face. Talk about déjà vu – that's more or less what Dad said to me.

'I really wasn't expecting you to go to these lengths, you know. A pizza and a salad would have been fine.'

Ah, Cary has laid the table on a par with Nicholas' attentive skills. My mouth is watering at the smell of the fragrant jasmine rice accompanying the lemon soul goujons.

'Stop looking at it and eat,' he insists. 'You've eaten very little for the past three days and now it's my turn to look after you.'

There's nothing at all like fear to focus the mind or get the heart to reveal its true nature.

'That's twice in as many days that you've rescued me now, and I'm going to prove to you that I'm worthy.'

'Twice? And how?' The fish is good, and this man can certainly cook.

'I'm going to sweep you off your feet and leave you in no doubt at all that admitting you loved me was a wise move.'

I almost choke on a forkful of rice I'm in the process of swallowing. Would the legendary Cary Grant have ever said something as ungentlemanly as that? Cressida would be horrified. Concern for her casts a fleeting shadow over my euphoria.

'You trapped me. Asking someone outright if they love you when you are in a confused state, then having the audacity to remember it the next day, is manipulative. To say the very least!'

But that's what happened. In fact, Cary declared his love for me first, but I'm so happy to see him almost back to his usual self, that I won't let on. Because I know he was telling the truth. You can't lie when even stringing a few words together is a challenge. Piecing it all together, when he first returned he was getting everything set up ready to arrive on my doorstep and claim my heart, like a true hero rescuing a damsel in distress. Not least, I will add, because he had this silly idea that I was attracted to Tim. That bit didn't make any sense at all, obviously, but he was delirious at the time.

'I want you in my life,' he'd muttered in a groggy voice. 'I never should have let you go. I thought it was too late and I didn't give you flowers.'

It sounded like he went downhill quickly. He admitted he wanted to call me but didn't want me to see him helpless and sick. My heart squished up then. Listening to Cary in the darkened room as he rambled on, filled me with joy and hope. Besides, at that point I'd already come to terms with the fact that I was hopelessly in love with him. You don't sit up all night watching over someone, fearfully, if they don't mean anything to you. There was nothing left to hide, or to doubt.

Every single word he uttered was from the heart because he wasn't in a state to dress it up or mask his true feelings.

'The only cloud on the horizon now we've sorted ourselves out is how on earth are we going to get everyone else back on track?' He frowns, the size of the problem does seem rather daunting.

We stop eating and look across at each other, uneasily.

'Still nothing from Cressida?'

'She's still on lockdown until she's met her deadline. Her phone is switched off every time I've tried, but that's so like her. She never knows where she's put it down, anyway. I've had a few email updates, but I can tell she's under pressure as they are just one-liners saying she's getting there. I don't want to add to her pressure or make her rush back before she's good and ready. She deserves to take all the time she needs to sort herself out.'

'Cressida is going to panic when she finds out about what you've been through and realises what could have happened. I texted Matthew once we knew what was wrong with you. He sent back two words – 'thank God' and that was it. I don't think he's very well at the moment.'

I've been holding that piece of information back.

'He's ill?' Cary frowns. 'I hope he hasn't had this flu thing because I'm fit and strong and look at the toll it took on me. Should we go and see him?'

'I suggest you phone him first to give him an update and ask whether there's anything he needs. He's a very private man and he'll only accept help if he wants it. Do you feel up to visiting my parents after you've spoken to Matthew? I haven't said very much to them, only that I'm spending a couple of days at Cressida's. They didn't ask questions but they will be concerned if I don't make contact soon. I think this is something we need to tell them face to face.'

'Let's not hang around, then. The chocolate brownies can wait. It's time to kick our families into shape. When we get back I'll ring Laurence. Scanning my phone, I see he sent another photo of baby Alice. Now I'm totally over the flu I can't wait to meet our newest little niece.'

Our?

'Cary, you don't think we're ignoring the proverbial elephant in the room?'

'Which is?'

'Can you really see us here, making a success of running this house together? And the whole baby issue. I know it's important for you, but even the thought of that terrifies me.'

He reaches out to grab my hand in his.

'It wasn't your fault. You didn't do anything wrong, Leesa.'

To my horror, I realise he heard every word I said that night when I let out everything I'd been bottling up inside of me. I wanted him to know but I didn't want him to remember.

'I can't take on that sort of responsibility, Cary, it would be too much. I simply wouldn't have a clue what to do. I barely managed to get through this incident with you and it served to remind me that when it comes to illness I go into blind panic mode. I'm no Sally, and that's the truth.'

He searches my eyes with his own but there's no concern reflected back at me.

'And I'm no Laurence. We will figure it out, I promise you. I love looking after kids and if we decide it's for us, then I'm more than up for a career change. I can be the house husband, or whatever the politically correct term is these days. I'm only sorry I can't do the giving birth bit. It doesn't seem like a fair exchange, but if you can face going through it then I promise I will take over.'

'House spouse is popular, I believe,' I retort, grinning at him. 'I can't promise anything other than that I will think about it. Just tell Sally if we do this, not to enlighten me about the process until we're past the point of no return.'

'I will and there's no pressure, whatever happens we're going to be happy.'

'You're really prepared to cook and clean and change nappies? And I'll closet myself away in the study, building a little empire to feed our growing brood? What if I can only face going through it the once?'

'By the time we throw in that dog and the two cats you mentioned when describing your dream, I think that will be more than enough to keep us busy. And bring this house to life again.'

I mull it over. Could it really be as easy as that? Everything suddenly slotting into place?

'I'm not sure I can earn enough to cover the costs of running this house. What if my business doesn't go from strength to strength as planned?'

Cary rises from his seat and walks around to my side of the table, then he kneels down next to me. Lifting my hand to his mouth, he plants a kiss on it.

'I think we'll have enough in the bank not to have to worry unduly. I'll sell the place in London and I'm considering taking up a couple of non-executive directorships I've been offered. But the big news is that I've been approached to join an official think-tank, tasked with pulling together an advisory report for the Secretary of State for Business, Energy and Industrial Strategy. It's time to drive forward and manage the energy legacy by shortening the timescales laid down to meet those targets. That's what delayed me rushing straight over to drag you back here.'

I can't suppress a grin at the mental image that is conjured up of Cary beating down my door or sitting around a table talking about one of the other passions in his life.

'I like a challenge and most of the work can be done from home. I could make a real difference, Leesa, just in a slightly different way to the one I'd originally planned. We can make this work. Strike that, we *will* make it work.'

I'm scared to venture forward into the unknown, I will admit that. But when your heart makes it impossible to say no, what can you do but jump on board and go along for the ride?

I don't need a man in my life to be happy, but I do need Cary. I was once in love with the idea of being in love. Then I decided that I was never going to trust a man again because, clearly, I didn't even know what love was. And suddenly, here I am and I can't help myself. It's either true love, or insanity. And now none of that matters, anyway.

'The answer is yes. But don't expect me to commit to a lavish wedding, even to please Cressida. Being the centre of attention isn't my thing and I'd probably end up tripping over my dress and spoiling it all as I walk up the aisle.'

Cary frowns. 'Hmm. How can we please everyone at the same time? What if we have a close family and friends only ceremony and then let Cressida arrange a big party here, after we come back from honeymoon?'

Ugh. Big party.

'Well, I survived the Santa Clause, guess I can survive the Wedding Clause. But first I have an idea about Christmas. We have sixteen days to make it all happen and get everyone together for the first time under one roof.'

Cary's face is a picture.

'And you think we can make that happen?'

'We make things happen every single day in our professional lives. It's time to get some invites out and apply a little pressure, where needed.'

'You mean Grandma and your sister?'

'Yes! We'll start making lists of what we need to buy. I want to welcome Cressida back and make her feel proud of us, and how we've looked after the house. Maybe she'll decide to stay on after all.'

'You'd do that?'

'Of course.'

'But what if she doesn't turn up?'

'Can you see Cressida enjoying Christmas without seeing her grandsons and great-grandchildren, especially when it's the first Christmas for one of them?'

Cary throws his arms around me and what was meant to be a happy embrace ends up turning into something else entirely.

An hour later and it's time to head out to begin sorting out the people we love. Our revised contract has now been signed, sealed and well and truly delivered – which makes us a truly formidable team. Life is about to get its ass kicked!

CHRISTMAS EVE

32

Counting Down

The big day is tomorrow, and Cary and I are nervously excited. We have badgered and cajoled every single person on our list to be here. It's going to be a huge Christmas celebration and the wonderful Nicholas is back in situ to help make it happen. And he will also have a starring role, but in the meantime there is a lot still to do.

When Cary agreed to his request to take early retirement because Nicholas felt 'the time was right', they both realised that it was for the best. It was acknowledging that it would be easier on Cressida when she returned, as everything would be different anyway. It was the right thing to do.

With Nicholas' direction we've all been working as a tight team and the house looks amazing. But without the help of some dear family and friends, we would have struggled to make the Christmas magic happen. And tonight, fingers crossed, Cressida will step over the threshold for the first time in some months for a little preview before the main event tomorrow.

'She will turn up, won't she?' Cary leans in to whisper as I stand alongside Nicholas, arranging canapés on a plate.

'Of course she will. She promised.'

Nicholas discreetly disappears, and I turn to face Cary, noting that anxious look of his.

'You look good; the house looks amazing and we're together. What on earth is there to be anxious about?'

He drapes his body around me, gathering me up in his arms as if I'm the most precious thing in the world to him.

'You're right. Nothing at all. With you by my side suddenly every day seems that little bit brighter. I know that we'll cope with the bad, and celebrate the good, together. A man can't ask for any more than that.' The kiss he gently bestows upon my lips is full of promise. A lifetime of love awaits us both.

'I'll leave you to it and go watch out for her taxi. Don't get anything on that dress, which looks totally stunning on you, by the way. In case I didn't say.'

He said. Three times already. Cary smirks as he passes Nicholas, who is clearly returning to chivvy us along. Nicholas can barely keep a straight face.

'I think we're almost ready, Leesa,' he announces.

'Well, we couldn't have done it without you, Nicholas. And Cressida will be keen to catch up with your news. She will have missed you, but it's all-change now, for us all.'

He nods in agreement. 'It's often hard to accept it when it comes, but although there is a tinge of sadness, there's so much happiness to look forward to, all round. I will miss the Grande Dame, though. She's like a beacon; she inspires everyone around her to be the best they can and she's always led by example. There will never be another woman in my mind who comes even close.'

Amen to that.

'Does Laurence have our special surprise in hand for tomorrow?'

Nicholas' eyes light up. 'He does. It still remains a secret at the moment and let's hope it stays that way. Cressida is going to love it.'

'And the outdoor arrangement?'

'Double-checked first thing this morning.'

'It's not too much, Nicholas, is it? I just feel everyone has been through a lot lately and Cary and I want the adults to be wowed as much as the kids. That's a tall order, isn't it?'

'It is but I'm confident you're going to pull it off.'

I laugh. 'I think *we're* going to pull it off.'

Cary dashes in through the door. 'She's here and Granddad is with her!'

The three of us exchange a look of total disbelief. If he's joking it's in poor taste. We hoped Matthew would come, but the two of them sharing the taxi and arriving together is hard to believe.

'This I have to see for myself.'

True enough, as Nicholas swings open the front door in the traditional welcome every visitor has received since Cressida took up the reins, Cressida and Matthew are heading up the path. Cary shoots me a worried look. Cressida is leaning heavily on Matthew's arm for some reason. He hurries out the door to assist, taking her other arm.

'My goodness!' Cressida exclaims, as her eyes begin to take in the lavishly decorated porch that now looks a little like Santa's grotto. Filled with greenery from the woods by Robert and his guys, the holly is awash with waxy red berries and the myriad of mistletoe proudly displays its almost transparent white globes. 'What a picture this is!'

It's clear to see that she has lost a lot of weight and all three of us are in shock.

'The fire is lit in the winter sitting room, let's head in there and make Cressida comfortable,' I direct, a sense of dread washing over me.

Glancing at Cary, then across at Nicholas, there are no smiles, just pure concentration as she's helped inside. She looks frail.

Once Cressida is settled down in her favourite armchair, with a soft pillow at her back, she quickly shoos everyone away.

'That's enough. I'm comfortable, thank you, and it's not as bad as it looks.'

Nicholas heads off to get a tray of drinks, having taken Matthew to one side to enquire specifically about Cressida's requirements. It's touching to see their mutual concern.

'Grandma, first things first. This is a bit of a… shock.' Cary sounds distraught and the effect upon him of seeing her looking so vulnerable is heart-stopping.

'I'm over the worst and on the mend. I have no intention of leaving you any time soon and that's why I elected for surgery.'

Cary and I sink down onto the sofa; as we do, he grabs my hand, and I give his a reassuring squeeze in return.

'I've had my aortic valve replaced. Blood was flowing back into my heart and causing me all sorts of problems. I didn't intend taking any risks at all, I can assure you both, but this was something I needed to do on my own. Well, I say on my own, but Matthew has been with me every step of the way.'

Matthew places his hand on her shoulder, taking over the story.

'We both felt it was the best way to handle this and ultimately it was about getting Cressida through it with the least stress. There have been a few complications, and this is the first time we've been able to get out of the lodge since the last trip to hospital. The operation was a success, but it is major surgery and unfortunately Cressida developed an infection in the wound. That has slowed her recovery but we've just had the all-clear.'

Cary and I sit, open-mouthed as it begins to sink in what she's been through.

'I can't believe you kept that from me, Grandma. Anything could have happened, what then?'

She looks at Cary with acceptance written all over her face.

'Sometimes you need to rely on your faith to get you through a sticky time. I'm not done yet, so stop fussing. A couple more weeks and the doctors say I'll be good as new. Now, what's been happening here?'

We sit for a long while talking about our plans for the future and our hopes that Cressida will return to be a part of it. It's only when Cressida runs out of questions that Cary begins to question her.

'So, you've been staying with Granddad since you came out of hospital? How did that happen? The last I knew you two hadn't spoken since, when, New Year's Eve?'

Matthew is now perched on a straight-backed chair which Nicholas has pulled up next to Cressida. The two of them look at each other and Matthew nods. When Cressida looks back at us her face shows determination.

'I'm not coming back here, Cary. This is the future for you and Leesa. The future I'd dreamed about for you but didn't really know if it would fall into place. People do silly things and often don't listen to what that little voice inside is trying to tell them.'

'You mean, I'm stubborn. Well, where do you think I got that from?' Cary is only half-joking but she smiles back at him.

'Touché. When you lectured me that night of our not-so-cosy dinner, it did make me take stock of my life.'

They haven't taken their eyes off each other while she's been speaking and now Cary is looking ill-at-ease.

'I had no idea you were ill, Grandma. It was very wrong of me.'

'No, very right of you, Cary. I headed off to spend a night at a small hotel in Cardiff to think. At the time I was waiting for the doctor to phone with the results of some tests and I had no idea what I was facing. If I had, then maybe I wouldn't have taken that next step.'

She turns to look at Matthew.

'Cressida turned up on my doorstep, unannounced, with two suitcases before I'd even had a chance to drink my first coffee of the day. The moment she walked over the doorstep I knew everything was going to be alright.'

They smile at each other.

'Well, I wasn't quite so sure of that, if I'm being honest. I thought if my time was limited then you were right, Cary. I needed to listen because it wasn't over.'

Matthew chuckles. 'And boy, did I talk. In fact, afterwards Cressida said I'd more than made up for all those years of silence.'

The ease with which they seamlessly pick up each other's conversation is wonderful to see.

'I moved into Matthew's guest suite. Once the doctor confirmed I needed open-heart surgery I focused on finishing off my work in progress. Matthew waited on me, attentively. And the dear man has continued to do so every day since. It hasn't been easy, and I did suggest employing a nurse, but we coped. Sometimes the hero in your life is absent for a while. A long while. But when you need him, he's there by your side and you realise that's all that counts.'

Matthew nods, endorsing every single word she's said, and my eyes fill with tears. I can't even look at Cary because he's silent, too, and I'm guessing there's a huge lump in his throat.

'We're not youngsters, we know that. The guest suite will be Cressida's new office and when she's completely well we'll move her into the lodge. Knowing Cressida, there will be a few changes to come.'

He glances at her, hesitantly.

'It's perfect as it is, Matthew. My days of putting up with building works are over and all I want is a little peace and quiet to write.'

'As soon as she's up to it, we will be heading off to Spain for an extended holiday,' Matthew adds, 'but we'll be available to fit in with your plans.'

They both look at us, expectantly. I'm still processing everything that's happened, but Cary is way ahead of me.

'It's going to be a no-fuss wedding, we'll warn you of that now. But tomorrow, well, it will be full of surprises and everyone will be here. It's the first time our two respective families will all be together under one roof. It won't be too much for you, will it, Grandma?' Cary's concern is very real and mirrors my own thoughts.

'If you two begin treating me like an invalid when I'm on the mend, then I'm going to get very cross indeed. I've done nothing but rest for the best part of three months now. I will be sitting down a fair bit and we will head off immediately after dinner, if you don't mind. But after a good night's sleep we're both really looking forward to joining in the fun.'

On the way to the car, Cressida hangs back and I catch her arm as the others go on ahead of us. It's clear there's something she wants to share with me and she waits until they are out of earshot.

'I wasn't abandoning Cary, Leesa, and I want you to know that. It was coming up to the anniversary of Katherine's death and for some reason, it was different this year. I never had the time to really let go of that anger I've always felt over losing her. It was all about being strong and keeping everyone going.

'But facing the prospect of my own mortality, I suppose, caused a chain reaction and I found myself thinking about the people I'd be leaving behind. Writing is cathartic for me and as I channeled my emotions into what turned out to be a story of love and loss, I was able – finally – to accept the unthinkable. That's not something I can bring myself to explain to Cary, but if the opportunity arises to explain to him that I wasn't running away from everything, I'd be very grateful to you. If indeed, it does make any sort of sense at all.

'I needed to heal my soul and I know that sounds rather indulgent, selfish even. But it's a fact.'

Tears begin to sting behind my eyelids as we draw to a halt, standing alone in the vast hallway.

'No, it doesn't.' My voice breaks and I stifle a sob. 'I had a miscarriage, Cressida, so I know a little bit about losing someone, albeit I never got to hold my baby girl in my arms. But it was the sort of loss that leaves a hole that can never be filled. Why would you want to fill it with something else, anyway? It's a special place, for them, isn't it? Your daughter is a big part of who you are and that love will remain in here forever.' I place my free hand over my heart, realising I'm speaking for us both.

'Last Christmas was my time to grieve,' I admit. 'Without even knowing it, Cary was instrumental in getting me through that time. I'm just glad you were able to share your moment with Matthew. Cary will understand that.'

Cressida squeezes my arm against her side, affectionately.

'The hard part is acceptance, isn't it? Even a mother's love can't change destiny. We simply have to be grateful for what we did have, knowing they touched our lives in a very real way.'

As we begin to walk forward once more, Cressida's words fill my heart with a strange sense of peace. What I saw as a failure on my part was really my inability to accept something that was never within my power to influence. Hearing someone else say that, someone who really understands, is like lifting a heavy weight off my back. It's finally time for me, too, to let go of the guilt.

'Never give up hope, Leesa. Life has wonderful plans for you and so does my grandson. He won't fail you.'

*

It's 6 a.m. and the house is buzzing with activity.

'Do you need help?' I ask Cary, who is on his hands and knees on the floor in the main hall, wrapping presents.

'No. I'm good. After this I'll head into the kitchen and get those sausage and bacon rolls on the go. Laurence is due to arrive shortly to help out.'

'Right, if you're sure you can cope, then I'll help Nicholas with the greenery for the marquee.'

Cary stands, easing out his stiff back and then scooping me into his arms.

'Thank you, Leesa.'

'Um… for what, exactly?'

'For being there when I needed you most, for not giving up on me and for compromising.'

'Fool, that's what life is all about,' I mutter, standing on tip-toe to plant a kiss firmly on his mouth. 'Now get back to work. If we want our visitors to enter Santa's Kingdom for a day they will never forget, then that sort of magic requires hard work.'

'You mean Santa's little helpers aren't on their way to sort it out for us?'

I wink at him and turn to walk away, calling out over my shoulder, 'I have news for you, you are one of Santa's little helpers.'

Heading into the dining room, the table is piled high with greenery.

'Nicholas, I'm ready to give a hand before I get the call to start ferrying around the hearty breakfast sandwiches. We need to keep Robert and his guys happy to make up for getting them up so early. Hopefully everything will be in place by nine at the latest and they will all be able to get off home to change and collect their families. Do you know, I can't remember ever feeling this level of excitement about Christmas before. Isn't that crazy?'

Nicholas smiles as we stand together bundling little bunches of holly, fir and ivy together. This could take a while.

In the meantime, up at the entrance to the drive Robert and his men are turning the front garden and drive into a snow scene. Today the forecast is dry and sunny, which is great but not very festive, is it?

We've asked everyone to come dressed for an outdoor winter wonderland experience. The marquee is heated, but the kids will no doubt be running all over the place, so it seemed like a good idea at the time.

Thick woolly jumpers, padded ski jackets, warm knitted hats and snow boots. Well, the temperature will require that, even if the sun is shining and now we need to work on creating that ambience. I can't help but laugh to myself – what a difference a year makes and what a year it's been.

With family, friends and all the neighbours invited to share in the fun there are going to be over seventy people arriving in less than four hours' time, now. This house will have brought a lot of people together over the years to share joyful times – birthdays, anniversaries and the like. For Cary and me this is a way of sharing our happiness with the people who mean the most to us. We are counting our blessings and sharing the love in our hearts.

33

The wooden gates to the drive are closed and the crowd in front of it is growing. Cary has Cressida's arm firmly tucked into his side and he gives Robert a nod.

As the gates are flung open the children cluster around Cressida and Cary, but it isn't only their eyes that are glowing as I turn to scan the smiling faces.

The North Pole has come to Porthkerry and there is a collective gasp. Virtually the entire area has a little dusting of snow as two machines spew out little mini blizzards. Stacks of white plastic snowballs, destined for the local children's playgroup once the festivities are over, have the kids running on ahead. Cary guides Cressida forward and I walk alongside them.

'This is beautiful, darlings. Look at everyone's faces. I can't quite believe it, and this is certainly a Christmas I will remember forever. We all will.'

She gathers us close for a group hug and I look over her shoulder at Matthew. He's not an overly expressive man but I can see that he's moved.

'The house is in good hands,' Cressida states, happiness radiating from her.

I step aside to let Matthew take Cressida's arm and Cary gets the hint, relinquishing his place.

Sidling up to me, he plants a kiss on my cheek as Matthew steers Cressida in the direction of Robert.

'We must be mad,' I whisper. 'But happiness is infectious, isn't it? And we have such a lot to celebrate and share.'

'Whatever happens in the future, today is a chance to bring everyone together for the first time but it also marks so many new beginnings. Ah, look who I've spotted – hi, little Alice. Can I get the first hold?' Cary is already marching up to Laurence, impatient to meet his niece in person for the first time.

Sally homes in for a welcoming hug, with Laurence closing in behind her.

'We couldn't be more thrilled that you're back,' she says, beaming from ear to ear.

'I've missed you all so much. Look at Alice, she's so tiny.'

We turn to look at Cary, peering down at a cute, little pink face which peeks out from a furry white snowsuit.

'She looks like a pile of snowballs,' Chloe says, appearing from nowhere. 'Mum, they have snowflake curtains and they're so pretty. Can I have some for my bedroom, please?'

Before Sally can open her mouth to speak, Cary chimes in.

'Of course you can, you know that Uncle Cary will always say yes, Chloe.'

Sally rolls her eyes, but she's not annoyed. 'Isn't that the truth?'

'Time to give her back, Uncle Cary,' Laurence levels at his brother. 'I'm off to find Grandma and Granddad. Thanks for the phone call last night. It was a shock, I will admit, as we've been worried sick. Though we've had our hands full as you can imagine. I understand why Grandma handled it that way. And are you good now, brother, considering what you've been through?'

I'm half-listening to two conversations at the same time. Sally is telling me how thrilled she is to see the kids so excited, thanking us for taking the stress out of their Christmas. As they try to gather up their brood to go in search of Cressida and Matthew, I yank the phone out of my ski jacket pocket.

I texted Mum, Dad and Beth this morning to say Happy Christmas and all three responded, but there's still no sign of them.

'What's up?' Cary appears at my side, looking down at my phone. 'Problems?'

'I hope not,' I reply.

'I'm introducing people as I move around but it's probably going to be easier for people to gather in groups once everyone is in the marquee. With so many kids running around it's a constant distraction but it's a good sort of chaos, isn't it?'

'Leesa!'

I look up and there's Beth, followed by Mum, Dad and bringing up the rear – Will.

'We've brought a gatecrasher. And look!' Beth holds out her left hand, the one that used to sport an engagement ring. It's missing still, but in its place is a shiny, white gold wedding band. Will holds up his left hand in a mock wave, flashing a matching ring and I gasp. These two wasted thousands of pounds and they go off and tie the knot, just like that? I look at Mum and Dad, questioningly.

'Were you in on this?' I tease, assuming they were.

'Not at all. First we knew was when they called around this morning to pick us up.'

I reach out and hug Beth, as Will and Cary do a manshake.

'Hearty congratulations, guys,' Cary adds. 'I think we'll be doing much the same thing but I'm awaiting my orders.'

Will laughs and leans forward to give his new sister-in-law a bear hug, literally lifting me off my feet.

'I knew it wasn't over,' I whisper into his ear. 'You're a keeper, Will, and I said that from the start.'

'We lost our way for a little while there and forgot what really mattered,' Will admits.

Beth sidles up to place her hand in his, gazing up at him.

'Who needs a flashy, diamond engagement ring when they have the man of their dreams? Our debts have been cleared and that's all behind us now. Some lessons are worth learning.'

Wow, I never thought I'd hear my sister say those words but, then, it was one huge learning curve, that's for sure.

'Big step for you, too,' Will continues. 'Juggling a busy career, planning a wedding and looking after this impressive house. Thank goodness you're an organiser.'

It is a bit daunting and I can see why that would register with him, given what he's just been through.

'I have a good man by my side and I know that somehow we'll manage. You are so right, Will, when you say it's all about remembering what's important and not getting caught up in things that don't really matter in the grand scheme of life.'

Cary catches the tail end of our conversation.

'Yes, a really good man.'

'One who is going to be hands on at home,' I add with a measure of satisfaction.

'Shh! Don't let Beth hear that. I'm useless around the house and I'm counting on her to sort all that stuff out.'

Cary claps him on the back. 'Every one of us is different, Will. What matters is that you find a way through it that works for you both.'

Dad and Mum have disappeared, and I cast around, wondering where they've gone.

'I introduced them to Cressida and Matthew. They've gone inside to have a chat and a hot drink. I didn't think you'd mind,' Cary explains.

'Aww,' Beth moans. 'I'm so excited to meet her. It will be a fan girl moment, but I'll try my best not to shriek!'

Oh dear, she isn't joking.

Beth links arms with me and pulls me to one side. 'I'm sorry I couldn't say anything but after the wedding fiasco I wanted to prove to Will that none of it mattered. Saying "I do" only involves two people when you get right down to it. The rest is just cosmetic.'

I look at Beth and I can see how happy she is; I feel so proud of the woman she's turning into. Some lessons come at a price that is worth paying, but that doesn't make it easy.

'Oh, I hope this doesn't upset you, but I bumped into Sheryl. She said to thank you and that she's decided to re-think her life. I don't know what she meant, exactly, but she made me promise I'd pass on the message. I was rather surprised the two of you were still in touch.'

Beth's eyes search mine.

'It's fine. We aren't, it was just a one-off. I'm glad she's okay but I don't think about the past any more. What's done is done.'

'Good,' Beth says with gusto. 'We'll toast the future together, in a bit. I'd better go in search of my husband – oh, that sounds so wonderful!'

We hug each other excitedly, before heading off in opposite directions.

I catch up with Cary and we continue to wander around, meeting, greeting and introducing. What I love is that it does look rather like we could be in a snow-covered resort. We are surrounded by a crowd of fellow snow worshippers, wearing fur trimmed parkas and brightly coloured skiwear. The air is still, but cold, so everyone has that rosy-cheeked, pink nose thing going on. Except the kids, who are all glowing and a little sweaty from all the chasing around they are doing. I can imagine the children's faces at the local playgroup when we arrive to fill a huge paddling pool with these plastic balls on their first day back after Christmas.

Cary eventually pulls me to one side. 'We have an hour and a half until it's time to serve the buffet. Robert says that the hog roast is coming along nicely and we can relax. Everything is in hand. Happy?'

'Ecstatic. You?'

'I can't believe how lucky we are, and we seem to be surrounded by good news. Grandma is on the mend; Granddad is back by her side, where he belongs; Beth and Will, well, they were meant for each other and I'm glad they managed to turn it around. That can't have been easy for them. Your mum and dad are beaming. And here we are – you and me, together as a real couple. Did it occur to you that it's our first anniversary? The day our verbal contract was put into practice.'

In all the excitement I'd totally forgotten.

'Come on.' Cary grabs my hand and pulls me away from the house.

'We can't just disappear.'

'Nicholas will take charge and we can swan back in at the last moment. Besides, next on the agenda is hot chocolate with marshmallows and gingerbread men fresh from the oven. That should distract them all for a while.'

He leads me out into the lane and we wander down to our bench to sit, staring out at the viaduct. With the azure blue sky above us so reminiscent of the first time I was here, it's magical. Overhead, the boughs of the old oak trees are decorated with huge balls of mistletoe and creeping ivy, as nature puts on its own festive display.

'The Santa Clause was a good start, wasn't it? The Easter Clause was a bit tricky, I will admit. But I think we've thrashed out the details for the Marriage Clause and, God willing, the Baby Clause.' Cary sounds content, as if he's signing off on our future plans with great expectations of what's to come.

'That's everything sorted, then. How did you refer to our arrangement, once? Civilised, I think was the word,' I remind him.

'Oh. What was I thinking? That isn't the way to a woman's heart, is it? You don't have to be Cary Grant to know that. Love, I've come to discover, is all-consuming, not civilised at all. How could it be? Because suddenly nothing else matters but that one thing; that one person. But you must forgive me as I had no idea at all where it was all heading and that was the old me. What I thought of as a convenient temporary fix turned out to be my grand passion in life. Now there's an idea for Cressida's next story. No prizes for guessing the moral of that one, though.'

Our laughter echoes around us.

I cast around, watching a man and woman heading in our general direction, a cute little puppy straining on the leash in front of them. As they get closer I don't recognise the breed but it's a jolly little thing. They head for the bench and I move over a little to make room for them.

'Hey little guy,' I put my hand down and ruffle his head as he tries to jump up on my lap.

'Here you go, Cary,' the man says, handing the lead to him but he doesn't take it. Instead he turns to look at me.

'Happy Christmas, Leesa.'

I clap my hands to my face in delight, leaving the puppy to jump around excitedly.

'What's his... her name?'

'That's entirely up to you. She's a cross between a beagle and a basset hound. She's the last of four pups and she needed a home. I didn't intend getting you a four-legged Christmas present, I will be honest, but when I popped down to the farm first thing this morning, we crossed paths. And that, as they say, was that.'

The man looks at me, nodding. 'She's the last one of the litter to go and dogs, like a lot of animals, choose their owners.'

A name pops into my head with hardly any conscious thought at all. 'Bibi. We'll call her Bibi.'

Cary pulls out his phone and taps away. 'It says here it's French for "lady of the house".'

'Perfect!' I exclaim.

The man shakes Cary's hand and the woman extends him a warm smile.

'We're thrilled you're able to take her. Our house is the one further down the lane on the left. We're just off to visit family in Bristol so can't make the party, but we'll arrange for you both to pop in for a drink soon and meet Bibi's parents. She has a sweet nature and deserves a good home.'

I stand, shaking their hands before I take control of Bibi's lead. A little thrill runs through me. Suddenly it all feels so real. Welcoming Bibi marks the beginning and I scan around, thinking this is the start of a new life and one I could never have imagined.

It's late afternoon and people head off home, stomachs full and throats hoarse from the Christmas karaoke session. I think our rendition of 'O Come All Ye Faithful' almost shook the huge marquee off its pitch. 'Gangnam Style' was the kids' favourite though and had them all prancing around, it was hilarious. Now to steer the family back inside, as Nicholas and Robert have already gone on ahead to prepare for us.

'It's been a wonderful day, Leesa. You two worked really hard to pull this off.' Mum gives me a hug, her eyes full of delight. At last my parents have had the Christmas they deserve and, for once, they were able to sit back and simply enjoy it.

'Right, everyone,' I shout above the general chatter, 'let's head inside for one last treat.'

There's no squealing from the kids because the noisiest ones are already inside. Cary and Matthew are either side of Cressida, but she doesn't seem to be flagging and I take that as a good sign that she really is over the worst.

We filter in through the French doors and on into the large open area at the foot of the stairs. The Christmas tree isn't quite as perfect as last year's, I fancy, but it's still an awesome sight to behold.

Robert and Nicholas have set up a semicircle of chairs several feet back from the base of the tree and we settle Cressida down in the middle of the row.

'What's this?' she asks, curiously.

On cue, the music strikes up and everyone scrambles to take a seat.

Laurence enters, dressed as a shepherd and carrying a folded screen. Following close behind him, Jackson is carrying a small manger in his arms.

As the backing track unfolds the story of Christmas, Laurence sets up the screen off to one side and Jackson rather ceremoniously places the manger in front of it. As we hear about the star guiding the Three Wise Men to the stable there's a lot of posturing between the two of them and I look around to see everyone is smiling. Is that a tea-towel on Laurence's head, I wonder?

From behind the screen Sally, who is wearing a long pale blue robe, quickly appears, placing baby Alice in the manger. Everyone begins to clap, falling silent only when they realise she is asleep. Tired out by a day of being handed around and fawned over, no doubt.

It's time for the Three Wise Men to appear and suddenly little Chloe enters far right, to a collective 'aah'. Walking slowly and with great solemnity in her cute white garment, she's holding up a cardboard banner on a pole. It depicts the three Kings riding across the hills on the backs of camels. She jostles the pole a little as the narrative describes their perilous journey. The stable is beginning to take shape and last, but not least, Daisy appears. She's dressed in a long white garment, too, and is carrying a box with three gifts. One wrapped in gold paper, one in silver and one in purple. She turns for a moment when she draws level with her great-grandma to give her a big grin and we all chuckle.

As the story draws to a close our little baby Jesus stirs, and the wailing begins. Sally stoops to pick her up, cradling her in her arms, making a poignant tableau when Laurence and the kids draw round her. The Christmas story has been told and Alice is now competing with the strains of a full choir singing 'O Little Town of Bethlehem'. There isn't a dry eye in the house and on the final note everyone is on their feet, clapping loudly. Sally bows and makes a quick exit with Alice to feed her.

'You guys were amazing,' Cressida announces, walking across to give each of them a hug in turn.

'We did it for you, Great-Grandma. Daddy said that you haven't been very well and he thought we should do something to make you feel better.'

'Oh, my cherubs, I do! I feel wonderful.'

What increases my joy is seeing Mum, Dad, Beth and Will feeling a part of this, even though for them it must all be a little overwhelming. I felt the same way on my first visit. But when all is said and done it's just a house, a rather grand one, but bricks and mortar all the same.

Cary appears from behind the screen, Bibi at his heels with her little tail wagging.

'No blips with the CD, well done, darling,' I pat him on the back as I plant a kiss on his cheek.

Suddenly the jolliest Santa I think I've ever seen appears just a couple of paces behind Cary. And what a job Cary has done of turning Nicholas into Saint Nick.

'I think it's present time. Ho! Ho! Ho!' he declares in a robust, bass tone to the accompaniment of loud squeals.

Cressida is standing next to me and whispers into my ear.

'Has Matthew brought the presents in from the car?' I nod, and she gives me a smile that says so much more. It comes from the heart; a very happy and contented heart that is strong once more.

Laurence assists Santa in sorting out the presents into piles. There are token gifts for the adults and some special gifts for the kids.

We move the chairs closer to the tree so that we can all watch as the little ones sit on the floor and begin the grand opening. Well, the tearing and the ripping. And yapping from an excited Bibi. But we all know it's not about the gifts, because we've already had the perfect Christmas Day.

Cary catches my eye and with a tilt of his head directs me to follow him. The present-opening stops for a moment as everyone looks up. Cary takes my hand and leads me over to the bottom of the staircase and proceeds to get down on one knee.

'Leesa Nichole Oliver,' he begins and I look across at my parents, frowning. Who told him about the Nichole? What other little snippets of information have they been sharing about me, I wonder?

'I have your father's permission to ask the question. Will you make me the happiest man alive and marry me?'

He pulls a pink plastic ring out of his pocket and I burst out laughing. It's one from the crackers on the buffet table.

'Yes.' With a little shove, he eases it over my knuckle and it appears to fit.

Cary stands and I assume he's going to kiss me. Instead he turns to our audience and does a rather theatrical mopping of his brow with one hand.

'Phew. If she's willing to accept a plastic ring then I know I've chosen the right one. I just wanted to say that you have all made today a wonderful occasion. It means so much to both Leesa and me, that you could all be here to share this moment with us.'

And then he does kiss me, to 'oohs' and 'aahs' from the assembled crowd, who break into another round of applause.

'Right, back to the unwrapping! Merry Christmas everyone!' he declares.

We stand hand in hand, and as things settle back down, he turns to face me.

'Merry Christmas my soon-to-be Mrs Leesa Anderson. God, that gives me a thrill to hear myself say that. As soon as we get a chance we will go ring shopping.'

I hold out my hand to stare down at my ring.

'I don't know, I think I rather like this one. I might not want to take it off.'

Slipping my arms around his neck, I sink into him, thinking I have everything I need right here. Cary rather skilfully scoops me up into his arms and carries me across the hallway. Glancing upwards, I start laughing as I gaze at the mistletoe.

'We'd better not waste it,' I say, a little breathless with excitement as our lips meet. His touch is gentle at first, then more insistent until we remember where we are.

As I cast my eye over his shoulder, surveying the festive scene and smiling faces, I begin to think about the series of coincidences that led to this moment. The sudden snowstorm and being stranded; getting to know Cary and his family, then losing all contact; and now, being given a second chance. We've both discovered that all you need to do is to listen to your heart, let go of the past and grab a slice of happiness with both hands when it comes your way. Like we're grabbing each other now.

'Right time, right place,' I mutter to myself. Then, as I gaze up adoringly at Cary, 'And best of all, the right man.'

I knew my very own mistletoe moment would come and it didn't disappoint. And neither did the hero of my story.

Realising that love is actually all around means there's always hope.

For everyone.

Acknowledgements

No man is an island …

That famous line from John Donne's prose – published in 1624 – has always stuck in my head. When it comes to the publication of a novel the author is simply the first link in a chain of participants. It takes a whole host of people to turn the equivalent of a four-inch stack of A4 paper into a polished, beautifully presented book.

To my awesome editor, Hannah Smith - it's a pure delight working with you lovely lady. Thanks go to Dushi Horti, Sue Lamprell and David Boxell, for their hard work in helping to make the words on the page sparkle.

Huge thanks also go to Laura Palmer, Nikky Ward and Vicky Joss for their tremendous effort behind the scenes to publicise and promote Lucy. You guys are amazing!

To my lovely agent, Sara Keane, who keeps me on my toes – I couldn't do this without your help and support!

There are some wonderful reviewers and readers who continue to follow my career and support me every step of the way – for that I'm eternally grateful. Please know that it's your wonderful reviews that spur me on.

But every single day I'm amazed by the kindness of my fellow authors and new readers I may never meet, who add to that support network and share the book love. It's truly a blessing.

I must also mention my wonderful family and close friends who put up with my obsession to write. They are so forgiving of my demanding, crazy working pattern which takes me out of circulation for weeks at a time. And not forgetting Lawrence, my rock, for getting me through the tough times and being there to celebrate the happy times.

For those who have taken the time to contact me via my website, or Tweeted me to share their reading experience, I feel both humbled and loved at the same time.

And, in reading this it means YOU, too, have played a part. Plucking my book from a shelf or downloading it on your reading device, is what keeps me writing. And I can promise you one thing… there are many more stories to come!

With much love and grateful thanks,
Lucy x

About the Author

Lucy lives in the Forest of Dean in the UK with her lovely husband and Bengal cat, Ziggy. Her novels have been shortlisted in the UK's Festival of Romance and the eFestival of Words Book Awards. Lucy won the 2013 UK Festival of Romance: Innovation in Romantic Fiction award.

Hello from Aria

We hope you enjoyed this book! If you did let us know, we'd love to hear from you.

We are Aria, a dynamic digital-first fiction imprint from award-winning independent publishers Head of Zeus. At heart, we're committed to publishing fantastic commercial fiction – from romance and sagas to crime, thrillers and historical fiction. Visit us online and discover a community of like-minded fiction fans!

We're also on the look out for tomorrow's superstar authors. So, if you're a budding writer looking for a publisher, we'd love to hear from you. You can submit your book online at ariafiction.com/we-want-read-your-book

You can find us at:
Email: aria@headofzeus.com
Website: www.ariafiction.com
Submissions: www.ariafiction.com/we-want-read-your-book

@ariafiction
@Aria_Fiction
@ariafiction

Printed in Great Britain
by Amazon